Callie's MOUNTAIN

*One Couple's Three-Part Romance
Sings Across the Misty Mountains*

VEDA BOYD JONES

BARBOUR
PUBLISHING

Callie's Mountain © 1995 by Veda Boyd Jones
Callie's Challenge © 1995 by Veda Boyd Jones
An Ozark Christmas Angel © 1996 by Veda Boyd Jones

ISBN 1-59310-907-5

Cover art by Corbis

Published by Barbour Publishing, Inc., P.O. Box 719, Uhrichsville, Ohio 44683, www.barbourbooks.com

Our mission is to publish and distribute inspirational products offering exceptional value and biblical encouragement to the masses.

 Member of the
Evangelical Christian
Publishers Association

Printed in the United States of America.
5 4 3 2 1

Dear Readers,

One summer my family went to North Carolina with my friend Cathy's family. Occasionally we hired a local high school girl to babysit our children. At dinner one night we were saying how nice she was, and Cathy's father, who was quite wealthy and generous, said quite casually that he thought he'd put the babysitter through college.

Callie's Mountain was born from that idea. My fascination with music led me to make Callie's benefactor a country singer. I continued Callie and Trey's story in *Callie's Challenge* and gave them cameo appearances in the novella *An Ozark Christmas Angel*, which takes place in Branson, Missouri, where singers perform in theaters. I love these characters, and it means so much to have this trilogy in one volume. I hope you enjoy these stories of love, respect, and faith.

I've always set my romance stories in places I've been, even if I fictionalize the place names. My husband, Jim, and I live in Joplin, Missouri, but we're planning to travel more to see places that could be settings for future novels. Who knows, we may be coming to your hometown soon.

Veda Boyd Jones

Callie's Mountain

To my sister, Elaine Jones, for always being there.
Thanks to Jimmie, Landon, Morgan, and Marshall,
who have taught me appreciation for different forms of music.

Prologue

Callie Duncan slipped her chemistry book on the lower shelf of the waitress station as the hostess ushered superstar Trey and an older man into the private dining room.

Callie was used to seeing celebrities. Actors, politicians, singers, and important businessmen often dined at Highridge House. But she wasn't prepared to see the famous singer, whose songs she sang along with on the radio. And Trey's tall good looks were even more impressive in person than on the cover of the *People* magazine her friend Sally had brought to school.

From the magazine stories Callie knew Trey's statistics: twenty-five years old, single, played the piano, and wrote his own songs. He'd graduated from Princeton when he was twenty-one and held a degree in business. He liked the color blue, chocolate ice cream, and watching late movies on TV.

Now, looking at the real live person, Callie took a deep breath and carried ice water and menus to the table. Part of her job training was to ignore celebrity status and treat all customers alike.

❦

Morgan P. Rutherford III, alias Trey, looked around the small dining room and nodded with approval. No crowds of screaming girls had greeted him. No one approached him for an autograph. That was one of the many things he liked about Highridge, North Carolina. The local people were used to celebrities and respected their privacy, and the wealthy crowd who flocked to the Blue Ridge Mountains in the summer sought the peace of the mountains and escape from the demands of city life. None of them would interfere with another man's need for seclusion.

But sometimes the solitude that Morgan needed carried with it a burden that bordered on loneliness. He hoped that buying the house on Regal Mountain would make him a part of a group, without interfering with his need for a life away from reporters and screaming fans.

"Dad," he said, taking a sip of ice water, "I appreciate your coming with me today. I wanted another opinion about the house."

"Glad to do it," his father answered. "It's a great house. Wonderful view."

They ordered and were soon served excellent meals. Their conversation lapsed as they tackled their dinners.

"Victoria wants to come up," his dad said at last. "Your mom thought it would be fun to spend some time in the mountains, too. You may be getting more togetherness than you bargained on." He chuckled.

"I don't see enough of Vic and Adam and their kids. I want them thinking their Uncle Morgan is a guy who can give them piggyback rides and buy them ice cream cones. And somebody they can talk to when they need to confide in someone. Like I can with you."

"Like now?" the older man said with a lift of bushy eyebrows. "What's bothering you, son? I know you wanted me up here for more than my opinion on a house. You've bought two other houses without asking for my approval."

"I never could pull one on you, Dad." Morgan tapped his fingers on the table, glanced over at the waitress who was reading a book at her work station, then took another drink of coffee. "I need something more," he said in a low voice. "That sounds crazy, I know. I just bought my dream house on Regal Mountain, my new album hit platinum—and I'm not content."

Morgan set his coffee cup down with a thump. The waitress immediately appeared with the coffeepot in her hand. "More, sir?"

"Sorry, I didn't mean to put the cup down so hard. But since you're here, I could use half a cup." He smiled at the waitress, whose blond hair was pulled back in a braid that almost reached her waist. She poured his coffee, topped off his dad's cup, and returned to her station in the corner of the room.

Morgan glanced at his watch. Just past eleven o'clock. He glanced over at the waitress, who had opened her book again. "Miss," he called, "are we keeping you?"

Callie looked up guiltily and swiftly made her way to his side.

"I'm sorry. Would you like something else? More cream?"

"No, I meant should we go? Is the restaurant closed?" He was used to eating late so he could avoid crowds, but the girl looked too young to be kept up late.

"The kitchen is closed," she answered, "but you can stay as long as you want."

She looked him straight in the eyes, her gaze calm and level. She had to be seventeen or eighteen, he thought, an age that almost guaranteed that she knew who he was, and yet she didn't flutter her eyelashes or give him the coy looks that teenagers usually directed his way.

"What are you reading?" he asked her.

"Chemistry. I have a test tomorrow."

"Senior?"

She nodded. "Can I get you anything else?"

"No, thanks," Morgan answered.

She returned to her post and opened the book again.

"So, why are you discontent?" his father asked.

Morgan shook his head and held out both hands in an empty gesture. "Maybe I got it all too easily. I didn't have to work for anything."

"Didn't you earn your grades in college?"

"Of course I did," Morgan answered, "but I didn't have to work at a job at the same time." He nodded toward the waitress. "She's just in high school, and she's working."

His father glanced at the girl who appeared absorbed in her textbook. "You've worked hard at your music."

"Yes and no. The songs just came to me. If I hadn't had connections, that first album could have flopped." Morgan studied the fine linen tablecloth. He had no idea how to explain to his dad what he didn't understand himself. "I feel like I have everything, and maybe it's time to give some of it away."

"Away?"

Morgan looked at the ceiling for an answer. "I already give to charities. I tithe to the church. I know this sounds hackneyed, but I feel I should give some of the money I've made to those less fortunate."

"I've always been against that," his father said. "My philosophy is that God helps those who help themselves. I don't believe in giving money to others, but I believe in giving opportunity."

"How do you give opportunity? Give a job?"

"That's one way."

"Callie," a woman's high-pitched voice called. Morgan looked up as the hostess who had seated them entered the private dining room and approached the waitress. The teenager shut her book quickly, and her head lowered.

"Yes, Mrs. Allen," she answered in a small voice.

The hostess spoke in low tones that Morgan couldn't catch, but the girl looked chastised. She kept her eyes on the floor and nodded several times. She looked at his table then looked quickly away.

Mrs. Allen walked to the table. "Would you like some dessert or more coffee, Trey?" she asked, using his professional name. His family had helped him think of it. One evening they had thrown stage names around, and Grandad had jokingly called his son, Morgan P. Rutherford the Second, by the name Deuce. It followed that Morgan P. Rutherford the Third would be called Trey. The name had stuck, and his adoring fans knew him by the single name.

"No, we're fine," Morgan answered. "Callie's taking good care of us." He smiled at the waitress who remained beside the work station, trying to reassure her that he didn't blame her for studying when she had a chance.

The hostess walked away with a final glance at Callie.

"Opportunity," Morgan mused, his mind going back to his dad's philosophy. "Callie," he called to the waitress.

She immediately approached the table with the coffeepot. Morgan placed his hand over his cup. "Callie, where are you going to school?"

"Highridge High School."

"And where are you going to college?"

She glanced at his dad as if looking for direction. "I'm not going to college," she said.

"Would you like to?" Morgan asked.

"Is this a trick question?" She laughed a humorless laugh. "Of course I'd like to go."

"Where would you go if you could?"

"Probably University of North Carolina at Chapel Hill."

"Then you're going," Morgan said. "Someone who studies chemistry at every odd moment deserves an opportunity." He raised his eyebrows at his dad and saw the nod of approval. A glance at Callie showed her disbelief. But he had decided, and he felt good about his decision. Callie was going to college. He would finance her education. Whether she succeeded or failed at college would be up to her, but she would have the opportunity.

Chapter 1

Callie reached for her phone. "Yes, Liz?"

"Morgan Rutherford to see you," the receptionist said in a breathless voice, her excitement vibrating across the intercom line.

"Send him in, please," Callie said calmly, although her heart pounded.

Why was Morgan Rutherford here at Brandon, Callender, and Clark's CPA offices? She fluffed her blond hair, wishing she had a mirror. Except for last year when he hadn't come to the mountains, she had seen him each summer after the night five years ago that had changed her life.

In his elegant home on Regal Mountain one day they had filled out admission forms for college and gone over financial costs. They had met three times that summer to finalize her plans. Each summer after that she had met with him while she was home between summer school and the fall semester. They had discussed her schooling, but often the conversation had turned personal, and they had shared their innermost thoughts.

Morgan had told her how he disliked performing live, how stage fright nearly overwhelmed him. Callie had confided her fears that her grandma was aging too fast. In Callie's mind, they had become friends, even though they only saw each other once a year.

Still, she had been stunned when last year he had shown up unexpectedly for her college graduation. What a stir he had caused on campus. The news that he was in the dorm spread like wildfire, causing the dorm mother to call campus security to ensure his safety. That was a day from her wildest fantasies. When the afternoon graduation exercises were over, he had taken her for a long drive, and they had stopped for hamburgers at a drive-through place and gone on an impromptu picnic. Morgan had apologized for the simple meal, explaining that fans swamped him whenever he ate in public. She was practically stampeded when she got back to the dorm, and she hadn't seen him since.

And now he was back in Highridge. Was he out at Regal Mountain? Rumor had it that his family members used the home more often than he.

"Hi, Callie."

She looked up into the same blue eyes she had dreamed about for five years. His dark brown hair had a little gray around the temples, she was quick to notice, and his face had a few lines she didn't believe were there before, but he still had the same neat, athletic build. He was thirty now, but he would turn thirty-one on June twenty-ninth. Callie knew because she had read every scrap of information printed about her benefactor in the last five years, from Who's Who to the tabloids, although she only believed a fraction of what she read there.

She stood and held out her hand, and he took it in his larger one. "Callie Duncan, you've cut off your braid."

"Yes." She touched a hand to her cropped honey-wheat hair. Short hair had seemed more suitable for a certified public accountant. "Morgan, it's good to see you again. Are you staying awhile?" She motioned for him to sit down, but he waited until she had resumed her seat before sitting down in the overstuffed chair in front of her desk.

"I hope so. It's been a long time since I spent any time here in the mountains. I need the peace."

"I'm sorry about your father's death," she said, not knowing what to say next, but feeling she should comment on his loss.

"Thank you. And thanks for your card."

She had received a formally engraved thank-you note from the family a year ago, but she hadn't known if Morgan himself had seen the card. Now she was glad she'd sent it.

"How's your grandmother?" He sounded genuinely interested, not just passing the time with a person he saw once a year.

"She's not as spry as she once was, but she's getting around all right. You'd never guess her to be seventy-five."

Her grandmother's health was one reason Callie had once given up her dream of a college education. A broken hip had the older woman bedridden for the last month of Callie's senior year in high school. She couldn't go off and leave Grandma alone. But Morgan had hired a woman to stay with Grandma until she didn't need help anymore. He had seen to everything, and in Callie's eyes, he was a hero.

"I was hoping you could have lunch with me. Catch up on old times," he said.

Her heart pounded. This scenario had occurred in her fantasies countless times, but this was reality.

"Morgan, I'm sorry," she heard herself say. "I can't. I have a client coming any minute for a lunch meeting."

"Oh. Well, another time then," he said. He stood and flashed her his famous grin, then strode out of her office before Callie could say another word.

This was not the way things were supposed to happen. He should demand that she cancel her meeting and go with him. She didn't even know how long he would be in the mountains. Would he really come another time?

Liz darted into her office. "I thought I'd faint when I saw him walk in. You never mentioned you knew Trey," she said, referring to Morgan by the name that appeared on his compact disc cases.

"There wasn't much to mention," Callie said. She had told only one person, Joe Lowery, that Morgan had put her through college, and that was because she and Joe had shared rides to school and had become close friends.

Grandma had looked on Morgan's financing her education not as a scholarship but as charity, and she had allowed Callie to accept the opportunity only with the stipulation that she pay back every cent when she could. Callie had agreed. Only last month she had sent Morgan the first payment in care of his company. Maybe that was why he'd looked her up.

"Trey is Morgan Rutherford," Liz said dreamily.

"The Third," Callie corrected. At Liz's questioning look, she elaborated. "His grandfather is Morgan Rutherford; his father was the Second; he's the Third."

"I have all his albums," Liz said. "When's his next one coming out?"

"I don't know. He writes all his own songs, so it takes awhile to produce an entire album." Callie admired his talent. His songs reflected his beliefs in tolerance and kindness to others. His music was popular, and he'd won four Grammys for his work.

"Trey hasn't given a concert in two years," Liz continued. "I saw him in Asheville four years ago. He's dynamite on stage. But you've seen him perform, haven't you?"

"Just on television, not in person. Listen, I need to finish this before Mike Warner shows up." She motioned at the report on her desk.

Liz walked out, and Callie closed her eyes, remembering Trey in the last TV special she'd seen. He had sat at the piano and stared into the camera, looking especially at her, she'd thought, until the song ended and screams erupted from the packed auditorium. He reached for a rose from the bouquet on the piano and tossed one to a girl in the audience, blowing a kiss at the same time. That blown kiss was his trademark.

At that moment Callie had realized she wasn't the only girl to feel attracted to Trey. Except, she had rationalized, she knew the real Morgan Rutherford III. Or was Trey, the man who played the piano, sang in front of thousands, and blew kisses to teenage girls, the real Morgan Rutherford III?

❦

That night while washing dishes, Callie mentioned her benefactor to Grandma. "Morgan Rutherford's back in town. He asked me to lunch."

"Did you go, Callie Sue?" Grandma's voice was sharper than normal, and Callie turned to look at her.

"No. I had a client coming in."

"Good. You know year-rounders and summer folk don't mix."

Callie had heard that phrase quoted to her since she was two years old. Normally she let it pass, but this time she needed answers.

"Grandma, why not?"

Grandma looked taken aback for a moment; then she picked up a plate and briskly rubbed it dry with a tea towel. "Summer folk are from a different world. They expect their money can buy about anything."

"I don't know about that. Look at Morgan. He put me through college. He changed our lives, Grandma." Callie pointed to the sink.

Grandma snorted. "We'd of done okay without running water."

Callie wanted to argue that. Their lives had been so much easier this past year, ever since she'd saved enough from her first few paychecks to afford the luxury of a hot shower, a real bathroom, and running water in the kitchen. Grandma had objected to spending all that money when they'd gotten along without indoor plumbing before, but Callie was adamant. Three years at the university had spoiled her, and since she couldn't get Grandma to move, she spent her money making the old home place more comfortable.

Yes, the changes had helped their lives, but one look at Grandma's stony face told her arguing would do no good. She dropped the subject of Morgan P. Rutherford the Third, although in her heart she prayed he would come see her again.

❧

Two days later, Liz buzzed Callie.

"It's him," she said breathlessly. "Line three."

There was no need to wonder whom Liz referred to. "Hello, Morgan," Callie said, pushing the other button.

They exchanged pleasantries for a moment, and then Morgan said, "I was hoping you'd have dinner with me tonight."

Callie caught her breath. She wanted to go, but in her mind she saw Grandma's disapproving look. Why did she feel this deep-seated duty to honor Grandma's wishes?

"Morgan, I already have plans for this evening," she said. She did have plans. She was meeting with church members interested in the building project. But she could skip it, couldn't she?

"We'll try it another time," he said. "Good talking to you, Callie."

❦

As soon as she got home that night, Callie confronted Grandma. "Morgan asked me to dinner tonight."

Grandma looked sharply at Callie, but didn't say anything. Was that fear Callie saw in her eyes?

"I wanted to go, but I told him I had plans."

"Tonight's the meetin'."

"I know. And I'm going because I have the financial report. But I think I'll go if he ever asks me again."

Grandma's eyes narrowed. "Year-rounders and summer folk—"

"Don't mix," Callie finished. "I know. We're from different worlds. He hasn't asked me to marry him, Grandma." Callie looked away from her grandmother's eyes, because that particular event was a part of her wildest dreams, too. "He just wants to have dinner. Probably wants to see how his investment turned out."

Grandma dropped the spoon in the gravy then fished it out with a fork. "Supper's ready. We'd better eat."

❦

During the building meeting at the small church, Callie forced her mind away from Morgan and onto the leaking roof and structural repairs needed for the old church. An alternative was to build a metal building, like other churches around had done. At the moment her tiny church had little money, and what they had would have to be spent on stop-gap measures. The group decided to buy more tar for the roof.

Back at home, Grandma followed Callie to her room. She stood inside the doorway, fidgeting with the straps to her purse.

"What is it, Grandma? Is something wrong?" Callie asked.

The frown line between Grandma's eyes deepened, but she shook her head and walked into the other bedroom.

❦

A week and a half later, Callie was working at her desk when Liz brought Morgan into her office.

"Callie," he said in a no-nonsense manner. "I just got back into town and found I'm to be at a surprise birthday barbecue for my mother's best friend. I hope you'll come with me."

He was back. She'd thought she would never hear from him again. "You want me to go with you?" she repeated.

"Yes. When do you get off work?"

"At five."

"Good. By the time I pick up a present for Mary, you'll be off and we can go. All right?" He actually looked like it mattered to him whether she went or not.

"Is this a fancy party?" she asked.

"No. It's a surprise barbecue at my house. You look just fine as you are. I'm wearing this." He gestured to his khaki slacks and blue-striped oxford shirt. The long sleeves were rolled up to his elbows, showing bronzed skin.

"Yes, I'd like to go," she heard herself say. "But I can drive there when I get off work. You don't have to pick me up."

"I'll be glad to follow you home," he offered. "Then you could ride to the mountain with me."

"Oh, no. Our road is a washboard after the spring rains, and a pickup is the only way to get in."

"All right. I'll leave word with Billy so you can come right up."

Billy's family had lived in the gatehouse at the foot of Regal Mountain as long as Callie could remember. His daughter had attended high school with her.

"I'll see you around five thirty," Callie said.

"Good." He grinned, waved, and disappeared out the door.

Callie reached for the phone. Times like this, she was glad she'd talked Grandma into letting her have a phone installed in the old farmhouse.

Grandma didn't sound at all surprised that she was going out with Morgan P. Rutherford III—nor did she sound pleased about it.

"You remember he's summer folk and only here for a few weeks, Callie Sue. Year-rounders and summer folk don't mix."

Callie wasn't going to get into an argument about this. "Yes, Grandma, but he just got back into town and needs a date. I should be nice to him. After all, he did put me through school."

"Be careful, Callie Sue," Grandma warned.

"Yes, Grandma. I'll see you later." Callie hung up the receiver with a bit more force than was absolutely necessary. She and Grandma rarely disagreed, but sometimes she felt she was treated like a fifteen-year-old instead of a woman who had turned twenty-three in April. Of course, she thought ruefully, if she continued to take out her frustrations on inanimate objects like the telephone, Grandma could be justified in treating her like a child.

With determination, Callie tackled the report on her desk, updating figures on the Mangrum file. Thirty minutes later she tidied her desk and stopped in the ladies' room on her way out.

She looked passable, she decided. Usually she wore business-like suits to the office. Because she had no meetings today, though, she had chosen a simple pink seersucker dress and sandals. At least she wouldn't be overdressed for the barbecue.

She drove slowly out of Highridge, not for her old pickup's benefit but because the road curved, climbed, curved again, and then turned back on itself, and she was stuck behind a shiny new sports car. Year-rounders knew the curves by heart and could take them at a pretty good clip, but summer people usually traveled with more caution.

Nine miles out of Highridge, the gates of Regal Mountain appeared. Callie turned onto Regal Road and waved at Billy, who stuck a card in a slot which swung open the wrought iron gates.

The climb up the mountain was much steeper than the road from Highridge. Callie shifted to low as the road snaked upwards with one switchback curve after another. Trees crowded the edge of the road and hid the mountain houses from each other. The higher the house on the mountain, the better the view and the more prestigious the family. Morgan's mountain retreat was near the top.

Morgan came out the front door the moment she pulled into his drive. "Good timing," he called as she climbed out of the cab of the old pickup. He patted the hood as he walked by. "Have you had any trouble with her?"

"Not a bit. Grandpa bought it brand new when he sold some land next to the highway. He built the grandest shed for it and polished it every weekend. I haven't given it the kind of care he did, but we have always maintained it. Until I started to drive, it only had 8,000 miles on it. Now it's nearing 70,000. Grandpa and Grandma used to go to town twice a month, but I'm there every day of course. I hope to get a car of my own soon, but I've been putting my earnings into fixing up the house."

Suddenly aware of how she was rambling, she fell silent. "I'm sorry," she said after a moment. "I'm sure you're not interested in hearing all that."

"Nonsense. I enjoy hearing about you."

They walked back to his home, and he led her into the living room. The long glass wall drew her toward the deck. "The view here is so incredible."

"I never tire of it myself—but I thought someone from around here would find the view rather commonplace." He moved ahead of her and opened the French doors, then followed her out onto the deck.

"Not me. The pullovers on the highway are not as spectacular as this. Although Grandma owns Eagle Mountain, we live at the foot of it, in the valley. When my ancestors settled here, they wanted flat land they could farm, not a mountain that would produce nothing and was inaccessible in winter."

"Has your grandmother ever thought of selling it?" he asked. He had moved beside her and leaned on the redwood railing, looking across to where other mountains reared their lofty peaks.

"I don't think so. Our place is three miles off the highway on a dirt road. Just getting a decent road to the mountain would take quite an investment, so I don't think we'd have buyers beating down the door."

"I'd like to see Eagle Mountain sometime. How far is it from here?"

"As the crow flies, probably two miles, but by road at least six. There's an old trail to it from this mountain that used to be used a lot for hiking. It's the peak to the right." She pointed, but she could tell he was looking toward the wrong one. "No. See the church steeple. It's hard to see because of all the trees. Now go to the second peak to the right," she instructed. "You've got it."

He had moved close to follow her explanation, his head beside hers as if to see through her eyes. His nearness had an unsettling effect on Callie. She had overcome her first anxiety at being with him because he had been so easy to talk to and acted truly interested in her background. But that was when he was at least three feet away. Now they were separated by mere inches. She could feel his breath on her cheek, smell the musky fragrance of his cologne, and she hoped he couldn't hear the loud beating of her heart.

She turned her head to look at him and found an odd searching look in his eyes. For a moment their gazes locked, and she felt he could see all the secret thoughts she'd had about him during the last five years.

The sound of childish laughter drifted up from below the deck, and Callie looked over the railing but couldn't see anyone.

"The kids and Victoria are downstairs decorating," he explained as he escorted her through the dining room and into the kitchen, where Wanda, the cook, was preparing a salad. Wanda good-naturedly warned Morgan to stay away from the charcoal grill, and then Callie and Morgan took the back stairs down to the family room. Again one wall was glass, and the sliding door opened onto a patio at ground level.

"Callie, this is my little sister Victoria, who's been my nemesis since the day she was born."

"Not true," Victoria inserted, as he introduced his niece and nephews.

Callie repeated each name to get them in her mind and guessed at their ages. Jake had to be around eight, Angie could be five, and little Dave toddled around the two-year-old mark. Adam, Victoria's husband, would arrive next week.

"You have your hands full, Victoria," Callie said. Then she thought better of that statement. Victoria probably had a full-time nanny and a cook and a housekeeper. Callie had no idea how the rich really lived.

"You've got that right," Victoria said. "Davie's turned into quite a night owl, and it's wearing me out. He gets up from one to three in the morning. I think he's getting more teeth. Here, Jake, can you tie this balloon over there?" She handed her son the balloon and patted him on the back as he headed for the light above a round oak table.

"What can I do to help?" Callie asked.

"You and Morgan can string crepe paper across the room. Mom and Mary should be back soon, so we've got to get a move on."

Together Morgan and Callie measured, twisted, and taped metallic red and silver streamers from the light fixture to corners of the room, forming a canopy above the table.

"Thanks for inviting me to this party," Callie said. "When do the guests arrive?"

"We're here. It's just a small get-together. I wanted you to meet the family."

"I see," Callie murmured, but she didn't really see at all. Did he want them to meet her because he had paid for her schooling? She had hoped he was interested in her as a woman, not as an investment. But she had known that couldn't be true. They were from different worlds, just like Grandma always said.

"Morgan, I really appreciate your putting me through school. You rescued me from waiting tables all my life," she said as she handed Morgan a piece of tape.

"I'm glad I could help, but I don't want to be thanked again. We went through all this at your graduation."

"I know, but you changed my life."

"You changed your own life, Callie. I just provided the opportunity. By the way, what was the meaning of the check I received?" He pulled out his wallet, extracted her uncashed check, and held it out to her.

In an effort to make light of the moment, Callie stuck her hands behind her back. "I intend to pay you back."

Morgan looked at her and then at the check. "It was a scholarship. I give five scholarships a year now."

"Then you can apply the money to the next student."

Morgan carefully placed the check back in his wallet and stuffed it into his back pocket. "We'll see," he said.

Chapter 2

Morgan could tell he'd said the wrong thing when he had offered Callie her check back. Even though she had stuck her hands behind her back in a gesture that reminded him of little Davie in a stubborn mood, she had drawn herself up to her full height, lifted her chin, and her eyes had challenged him to defy her decision.

He glanced at his sister and saw her interest focused on Callie. Vic had always been sweet and kind, the champion of the underdog. But when she was riled, look out. He realized he had just seen the same kind of look in Callie's eyes—and it wasn't one he wanted to face right now.

"We're through here. Let's check the barbecue," he suggested and opened the door onto the patio. The spicy aroma of barbecue filled his nostrils and despite Wanda's warnings, he lifted the lid of the charcoal cooker and checked the ribs, letting the heat out in the process.

Callie was looking over the grounds and again staring at the view. What was it about her that fascinated him so? He hadn't realized what that night five years ago would mean to him. It was the beginning of a satisfying feeling that he was making a difference in people's lives, but with Callie, it meant much more than that to him.

He had enjoyed the planning sessions with Callie when they had discussed her college career. The first time she had ended up spending most of the day, and he had told her things he hadn't told anyone else. She was a good listener. Instead of breaking into his monologue, she looked questioningly at him, silently urging him to go on. And he did. He told her of his reluctance to perform live. He didn't mind the recording studio, but being out in front of an audience scared him. If he forgot the words or sang off-key, he could not try again. He told her he was going to cut back on concerts, maybe stop them altogether.

"If you ask God, He'll help you do what you need to do." She stated her religious belief so simply and trustingly. Although he considered himself a Christian, he rarely talked about God to others. He tried to show his Christian belief through his actions, but in his line of work, religion wasn't mentioned much.

Since that summer day with Callie, he had prayed for help before each performance and had felt a guiding Hand from above. He still didn't like performing live, but the thought of singing in front of people no longer paralyzed him. He had Callie to thank for the new closeness he felt with God.

He glanced at her quickly, admiring the pale gleam of her hair. Once she had started school, she worked hard, taking heavy class loads each semester and going two summers as well. She wrote to him, in care of his house on Regal Mountain, telling him her plans, what classes she was taking, and sent him a grade report each semester. She graduated with honors at the end of three years.

At the end of each summer session she returned briefly to Highridge, and Morgan had made sure he was there to see her. She sent him a graduation announcement but was obviously surprised when he showed up for the event. That was another day he wouldn't forget.

His impulsive visit to the university might have started as a lark, seeing how his first scholarship student had turned out, playing Professor Higgins to her Eliza Doolitle. But after seeing the metamorphosis of Callie Duncan, he was mesmerized. Oh, he had seen the changes coming from summer to summer, but the young woman with an air of confidence he saw at graduation bore little resemblance to the nearly servile teenage girl he had met at the restaurant.

She was delighted that he had shown up; he saw that immediately. That the other coeds were so excited by his presence was part of it, he recognized, but he believed she had felt as much as he had that sharing her special moment of triumph had formed a bond between them. On that day, he was the listener and heard all her plans for her future.

He had wanted to see her last summer, but his father's death had kept him busy in Atlanta, sorting through papers, learning about the businesses from his grandfather, so that he hadn't made it to the mountains. But now that he was back, he intended to see her until he found out if that something special he had felt toward her still existed and why.

"Smells good," Callie said. "But didn't Wanda tell you. . ."

He cut her off by placing his finger to his lips, as if they were conspiring together, as he put the lid back on the cooker.

"Isn't it a bit early in the summer for your trip to the mountains?" Callie asked.

What could he say? Because he wanted to see her, see if he could get her out of his mind, he had rearranged his entire summer calendar. But if he said that, it would scare her for sure. When she wouldn't go out with him the first two times he'd asked, he'd retreated to Atlanta, but he had returned to try one more time. He'd decided if she refused this time, that would be the end of it. He wouldn't ask again.

"Yes, it's early. But I'm overdue for a long vacation this year. Last year I didn't get away at all, with all the details of taking over the office."

"So you're in charge now? What about your grandfather?"

"He'd already handed over the reins to Dad, and he didn't want them back. He said he knew I'd be ready to take over when the time came. Unfortunately it came too soon."

"What does this mean to your singing career?"

"I don't know. I need time to think about that. That's one of the reasons I came to the mountains. I can hire competent people to oversee the corporation." And he could. Even though his family owned six subsidiaries, from a retail chain to movie theaters to a small airline, he had top executives running each company. Did he want to be CEO and oversee the works—or hand that authority to someone else?

"But do you want to hand over your control?" she asked.

"I don't know," he repeated. "I'd like to talk it over with you."

"With me?" Her eyes widened as she looked straight into his eyes.

"Yes. You listen. You don't tell me what to do. Know what I mean?" He placed a hand on her shoulder.

She nodded. "Would it be something like graduation day when you listened to me decide which accounting firm to go to work for? The big one in Asheville or the smaller one here in Highridge. I knew all along I needed to come back and help Grandma, but I still had to walk through all the steps of the decision. You helped me to do that."

He nodded and smiled. She understood the pull they had for one another. She didn't treat him like a big star and bow down to his every wish. Other than the gratitude she felt about the scholarship, she treated him like a normal guy, which was what he was. A normal guy who was worth millions and whose name was a household word across the nation. Most people didn't see past the glitz to the real Morgan Rutherford.

"They're coming." Angie rushed out on the patio. "Grandma's back."

The group lined up behind the table, where Vic had placed a large cake.

"Morgan, the piano," Vic said as she lit candles.

Morgan took his place at the upright piano and waited for his mother to bring Mary downstairs. The kids poked and shushed each other while they waited. Finally, Morgan heard footsteps on the stairs.

"I need to put these things in the family room," his mother's voice drifted down. "Thanks for carrying, Mary. I shouldn't have bought so much."

As soon as the two women appeared at the bottom of the stairs, Morgan struck up "Happy birthday to you," and Vic, Callie, and the kids sang along.

"For me?" Mary said.

Mary had lived next door to the Rutherfords in Atlanta as long as Morgan could remember and was an ex officio member of the family. She had never married, but had unofficially adopted Morgan and Vic. Whenever they were in trouble at home, they had escaped to Mary's house.

She blew out the candles then turned to hug the kids.

"Morgan, when did you get back?" His mother kissed him on the cheek and demanded a bear hug in return.

"A couple of hours ago. Mom, this is Callie Duncan. Callie, this is my mother, Dorothy Rutherford."

"Hello, Mrs. Rutherford."

"Hi, Callie—and it's Dorothy. Mrs. Rutherford was my mother-in-law," she said and smiled.

Morgan was proud of his mother. She had been a tower of strength when his dad had died. Once he had discussed their marriage with his father, who admitted that a great deal of his success could be attributed to Dorothy. She was behind her husband every step of the way, loving him, admiring him, encouraging him. Her shrewd brain had been hidden behind his dad's forceful personality, but his dad had always listened to his wife's opinion in important decisions.

Morgan introduced Callie to Mary, and the group watched Mary open her presents. Mary opened the card on Morgan's gift and read it aloud. "Happiness always to the birthday gal. Morgan and Callie."

Callie glanced swiftly at Morgan, who sat beside her on the couch. "I knew you didn't have time to pick up a gift. Besides, you hadn't even met her then," he whispered.

"Thank you," Callie whispered. She watched the family joke around and was surprised when, before sitting down to the barbecued ribs, salad, and hot bread, they joined hands in prayer. This was not at all what she expected from Trey's family. But she'd learned five years ago that Morgan Rutherford III and Trey, the singer, were two separate identities for the same person. Something like Superman and Clark Kent. But unlike most people, she would equate Morgan to Superman and Trey to Clark Kent.

She enjoyed dinner. At first she smiled and said all the customary things, while the butterflies in her stomach danced wildly. But by the time dinner was over, she relaxed. Victoria obviously adored her older brother. Dorothy was as down to earth as Grandma. The older woman was not as polished as Morgan's mother, but Callie could see the same hard working, determined core in them both.

At one point when Dorothy and Callie sat by themselves, Dorothy mentioned her husband, and Callie murmured her sympathy at his death. Dorothy shrugged. "God has smiled on my life. I loved a wonderful man, and he loved me. We had a joyous life together. And when I think of him, I smile. Oh, sometimes I miss him so much I sit down and cry my eyes out. But his motto was, 'If you're not enjoying life, you're doing something wrong.' So I keep going, trying to do the right thing. And I have his children, and that helps. Morgan is his father all over again. Vic has his fire, too." Dorothy was silent a moment and then changed the subject.

❦

The next morning Callie climbed out of bed and walked over to the window. Another beautiful June day. As she padded to the small closet hidden by a printed cotton curtain, her mind was on the night before. She picked out a yellow skirt and a white short-sleeved cotton shirt. She'd change before Morgan picked her up for dinner. Tonight! She'd been surprised when he'd asked her, but then he'd mentioned earlier that he wanted to talk about his singing career. That he would confide in her thrilled her heart. Maybe there was a chance that he would see her for herself and not merely as his protégé. Her happy mood continued through a quick shower, and she hummed to herself as she dressed. She fairly skipped into the kitchen.

"Morning, Grandma," she called to the wiry little woman standing in front of the wood-burning cookstove. "The coffee smells wonderful," she said as she poured herself a cup from the old percolator on the stove.

"You got in mighty late last night." Grandma frowned.

"Yes. It was a wonderful party," Callie said dreamily.

"Now don't you be gettin' high flyin' ideas, Callie Sue. Year-rounders and summer folk don't mix."

Callie nodded automatically, but she wasn't really listening. "Grandma, I have a date for dinner with Morgan tonight. He's going to pick me up here at seven thirty. Please be nice to him. And I promise I'll remember that he's leaving in a few weeks. But there's nothing wrong with me seeing him while he's here. Nothing at all."

"Callie Sue, I just don't want to see you hurt," Grandma explained, her voice strained. She tapped the plastic spatula against the stove.

"I won't be. Is one egg for me?" She wanted to change the subject before Grandma got warmed up to her aversion that bordered on fanaticism.

"It is." Grandma scooped the eggs out of the iron skillet and onto two plates. Plucking two pieces of toast from the inside of the massive stove, she added those to the plates, dropping one slice in the process. She picked it up and put it back on the plate, then took her seat at the table, and the two women bowed their heads. Instead of the usual grace, Grandma said, "Lord, please help me tell her what has to be said. Amen."

"Grandma, what's wrong?" Callie could see her grandmother was greatly disturbed.

"Lord knows I never wanted to tell you this, but I think you'd better know for your own good." Grandma fidgeted with the cup in front of her.

"Grandma, what is it?" Callie put down her fork and watched with growing alarm. Grandma hadn't looked this distressed since Grandpa had died.

"Callie Sue, you know your ma died when you was born. And we always told you that your pa was killed before that in an accident. Well, your pa wasn't killed. He just went away."

"Just went away?" Callie echoed.

"Daisy Lou was only seventeen when she died. So young." Grandma shook her head. "She got mixed up with a summer feller, and when he left, it broke her heart. As soon as she found out she was pregnant, she wrote him, but he never came back."

"Grandma." Callie felt as if she'd been hit in the stomach.

"Who was he?" she whispered.

"I don't know his full name. Daisy called him Phillip. She never would tell us his name, but on the day she died, the day you was born, she called his name over and over." Her eyes teared as she spoke of her only child. Grandma's other four children had been stillborn.

"Then my father is alive." Callie's thoughts muddled her mind. "Phillip," she repeated his name. "Phillip." With tortured eyes she looked at Grandma. "How old was he when he and my mother. . ." Her voice trailed off.

"He would've been a little older than her, probably twenty. I don't rightly know. I only seen him one time, in Highridge, and I didn't know then that Daisy Lou was seein' him." She snorted. "I ought to of known. I seen he was makin' eyes at her. Your ma was a real good lookin' girl, Callie Sue. You take after her," she added and patted Callie's hand.

"Did she love him?" Callie needed to know.

"Oh, yes, she loved him. She wouldn't tell Orie his name 'cause she was afraid he would of hurt him if he'd found him. And he probably would of. He was that mad."

"After I was born, did you try to find him then?" Callie had to know everything.

Grandma shook her head. "No, we didn't want to find him then. Daisy Lou was gone, and we was afraid he might try to take you away from us. I couldn't of stood that. You was all we had left of her."

"And he never tried to contact you?"

"Never. He never did," Grandma said and sniffed.

"What did he look like?"

"I only seen him that one time, like I said. I recall he was pretty tall, had dark hair. That's all I can say, 'cept I reckon he had eyes that pretty shade of green like yours. Daisy Lou had hazel eyes."

"How could they meet without you knowing?" Callie jumped up and began pacing the room.

"Daisy Lou cleaned house for a couple of families on Regal. She'd just walk over there on the trail. It's not far, under two miles. She must of met him there. She knew we wouldn't like her seein' any of them summer folk, so she snuck out at night to meet him. That's all she'd tell me about it." Grandma pushed out of her chair, walked around the table to where Callie stood, and put her arms around Callie's shoulders.

"Callie Sue, I only told you so you would know the danger in bein' with summer folk. It broke your ma's heart. Don't let the same thing happen to you." Grandma was crying.

Callie put her arms around Grandma and the two women, one stunned, dry-eyed, the other with tears running down her wrinkled cheeks, held each other in silent comfort.

Grandma pulled away and reached in the deep pocket of her large apron and pulled out a handkerchief. She dried her eyes and blew her nose.

"Callie Sue, you mean more to me than anyone on this earth. Please, please be careful of the summer folk." She replaced her hanky and began clearing the table.

Callie stood still, trying to evaluate all she'd heard. She watched Grandma carry their plates of eggs and toast to the new kitchen sink. Grandma, who never wasted food, tossed their breakfast in the garbage. "Grandma, I'm not going to break my date with Morgan for tonight. He put me through college. I owe him something, and he only wants to talk. That's fine by me. But it won't go any further than that. My mother was seventeen. I'm twenty-three. I know what I'm doing." She stepped over to Grandma and hugged her. "Trust me, Grandma," she pleaded.

"I do, honey." Grandma nodded and stuck her hands in the soapy dishwater. "The Lord knows I do."

"Good. I've got to get to work. Anything you need in town?" Callie asked as if the other subject was closed.

"No, honey." Grandma turned around and looked at her. "I'll see you this evenin'."

Chapter 3

In a daze, Callie walked out to the pickup. Once inside, she lay her head on the steering wheel, all pretense gone out of her. Grandma was so upset, Callie couldn't show her true reaction to the startling revelation. She didn't even know her true feelings, just that she felt numb.

She started the pickup and drove by memory toward Highridge. Her mind whirled, sorting out the hurt and disbelief. She was illegitimate. For five miles her mind stuck on that thought.

"Dear God, help me handle this," she prayed aloud.

What were her parents like? She had never known them and had thought she never would. Now there was a possibility she could find her father. She had thought Grandma and Grandpa had adopted her after her mother had died. They had told her over and over that she was their little girl now, and of course her name was Duncan, just like theirs. Now she knew it was Duncan, not because they'd adopted her, but because her father hadn't married her mother and they didn't even know his name.

Did she want to find her father? He had deserted her mother, who had loved him enough to protect him from her pa's wrath. Maybe he had never received the letter; Callie tried to find an excuse for him. But what if he had just used her mother, discarded her as a summer fling, and turned his back on his responsibility as a father? What sort of man would do that? Did she want to meet a man who had disowned her?

She parked in her assigned spot at the office. During the day she tried to focus on the numbers and statistics in front of her, but her mind kept wandering to her mother. When Callie was thirteen or fourteen, she had been curious about her, and Grandma had painted a glowing picture of Daisy Lou. But obviously that wasn't the whole truth. What had her mother felt when she had waited until her folks were asleep to slip out of the house and up the path to Regal Mountain to meet Phillip? Did he meet her halfway? Did he take her places in a fancy car?

Her mind tossed out ideas, discarded them, and thought up new ones; but by the end of the day, she had accepted the idea that her father was still alive and that except for knowing that fact, she was still the same person she had been yesterday. The past could not change the type of person she was, she told herself as she headed the pickup back home. And she wasn't going to let it upset her.

She hadn't decided about searching for her father. She needed more time to think about that. For now she would heed the warning Grandma had given her. Morgan would be only a friend, which was exactly what he was anyway.

The sad part was, she had wanted him to be more. So far he had lived up to all the dreams she'd had of him during the five years since their first meeting. Was it fair to judge him by her father's behavior?

She had not resolved that argument when she turned into the rough drive up to her home. As the white clapboard house came into view, she felt a surge of pride that she'd been able to help Grandma fix up the house. With the fresh paint, she thought the house had a new air of cozy neatness.

She parked the pickup in the shed and walked slowly to the house, schooling her face so Grandma wouldn't see the anxiety that still lingered in her eyes. She tried to put the morning's revelation out of her head and turned her thoughts instead to the evening ahead.

Although she had warned Morgan about the three miles of gutted road that led to their house, he had insisted he would pick her up for their date. Despite the jumbled thoughts she had had about summer folk during the day, she couldn't stop her pulse from quickening at the thought of seeing him again. She sure hoped Grandma would be nice to him.

❧

Morgan turned the maroon van onto the dirt road that led to Callie's home. The van had a much higher wheel base than his sports car, and Callie had repeatedly cautioned him about her rough drive. The first few hundred yards weren't bad, but the road deteriorated quickly as it gradually climbed a gentle slope. He decided the rains must run right down the deep rut where the left tire should go. No drainage ditches lined the sides, so he hugged the right side and tried to dodge the largest potholes.

As he rounded a sweeping bend, the old farmhouse came into view. He stared at the homestead as he drove the remaining yards to the house. All that Callie had told him about the place her grandmother and grandfather had built together hadn't prepared him for the dilapidated structure.

The entire house had been newly painted white, but paint couldn't hide the decayed wood of the eaves and window ledges. Fieldstone piers struggled to hold up the sagging front porch. Two fieldstone chimneys, one at each end, towered over the one-and-a-half-story house, giving the impression of sentinels guarding the place. The house lacked any lawn at all, but was surrounded instead by bare rock and dirt, worn smooth, and the wild ground cover of vines and scrub brush.

He could see four outbuildings not far from the house and guessed one to be the garage Callie called the shed. He could see why. He had thought she was kidding when she'd told him they had gotten running water the year before, but the outhouse, the farthest out of the buildings, bore evidence that she had been serious.

At least half an acre was fenced off to the left of the house, and the garden rows inside were straight and perfect, early June peas climbing high on a hog wire fence, corn standing a foot high, and tomato plants lining one edge. Other plants he didn't recognize peeked out of the ground, all neatly weeded, obviously the vegetables that would feed the Duncans through the year.

Morgan climbed out of the van and walked up the slab stone steps to the front porch. Three rockers, their wood gray and splintery from exposure to the elements, sat surrounded by flowers in old coffee cans. Handmade pillows that would have been the envy of many mountain tourists lay in the seats of the chairs.

He knocked on the screen door and waited a moment before it was opened by a wiry little woman, gray hair fastened in a bun on the back of her head. Her face was lined from many years of hard work. She didn't smile as her piercing hazel eyes assessed him.

"How do you do?" Morgan said, offering his hand. "I'm Morgan Rutherford, here to see Callie." He wasn't sure she was going to shake hands, but at last, reluctantly, she put her small wrinkled hand in his larger one. Her grip was remarkably firm for such a frail-looking woman. Her small frame must have made him first think she was feeble, he realized, for he noticed now that her back was straight and she held her head high and proud.

"I know." She acknowledged his introduction without volunteering her own name. "I'll fetch her. Come in." Her tone was belligerent.

She held the screen open while he crossed the threshold, then immediately left him and disappeared through a low doorway that led toward the back of the house. Since he had not been asked to sit, Morgan stood near the door, hands in the pockets of his gray slacks.

He looked around with interest. The room, shabby, with old furniture stuck here and there, was nevertheless immaculately clean and cozy. A large hand-braided rag rug covered most of the wooden floor. An old-fashioned sewing machine, with scraps of white fabric on the bench beside it, stood in one corner. A stone fireplace dominated the north wall, and on the mantle sat pictures of Callie, one of her grandmother and apparently her grandfather in their younger years, and a picture of another young girl who looked much like Callie.

He heard Callie's muffled tones before she appeared in the doorway. When she came into the room he couldn't hide the admiration he felt. She wore a plain white dress with short sleeves and a red belt that cinched her narrow waist. Her high heels were also red. She needed a halo to complete the picture, for she reminded him of an angel. On second thought, her golden honey hair could be her halo.

"Hello, Morgan." She said his name with that same soft quality he remembered from last night. Most people called him Trey, and it was refreshing to hear his own name from the lips of a beautiful young woman.

"Hi, Callie." He didn't know what to say. "You look wonderful. Pretty dress." The compliments sprang to his lips automatically, the deportment lessons from his childhood coming to his rescue. Not that he didn't mean them; she looked stunning.

"Thanks," she said and smiled. "Grandma just made this dress for me today."

Grandma had followed Callie into the living room, and Morgan's gaze followed Callie's to rest on the pugnacious woman, her hostility toward him a tangible thing. Why she disliked him, he didn't know, but he did know he'd have to win her over if he ever hoped to know Callie better.

"You're very talented, Mrs. Duncan. Did you also make the pillows on the rockers?" He motioned toward the front porch.

"Yes."

"They're very nice. Do you display any of your work at the craft stores in Highridge?"

There was a pause, and Morgan could tell by the look in her eyes and the grim set to her mouth that he'd said something wrong.

"We don't have no need to sell stuff to summer folk," she said gruffly.

"I didn't mean to imply that you did, just that your workmanship is excellent." He could tell he was digging a bigger hole for himself. Callie bailed him out.

"Grandma's been sewing for me since I was a baby. She's taught me, but I can't hold a candle to her. Shall we go, Morgan? I'm famished." She picked up her purse and turned briefly to her grandmother. "I won't be late." She kissed the old woman on the cheek and gave her what looked to him like a reassuring look. Why would she be reassuring her grandmother?

Morgan wanted to take her hand, but he walked her to the van with a couple of feet separating them, since Mrs. Duncan's disapproving eyes watched him like a hawk. He felt as if he were sixteen and on his first date.

After he had helped Callie into the van and slid behind the wheel, he breathed a heavy sigh. "Is it me or the summer crowd in general?"

"You're very perceptive, Morgan," Callie answered, a quickly hidden flash of pain in her eyes. "It's what you represent." She hastily added, "I mean, in Grandma's eyes, you stand for all the summer people."

"Is there a reason why she distrusts us?" Morgan wanted to look at her to see her eyes again, but the rough road took all his attention as the van crawled along at ten miles an hour.

Callie was silent for so long he didn't know if she was going to answer or not. Finally, she said, "She had a bad experience with a summer person once and tends to hold a grudge. Isn't this road all that I promised?"

"That and some more. Are you going to get it fixed?" he asked, following her lead and sticking to a neutral subject.

"We've been working on it," she said shortly. After a moment, she added, "Sorry, I didn't mean to snap. It's hard work, and I only have Saturdays. Grandma's a stickler for Sunday being a day of rest."

"I see," Morgan said, hiding his surprise that she had been working on the road herself. He had naturally assumed she would hire workmen to do such heavy work. He searched for another neutral topic and found one in the wild flowers growing profusely on each side of the so-called road.

"I understand there are more varieties of wild flowers here than in any other part of the United States. That's an odd shade of orange." He pointed to a species. "What's it called?" He knew he probably sounded like a tourist, but this was such a different Callie than the one he had seen last night, and he didn't know why.

She looked at him oddly. "I don't know the name. Are you interested in the wild flowers here? You hardly seem the type to traipse through the woods with a little notebook, cataloging flowers."

He chuckled at the picture she painted of him. "You're right. I'm not the type. But Mom enters the wild flower arranging contest each summer in Highridge."

"When did you start coming here? Do you have any relatives living here?"

"No, no relatives. That spring we met was when I bought the house. I'd visited an old friend, Robert Garrigan, the summer before."

"Robert Garrigan, the mystery writer?"

"He's from Atlanta. Lived around the corner from me when we were younger."

She seemed almost relieved at his information, and the easygoing Callie of the night before returned.

"Where are you taking me for dinner?" The sparkle was back in her eyes.

"I thought we'd go to Collett's. Do you like it?"

"I don't know. I've never eaten there."

"Never?" He was amazed. She had lived here all her life and never eaten at what he would have called the main eating establishment in Highridge.

"Never," she repeated. "Collett's, like two-thirds of the shops and restaurants in Highridge, is only open in the summer. Year-rounders could never support such an expensive place."

"I didn't realize so many of the places closed down." They had reached the main highway, and Morgan could glance at Callie now and again as the road, although curvy, didn't demand as much attention. He hesitated a moment, then said, "Do you hold a grudge against summer people, too?"

He knew he was treading on dangerous ground from the guarded look in her eyes. She had seemed comfortable with his family last night. What could have happened between then and now to change her attitude?

"No," she answered slowly. He thought that was all she would say, but she volunteered, "I don't even know the one Grandma dislikes so."

"Someone I might know?" He was prying, but he was curious about the person whose past he was going to have to overcome.

She was silent for over a mile. "His name is Phillip," she said in a small voice. "I don't know his last name."

Morgan had hurt her, and he didn't know how. But he didn't want to hear that tone of voice ever again. "I don't know any Phillip on Regal Mountain," he said and grimaced, thinking he would sure like to know him. In fact, he'd like to find out what this was all about so he could make sure this Phillip could never hurt her again.

"Vic wants to see you again," he remarked, changing the subject once more. "She's only here another week before her husband joins her and the kids, and then they take off for Maine to visit his family. Could you come to the house for dinner next week?"

"Sure. I like your sister and her kids."

"They're a handful, but fun, happy kids."

They discussed the safe topic of his family until they arrived at Collett's and were ushered to a table beside the open-air balcony that ran along Main Street. French doors closed out the cool night air. The restaurant wasn't full, since it was still early in the season for the summer crowd. By the end of June, the place would be booming, and booking a table at the last minute would be impossible, even if his name was Trey. Then the balcony would be the most popular spot in Highridge.

Morgan was relieved to see no teenagers in the room, which assured them a peaceful dinner without autograph seekers. His older fans rarely approached him, and only at the beginning of the summer season was he hounded in Highridge. Once teenagers got used to seeing him in the restaurants and on the street, except for the brashest ones, they usually left him alone.

After they studied the menu, Morgan ordered for both of them. No sooner had the waiter disappeared when he reappeared with water glasses and a stuffed artichoke salad.

"The movie house is busy," Callie said. She motioned toward the windows where the theater across the street was visible through the balcony railing.

"I wonder what's playing," Morgan said. "Back home you can go see any movie you want, any night, and yet I rarely do. Here, with only one movie theater, it's exciting to go."

"I know what you mean. At Chapel Hill we had several theaters, but it wasn't the thrill it is here, waiting for a special movie to finally come."

"Tell me about the university, Callie. What was it like for you in Chapel Hill?"

"I was scared at first. Although it was a dream of mine for a long, long time, I had always thought I couldn't go because of the expense. And when I finally got there, because of you. . ."

"Whoa," he interrupted as he heard gratitude in her voice. "Forget the financial part of it. We agreed we wouldn't speak of it again. I want to know how you liked it, what you did." They hadn't had time to discuss those years at her graduation.

"I was terribly homesick at first. I wanted to come home for Thanksgiving, but it was too expensive. I did get to come home over semester break at Christmas. I found an ad on the bulletin board. A student from Franklin needed someone to share gas with him. From then on, when he came home, I had a ride."

"Do you still see him?"

"Once in a while. We were both fortunate to get jobs back in this area. Joe works in a bank in Franklin."

"Did you date while you were in school?" What a stupid question. Of course she dated. What did he expect?

"Yes, I went out," she said and laughed. "How else would I get to go to the movies?"

"You mean you used men just to go to the movies?" he teased.

"No. I was very selective and only went out with the ones I liked. I only use men to get steak dinners," she said solemnly as their steaks were set down in front of them.

She winked, and Morgan laughed out loud. After a stale recording studio, she was a breath of fresh air.

Chapter 4

"Grandma, he's just coming over to help with the road," Callie explained. "No harm in that is there? Morgan's just being neighborly."

"Neighborly?" Grandma snorted. "We got good neighbors, and they ain't that close-knit bunch on Regal. I doubt you'd see them being neighborly to year-rounders."

Callie ignored Grandma's jab at Regal. What could she say anyway? Regal Mountain was known as an exclusive and closed society.

"I mentioned we've been working on the road on Saturday afternoons, and he said he'd come over and help. I couldn't tell him not to come since he offered. It's not like I asked him to help us. Besides, Grandma," Callie added, trying to persuade the woman to her point of view, "he's a man and a lot stronger than us. He'll be good labor."

"Humph. He's comin' over here just to see you again. I don't want you hurt, Callie Sue."

"I'm not going to get hurt," Callie protested. "He's probably only going to be in Highridge a couple of weeks longer anyway. He'll be gone before you know it."

She turned back to the noon meal dishes, not waiting for a reply from her grandmother. Grandma was right, of course. Morgan was coming over to see her. And she was glad. He had done nothing to disillusion her five years of dreaming about him. He was kind, sensitive, strong, had a great sense of humor, and he seemed to like her, too.

She wouldn't get hurt. She knew it was only a summer friendship, if friendship is what it could be called. He had kissed her last night—and it wasn't a kiss of friendship, but the kiss between two adults who were drawn to each other. She closed her eyes, remembering how he had walked her to the front door, his arm draped around her shoulder.

Before he said good-bye, he had pulled her to him in a warm embrace, leaning down to kiss her ever so gently and lingeringly.

"Callie Sue?"

She opened her eyes and realized she was still washing the same plate she had picked up a full minute earlier. "Yes, Grandma?" she answered guiltily.

Grandma stared hard at her for a moment then said, "Nothin'," and walked into the other room, muttering under her breath.

Callie washed the rest of the dishes and scurried outside where Grandma was already getting tools out of the workshop.

"You reckon he'll bring any tools with him?" Grandma asked. "Maybe a big ol' road grader?"

Callie chuckled. If Grandma could tease about him, even if it was about his money, maybe she was beginning to soften a bit.

"I doubt if he'll bring anything," she answered. "Except muscles and we can sure use those."

They walked a hundred feet down the drive and set to work, one on each side of the one-car lane. In places grass grew up between the paths of the tires.

Callie pushed the shovel into the soft ground beside the road and carried the dirt to the closest rut. While she worked, her mind jumped back to last night and her conversation with Morgan. Although she had tried to block it out, her parentage had continued to occupy a great deal of her thoughts, and she had been greatly relieved to discover that he had never had relatives on Regal. Therefore, they couldn't be related. That had been part of her fears when Grandma had told her about her father.

She decided that since she had never known her father, whether he was dead or alive didn't matter. He hadn't been there during her childhood, and she didn't need him now.

As her thoughts circled in her mind, her body worked with the shovel. After fifteen minutes of filling holes, her shoulders ached.

"No wonder we don't make much headway, Grandma," she pointed out, noticing that Grandma was also leaning on her shovel. "We tire out too fast."

At the sound of a car engine coming slowly down the lane, they turned their heads and watched Morgan maneuver the maroon van to a standstill a few yards past where they were working. He climbed out of the van, wearing worn blue jeans and a white tee-shirt that stretched across his wide chest. His clear blue eyes assessed the situation.

"Good afternoon, Mrs. Duncan, Callie," he called.

"Hello, Morgan," Callie answered.

Grandma merely nodded.

He slammed the van door and walked toward Callie and took the shovel out of her hands. "How exactly are you tackling this road?" He got straight to the point, not mincing words with pleasantries.

"We're just shoveling dirt into the holes," Callie said and shrugged.

"I see." He turned back toward the house and traced the road with his gaze. "When it rains, this road becomes a river, doesn't it?" He addressed Grandma, since her shrewd eyes had been watching his every move.

"It does."

"Well, then," he said, "it seems to me you need a drainage ditch on each side of the road. Otherwise, you'll be doing this every year as the spring rains wash out new ruts."

Callie exchanged glances with Grandma. "We do fix the worst of it every year. Although it's really deteriorated fast since it's just been Grandma and me."

In silence, Morgan walked to the side of the road and down a hundred yards or so, then back up to the women. "It appears there was a ditch of sorts here some time ago, but it's filled in over the years. See the sunken area over here," he said and pointed to a grassy area two feet from the edge of the road.

Again Callie and Grandma exchanged looks. "I reckon there did used to be one there," Grandma admitted, a touch of respect in her voice. "Orie always took care of the road afore he died. Callie Sue and me let it go for a couple of years, then started fillin' in the chuckholes. I never thought about that ditch."

"I didn't either, Grandma," Callie hurried to add, knowing

Grandma was mentally whipping herself for not seeing the obvious. "And while I was in Chapel Hill, the lane didn't get much use, so it just got worse."

"I'll work from the yard toward you," Morgan said. "Callie, get the dirt to fill the ruts from a straight line like this." He drew a line with the shovel along the side of the lane. He handed the tool back to Callie. "Mrs. Duncan, do you have a pick?"

"Yep. In the workshop." She started in that direction, but Morgan stopped her, placing a hand on her shoulder.

"I'll get it. Second building?" He pointed to a shed.

"Yep."

Morgan set off for the workshop, and Callie and Grandma started work again.

"Can't believe I didn't think about that ditch," Grandma mumbled to herself. "Summer folk tellin' me how to get water to run off. What a day!"

What a day, Callie echoed in her mind, when Morgan returned. He had assumed command of the road gang, and although he worked three hundred feet away from them, he was still in charge.

After a half hour of hard labor, Morgan called, "Mrs. Duncan, do you think we could have a cool drink in a few minutes?"

Grandma went into the house while Callie and Morgan worked on. The day was not hot, the temperature probably only in the mid-seventies, but Callie could feel the sweat on her forehead and down the middle of her back. Moving dirt was back-breaking labor.

"Bring your shovel up here," Morgan called. He showed her where to put the dirt he had loosened with the pick, having dug down about six inches and across about a foot. "We don't need a wide ditch, just enough for the water to run off."

He had a fine sheen on his face from his exertion, but he kept up a steady rhythm with the pick as if he were accustomed to manual labor, though Callie knew he was more at home behind a microphone in a recording studio—or lately behind a desk in the corporation headquarters.

"This is going to take forever. How far does your land extend,

Callie?" Morgan took a handkerchief out of his hip pocket and rubbed his face.

"The county road dead-ends into our lane, so it's hard to tell the difference. We have about a quarter of a mile. But the county road hasn't been maintained in years. There are only three houses on it, and we're the only one for the last two miles, so I guess other roads with more use get the county money."

"Hmmm. Your grandmother's on the porch. Let's take a break."

They laid down their tools and walked up to take their places in the rocking chairs and drink the ice water Grandma had brought out in a tin pitcher. Morgan drank three glasses before the trio marched back to the lane. This time they worked closely together, Morgan loosening the dirt with the pick, Grandma and Callie shoveling it into the potholes.

After another half an hour Morgan asked Grandma to bring out more water. "She shouldn't be out here doing this kind of work," he told Callie when Grandma was out of earshot.

"I know, but I'm not going to tell her that." Callie smiled. "She knows her limits, but she'll work hard until she gets there."

"Can you think of something else for her to do?"

"Will you stay for supper? I'll ask her to fry some chicken and fix a big meal. That'll keep her busy. How about an apple pie? That she can start baking now."

"I'll stay. Can't resist apple pie." He laughed.

Callie scurried off to inform Grandma that Morgan would be staying for dinner. When Callie returned with the glass of water for Morgan, he casually rested one arm around her shoulders as he drank. His touch sent her senses reeling, but all too soon he finished his drink and withdrew his arm as he handed her back the glass.

The rest of the afternoon he worked tirelessly. Callie couldn't keep up with him, so he alternated between the pick and the shovel. At the end of the day, they had completed only a fourth of the lane, but Callie was more than satisfied with their work. She was exhausted, but after washing up, Morgan looked as fresh as when he'd started.

"Aren't you tired?" she asked. She stood in the living room and pushed her elbows behind her to ease her aching back muscles. "You worked circles around me, and I'm about to drop."

Morgan knew that his muscles would scream at him tomorrow, but he didn't admit it. "Right now all I can think about is that apple pie you promised. It smells wonderful in here."

"Come and get it," Grandma's voice carried into the living room.

When they were all seated, Grandma asked Morgan to say grace. Without missing a beat, he held out his hands to take Grandma's and Callie's hands. "Father, thank You for this day. And thank You for the food we are about to receive and for the good woman who has prepared it for us. Amen."

Callie felt a squeeze from Grandma's hand and glanced at her. The older woman had a puzzled look on her face, as if she didn't know what to believe.

Grandma had fixed enough to feed half a dozen, but Morgan did justice to the meal, and Grandma had a self-satisfied smile as she watched the big man heap thirds of mashed potatoes and gravy, fried chicken, fresh biscuits, and fresh green onions and radishes on his plate.

"Excellent meal, Mrs. Duncan," he complimented Grandma.

"Them onions and radishes are the first of this year's crop," she said proudly.

"I noticed your garden last night. Looks like it belongs in a magazine," Morgan observed.

Grandma flowered under his praise. "Well, I do take good care of it. After all, it feeds us all year. I can most everything. The apples in the pie are from last fall."

"I didn't notice an orchard."

"It's around back. I'll show you," she said then bit her lip, as though taken aback by her own offer.

"Why don't you both walk around while I start on these dishes," Callie said. "We can have dessert on the porch in a few minutes."

"Good idea," Morgan hastily agreed, getting up from the table. "I need to walk off this meal before I start on apple pie." He pulled out

Grandma's chair and walked her to the back door. "Be back soon."
He winked at Callie.

Grandma looked disgusted, as if she'd been taken in, but with
her head held high, she walked out the back door that Morgan held
open for her.

❧

The next morning as Callie drove the old pickup down the lane, she
said, "Look how far we got yesterday. Without Morgan, we wouldn't
have gotten nearly that much done."

Grandma grunted, "He helped."

At Sunday school, Callie stood and gave the financial report.
The Sunday school president, who had been at the building meeting,
organized a workday to tar the roof.

"We've got to decide on a way to raise money," the elderly man
said. "We won't be able to build a new church for fifty years if we
don't come up with some way to bring in the dollars. Since we got a
preacher this week, we won't spend time on it now. But next week,
we've got to make some decisions."

He sat down and let the biweekly preacher take the pulpit.
"Worry is not for the Christian soul," the preacher began. "James
Russell Lowell said, 'The misfortunes hardest to bear are those which
never happen.' And Luke said in chapter 21, verse 34, 'Be careful, or
your hearts will be weighed down with. . .the anxieties of life. . . .'
Worry is futile. We should be free from concern. We should face life's
troubles as they come and turn them over to God."

Face life's troubles as they come, thought Callie, *and turn them over
to God.* She didn't hear the rest of the sermon. Instead she talked
silently with God, telling Him of her worry about not knowing who
her father was, her worry about Grandma not liking Morgan, and her
worry that her feelings for Morgan were not returned.

By the time the small congregation stood for the closing hymn,
she felt a great burden lift from her shoulders.

Chapter 5

Good morning, Vic." Morgan greeted his sister with a lazy smile. "Is there plenty of coffee?"

Vic poured him a cup and sat down with one of her own at the kitchen table. "What are you up to this fine Monday morning, Morgan? Do you have to work?"

"I was just about to ask you the same question. Where are the kids?" He took a sip of the hot brew and set down his cup as Wanda came in.

"Hot muffin, Morgan?" the cook offered, pulling a tray of delicious smelling muffins from the oven.

He sniffed. "Blueberry?"

"Of course. I know your favorite."

"You're too good to me, Wanda." He buttered two of the steaming muffins.

"I know it, and don't you be forgetting it either."

Dorothy entered the kitchen. She reached for a cup of coffee, then looked over her shoulder at Morgan. "How was your visit with Callie? You never mentioned it yesterday."

"So that's where you were Saturday night." Vic's eyes sparkled with curiosity. "I thought you were over at Robert's."

"I had dinner with Callie and her grandmother. We worked on smoothing out their drive, and I thought I'd go back over today and do a little more."

Victoria laughed. "I do believe you've met your match, Morgan, if she can get you out leveling a gravel drive."

"I didn't say it was gravel. In fact, it's a dirt drive. I'm digging a drainage ditch along side it." He knew he was letting himself in for it, but he wanted Vic's help.

"This is better than I thought," she said and giggled. "The Grammy-award-winning singer and new CEO of the Rutherford Group digging ditches to impress his love."

"I think it's quite admirable," Dorothy said. Morgan saw a knowing look in her eyes.

"Thanks, Mom. Now, Vic, I thought we could take the kids over to Callie's and work on the lane awhile. Have a picnic."

"No fooling? Okay, why not? The kids are still in bed, but it won't take them long to get around."

"No hurry. I need to make a few calls and run into Highridge on an errand. We'll leave here around ten thirty. Pack a good lunch, Vic."

Morgan carried his coffee cup with him to the study and called the office in Atlanta. He spoke briefly to his secretary, then was transferred to Charlie Lockard, his right-hand man. Morgan consulted his list on a yellow legal pad and jotted down notes beside each item. In concise terms, he directed Lockard, crossing some items out, adding more to the bottom of the list.

"Keep me posted on the contract renegotiations with the airline attendants, Charlie. I'll be out the rest of the day, but you can leave a message. Switch me back to Rochelle, please."

He dictated three letters to his secretary and asked her to collect more data on two of the new items on his legal pad. Making choices was difficult enough without meeting the people involved. He needed every scrap of available information that would help him make the best decision.

"Your manager has called twice. I told him I'd be talking to you, but I didn't tell him you were in the mountains. Don't be surprised if he doesn't call there next, though. He's pushy."

"That's why he's a good manager," Morgan said. "I'll call him." He didn't want to talk to Harry Caywood, though. Morgan didn't know what he was going to say. He had a corporation to run—and he had a singing career to promote. Or did he?

He hadn't talked to Callie about it the way he had planned. The evening they had gone out to dinner, she had seemed troubled, and he didn't want to bring up his own problems. He'd given his future plenty of thought, but he had a feeling that talking it out with Callie would help him put everything in perspective.

With reluctance he picked up the receiver and pushed Harry's programmed number. He didn't like what he heard. He'd been asked to star in the Super Bowl half-time show. It wasn't even football season, but the show had to be lined up.

"I'll call you in a few days with my decision," he told Harry, but his initial reaction was to say no.

"What's to decide? We're talking the Super Bowl. You know how many millions watch that? You've got to do it, Trey. It's been too long since you've been on tour. You need the exposure."

"I'll consider it and call you by Wednesday," Morgan assured his manager before hanging up.

A frown line remained etched on his forehead, but Morgan was pleased with how quickly he had finished his morning's work. He rewarded himself by taking another muffin with him as he cut through the kitchen on the way to the garage.

He drove straight for Pressman's Grocery Store. He could have called Darrell Pressman, but some things were better done in person. He took Darrell out for coffee and explained the county's negligence in caring for the road that led to Eagle Mountain.

Darrell, the sixty-odd-year-old grocer and county commissioner, was receptive, even ingratiating. Morgan might have felt a twinge of guilt at using his position as a wealthy taxpayer in the county to persuade a county commissioner to get that road fixed, but on this issue he felt vindicated because of the years of neglect.

After delivering Darrell back to his place of business, Morgan swung his car onto the highway and headed back to Regal Mountain. He felt another twinge of guilt at his plan to win Callie's grandmother. After yesterday's walk to the orchard, if all went according to his expectations, today might harvest even greater rewards. Callie was no fool, and she knew what he was doing. She'd seen right through him, but she had seemed pleased.

Vic and the kids were ready when he arrived back at his mountain home. They piled into the van amid laughter and kidding that continued until they reached Callie's turnoff. As he maneuvered the van down the difficult road, Morgan called for quiet and explained the situation. He impressed upon the kids that they were to be extra polite to Mrs. Duncan.

Callie's grandmother was in the garden when Morgan brought the van to a halt. He directed the others to stay in the van until she had given them permission to have their picnic.

As Morgan walked toward her, she straightened up, her pose one of questioning mistrust. Surely, Morgan thought, Saturday's work had made some headway with her.

"Good morning, Mrs. Duncan." Morgan didn't wait for her greeting but continued, "I was hoping you wouldn't mind if I worked on the lane a bit more. I brought helpers today. My niece and nephews need some planned activity," he said as if confiding in her. "I thought a little shoveling would use some of their energy and make sure they were tired enough for a good night's sleep." He added for good measure, "I'm baby-sitting tonight." The idea had just occurred to him, but he thought it was a good one. Vic would be glad for a night off.

Mrs. Duncan smiled. "Young uns can sure wear a person out if you don't beat them to it."

"Then you don't object to us working on the road?"

"Nah. But tell me, Morgan"—his ears pricked up at her use of his given name—"you out to impress my Callie Sue?"

"Yes, ma'am, I surely am," Morgan said and grinned. He waved for the troops to unload.

Morgan introduced his sister and the kids then took them to the workshop for tools. They made a curious parade, him leading the way, Victoria behind, the children following, each shouldering a tool. Even little Davie carried a tiny spade that Mrs. Duncan must use for repotting flowers.

After fifteen minutes of concentrated effort, Davie and Angie deserted to play in the shade of a tree. Jake manfully did his best to keep up with Morgan and Vic. When at last Jake left them to find out what his sister and brother were up to, Morgan told Vic that he'd watch the kids so she could take their mom out to dinner. As he figured, Vic didn't refuse the offer.

Lunch was a festive occasion. Wanda and Victoria had packed roast beef sandwiches, a thermos of gazpacho, and the ever popular peanut butter and jelly sandwiches. Morgan dispensed cold cans of soda from the ice chest. He'd asked Mrs. Duncan to join them under the shade of a huge oak tree for lunch, but she had refused, saying she had work to do indoors.

Morgan and Vic got back to work while the kids played by the side of the house.

"I'm going to have blisters soon, Morgan," Victoria complained. "Why not get some heavy machinery out here to dig this thing?"

"Would defeat my purpose. I'm trying to prove to Mrs. Duncan that all summer people aren't snobs out to use the year-rounders. That we work the same as they do."

"You picked a hard way to do it," she grumbled. She tossed more dirt on the lane, then lifted her head in alarm, looking around. "Have you seen the kids? They were over there a minute ago." She dropped her shovel and ran toward a path leading up Eagle Mountain, yelling Jake's name.

Morgan went around to the back of the house, calling their names.

"In here, Uncle Morgan." Jake poked his head out the kitchen doorway.

"I've found them, Vic," Morgan called to his sister and hastened to the back door. "What are you doing in there?"

"We're helping Grandma bake shortnin' bread," Jake explained, holding the screen door open for Morgan.

"Mrs. Duncan, I'm sorry the little scamps got away from us," Morgan apologized. He looked from one to the other of the children standing around the yellow oil cloth-covered table. Angie, flour covering the tip of her nose, was pushing a cutter into the dough. Davie was licking a spoon.

"They're no trouble, Morgan." She had a twinkle in her eye. "Reminds me of when Callie Sue was little or when her mom was a young un." A far away look came to her eyes. "My Daisy Lou loved makin' shortnin' bread and loved eatin' it more. Just like these little fellers, I reckon."

Morgan blinked, and he hoped it was the only outward sign that he'd been handed a revelation. He had assumed Mrs. Duncan was Callie's paternal grandmother because they had the same last name.

Vic knocked on the back door, and Morgan opened the screen. "Here they are," he said. "Mrs. Duncan says they're not being a bother." He turned back to Callie's grandmother. "I'm hoping Callie will help me baby-sit this evening, Mrs. Duncan. Would you mind if I used your phone?"

He excused himself to the living room and phoned Callie at work. After she agreed to help him, he returned to the kitchen and found Vic and Mrs. Duncan sitting at the table, glasses of lemonade before them as they exchanged views on child rearing.

"Just give 'em lots of love, and they'll turn out all right," the crusty old woman advised. "As long as you add the hickory stick from time to time as needed." She chuckled.

"Now, Grandma," Vic started.

Morgan stood framed in the doorway, taking in the scene before him. He was breaking his back trying to get on Mrs. Duncan's good side, and Vic just waltzed in and started talking like they were old friends.

"I'm going back to work for a few more minutes," he said. "When you finish the cookies, we'll go. Mrs. Duncan, Callie is coming to my house after work. She said to tell you she won't be in too late."

The apprehensive look was back in the old woman's eyes, and Morgan forced himself to smile and walk outside without slamming the screen door.

That old woman had let his sister and kids call her Grandma. She had taken them into her home and into her heart, if looks weren't deceiving. What had he done to deserve being treated like an outsider?

He tackled the ditch, working his annoyance off as he swung the pick and tossed dirt from the shovel. His intelligent mind sorted through the facts as he knew them, making lists just like on the yellow legal pad in his study.

Mrs. Duncan didn't like him paying attention to Callie. That much was clear. And why was that? According to Callie it wasn't a personal dislike, just a mistrust of summer people. Who was that Phillip anyway?

In midswing Morgan stopped, the pick dropping to the ground with a thud. Phillip was Callie's father! It all fit together now. The cad must have gotten Daisy pregnant during a summer fling and then left her. That's why Callie's name was Duncan. Callie had asked him indirectly how long his family had been coming to the mountains. She wanted to make sure they weren't related. That was it. It had to be.

He picked up the tools and started for the workshop. It was doubtful that any amount of shoveling would convince Mrs. Duncan he was not like Phillip, using her granddaughter for his own pleasure, then leaving her high and dry when fall came.

He was hot, tired, discouraged, and longing for a shower. He wanted to get away from this place. Here he was an outsider, and he didn't know how to belong. He was used to being in control, being respected for who he was and what he was, for his singing talent and for his shrewd business sense. Here he represented dirt under the old woman's feet.

Morgan called to Vic and the kids, loaded the ice chest and picnic basket, and sat in the van waiting for them, his eyes closed, his mind whirling with what he had figured out.

Finally his relatives trailed out of the house, Mrs. Duncan walking them out to the van. His good manners rescued him, and he thanked her for letting them picnic there.

As he drove off, the kids and Vic called their good-byes to Grandma.

"She's not your grandma," he snapped, then was aware of four pairs of startled eyes upon him.

"Sorry," he muttered and drove them home in silence.

Chapter 6

Callie knocked once on the front door and immediately heard running footsteps. The door opened, and Jake stood grinning up at her.

"Come on in, Callie Sue. Uncle Morgan's in the kitchen fixing dinner." He motioned her to follow him.

He had called her Callie Sue. How odd.

"Hi, Callie," Morgan greeted her. He was dressed casually in a green striped knit shirt and a pair of khaki shorts. Davie stood on a stool beside him, and Angie monopolized his other side. In one hand Morgan held a slotted spoon and in the other an apron. He tossed the apron to her. "I was hoping you'd give me a little assistance. It's Wanda's night off, and Mom and Vic left a few minutes ago."

"What are we making?" Callie asked, laying her purse on the counter and tying the apron around her waist. Lot of good a fancy apron would do her, she thought ruefully; she always spilled things on herself.

"We're making pizza," Angie answered. "You know, you're prettier than Grandma said."

"Thank you." Callie wondered if Dorothy had discussed her with the children after the surprise birthday party.

"We went to your house today," Angie said.

Callie glanced at Morgan.

"I took them with me," he explained. "They helped work on the lane."

"We sure did," Jake said. "We had a picnic, and Grandma let us make shortnin' bread. They were good."

"Grandma's a good cook," Callie replied as her mind assimilated the fact that Grandma liked the kids or she would have shooed them out of her kitchen. Besides that, she'd let them call her Grandma.

"Let's see if this pizza is as good." Morgan obviously wasn't expanding on the visit to Eagle Mountain.

Callie grated cheese then helped clean up the kitchen while the pizza baked. They carried it to the deck and ate amid laughter and chatter. The kids were full of the different things they had seen at Grandma's and explained them to Callie as if she hadn't lived there all her life.

With supper over, the kids carried plates into the kitchen and brought back their Candy Land board game. After the third game, Morgan called a halt.

"Time to get ready for bed," he announced. "Quick baths then to bed, little friends."

Groans and entreaties issued from the kids, but at Morgan's firm voice, they scurried to the bedroom wing of the house.

"I'll supervise Davie," Morgan told her. As soon as he headed for the bathroom, Callie rinsed the dishes for the dishwasher. She had the room spotless when Morgan returned, three kids in pajamas in tow.

"Morgan's going to tell us a story," Jake said.

Davie reached for Callie's hand and pulled her along. "Come on," he said.

Morgan tucked Jake and Davie into twin beds then sat in the rocking chair with Angie on his lap. Callie took an upholstered chair in the corner and watched entranced as Morgan told a story of kids mountain climbing and meeting a ferocious bear. By the end of the story, the kids had tamed the bear and taken him home to live with them.

"A little corny," he said under his breath and grinned.

"It's a great story," Callie whispered back. "But they're not asleep."

"Sing us a song, Uncle Morgan," Angie said. "The angel song."

"Then it's lights out, and you go to sleep. Promise?"

"Promise," the three kids said in unison. Callie chuckled. This obviously was the evening ritual.

"May you sleep with the angels, my little ones," Morgan crooned in his tenor voice. "May your dreams be the kind that come true. If you sleep with the angels, my little ones, little ones, then God will be smiling on you."

As he sang the verse one more time, Callie closed her eyes. The vision of Trey sprang in front of her eyes. Although she didn't know the song, the voice was the same one that sang on her stereo. She opened her eyes, and there was Morgan. Two very different personalities in one person.

He smiled at her when he finished the song then carried Angie across the hall to her bed. Callie sat in the corner until he returned and asked Jake to say the prayer. After he kissed the boys good night, he held out his hand to Callie. Together they walked down the hall to the living room.

"Shall we sit on the deck?" Morgan asked. "Or is it too cool for you?"

"I'll be fine," she said.

Morgan grabbed an afghan from the couch and opened the French doors onto the deck. He led Callie to the platform swing and sat down beside her.

"I've been wanting to talk to you," he said as he spread the afghan around their shoulders.

"About your careers?" Callie asked. "Which one do you prefer?"

"That's the problem. I like parts of both. Callie, you know I like making records. That's the fun part of singing. I've pretty much limited myself to recording and cut out the live performances, and not just because I'm afraid. You were right years ago about the power of prayer. Each performance I asked God for strength to get through the concert, and He gave it to me. I never forgot a word or a note. Now, though, I don't have the time for tours. Reporters bother me. I thought no concerts would put an end to publicity hounds, and it has to an extent. At least up here I don't have to worry about that." He reached for her hand and held it.

"What do you like about the corporation?"

"I like contributing to a company Grandad and Dad built. It's my heritage. I want it to continue as a company so Vic's kids and maybe someday my children will have the same opportunity I've had. I like the decision making. I guess I like the power."

"Is there something wrong with that? Power isn't bad. Someone has to make decisions, and I'd feel safe having you in charge of my business. You'd weigh every issue fairly and make as wise a decision as you could. Right?"

"I like to think that. But will other business leaders think I'm making wise decisions, or will they think I'm an airhead singer who's been handed a corporation as a toy?"

Callie turned in the swing so she could see his face in the dim light that filtered outside from the living room lamp. Morgan shifted, too, and rearranged the afghan so that they still had cover from the cool mountain air. He pushed the swing gently with his foot.

"I suppose that depends on your decisions," Callie said thoughtfully. "You shouldn't be afraid of what others will think of your singing career. You're an individual. You can't rest on your grandad's laurels or on your father's. You have to be who you are. And you are a wonderful singer who happens to be a businessman, too."

"You think so?"

"Of course. Hey, if an actor can be president of the United States, a singer can head a large corporation. The two careers don't conflict. They could actually complement each other." Callie grinned. "You could sing at the company Christmas party."

Morgan stopped the gentle sway of the swing and sat up straight. "I've been asked to sing at Super Bowl half time."

She raised her eyebrows at him. "What are you going to do?"

He took a deep breath and let it out slowly. "I don't want to do it. Besides the thousands at the stadium, there would be millions watching on TV—live."

"Then don't do it."

"Just like that?"

"Exactly. As a full-time singer you were busy—on the road performing and recording at home. Now that the business takes lots of your time, you've cut out the touring because it's the part you dislike and is too time consuming. Don't make an exception and go back to it. You've earned the right to do what you want."

He took her hands in his. "You have such a clear way of stating the obvious. I've gone over that very logic; then I get bogged down with—will no performances hurt my image? Will fans keep buying my records if I don't perform occasionally? I don't think so, but if not, I don't have to depend on singing for a living."

He leaned over and kissed her, not once, but twice.

"Oh," she said when he drew back.

"Yes, oh."

They stared at each other; then Callie drew back. She'd promised Grandma she wouldn't get involved with a summer person, and this wasn't how to keep that promise. But Morgan was not a typical summer person. She put her hands in her lap.

As if reading her mind, Morgan said, "I think I know who Phillip is."

Callie gasped. "You know my fa. . ." She stopped herself before she finished the sentence.

"No. I know Phillip is your father. I figured out today that Mrs. Duncan is your maternal grandmother. All along I thought she was your father's mother."

Callie stood up and walked to the deck railing. She stared out at the darkness, broken far below by lights from houses that twinkled like the stars above her. She shivered and hugged herself for warmth. The cool night air did not chill her as much as the realization that Morgan knew she didn't know who her father was.

He came up behind her and spread the afghan over her shoulders like a shawl. He pulled her back to lean on him. "Your grandmother thinks I'm like Phillip," he stated.

"Yes. She doesn't trust summer people. Especially those on Regal Mountain."

"But you trust me?"

"Yes. I've only known about Phillip for a few days. She had told me he was killed in an accident before I was born."

"And you never questioned that?"

Callie turned to face him, glad he kept his arms around her for support. "At first I did. I wanted to see pictures of him, but we didn't have any. I asked lots of questions, but Grandma never answered them, so I quit asking." She said in a small voice, "If it wasn't for you, she wouldn't have told me."

"Do you want to find your father?"

Callie was silent for a long moment, searching her heart for the truth. "I don't know. One minute I want to know who he is, to know something about his family. The next minute I never want to know a man who would turn his back on me."

Morgan nodded and pulled her closer. Callie rested her head on his chest. This was what she needed. Comfort.

"If you decide to find him, I'll help you." When she didn't respond, he continued. "This has nothing to do with you. You are who you are, no matter who your parents were. You're a lovely, kind, God-fearing woman. Your ancestry has nothing to do with the kind of woman you are. Oh, your grandmother does, because she raised you and instilled her beliefs in you. But genes don't matter that much. It's what you do with them that matters."

Callie started to lean back, but he cupped her head with his hand and held it against his chest. She wanted the moment to go on and on, but it ended with the sound of the garage door opening.

"Whatever decision you make, I'll support it," he said and led her back to the swing. "But if you want to find him, we will."

Dorothy and Victoria breezed onto the deck, greeted them, and took chairs beside the swing.

"How was your night out?" Callie asked.

"More importantly," Victoria said, "how was your night in? Did the kids behave?"

"Perfect angels," Callie said.

"Now, why are they better for you than they are for me? That's kids for you. By the way, I had a pleasant visit with your grandmother today. The kids and I went to help with the lane and had a picnic. I like her. She's quite a character."

"That she is," Morgan agreed. He had nonchalantly settled his arm around Callie's shoulders, and she welcomed the protective gesture. She still felt flustered from their discussion.

"Where did you go for dinner?" she asked to make conversation.

"Collett's," Victoria answered. "They have a scrumptious cheesecake that I can't resist. Didn't you and Morgan go there? Did you try it?"

"No. I mean, we didn't try it, but we did go there."

"What do you do for entertainment, Callie?" Dorothy had wandered from the chair to the deck railing where Morgan and Callie had stood just minutes before.

"I go to movies with friends, but more often Grandma and I have friends over to visit, play music, or play dominoes."

"Do you dance at your music parties?" Victoria's animated voice held real interest. "That mountain stumble or something that we saw a few years ago. Do you remember, Morgan? We went down to Dillard for some special celebration."

"You must mean clogging," Callie said.

"Yes, that's it. Do you clog?"

"Sure. Would you like to learn how?"

Victoria chuckled. "We tried it at that festival. What a disaster. I felt like I had two left feet. Morgan wasn't any better."

"Wait a minute. I can clog circles around you, Vic," he teased. "Why don't we all go to Dillard tomorrow night? Have a little contest. Don't they have a tent show every night, Callie?"

"They do."

"I'm game. How about asking your grandmother to join us, Callie? I'll bet she's a real clogger."

"She is. I don't know if she'll come or not, but I'll ask her." Callie reluctantly stood up and smiled at Morgan. "I must be going. Tomorrow's another day at the office."

"It's nice to see you again, Callie." Dorothy led the way to the living room. "I'm looking forward to tomorrow night. And do encourage your grandmother to join us. I'd love to meet her."

"I'll ask her. Will you take the kids? I think they'd have fun."

"Only if you'll help me keep an eye on them," Vic said.

"Of course, Vic," Morgan said. "We'll each take one in tow."

Callie folded the afghan and laid it on the arm of the couch. She picked up her purse, and Morgan ushered her to the door.

"I'll see you tomorrow," Callie called to the Rutherford women.

They called good night as Morgan walked her outside to her pickup.

"Remember what I said. If you want to find him, we will. If you don't, we'll never discuss it again." He pulled her close and kissed her.

When the kiss ended, Callie clung to him. "I must go," she whispered, but made no move to withdraw.

"Yes," Morgan said, but his arms tightened around her. He kissed her again and finally let her go.

"We'll pick you up around seven tomorrow night. Let's eat at the Dillard House before the clogging begins."

"Sounds good." Callie climbed into the pickup. Morgan shut the door, stepped back, and blew her a kiss, the same gesture she had seen on his TV special. Was this Trey or Morgan?

Her mind reeled as she inched her way down the mountain to stop at the gatehouse and insert the plastic card that opened the gate. When she had arrived earlier, Billy had stopped her and given her the card, telling her Morgan had instructed him to give it to her so she could come and go whenever she needed. She shook her head, her lips faintly curved; Morgan seemed to be after more than a friendship.

She watched the gates swing open and drove the pickup onto the highway toward home. What did he want from her, and what was she willing to give? *Everything*, her heart answered, but her mind couldn't see a permanent relationship between them. She didn't fit into his high-powered world. She liked his family well enough, and they seemed to like her, but for all that, they were millions of dollars apart. The likelihood that he could settle down with someone like her seemed remote.

So what did he want? An affair? She didn't believe that. He was a God-fearing man. But memories of her mother and the unknown Phillip flooded her mind. For a moment she knew how her mother must have felt, loving Phillip the way she had. But did she love Morgan?

Yes, her heart answered again. She had loved Morgan for five years.

For most of that time, he was a pipe dream of hers, based on what she knew of him. But the last few days had proved that in this case, fantasy and reality were the same. He was the man of her dreams, and he lived up to them. A big star, a singer, a caring man, a Christian. All those things in one man. If only he could truly love her.

Callie turned onto the dirt road from the highway and automatically slowed the pickup to a crawl, preparing herself for the bumps and ruts. They were gone! The road had been graded! She picked up speed a bit and marveled at the ride.

When the county road turned into their lane, the ruts returned, then ended again at the point Morgan and Vic had reached with their slow, painstaking labor. The light was on in the living room, and Callie parked the pickup in the shed and raced to the house.

"What happened to the road?" she demanded of Grandma as she burst into the front room.

"It was graded," Grandma replied calmly. She was sitting in the big green chair beside the lamp, one of her beloved paperback westerns in her hands.

"I know that," Callie stated. "But when, how, why? Did you hear it?"

"Whoa! Sit down, and I'll tell you all about it. Want something to drink?"

"Quit stalling. That road hasn't been touched in years, and now it's as smooth as velvet. What are you hiding, Grandma?"

"Nothing. Frank DeShaver came by on that big road grader of the county's and said he was ordered to come over here and get that road in shape today. He came not long after Morgan and the kids left and worked until almost dark."

"But what prompted it after so many years of neglect?" Callie stood with hands on her hips, wanting to get to the bottom of this puzzle.

"Humph," Grandma snorted. "It was politics. Frank told me it was Darrell Pressman hisself who called and told him to do it this afternoon. Seems Morgan paid him a little visit this morning and threw his weight around to get it done." Grandma didn't seem too pleased that Morgan had gone to all that trouble for them.

Callie sat down hard on the footstool in front of Grandma's chair. "Morgan did that for us?"

"Yep. He did it for you. Don't it gripe you that someone who only comes here for a few weeks a year has more say in what goes on here than us year-rounders?" She frowned.

"He may not live here year-round, but he pays a sight more money in land taxes than we do, Grandma. Even with us owning Eagle Mountain. That's undeveloped land, and it doesn't touch the kind of money Morgan and his friends pay for their big fancy homes on Regal Mountain." She got up from the footstool and stood once again with her hands on her hips, facing Grandma. "Money talks. That may not be right, but it's how the world runs. And for once we know somebody who has some power to do things. Morgan did nothing wrong. He just righted a wrong, if you want to look at it that way. He wouldn't use his influence to do anything illegal."

"No," Grandma said. "Frank said he was told to do the road, but he couldn't touch our lane since it wasn't county property. He said he's done that kind of thing before when persuaded right. But he was told Morgan was takin' care of our lane hisself."

Callie smiled a big broad smile. "See. He's a good man, Grandma. I know he's a summer person, but he's a good man. He and his family are taking me to Dillard tomorrow night for dinner and clogging. They've asked you, too. What do you say? Wouldn't you like to go? Then you'd have the opportunity to thank Morgan for all that's been done for us." She was preparing for a major battle with Grandma, but was surprised when Grandma agreed.

"Might not be a bad idea," the old woman said with a gleam in her eye. "Long as you're goin', I might as well go, too. Who all's goin' to be there?"

"Dorothy, Morgan's mother, and Victoria and the kids who you met this afternoon."

"Yep. That Vic's a good 'un. Got good kids, too." Grandma nodded her head in agreement as she got up from her chair. "Sure, I'll go." She told Callie good night and walked toward her bedroom.

Callie heard her mutter, "Sure, I'll go. Keep my eye on things."

Chapter 7

The wind had picked up in the night and blown in a cool front that threatened rain. Morgan had awakened to fog so thick he couldn't see the great oaks that stood ten feet from his bedroom window. The fabulous view that he knew lay beyond the fog might have been only a figment of his imagination.

And what else was in his imagination? He thought Callie cared for him—but did she really? He had dreamed about her last night. When he awoke, he found himself praying that she had had a safe drive home on the curvy roads—and praying that she loved him.

Falling in love with her hadn't been love at first sight. That night five years ago in the restaurant he had been intrigued by her because she hadn't fallen all over the big star, but nothing more.

Instead, his feelings were love at second sight. On the day they had spent together filling out her college application, he had fallen for her. She had been shy at first, but then she had opened up and talked to him. More importantly, she had listened. He had felt so at ease with her, that he'd confided his hopes and fears.

Since that time, he'd unconsciously been waiting for her. He had dated other women in those years, but still had not committed himself to a lasting relationship. He had fooled himself into thinking he wasn't ready to settle down. Now he realized it was Callie who had kept him single.

He threw the light covers off and rolled out of bed, his bare feet hitting the thick carpet with a soft thud. With the habit of years, he walked to the bathroom and showered. He knew he was an anomaly in show business, but morning was his favorite time. He had grown up emulating his father, who was always dressed and ready to face the day when Morgan saw him. At a moment's notice his father could leave the house to settle a business crisis or a personal emergency. He was never caught off guard, and it was a trait Morgan admired.

Freshly shaved, clean, and dressed, Morgan headed for the kitchen and a cup of Wanda's unbeatable coffee. One of the things he looked forward to when meeting the family in the mountains was a cup of Wanda's brew and a talk with his mother, who was as early a riser as he was. He could always go to his mother's house in Atlanta, but his life was so busy there, he rarely had time for a visit. He called her regularly, and they had a good relationship, but she was as busy as he was, and their good intentions to see each other rarely materialized. When they did manage to meet, they squeezed a lot into their short time together. Except this time. He had been here almost a week and had spent most of his evenings with Callie. His mornings were spent in his office, and likely as not, Dorothy was running errands, sightseeing, or shopping in the afternoons.

He poured himself a cup and sat down at the kitchen table alone. A moment later, Dorothy walked in.

"Good morning, Morgan." Dorothy smiled at him as she crossed to the coffee maker.

"Morning, Mom." He looked at her with a straightforward gaze. "I've just been thinking about you. We haven't had time for a good visit, have we?"

Dorothy sat down across from him and smiled. "She's special, isn't she?"

"Yes, she is." He had no need to ask who. They may not have seen a lot of each other lately, but they had always communicated on the same plane.

"And does she feel the same way about you?"

"I don't exactly know." He shook his head. "I think she does, but she has a lot of ingrained biases. Her grandmother distrusts all summer people."

"You put her through college for your benefit, didn't you?" Dorothy's eyes were not accusing, just concerned.

"No," he said. "Well, not at first, but maybe it developed into that. She needed a broader background and more confidence in herself." He pushed away from the table, walked to the glass wall, and stared out at the fog. "That sounds very manipulative, as if I'm trying to change her into what I want her to be. Yet it's not that way." He stood with his back to his mother, his hands in his slacks pockets. "She's so intelligent; she needed the opportunity. It was a risk. She could have met someone at college, and I would have been out of the picture." He turned and looked at her. "But it didn't happen that way, and I'm not sure how it will turn out. I came here this summer to get to know her better, to see what might happen between us."

"You are so much like your father, Morgan. You want to have as much information as possible before you make a decision. But this time, your list of pros and cons isn't going to help." Her eyes danced as she looked at him. "Seems to me your future is in the hands of a little gal from the mountains."

He smiled wryly and acknowledged her wisdom. "You're probably right. So where do I go from here?"

"What? The dashing bachelor needs help dealing with a woman?" She laughed. "Wouldn't the tabloids have a heyday with that!"

"It's not funny, Mother." His eyes asked for her understanding.

"No, it's not. But don't worry about it, Morgan. I trust Callie's judgment—and she couldn't do better than you."

"Thanks. I hope your confidence in her and me isn't misplaced." He leaned down and kissed her cheek. Glancing at his watch, he changed the subject. "I've got to call the office and see what was accomplished with our flight attendants. I'd hate to fly to Kansas City to sit in on negotiations."

"Have you eaten?"

"No. I'll eat when Vic and the kids are up."

As if on cue, Victoria sauntered into the kitchen.

"Morning, Vic," Morgan patted her head as he passed her. "Call me when breakfast is ready."

Closeted in his study, the shrewd businessman took over, and Morgan reviewed the information he'd been faxed the previous afternoon. When Vic called him for breakfast, he told her to go ahead and eat, that he would be a few more minutes. He took another hour to complete his agenda, and he was grateful when Wanda brought in a fresh cup of coffee.

The house was empty when he finished jotting notes to himself and called his secretary again to dictate letters. A note on the refrigerator told him he was on his own for lunch. The others had gone to Asheville on an impromptu excursion with some friends and wouldn't be back until late afternoon.

Morgan called his manager and rejected the Super Bowl offer. Harry growled, but Morgan told him straight out that he wouldn't be doing any performances. He'd commit to presenting a Grammy, if asked, but not to singing in public. Callie had said he'd earned the right to do as he pleased, and he agreed.

His thoughts turned to Callie. He still had to convince her grandmother that he was worthy of Callie. And there was the matter of Phillip. Callie might not know it yet, but he was certain she wouldn't be satisfied until she knew why her father had deserted her mother. Knowing the real story might make Mrs. Duncan feel better about both Phillip and Morgan. Morgan wouldn't start the search without Callie's okay, but he decided it wouldn't be long before she came to the realization that she had to know.

Left with the day to himself, Morgan prowled the house like a caged animal. The fog had turned to heavy drizzle and any thought of outside activity was nixed. He tried to read a novel, but couldn't concentrate.

His muscles cried for attention. For two days he had shoveled dirt and now they needed some exercise to ease the stiffness of the unaccustomed strain. He worked out regularly at his home gym in Atlanta or played racquetball with a friend, and he needed some sort of workout now.

Knowing it wasn't the smartest thing to do for his voice, but nevertheless determined to get outside, Morgan donned an old sweat suit and running shoes and took off into the drizzle. He ran over to the clubhouse, a fairly flat run. From there the road turned up the mountain and ran by Reynolds', past Newmans', and peaked at Houstons'. He turned around and flew down the mountain, past his own house and down, down.

He stopped when he reached Robert Garrigan's and rang the doorbell. No answer. His old pal from Atlanta was either not in or at the computer plotting his latest mystery. He didn't like being interrupted and didn't answer the door or phone when he was writing. Morgan didn't blame him. He certainly didn't allow visitors at the studio when he was recording.

He turned and started back up the mountain. After a couple of blocks, he slowed to a walk and looked over at Prescotts'. Dianne Prescott stood looking out the picture window at the rain. Although he hadn't seen her in a couple of years, in other summers in the mountains they had dated.

She had seen him and waved. He walked to the front door, which opened before he reached the first step.

"Trey, when did you come to the mountains?" She had always called him by his stage name, probably because that was what attracted her to him, but she was as gorgeous as ever. The two years since he'd seen her hadn't aged her one day. She wore turquoise slacks and a long blousy white top trimmed in turquoise, the same color she'd been wearing the last time he'd seen her. Her eyes glittered with excitement.

"Hello, Dianne. I arrived Thursday. Yourself?"

"Just got in yesterday, in time for this dreary weather. The whole family's due in by the end of the week. Big reunion. We're having a party Saturday night. I hope you'll be able to come."

"I'll check and see," Morgan replied noncommittally.

"Come in, Trey. We can catch up on news." She looked him up and down and smiled persuasively.

"No, thanks. I'm drenched and need to finish my run before I get cold. I'll see you later, Dianne." He waved a salute and turned back for the run up the mountain, aware that Dianne stood on the porch and watched his retreat.

The last summer he'd seen her, she had just been divorced after a one year marriage. She'd wanted to continue their dating relationship and had called him in Atlanta, but he hadn't complied. He wasn't sure that as a Christian he should date her, especially since he didn't know the facts of her marriage and divorce. Besides, she was a summer date, not someone he wanted around on a permanent basis. She'd not taken his rejection well, but she seemed to have forgiven him now for ending their dating relationship.

Morgan made the rest of the jog in good time, and once inside the garage, he took off his wet shoes and socks and darted for his room. Testing his voice, he sang in the shower and heard no telltale raspiness.

He needed to write the songs for his new album. That had been one of his goals while on vacation from the corporation, if he decided to continue singing. Although he had talked only briefly with Callie about his two careers, his thoughts had solidified since last night. No concerts was an easy decision. He'd further concluded that he could put out a new album every two years without disrupting his corporate life. True, Harry would growl that he had to record one album a year, but he'd come around eventually. Harry always growled. He'd actually taken their no concerts conversation better than Morgan had thought he would.

He wanted to tell Callie. He glanced at the clock—almost twelve—he might catch her. He dressed and drove into Highridge, carefully manipulating the wet, slick turns. The receptionist at the CPA firm got wide-eyed when she saw him.

"Is Callie in?"

"She's on her lunch break," she said. "She usually brings her lunch and eats at her desk. Go on back."

"Thanks." Morgan walked down the long hallway until he reached Callie's office. She sat in her chair with her back to the door and her feet propped up on her work table, a paperback novel in her hand.

"Hi," he said softly.

She whirled in her chair, dropping the book.

"Hey, Robert's latest book," he said, picking it up and handing it back to her.

"Since you knew him, I thought I should know what he wrote.

What are you doing here, Morgan?"

"I thought I'd take you to lunch."

"Oh." She smiled up at him. "That's a lovely thought, but I only have fifteen minutes left. I had an early lunch since I have a twelve forty-five appointment. Want to share?" she asked and motioned to a chair. "I have some chips left and an apple. Want a drink?" She handed him the canned soda on her desk, and he took a long drink, exulting in the fact that her lips had touched the same place as his.

I'm as silly as a teenager, he thought. Once again a teenager on a first date.

"I've decided to sing and be CEO of the Rutherford Group," he said without preamble.

She nodded. "You can do both. It just requires balance. If you see that you want to do more recording, you could appoint someone to oversee the business. However, I don't know how you'd work it if you wanted to do less singing. You can't appoint someone to take your place as a singer."

"I know. One album every two years is my plan. I've been using studio musicians for the albums since I laid off the concert tour. Most of them are the same guys who went on that last tour with me, but I just pick them up when I need them, so they aren't depending on me for a livelihood."

"Sounds like you've got it all worked out."

"Not the details and not the songs. I have a few songs that will work, but all of them aren't written. The house is empty today, so I'll be able to work this afternoon. I was hoping for a little inspiration."

"Inspiration? From me?"

He walked around the desk and pulled her to her feet and into his arms. He kissed her soundly then stepped back.

"That ought to do it. I'm working on a love song this afternoon." He chuckled at her expression and walked to the door. "I'll see you tonight. Till then." He blew her a kiss then walked out the door.

Notes were already flitting through his mind. By the time he arrived back on Regal Mountain, he had a full-fledged melody. He sat at the grand piano in the living room, pencil in hand, manuscript paper on the piano top, and hit keys and wrote down notes. "Callie's Song," he said and hummed before he played a few more notes and scribbled them down. Within an hour, he had the entire melody down, including chords.

If he could get the others done that quickly, he could meet with the arranger in a couple of weeks and get each score finished. Normally he used a violin, drums, and a bass guitar, but on occasion, he'd add a sax and other brass instruments. Each song demanded different instruments to make the emotion come through.

"We're home," Vic called from the kitchen.

Morgan had been so absorbed in his work, he hadn't heard the car pull in. The chatter of kids coming inside and the ringing of the phone coincided.

"I'll get it," Vic said.

"Come listen to this," Morgan called to the others. The kids and Dorothy joined him in the living room. He played the new song.

"It's beautiful," Dorothy said. "What's it called?"

"I don't have all the words down yet," he hedged. She looked over his shoulder at the title he had written down and raised her eyebrows.

"Mmm. She'll love it," she said.

"Morgan, a message for you," Vic said as she waltzed into the living room.

Morgan's mind flew to the labor negotiations. "Charlie?"

"No, dear brother. A voice out of your past."

He immediately knew. "Dianne?"

"Yes. She invited us to a party Saturday night. I asked if we could bring a guest and of course she agreed, not knowing I meant Callie."

Morgan frowned. "That should prove interesting. I told Callie we'd pick her and Mrs. Duncan up tonight at seven. So everybody be ready by a quarter to. I'd better call the office again." He took his music notebook and headed back to his study. He wanted to write the poem that would make this especially Callie's song, but he needed peace and solitude to do that.

Not to make a liar out of himself, he called the office and learned the flight attendants' negotiations were hitting some snags. He called Kansas City and talked to Charlie Lockard, who had flown out there the day before. By the time he'd finished tying up details, it was time to get ready for clogging at Dillard. "Callie's Song" would have to wait.

At fifteen minutes before seven, the family climbed into the van and set off for the Duncans'. Vic commented on the newly-graded road, but Morgan didn't explain his part in it. As he turned the van onto the rutted lane, he noticed a red Trans-Am parked in front of the house. Callie, Mrs. Duncan, and a strange man sat in the rocking chairs on the front porch.

Morgan left the others in the van and walked to the porch, assessing the man on his way. Although he was sitting, Morgan could tell he was lean and fairly tall, but not as tall as himself. He had straight blond hair and sported a thick mustache. He was laughing with the women but kept his gaze on Morgan.

"Good evening, Morgan." Callie stood as he climbed the slab rock steps. "I'd like you to meet Joe Lowery. Joe, this is Morgan Rutherford."

The two men shook hands, much like two boxers eyeing one another in the ring, assessing the other's ability and chance at success.

"Joe had business in Highridge and stopped off here hoping he could eat supper with us," Mrs. Duncan announced, her eyes dancing. "He does that whenever he's in town. He's a banker in Franklin," she informed Morgan proudly.

"I see," Morgan said. After a pregnant pause, he added, "Why don't you join us for the evening, Joe? We're going to Dillard for dinner."

"Thanks, Morgan, I'd like that. I haven't visited with Callie Sue and Grandma in quite awhile, and I was looking forward to it." Joe accepted the invitation with a big grin. Somehow Morgan had known he would.

"Tell you what," Joe continued. "Why don't I drive Callie Sue and Grandma down there since it's a straight shot from Dillard to

Franklin for me to go on home. Then you can bring these two ladies back here later."

The evening was not going at all like Morgan had planned, but he smiled and agreed to Joe's plan, since Grandma looked at him as if he had no choice.

Morgan ended up following Joe's car down the steep and curvy road to Dillard and parking next to him on the huge parking lot beside the Dillard House.

The country meal was served family style with large bowls of corn-on-the-cob, green beans, mashed potatoes, gravy, ham, fried chicken, and biscuits. Conversation halted as bowls were passed around. The kids provided a continuous chatter from then on, and the adults chimed in, soon breaking off into their own conversational groups.

Morgan watched the various participants. Mrs. Duncan eyed Dorothy suspiciously for a short while, then seemed to warm to her as Vic played moderator. Callie conversed at length with Joe, but tried to involve Morgan, too. He didn't know the people they discussed, and although Callie explained a bit, the conversation meant nothing to him. To add injury to insult, Joe asked him what he did for a living. Normally Morgan would enjoy not being recognized as Trey, but this meant that Callie hadn't talked about him to Joe. Morgan would have thought his name would have come up. He found himself talking to the kids and letting the adult conversation flow around him. He didn't like it, not one little bit.

Clogging in the tent show was as little fun for him as the dinner party had been, even though the main guitarist, a man at least in his sixties, knew his music and conveyed it to the audience. A young woman in a short, square dance dress and shiny white patent leather shoes with taps illustrated the mountain dance. When the audience was asked to join them on stage, all the kids, Vic, and Joe trooped forward. Morgan, however, wasn't in the mood to join the group.

At last Callie persuaded him to follow her. Try as he might, though, the steps were too difficult for him, requiring that he move from the knee down, holding the upper body straight. At the partner switch, Callie clogged with Joe, and Morgan and Vic sat down. The next partner switch, Callie clogged with little Davie, and Joe claimed a seat beside Morgan.

"How long have you been here?" Joe asked suddenly.

"Almost a week," Morgan answered. "Why?"

Joe grinned his lazy grin. "Just wondering how long you'd been seeing Callie Sue."

"Almost a week," Morgan repeated.

"Didn't lose any time," Joe observed. His eyes held a glint of amusement. "I appreciate you sharing her tonight. I've not been able to see her in quite awhile." His eyes turned thoughtful as he continued. "I may be out of line here, since I just met you, but don't hurt her."

"I have no intention of hurting her," Morgan protested.

"Just see that you don't. She's an awfully special person, and she feels indebted to you."

Morgan digested this information. "I thought you didn't know who I was?"

"Just wanted to see how you'd take not being recognized. Back to Callie. She's grateful to you for educating her, and she's built you up into some kind of hero."

The dance was over, and Joe and Morgan stood as Callie and David walked back to them. Joe's revelation had been a blow. Morgan knew Callie was grateful; she'd told him several times, but he didn't want that to be the basis for their relationship. He hadn't mentioned that check to her again, and now he decided to cash it. If she started paying him back, maybe she'd lose that grateful attitude.

After good-byes to Joe, the rest loaded into the van for the ten-mile drive back home. The kids were quiet, tired from a late night. The women spoke softly among themselves, leaving Morgan alone to brood.

"Morgan?" Callie's voice interrupted his thoughts. She was sitting in the captain's chair across from the driver's seat and leaned toward him so they could have a private conversation.

"Yes, Callie?"

"Thank you for inviting Joe. I'm sorry I didn't get to talk with you. Joe and I are old friends, and I haven't seen him in quite some time," she explained.

"You're welcome." He knew he was being short with her, but he couldn't seem to help himself. He was jealous. For the first time in his life, he was jealous. Not that his other women friends hadn't had flirtations when he was around. They had. But he'd known all he had to do was give them a sign he wanted them beside him, and instantly they'd be there. With Callie, he didn't think that would work. He knew she cared for him—but when an old friend came calling, she showed that she truly cared for him, too. Morgan, however, wanted her all to himself.

As they turned onto the dirt road, Callie again attempted conversation. "I didn't mention it at lunch, but we are grateful for your influence in getting the road graded for us."

"You're welcome," Morgan muttered. There was that word again, grateful.

"Grandma is impressed with your persistence in getting our lane smooth, too," she added.

Terrific, thought Morgan. What is that supposed to mean? That I should get over here tomorrow and get the job finished? He immediately dismissed that. Callie was too straightforward to manipulate him that way.

He knew he was acting like a spoiled child—but he had hoped that the two of them could have laughed together tonight, conversing with his mother and Callie's grandmother. As it was, he'd have to ask Vic how the two older women had gotten along.

He brought the van to a halt and hopped out to walk around and open the side door for Grandma, and then Callie's door. He walked them to the porch. The porch light shone brightly, and flying insects of various sizes and shapes buzzed around it.

Grandma held out her hand to Morgan. "Thanks for takin' us tonight, Morgan." With a mischievous light in her eyes, she added, "And I'm glad you asked Joe." She stepped inside the door, but Morgan could still hear her soft chuckle.

Morgan took Callie's hands in both of his and pulled her around the corner of the house where shadows gave some privacy.

The good-night kiss didn't last long. After all, his family was sitting in the van, and there was no telling where Mrs. Duncan was.

"Callie, see me tomorrow night?"

"Yes," she whispered.

"I'll be here after work, and we'll decide what we want to do."

"Okay." He gave her another kiss. "Good night, Morgan," Callie said softly and stepped inside.

Morgan strode to the van with a much lighter step.

Chapter 8

Callie waited until she heard the van roar into life and start out the drive before she turned off the porch light. She stood in the dark a moment longer, then sighed and turned on the lamp in the living room. Grandma ambled in from her bedroom.

"What did you think of the evening?" Callie asked.

"Well, it was nice of him to ask Joe."

"Yes," Callie said. "He was a good sport about it. He's going to pick me up here tomorrow evening after work." She walked over to the fireplace and looked at the picture of her mother on the mantle. When Grandma's opinion wasn't forthcoming, she spun around. "Aren't you going to say summer people and year-rounders don't mix?"

"No. You know that. Money makes a big difference in a person's life. Makes them expect different things. But I reckon Morgan's a good man. He can't help being born rich, and his ma's real proud of him. And a ma can generally tell how good their young uns turn out. That Vic's a good un, too."

"Morgan's a gentleman."

"Oh, he may be a gentleman, but he's also a full growed man, and he's a man who gits what he wants. Don't think I've been fooled by his manners and his hard work on our lane. He's after you, and he intends to get you. He's just biding his time, tryin' to get on my good side." Grandma gave a sly smile.

"And is he on your good side?"

"Hmm," Grandma said noncommittally. "I know he's already got you on his side. But be careful, Callie Sue. Don't give in to him."

"Grandma!" Callie exclaimed.

"Let's call a spade a spade, Callie Sue. I didn't marry Orie because he was the only man around. I married him because I loved him and wanted to live with him and bear his children. I know how it is. I've been there. And so has Dorothy. Don't think she don't know what's goin' on. She told me she'd never seen him so determinedly pursue anyone before. Them's her words, 'determinedly pursue.' "

Callie stretched her arms over her head and yawned. She didn't want to continue this conversation. Grandma looked like she was warming up to a lecture. Callie claimed tiredness and the need to get up early in the morning for work, and then she fled to her room to be alone with her thoughts.

So Morgan was determinedly pursuing her. Good. Because she knew she had fallen deeply in love with him, and she needed some assurance that he might feel the same way.

She was still amazed that a superstar like Trey could be such a fine man. A Christian, too. His family upbringing had stayed with him even though he must have been tempted by the trappings of show business. Not that she knew much about show business, but she read the tabloid headlines while she waited in supermarket lines.

The first time she saw his picture on the cover, she had almost fainted. That had been the summer before her college days. With the innocence of a teenager, she had asked Morgan about it the next time they met to discuss her financial matters. He had discounted as pure fiction his alleged liaison with an actress. The picture had been taken at the Grammy Awards months earlier. He had been standing beside the actress, but she wasn't his date. Since then he had been on the cover each time a new album came out. Publicity, he told her. He wasn't having an affair, he hadn't been abducted by aliens, and he wasn't running away to join a guru in India. He assured her he was a dedicated Christian and his morals were high. Certainly he was a gentleman.

He had behaved well tonight, although she could see the thunderclouds on his forehead. She thought he might even be jealous. Not that jealousy was a good emotion to arouse in someone, but it did mean he wanted her to himself.

Joe had sure played up to her. If she didn't know better, she'd have thought he was interested in her, instead of feeling brotherly toward her the way he always had. He knew how she felt about Morgan; they had discussed it on their trips back and forth to school. When he had told her good-bye tonight, he had confided that he'd wanted to see what kind of man Morgan was. He'd liked him, he said, though he hadn't expected he would.

The next day, Callie slipped an extra piece of peach pie in her lunch sack, hoping Morgan would join her during the noon hour. She was disappointed when her lunch hour came and went without Morgan appearing at her office door.

The minutes between four and five dragged by as Callie consulted her watch every five minutes. At exactly five, she hopped in the pickup and swung it onto the highway.

She was unprepared for the sight that met her eyes when she turned into her lane. Morgan and another man were resting on their shovels. As she drew nearer, she recognized Robert Garrigan from the cover picture of the mystery she was reading. Both men were dressed in cut-off shorts and tee-shirts, both were covered with dirt and sweat, and both sported wide triumphant grins as she pulled the pickup to a stop.

"We're finished. What do you think?" Morgan gestured down the wide sweep of lane. A drainage ditch on each side framed the smooth surface between.

"Looks wonderful. But I'll give it the ultimate driving test. Hop in."

The men jumped in the back of the pickup, hauling the pick and shovels after them. Morgan gave the go ahead sign to Callie, and she drove slowly up the lane, then increased her speed.

"I can't thank you enough," Callie told Robert after Morgan introduced them. She shook his hand and extended her hand to Morgan. He took it, only to pull her into his arms.

"You can do better than that," he said, stealing a quick kiss.

"What? You expect favors for work?" Callie teased.

"Any way I can get them," Morgan leered.

The glow of accomplishment was on both men's faces. Callie

demanded an explanation.

"After I finished my office work early this morning, I called Rob and asked him if he was up for the experience of a lifetime. He accepted, and we came right over. I didn't anticipate working all day, but we had accomplished enough by lunchtime, we thought we'd just keep at it. Grandma fed us lunch."

"And what a lunch," Robert chimed in. "Real home cooking."

"Then we got back on the lane, only taking time out for some water breaks. Speaking of which, I could use some right now."

"Yes, and not just on the inside," Callie said and laughed. "You're filthy. Come on, rest on the porch, and I'll bring out something cold."

She ran into the house and found Grandma lifting a tray of iced tea. "I heard you drive in, so I figured they'd be quittin'."

"They're finished."

Grandma smiled. "Two able-bodied men can do a lot more physical labor than the two of us."

Callie took the tray from her and carried it to the porch.

"Get your swimsuit, Callie," Morgan said. "We'll have a swim, then have dinner. Sound okay?"

"Great." She left the two men laughing on the front porch while she stuffed her suit, cover-up, a towel, and some makeup into a canvas shopping bag.

"Ready?" she asked, back on the porch in record time. Morgan and Robert got to their feet, and Morgan took her bag, then tossed it in the air and caught it.

Callie laughed. Morgan P. Rutherford III, alias Trey, was playing like a schoolboy. Quite out of character for him—but then digging a ditch was a bit out of character, too. What would his corporate officers say if they saw him now? And what would his fans say if they saw this side of the singer?

"Let's go." Morgan took her hand and pulled her toward the van. "Don't worry, Grandma, I won't keep her out too late," he called.

Robert was shaking Grandma's hand and telling her he'd enjoyed lunch, and Callie could tell Grandma liked him. Morgan helped her into the van and yelled for Robert to cut the chatter so they could get to the pool.

"Grandma?" Callie echoed Morgan's word, her brows raised.

"She said Mrs. Duncan was too high and mighty, so I might as well call her Grandma like everybody else." He grinned triumphantly. Callie nodded.

"We've made great strides today, Callie."

"You must have. I know she's impressed that you worked on the lane yourself instead of using money to hire someone else to do the hard work."

"I would have, but I knew her low opinion of summer people, so I had to show her a different side. Come on, Rob," he yelled out the window.

As soon as Robert was in, Morgan took off, the van humming along the lane.

"Smooth as silk," Morgan bragged.

"Smooth as velvet," Robert added.

"Smooth as butter," Callie chimed in.

They described the road in as many ways as they could until they arrived at Regal Mountain. Morgan dropped Robert off at his house and urged the van up the steep climb to his own home.

He helped Callie out of the van and draped an arm around her shoulder as he ushered her into the house. "We'll change here and walk to the pool."

"Hi, Callie, Morgan," Dorothy greeted them as they swung through the living room on their way to change. "Morgan, what have you been up to? You're covered with dirt."

"Rob and I finished Callie's road. It's as smooth as glass," he said with a wink at Callie. "I feel as if I've just finished a corporate merger or had a record go platinum. And we're going to celebrate. I'll meet you back here, Callie."

She changed quickly into her suit and a white terry-cloth cover-up. The living room was empty when she returned. She wandered onto the deck and gloried in the fantastic view. Was it just a week ago tomorrow that Morgan had brought her here for that birthday party? She'd seen him so much since then, that she felt she knew him well. Well enough to turn a schoolgirl crush into full-fledged love, the deep love a woman has for a man. If only she knew for sure how he felt about her.

"Ready?"

She turned at Morgan's voice. His hair was wet. Obviously he'd thought it better to get some of the dirt off before polluting the pool.

Holding hands, they walked to the pool, a distance of about three blocks. Only one other house separated Morgan's house from the clubhouse.

The fenced-in, blue, kidney-shaped pool was three times the size of the average back yard variety. A handful of young people were grouped on one side of the pool, music blasting from their portable radio. As they approached the pool, Robert pulled up in his low slung sports car.

"Perfect timing," he called as he climbed out of the car. They claimed the corner spot, the furthest away from the noisy young people, and set up camp, towels laid down in a row. The teens had recognized Morgan and were watching him with fascination.

"I'm headed in," Morgan announced. "Coming, Callie?"

"In a minute." She watched Morgan mount the diving board. He executed a perfect jackknife that barely splashed water and came up gasping for air.

"Is it that cold?" Callie called. It was only June, and the cool mountain night air would keep the water from warming.

"No, just takes getting used to. Take the plunge. It's better to do it all at one time." Morgan began swimming curvy laps.

"Are you going in, Robert?"

"Sure. I've worked up a good sweat today."

"Yes, I know how hard you worked. Thanks again. Fixing that lane would have taken Grandma and me several months of Saturday afternoons." She paused as one of Morgan's songs came on the radio. She glanced at him, but he showed no reaction to hearing his own voice, his smooth strokes still steady and rhythmic. Callie turned back to Robert. "How did you let Morgan talk you into manual labor? It's not what I associate with a mystery writer."

"I'm always looking for new experiences. Material for my stories, you know. Just might put this experience in my next book. Morgan told me about Grandma, too, and I wanted to meet her. He said she was one character I should write about. Besides, I got to spend the day talking with Morgan, and it's been a long time since we've spent that much time together. He's a special guy."

"Yes, he is," Callie agreed.

A car droned in the distance, then grew louder, until a white convertible pulled into the parking area. Robert and Callie both turned to watch a tall brunette alight gracefully from the car. Robert's eyebrows arched skyward.

"Dianne Prescott," he muttered. "Here comes trouble with a capital T."

"Oh?"

Dianne sauntered through the gate and waved prettily to Robert and Callie as she headed for the group of teens.

"Ten-minute warning. We have early dinner reservations." She glanced at the pool. "Trey," she purred.

"Hello, Dianne."

"Hi, yourself. Did you get my message? I talked to Victoria about the party. Can you come?" The radio had been turned off as the young people gathered their belongings, and her voice easily carried to Callie and Robert on their towels.

"I'm still not sure. I'll let you know before Saturday."

He swam to the edge of the pool toward his towel. Dianne walked around and stood beside him as he heaved himself out of the water.

"Hey, I thought you two were coming in?" he called.

"We are," Callie answered. She didn't know why, but she wanted to be by him, some primitive urge to stake her territory, she supposed. She slipped off her cover-up.

"Aren't you going to introduce me to your friend, Robert?" Dianne cooed.

"Sure. Callie, this is Dianne Prescott. Or is it Newcomb?"

"Prescott. I took my maiden name back after my divorce. That was a mistake, but past history now and best forgotten." She waved her hand airily. "I'm glad I've run into you, Robert. We're having a party Saturday night. Our house. Eight o'clock. You may bring a date." She cast a glance at Callie.

"Thanks, Dianne. What's the occasion?"

"Family reunion. First time in many years we'll all be in the mountains at once. The whole family will be here for a month. That crew over there," she nodded toward the teens, "are my nieces and nephews. Jerry's, P.J.'s, and Sandra's kids. This is the first time P.J.'s had his kids since his divorce."

"I haven't seen your family in ages. Might be fun," Robert said.

Morgan watched the interaction and reached his arm toward Callie. She did nothing to resist when he pulled her down beside him and pushed her unceremoniously into the water, before he jumped back in beside her.

She came up gasping for air. "Not cold? It's broken ice!" she exclaimed.

"Race you to the board and back," he challenged.

She didn't answer, but started for it, knowing that even with her head start, she couldn't beat him. She had watched his even strokes and figured he must have a pool in Atlanta.

He beat her easily and stood waiting for her at the shallow end of the pool. Callie conceded defeat and dove under the water to grab both his feet. He went under. In a lightning quick move, he changed directions and retaliated from behind, lifting her by her waist and tossing her into the water as if she were a featherweight.

Callie came up sputtering. "I think we're even."

"Probably." He was a foot away, treading water. "If you do any other despicable thing, I can't even answer for what might happen to you."

Callie glanced across the water at Dianne and Robert. Even from this distance, she could see the icy set to Dianne's face and the fascinated stares of the teens. Robert was grinning.

"Coming in, Robert?" Callie coaxed. "The water's great!"

"Sure it is," he drawled. "I heard your reaction. Broken ice."

With backward glances at Trey, Dianne's youth group trooped out the gate, and Dianne followed them. "I'll see you Saturday night," she called over one shoulder.

No one replied for a moment, until Robert tossed off a nonchalant, "Sure thing."

"Do you know Trey?" Callie heard one of the girls ask her aunt.

"Very well," Dianne answered.

Callie swam to the ladder and climbed out, running for her towel to warm up. Morgan followed at a more leisurely pace.

"I don't believe Dianne likes you," Robert said dryly to Callie, "even though she thinks we're a couple." He grinned.

"Hands off, buddy," Morgan said. "She's mine. I saw her first."

"Just my luck," Robert moaned. "How'd you meet this fellow, Callie?"

Callie glanced at Morgan for approval, and he gave a barely perceptible shrug of his shoulders. "Morgan put me through college. He gave me a scholarship. I don't know where I'd be if it weren't for him."

Morgan straightened. He didn't like that grateful note in her voice.

Robert looked hard from one to the other. "I smell a story."

Callie shivered as a breeze blew across her damp skin.

"Cold?" Morgan murmured.

"I'm okay," she answered.

"Am I glad I didn't go in," Robert said. "Although I could use a shower and a good meal. Where are you taking us, Morgan?" He laughed at his friend's expression. "You did say we were celebrating, didn't you?"

Morgan scowled good-naturedly as Robert included himself in the dinner invitation. "Think you can round up a fourth? I'm not sharing Callie anymore."

"Think I should ask Dianne?"

"Not on your life." Callie could sense the seriousness in Morgan's tone and wondered what his relationship was with Dianne. She wanted to ask but refrained. Maybe he would volunteer some information.

"Just teasing. I'll call Marilyn. She arrived yesterday to visit her parents." Robert picked up his towel. "Want a ride?"

"No, we'll walk," Morgan said. "I need some time alone with Callie."

"So where are we going? Black tie or Bermuda shorts?" Robert leaned against the open door of his car.

"Men! Always concerned with what they're going to wear," Callie teased. "I'm wearing what you saw me in earlier."

"Of course," Robert said. "How about Murphy's? I could meet you there."

"Good idea," Morgan agreed. "Eight thirty? I'll call for reservations. If it doesn't work out, I'll ring you."

Robert nodded and climbed into his car. With a quick wave, he backed around and headed down the mountain.

Arm in arm, Callie and Morgan walked toward his house. "I forget how petite you are until I'm right beside you," he said.

"I never forget how tall you are," Callie returned. "I like Robert. He seems like a good friend."

"He's my best friend. I haven't seen much of him lately, but I enjoyed our visit today."

"He said the same thing."

"Sometimes I get too involved in work and don't take enough time to be with the people I care about."

"Is that why you've taken some time off this summer? How long do you plan to stay?" She tried to sound as nonchalant as she could, but she had to know.

He smiled down at her. "I'll be here another week, then I'll come back on weekends. I've been working in the mornings, calling the office to stay on top of things. Looks as if I'm not as indispensable as I thought."

"Does it bother you that things are going well without you? That could give you more time for your songs."

"That's what I've been thinking, too. I've finished one and have the lyrics for another. Usually I do the melody first, but not always." He squeezed her shoulder. "Enough about business, I'm on vacation. Let's talk about other things, like why didn't you try some other tactic in the pool? Something that would have justified me doing something like this?" He stopped walking and took her in his arms, slowly lowering his lips to hers. She clung to him like a sailor to a life raft tossed in a storm. He pulled her closer, but the beep of a horn brought her back to the reality that they were kissing at the side of the road. They broke apart.

Victoria and the kids sailed by with Jake leaning out the window with a whistle. The other kids waved and grinned as if they had caught Uncle Morgan doing something wrong.

"Aren't nieces and nephews wonderful?" Morgan asked.

"I don't know." A thought struck her. She might actually have half brothers and half sisters. Maybe even nieces and nephews. She turned startled eyes to Morgan, who looked as if he were reading her thoughts. A concerned line creased his brow.

"Have you decided? Do you want to find him?"

"Yes," she said immediately. "No," she amended. "I don't know."

Chapter 9

L et's go change," Morgan suggested. "Then we'll talk about it." He took Callie's hand as they walked the remaining few yards to his house.

Inside, Vic's kids had destroyed the quiet of the house. They ran around laughing and giggling. "K-I-S-S-I-N-G," Josh sang out when Morgan and Callie entered the living room.

Morgan winked at Callie. "You can go ahead and rinse the chlorine off. I'll call Murphy's and then clean up."

With kids all around, Morgan didn't bring up the subject of Callie's father again until they were on their way to Highridge. "So," he slid into the topic, "you don't know if you want to find him or not."

Callie took a deep breath and let it out. "I want to know who he was if it turns out he cared about my mother and there was some reason he never returned to her. But what if he left on purpose? What if he didn't want the responsibility of a child?"

"That's the risk you'd have to take. The truth may not be what you want to hear. But will you be satisfied with a question mark for your father?"

Callie closed her eyes. "This is hard, Morgan. I've prayed about it, but I still don't have an answer. I don't want to hurt Grandma, and I don't want to be hurt myself. I keep thinking that it makes no difference. It doesn't change who I am. But there are so many unanswered questions. What if I have half brothers and half sisters? What if I've inherited some strange disease?"

"Don't borrow trouble, Callie. But if we find him, you must be prepared for the worst. He may not want to meet you or—"

"I may not want to meet him," Callie interrupted. "I just want to know the story."

"Then we'll find him," Morgan said with finality.

"Where do we start?"

"I'm not sure. Let me talk to some people. It can't be that hard to find someone who lived on Regal Mountain twenty-four years ago."

"What if he didn't live on the mountain? He could have been visiting. Grandma saw him once in town. Maybe he lived there for the summer."

Morgan nodded. "That's possible." He turned his sports car into Murphy's parking lot. "I don't see Robert's car," he commented. "They must not be here yet."

"Tell me about Marilyn," Callie prompted as he helped her out of the car.

"Marilyn's a good person. You'll like her. I've known her about six years. Her dad owns the Byer Drug chain. Instead of working for him, she struck out on her own and is quite a successful stockbroker in New York."

"Does she see Robert often?"

"I don't know. I met her here when she was visiting her parents. I think that's where Robert met her, too. They've been friends for quite some time. I know he sees her whenever he's in New York at his publisher's, but I don't think there's anything romantic between them." He shook his head, a brief movement. Callie had noticed earlier that all his movements and gestures were abbreviated, as if the slightest signal from him was to be obeyed. She'd seen Trey do that same motion on his TV special as he communicated with his band.

"There he is," he said and lifted a hand toward his friend. Morgan and Callie stood by the door to Murphy's and waited for Robert to park his car and join them.

"Marilyn will be a little late," Robert said in greeting. "She said by the time we finish hors d'oeuvres she'll be here."

The restaurant bustled with people, but they were seated immediately at a table near the fireplace. Booths lined each wall, while round tables dotted the floor.

Across the room, Morgan spotted Dianne Prescott with her family. Adults sat around one large table, while the younger members of the Prescott clan sat at a table beside them. One of her brothers was taking candid snapshots of the group.

Callie looked to see what had captured Morgan's interest.

"A friend of yours?" she asked, then regretted her words the minute they slipped out. His relationship with Dianne was none of her business.

"I dated her several years ago," Morgan said. "There was nothing between us. Just friendship."

Several heads had turned toward them, including Dianne's.

"Hi, Trey," she said and waved.

Morgan raised his hand and smiled. "I think we may be descended upon." A moment later, three of the Prescott teenage girls edged up to the booth and asked for Trey's autograph. Without hesitation, he scribbled his pseudonym on a menu, a cloth napkin, and a note pad. Dianne's brother snapped a picture as Morgan teased them. After gushing about his great albums, the girls left amid many giggles.

"There'll be a few more, then we'll be left alone," Morgan told her. "Once it starts, it goes on for a while."

Sure enough, another group of teens approached, followed by another. Within minutes, the furor died down. Callie figured every teen in the place now owned a genuine Trey autograph.

By the time they finished their shrimp cocktail, an older gentleman, who'd been sitting with the Prescott's earlier, stopped by their table.

Morgan stood and shook his hand. "Cooper Prescott, it's been too long. How are things with you?"

"Fine, fine," he replied. "Real fine now that I have all my family around me for the summer. I was sorry to hear about your father, Trey. We were out of the country when he died. Please accept our sympathy."

"Thank you," Morgan replied.

"You are coming to our party Saturday night, aren't you?"

"We hope to," Morgan said.

"Good, good. We'll visit then." Mr. Prescott returned to his seat.

"Callie, would you like to go to the Prescotts' party Saturday night? Are you going, Rob?"

"I hadn't asked Marilyn yet, but I'm game."

"Callie? Vic's going, too."

"Yes, that would be nice," she said. But from the looks she'd received from Dianne, she wondered what she'd gotten herself into. She'd never felt very secure the few times she'd been around summer people when they'd come into the office. Going to a summer folk party might not be a good idea. She tried to ignore the table to their right, but she was aware of piercing stares from several members of the Prescott family.

Morgan was also aware of the daggers Callie was receiving from Dianne, and, in fact, from several of the Prescott group. Mrs. Prescott kept glancing their way. Surely she wasn't upset that he was out with someone other than her daughter. What did she expect? He had not been out with Dianne for over two years now. And her brother was a puzzle, too. He had more than once caught Jerry—or was it P.J.?—casting a curious glance at Callie. He had never kept the two older brothers straight. They were so much older than Dianne and Sandra that they had no longer been part of the Prescott household when he was on the scene.

Maybe taking Callie to their party was a mistake. And yet he wanted to go. Some perverseness in his nature wanted him to flaunt Callie to all his friends. And he knew the whole mountain would be there.

The Prescotts were a close group, but they threw a wonderful party, he remembered from summers past. He genuinely liked them, yet he was relieved when they left.

A moment later, Marilyn arrived. Morgan stood and kissed her on the cheek. Robert introduced the two women, and Marilyn extended her hand. Callie liked her instantly. The dark-haired beauty was open and friendly, her brown eyes dancing from Morgan to Callie as if she were assessing something. Callie heard her say softly, "You were right, Robert." She didn't explain her remark, but exchanged a conspiratorial look with her friend.

The waiter came and took their orders, and the foursome settled down to some lighthearted conversation. Marilyn was an entertaining woman, telling of her adventures in New York with her firm. She and Robert exchanged several secretive glances that led Callie to believe that something was between them besides just friendship.

After their meal, Marilyn and Callie excused themselves and threaded their way through the tables toward the ladies' room.

"I'm glad Morgan's found you," Marilyn said without preamble as soon as the two women were alone.

Callie didn't know what to say. "Found me?"

"Yes. You do love him, don't you? Robert said you did, and it looks that way to me."

Callie stared into her new friend's eyes. "Yes, I do," she admitted with a sigh.

"No reason for sighs. It's just as obvious that he loves you. He needs to settle down, and you're just the one he's been looking for."

"Thank you," Callie said and laughed, liking this woman more and more. "And what about you and Robert?"

"Tit for tat, huh?" Marilyn asked. "All right. We've been friends for a long time."

"Not good enough," Callie teased. "I was honest with you."

"Can you keep a secret?"

Callie nodded.

"I arranged this trip to the mountains when I knew Robert would be home. We've been seeing quite a bit of each other lately when he comes to New York." Callie heard an unsure quality in Marilyn's voice that belied her sophistication.

"Does he know how you feel?" Callie asked.

"Not in so many words. But I show it, don't I?"

"To me, yes. To Morgan, no. He says you're just friends. Sometimes men have to be hit on the head before they realize what's going on."

"You may be right," Marilyn agreed. "Shall we join our thick-headed men?"

Morgan looked up as Callie and Marilyn made their way back

to the table. He rose to his feet beside Robert and pulled out Callie's chair, then sat back down.

"Robert, when did you start writing mysteries?" Callie asked. "You're very young to have published so many."

Morgan noted that Callie leaned across the table toward Robert as she spoke. He liked that about her. She focused on whoever she was talking to, making that person feel special.

"Such a flatterer, Callie. I've been writing since I was twelve, but nothing got published until I was twenty-seven. Since then I've been turning out two mysteries a year."

"Two a year! How can you think of that many plots?"

Robert shrugged. "They just come when I need them. I have one detective, Sinclair, who's in every book, and in a way there's a definite pattern to a mystery. I fill in the outline. The hardest part for me is finding the right names. Maybe I'll use Callie next time I need a lady in distress. Or better yet, a villainess," he teased.

Callie laughed. "Have you used Marilyn in a book yet?"

"She's Sinclair's girlfriend. Sometimes she's not in a book, but usually she puts in an appearance. Lately she's gotten involved in the plots."

"Isn't that interesting?" Callie smiled a mischievous smile at Morgan. He watched the glint in her eyes and suddenly knew that Robert and Marilyn were more than just friends. He wondered if Rob knew.

He looked at his friend and could almost see the lightning that snapped between him and Marilyn.

"Marilyn, are you ready to go?" Robert asked in a dazed voice. "I think we'll be off."

"Sounds good to me," Morgan agreed. He left money for the check. Robert and Marilyn walked ahead, holding hands. Morgan took Callie's hand and followed.

In the parking lot they said good night, promising to see each other at the Prescotts' party Saturday night.

As Morgan and Callie headed along the curvy road to Callie's, she laughed out loud. "Was it my imagination, or did Robert just realize he's in love with Marilyn?"

"I thought so, too," Morgan agreed. "But you knew, didn't you?"

"I suspected."

"Robert's a wonderful guy, but he's a writer. He gets preoccupied sometimes and doesn't see the tree for the forest. He's a master at describing characters' emotions, so I'm a bit surprised he didn't recognize his own. Of course, I didn't see it, either," he admitted. "But I'm perfectly aware of my own." One glance at her face and he realized this wasn't the time for a declaration of love. "I'm having a great vacation," he said instead. "And you're the reason."

Chapter 10

What was wrong with her? With her elbows propped on the high bureau, Callie rested her chin in her hands and stared at her reflection in the old mirror. She was certain Morgan had been going to tell her he loved her, just as she had prayed and dreamed for years. Yet, she knew she'd turned beseeching eyes to him, begging him not to say those three words.

Why? Was it her promise to Grandma that she wouldn't get involved with a summer person? She didn't think so. Even Grandma liked Morgan now.

"You are an idiot," she told her reflection in a low voice that wouldn't wake up Grandma. "But we're worlds apart. It isn't that silly summer person thing. It's the difference in the have and have-not society. He has so much. Yet," she argued with her reflection, "he hasn't abused his wealth."

She remembered one of their topics at dinner. Her dinner companions were well-traveled, discussing their travels around the world. She, on the other hand, had been in three states: Georgia and North and South Carolina. Not that she didn't want to travel. The opportunity just hadn't come up.

So where did that leave her with Morgan? She didn't know. She had committed herself to go with him to the Prescotts' party, but she wasn't looking forward to it.

The fact that he had dated Dianne Prescott was another thought that muddled her mind. Was that the kind of woman who interested him? He liked Marilyn as a friend, and she, too, oozed sophistication. How did a local girl measure up to that crowd?

Maybe going to the Prescotts' party was a good idea after all. There Callie could see exactly how the other half lived. Maybe it wouldn't be as bad as she thought. Certainly, Morgan didn't live the way she thought a singing star would. He attended church in Atlanta, although he hadn't found a church home in Highridge.

This Sunday he was going to her country church and eating dinner with her. But that was the day after the Prescott party. Would he still see her in the same light if she didn't fit in with his social set?

Callie turned off the light at last and crawled into bed. In her nightly talk with God, she asked for guidance in her relationship with Morgan. Within minutes she had fallen asleep and was surprised when the rooster announced that morning had come.

Callie walked into the kitchen dressed in jeans, a short-sleeved shirt, and sneakers. "Morgan's coming to church with us Sunday," she told Grandma.

"Oh, he is?" Grandma nodded her head as though she weren't surprised. "You going to work like that?"

"Remember? Today is when I'm working at Seymour's ranch up north. I'll be home late. Bill Connell is going again this year. He knows more about farm equipment than I do."

This was Callie's second year to do a fiscal year-end report for Seymour's. Every tractor, every horse, every chicken had to be counted. It was outside work, and Callie was pleased Mr. Seymour had asked especially for her to work on his account. They had hit it off last year when Bill had taken her along to show her the ropes.

The day flew by as Callie and Bill counted and recorded everything on the ranch. Last year it was a two-day job, and it would be again. They quit at six and started the long drive back to Highridge. After a dinner at a fast-food hamburger place, they were back on the road, and Callie pulled onto her smooth-as-silk lane after nine o'clock.

She had told Morgan she'd be late on both Thursday and Friday, but now she wished she'd told him she would see him before the big event Saturday night.

In the privacy of her room, she put his compact disk on her portable player, her one extravagant purchase during her college days.

His voice flowed through the earphones, but she pictured Trey singing, not Morgan. Maybe that was another thing that bothered her. Trey and Morgan were two different people to her. She needed to mesh his two separate identities in her mind.

❧❧

The following day was a repeat of the first, except she and Bill finished their work at the ranch by four. By six thirty she was home.

She hoped Morgan would call, but the clock ticked slowly toward bedtime, and the phone remained silent.

❧❧

By Saturday Callie was a nervous mess. She called Marilyn and learned the dress for the party would be casual. Callie decided on navy blue slacks, a cream-colored blouse, and a multi-colored patchwork vest. Grandma had made the vest out of different leftover fabrics and decorated it with beads, buttons, and ribbons. Callie had seen one similar in an exclusive Highridge dress shop, and Grandma had done a marvelous job of tailoring it.

Morgan arrived exactly at eight o'clock. The moment they drove out of sight of the house he stopped the car and leaned over and kissed her.

"I have missed you," he said. "I ended up flying to Kansas City to sit in on negotiations with the flight attendants. I flew back into Asheville exactly," he glanced at his watch, "three hours ago."

"Is the strike settled?" Callie asked. She'd been wondering why he hadn't called her. Now she knew.

"Settled before they walked out, which would have been at midnight tonight. We made a couple of concessions, but they made a couple, too. I think both sides came out feeling pretty good." He started the car again.

"Did your being a singer hamper negotiations?" Callie asked, remembering that he had voiced that reservation earlier.

"Actually," he said thoughtfully, "I think it helped. This sounds egotistical, but the attendants knew my music and were impressed that I was there. I hope they saw me as a businessman and not only a musician."

"Did anyone ask you to sing a number?"

"No," he said and laughed.

"Then I think you're safe. You can mix both careers."

"I hope so," he said. "Listen, about tonight. Vic's husband Adam is here. They're leaving in a couple days for Maine to visit his family. They'll be at the party. So will Mom."

"Good. I'd like to meet Adam."

"You'll like him. He's good to Vic. You'll see."

Morgan parked the car at his house and introduced Callie to his brother-in-law before they walked down the hill to the Prescotts'.

Victoria positively radiated love for her husband. He kept her arm tucked in his as they walked side by side. Every few steps he'd whisper something to her, and she'd whisper back.

Dorothy walked beside Morgan and Callie. "Two weeks is a long time to be apart," she said, nodding toward the couple who walked ahead of them. "He's a good family man."

As the group neared the Prescotts', Callie was glad they had walked down the mountain. Cars lined the road on both sides.

"Is this the social event of the season?" she asked.

"Not really. But any excuse to get together is a winner. There will be some interesting people here. You'll recognize some actors. You won't know some of the corporation presidents, but they're powerful people in the business world."

"I see." Morgan's words made her feel apprehensive. Year-rounders and summer folk don't mix; the expression she had heard all her life reared up in her mind, and her step faltered.

"Isn't that Robert and Marilyn?" Callie nodded toward a couple walking toward them.

"Yes. Robert's house is just around that curve. There are only a couple of houses between his and the Prescotts'."

They waited for the other couple to join them; then a maid admitted them to the house, and the group found themselves surrounded by partygoers. A young girl in a black caterer's uniform passed them with a tray loaded with hors d'oeuvres. She lowered the tray, and Callie tried a tiny new potato topped with caviar. She didn't care for the taste.

Callie saw Dianne the moment they entered the massive great room. She looked like the reigning queen of the prom, smiling and nodding at her subjects, dressed in a form-fitting black, below-the-knee dress. The neckline was cut almost to her waist, and it had no back at all.

"I thought this was informal," Callie whispered to Marilyn.

"It is. Do you see anyone else dressed to kill?"

Marilyn wore a silk turquoise jump suit. Victoria was in a two-piece lounge set. Callie glanced down at her patchwork vest that had seemed so elegant an hour ago. Now it seemed to shout that it was homemade.

Morgan put his arm around Callie and escorted her further into the room.

Dianne looked up from the admiring males around her and straight at Callie. Her eyes lost their smile, although she kept one painted on her lips.

She made her way to Morgan's side and slipped her arm through his. "Trey, I'm so glad you could come. Good evening, Marilyn, Robert." She ignored Callie.

"You remember meeting Callie at the pool?" Morgan remarked, as if unaware of the cut to Callie, although his eyes relayed a different message.

"Why, yes. Callie." Dianne nodded to her.

"Good evening, Dianne. It's a lovely party."

"If you'll excuse us a moment, I have someone I want Trey to meet," she purred.

Morgan started to object, but Callie stopped him. "That's fine. I need to freshen up anyway. I'll see you in a few minutes." She turned to Marilyn and asked if she knew where the powder room was.

Marilyn led the way to a huge main floor rest room with a vanity area divided off from the toilet area by a louvered door.

"Sorry to drag you in here, but I didn't want to lose my temper with that woman. A retreat seemed the best course," Callie explained, examining her reflection in the mirror and willing the flush on her cheeks to go away.

"Don't pay any attention to Dianne. She's just jealous. She and Morgan used to date in the summers. Now that she's divorced, she wants to start it up again with Morgan. He's too smart for that. Besides, he's found you." She patted Callie on the arm. "Come on, let's go find Robert."

"Wait. What about you and Robert? Something's happened between you two."

Marilyn smiled. "He insisted on talking to my parents earlier this evening. Can you keep a secret?"

"Of course."

"Next week my parents are giving a party at the clubhouse," she paused a moment, "to announce our engagement."

Callie hugged Marilyn. "Wow. Once he realized what you meant to him, he moved quickly."

"I know. We're getting married in August, and Robert's moving to New York. My work is there, and he can write anywhere. We'll keep the house here for summer vacations and weekends."

"You've got it all figured out."

"Yes. We've talked nonstop since the other night. I can't tell you how happy I am."

"You don't have to. It shows."

They rejoined the party and found Robert conversing with one of the Prescotts.

"Hi, P.J.," Marilyn greeted the man. "It's been a long time."

"You're all grown up, Marilyn. Last I remember you, you were a brat in pigtails." P.J. laughed and put his arm around Marilyn, but all the while he was staring at Callie.

"Callie, this is P.J. Prescott," Marilyn said. Before she completed the introduction, Morgan appeared, no Dianne tailing him now but with another man in tow instead.

"Callie, this is Phillip Anderson. He's been coming to the mountains for over forty years."

Callie gasped and turned questioning eyes to Morgan, who merely shrugged. She took a deep breath and extended her hand to Phillip, and he smiled down at her from well over six feet. He had to be in his late fifties or early sixties. She hadn't thought of her father as being that old. Hadn't Grandma said she thought he was twenty or so that summer? That would make him only forty-something now. Of course, people carried age differently. He might have been quite a bit older than Daisy at the time of their ill-fated love affair.

In the dim lighting, she couldn't make out the color of his eyes. Were they the same shade of green as hers? Or were they hazel? Maybe the green eyes came from a grandparent. She vowed to read about genes and heredity.

"You must love the mountain to come back year after year," she forced herself to say casually.

"Yes. There's peace here. When I was young my mother brought us for the summer and Dad joined us on weekends. Now I come when I can. Two weeks here, another week there, and lots of weekends."

"Phillip," someone called to him, and he excused himself to join another group.

"Callie?" Morgan pulled her away from the others. "I didn't mean to spring him on you like that. I've met him before, but I'd forgotten about him. What do you think?"

"I don't know. I didn't think of my father as that old."

"I didn't have a sense of him being the one we're looking for either, but you never know. I'll find out what I can about him."

He steered Callie to another corner and introduced her to a couple of actors whom Callie had seen on TV. She knew her mouth hung open, just like those teenagers who besieged Morgan in public, and she stuttered when she said hello. However, in a short time they put her at ease, and she saw that they, too, were normal people just like Morgan. Maybe she had exaggerated the difference between summer people and those who lived in the mountains year-round.

He introduced her to their hostess, Elizabeth Prescott.

"It's a lovely party," Callie murmured.

A perfectly coiffed and made-up Mrs. Prescott merely nodded with a strained, "How do you do?" and moved on. Callie revised her earlier opinion. There were differences between year-rounders and summer folk.

Morgan escorted Callie around the room, introducing her to others, but she couldn't remember all the names. She smiled automatically and said, she hoped, all the right things. Twice she caught Dianne watching her.

Marilyn and Robert joined them again, and this time Marilyn initiated a trip to the powder room.

"Why is it women can't go to the rest room alone?" Robert shook his head at Morgan.

Marilyn waved her finger at Robert and laughed. "It's a female secret you'll never know."

As soon as they entered the large rest room, Marilyn went through the louvered door to the inner area, leaving Callie in front of the large vanity. She stared at her reflection and applied lipstick. A moment later Dianne opened the door.

"Well, well. If it isn't Trey's newest little flame."

"Hello, Dianne."

"Until tonight I thought you were with Robert. Silly of me. I should have realized Marilyn wouldn't let him get away so easily."

"Excuse me, Dianne." Callie snapped her purse shut and moved toward the door.

Dianne stepped in front of her.

"I understand you're from around here, Callie. You know, Trey's just using you for a summer dalliance. That's his style. I'm surprised he'd stoop to a little hillbilly, but he came to the mountains early this year and pickings must have been slim. Now that women on his own social level are here, you'll be yesterday's memory."

Her heart pounding in her chest, Callie stood rooted to the floor. Her first instinct was to strike back. Her second was to run.

She did both, saying with tight lips, "I refuse to lower myself to your social level, Dianne," before she flounced out of the bathroom. A quick glance around the great room didn't locate Morgan, so with a determined step, she headed for the front door.

Outside, she stood statue still on the front step, wondering what to do.

Chapter 11

Callie followed the front walk to the street. She heard the door open behind her but didn't turn around.

"Callie." Marilyn's voice stopped her, and Callie waited for her to reach her. Marilyn put her arm around Callie's shoulder. "Stay here. I'll go get Morgan."

"No. I'm too mad and confused to see him right now."

"I heard it all through the door, but I couldn't get myself put together and out there before you were gone. Oh, that woman has nerve!"

They fell into step together and walked around the curve to Robert's house.

"Forget Dianne. Like I told you before, she's jealous."

Callie nodded in the dark, but her heart was torn in two. "Would you take me home, Marilyn? Tell Morgan that I'll see him tomorrow. I can't go back, and I'd rather be alone."

"All right, Callie, if that's what you want. But I think Morgan would rather see you himself." Callie shook her head vehemently, and Marilyn didn't pursue it. She motioned to the sleek sports car parked in Robert's drive. "Climb in."

Callie sat in the passenger seat, silent on the trip home, but her head was crowded with thoughts. She ran her hand over the luxurious upholstery. Everyone on the mountain drove a sports car, while she drove a pickup. Year-rounders and summer folk don't mix; the thought repeated itself over and over like a broken record. By the time they arrived at her house, Callie was feeling hurt as well as angry.

"Can Morgan call you?" Marilyn asked. "That is, if I can keep him from marching over here?"

Callie leaned over and hugged Marilyn before getting out of

the car. "Thank you for being such a good friend. I've only known you briefly, but I know you're a truly good person. And yes, please have Morgan call me. I owe him an explanation." With that she shut the door and walked to the front porch where Grandma had left the light on.

Grandma was already in bed, and Callie was glad. She didn't want to explain anything now. She carefully closed Grandma's bedroom door and sat down in the rocking chair beside the phone to wait for Morgan's call. She got up and turned off the porch light, then returned to the rocker to sit in the dark.

By instinct, she reached for the phone as it started to ring, picking it up before it had pierced the air with more than a sharp ping.

"Hello, Morgan," she said.

"What happened?" She could hear the scowl in his voice.

"Dianne and I had a disagreement," she said simply, "so I left."

"Why?"

"Because I'm not of her social standing. I believe the party was only for Regal Mountain dwellers."

"I'll be right over."

"No. Morgan, no. Grandma is already asleep, and I'm suddenly exhausted. I'll see you in the morning as we planned."

"Callie, I'm so sorry. I'll take care of it." He sounded menacing.

"Please, Morgan. It's over, and I'm all right. Let's forget it. Okay?" she pleaded.

"I'll see you in the morning, Callie. Nine o'clock sharp. You did say you're fixing dinner for me after church, didn't you? I trust you're as good a cook as Grandma." His attempt at light chatter didn't conceal the sharp edge of steel in his voice.

"I'm a good cook," Callie said. "Good night, Morgan."

She hung up the receiver and sat in the dark awhile longer. Morgan wouldn't let the incident go unnoticed. But what he would do, she didn't know. She didn't want to be an embarrassment to him.

"Dear God, what do I do?" she whispered into the dark. "I know You teach forgiveness, but I need help with that. I know Dianne is hurting and wants love from Morgan—but I want love from him, too. Only is that enough? How can two different worlds work together? Please, Father, help me see the way."

Father. And what of her earthly father? In her heart she knew that Phillip Anderson wasn't the man. Wouldn't she have felt some sort of emotional pull if he'd been related to her?

What would her father look like now? Grandma had said he was pretty tall and had dark hair. That hair could be gray now, like Phillip Anderson's. Grandma had only guessed that he'd have green eyes. Still, Callie knew it was someone else.

She'd been rocking back and forth, back and forth, and finally forced herself to get ready for bed. With care, she hung up her homemade vest. Why had she let those people make her ashamed of it? Grandma had sewn each seam with loving care. Never again would she let summer people make her feel ashamed of her clothes or anything else.

She knew she was making generalizations about summer people. The Rutherfords had been more than kind to her, and she felt a special kinship with Marilyn and Robert. But did her father fit in the uppity class or the kind class?

So many unanswered questions. She crawled into bed and wished for morning—and was stunned when she opened her eyes to see the pink shades of dawn stream through the window.

She put on a pot of coffee before heading toward the shower. Rarely did she wake up earlier than Grandma, who usually lit a fire in the cookstove and started coffee in the old coffeepot. Grandma said coffee tasted better when it was fixed the old-fashioned way, but Callie had invested in a drip coffee maker anyway. When she got out of the shower and into her robe, the coffee was ready without the fuss of feeding the fire.

Grandma was up and in the kitchen. Grumble as she might, she was drinking a cup of Callie's brew.

"How'd it go last night, Callie Sue? You was in pretty early." Grandma's shrewd eyes bored into Callie's. Callie sighed, knowing Grandma would have the truth and now.

Callie took a deep breath. "Dianne Prescott, who once dated

Morgan, told me I was not of her social level."

"What did you do?"

"I didn't want to cause a scene, although I told her I wouldn't stoop to her social level. It was her house, so I held my head up high and walked out."

"And what did Morgan say?"

"He wasn't around, so I asked Marilyn, Robert's fiancee, to bring me home. Morgan called. You heard the phone?"

"Yes, but I couldn't make out the words," Grandma admitted.

"I have no idea what he said to Dianne, but I'll bet it wasn't pleasant. He wanted to come over, but I told him I was going to bed, and I'd see him today."

Callie got to her feet, not wanting to discuss Dianne Prescott any further. Instead, she scurried around and peeled potatoes and set them in water.

"What's for dinner, Callie Sue?"

"Pork chops, scalloped potatoes, spinach salad, applesauce, and strawberry shortcake. Oh, and hot biscuits. Do you think we need some peas?"

Grandma gave her a sharp look. "Now don't go thinkin' you gotta put on airs for Morgan. We're plain folk, Callie Sue. He has to want you the way you are. You can't be something you ain't," she admonished with a wave of her index finger.

"You're right, Grandma. But did you ever fix dinner for Grandpa when you were dating?"

Grandma paused for a moment. "I see what you're tryin' to say, Callie Sue, and I guess it don't hurt none to fix somethin' special for company once in a while. I'll go pick some spinach. You sure you don't want to boil it?"

"I'm sure."

Together the women made as many early preparations for dinner as they could then dressed for Sunday school.

Morgan arrived exactly at nine. He joined the two women for coffee in the kitchen and apologized to both of them for the events of the night before.

"What did you do, Morgan?" Callie asked.

"Rob and I waited for you and Marilyn. When you didn't come, we started looking around. Dianne told me you had a headache and had gone home, but we didn't buy that. We walked to Rob's house and discovered Marilyn's car gone, so we waited there until she returned. Then we went back to thank Mr. Prescott for inviting us, and we left. And so did half the party. There was pretty much a mass exodus, even though many of the guests didn't know why they were leaving early. I guess they figured it was the avant-garde thing to do. So the Mountain had an early night." He laughed.

The trio finished their coffee and loaded into Morgan's van for the ride to Sunday school. Morgan was surprised at the dilapidated condition of the old church. From his view high on Regal Mountain he had seen it many times, the tall, sharp steeple a landmark. From a distance it appeared pristine white, but up close, multiple cracks in the stucco gave the structure a gray look.

"We have a building fund," Callie said, reading his expressive eyes. "We may put up a metal building and tear this down."

"A metal church? When was this built?"

"I don't know."

Grandma went inside while Callie and Morgan walked the perimeter of the building, looking for a cornerstone. They couldn't find one.

"We'll ask at the Sunday school meeting."

"Meeting?"

"We only have about fifty members, so we meet as a group, then break into classes."

Morgan hadn't seen anything like it. Inside the church, a wide aisle separated two rows of antique wooden pews. Morgan mentally measured the large room by counting ceiling beams and adding up the water-stained distance between them. He guessed fifty feet by twenty-five feet. The interior walls were wood, not cheap paneling, but tongue-in-groove wooden boards. A large gas heater sat at one side of the back door, the only entrance to the church. He imagined the stove had replaced a wood-burning one.

An old man of about eighty years pounded a gavel on an old podium. From his front pew seat, Morgan could see the square-headed nails that held the podium together.

The meeting began with the reading of the minutes of last week and the treasurer's report. Callie reported the building fund had one thousand, five hundred, and ninety-two dollars in it.

"We need to hold a pie supper or something to raise money for the new building," the old man said. "We're years away from getting a new place."

Callie raised her hand. "How old is this building?" she asked.

"Built in eighteen-aught-four," he answered without hesitation. "Been updated a few times."

"Is it possible to restore it?" Morgan whispered to Callie.

"Can we fix it up instead of tearing it down?" she asked. "It's such a pretty place. Have any of you been down to Mt. Shira and looked at their new metal building? It's bigger all right, and has rooms for Sunday school, but we don't have that kind of membership."

"No, missy, but we need something that will stand up. I think we'd all rather have this place fixed, but it needs big repairs."

"What we need," Grandma said, "is a bigger moneymaker than a pie supper." She cast a sly look at Morgan, who sat beside her. "What we need is a big-name singer to star in a tent show."

Callie gasped. How dare Grandma put Morgan on the spot like that.

"You happen to know anybody like that?" the old man asked, unknowingly putting Morgan in his place.

"Yep. This here fellow is a singer by the name of Trey." Muffled squeals were heard from the seven or eight teenage girls present. "He'd draw a big crowd. We just need to advertise. I'll bet we could make ten thousand dollars in one night, if we had a big enough tent."

"I take it you kids have heard of this Trey?" the old man said and pointed at Morgan.

Morgan felt his face flush. He'd been so relieved when his last tour was over, and he'd made the firm decision that he wouldn't perform live again. He didn't mind studio work or even the videos he shot for music TV stations, but live work was different. "What do you say, young fellow?" the elderly man asked.

He would have to call the musicians up to the mountains. He could have a house party, though, for his family would be gone in another few days. Even if the church scheduled the benefit for after his return to Atlanta, he could come up for the night and certainly the weekend.

"You don't have to do this," Callie whispered.

Morgan glanced at Grandma. "Yes, I do," he whispered back. "She's asked me. I can't turn her down."

He stood up. "I'll be glad to headline a performance," he said, "on the condition that the money raised be used to renovate this building instead of tearing it down and replacing it with a metal building. There's too much history here to let it be destroyed."

The meeting continued with a quick vote for keeping the old church. A committee was set up to look into how much it would cost to replace the roof and the windows, restucco the outside, and get a bigger heating system.

Callie and Grandma were put on the committee for the tent show. Four others were selected to help, including two teenagers, even though all of them had volunteered.

The meeting adjourned, and the group broke into Sunday school classes. Morgan went with Callie to the back left of the room. Three other singles joined them, and Callie opened her quarterly and shared it with Morgan.

"Anger is one letter short of danger," the leader, Jean Rogers, read. "I've heard that all my life," she said, "and I believe it. The Bible has taught us to turn the other cheek, and we've been taught to hold our tongue when in an argument. But do we all do that?"

"I think we have to stick up for ourselves, too," Tommy Ray spoke up. "I know the meek shall inherit the earth, but isn't there a point where we should be heroes instead of wimps?"

"I think we have to stand up for what we believe in," Callie said. "There are lots of ways to interpret 'meek.' Meek can mean obedient. And our obedience is to God, not to those who would lead us astray."

The others agreed, and the discussion continued. Callie thought back to last night when she had walked out of the Prescott home. The best route would have been silence, but she had gotten in her one barb first.

"What we need to learn is tolerance for others' opinions," Morgan was saying. "We're not to judge others' behavior, but we're to be in control of our own. So when others make us angry, we have to choose which course of action is best. Stand up to that person or walk away."

"But we have to decide," Jean inserted. "We shouldn't let the other person force us into a quick decision. My dad told me long ago that we didn't have to do anything—except live with our choices."

Thirty minutes later, the old man who had presided over the Sunday school rang a hand bell, and Jean tied up the discussion. Morgan and Callie moved back to the front of the church and sat by Grandma. When the song leader called out the first selection, the small congregation stood and sang "The Old Rugged Cross."

Callie and Morgan each held a side of the song book. Her soft soprano mixed with his rich tenor. She loved his voice, and for the first time, hearing him sing the hymn, she connected Morgan and Trey as one.

"Peace in the Valley" and "In the Sweet By and By" completed the singing portion of the worship service. The old man read from the Bible, offered a prayer, and dismissed the congregation.

"No sermon?" Morgan asked, as they made their way toward the back door.

"Only every other Sunday. We share a minister with another church. We don't have weekly preaching, but we do gather to worship."

"That's what church is for," Morgan said.

Outside, several people gathered around Callie and Morgan, waiting for introductions. The teenagers, with awe-filled eyes, shook Morgan's hand.

"I saw you in Asheville four years ago," one girl said. "I can't believe you're here," she squealed.

When they were finally back at Callie's house, she swung into action in the kitchen.

"What can I do?" Morgan asked.

"Just sit and talk to me," Callie answered and fed kindling into the big stove. She mixed white sauce as they discussed the tent show.

Morgan helped Grandma set the table. Callie glanced over and saw Grandma was using the good dishes, the ones they had gotten many years ago at a service station with each fill-up. Rarely did Grandma think the occasion warranted the good dishes, and Callie couldn't suppress a grin as she caught Grandma's eye.

Grandma gave a sniff and a look that said, "Don't say a word about it."

Chapter 12

Morgan had to take some action to find Phillip. He had thought of hiring a detective, but Callie had nixed that idea. A detective might arouse too many suspicions, asking questions and all. She wasn't ready for Grandma to know anything about her search.

Morgan didn't know where to turn. He could hardly go door to door asking who had owned each house twenty-four years ago. He didn't even know who had owned his house back then. He needed some advice from a detective.

Sinclair—that's who he needed. Robert's fictional detective.

He picked up the phone in his office and punched in Robert's number. The answer had been staring him in the face. Robert had taken classes in police procedures so his mysteries would be realistic. He could count on his friend to help him. He knew he could.

The phone rang four times; then the machine answered.

"Pick it up, Robert. I know you're there, and I need your help," he said as soon as he heard the beep.

"How do you know I'm here?" Robert answered. "And what kind of help do you need, Morgan?"

"I need Sinclair to solve a mystery. Can I come over?"

"Give me thirty minutes to finish this section. Front door's open."

Morgan read some letters that had been faxed earlier, called his office, and dictated responses. Then he called his manager.

"You're going to what?" Harry's voice was so loud that Morgan moved the receiver away from his ear and switched to the speaker phone. If Harry was going to yell, at least Morgan didn't have to hear his voice directly in his ear.

"It's not a full-fledged concert," Morgan told his manager one more time. "No warm-up act. Just me. I'll sing for an hour or so. It's a benefit performance. Aren't you the one who wanted me to get back in the public eye?"

"Couldn't you have picked a big charity so you could get more publicity out of this? Once you start doing this stuff free, every little cause will call me up. Will he do this? Will he do that?"

"That's why I pay you the big bucks, Harry. To handle that sort of thing. The benefit is a week from Saturday night. Are you coming up?"

"I suppose I'll have to," he growled. "How many musicians do you need?"

As soon as he finished with the details, Morgan walked down the mountain to Robert's and let himself in the front door.

"Coffee's on," Robert called from his office. "Be just a minute."

Morgan poured coffee into a china cup and smiled to himself. Robert was more the mug sort, but he had bought the house furnished and had not seen the need to personalize anything in it. Now, seeing Robert with a fine china cup and saucer in his hand seemed natural.

"Okay," Robert said as he entered the kitchen. "What's the mystery?"

"I can't tell you everything. I mean, I can tell you all I know, but I can't tell you why I need to know."

Robert picked up a pad of paper and pencil from the counter and sat down at the table. "Start from the beginning," he said.

"I need to find the full name of a man called Phillip who lived on Regal Mountain twenty-four years ago. At least in the summers. Or maybe in town. He's tall and had dark hair back then. Now he could be anywhere from forty-three to fifty something."

Robert looked puzzled. "You want to know the last name of a man called Phillip who lived here or in town twenty-four years ago?"

"That's right. How can we find him?"

"If he lived on Regal Mountain, we might find out from Billy."

Morgan hit his head with his palm. Of course. He should have thought of the caretaker. Billy might have records from the time Regal Mountain was first developed. "Let's go," Morgan said.

"Not so fast. You can't tell me why?"

"No. At least not yet. And could you pretend you're doing research for a book? Maybe checking out a procedure your detective would use?"

Robert nodded.

"I owe you one. Hey, you want free tickets to a concert I'm giving for Callie's church?" Morgan explained about the upcoming tent show.

"You've got it bad," Robert said and shook his head.

※⁒

"He's got it bad," Marilyn said, when Callie called her for advice about the tent show.

Callie had a half hour between client meetings and had worked on a schedule of details necessary for the concert.

"I don't know about that. My grandmother put him on the spot. What could he do?"

"He could have said 'no.' It's a simple word."

Callie laughed. "I suppose he could have, but he said he'd do it. But getting back to why I called—have you ever put on an event that needed publicity?"

"Not what you're needing. The functions I've had to organize had a guest list. What you need to do is find out the fastest way to get the word out. Radio and TV ads would work. But you have a small budget, don't you?"

"No budget. I checked on tent rental, and our tent show is now an evening under the stars."

"How about lunch, Callie? I'll work on some ideas, and we'll go over them."

By lunchtime, Callie had worked on a list of her own, and she and Marilyn put their heads together over a pizza.

"Most important thing is publicity," Marilyn said. "If people don't know about it, they can't come. With no money, you can't advertise unless you barter. We give the radio so many tickets to give away. The same with the TV station."

Callie was glad to hear Marilyn use "we," as if she were going to work on this project. "Closest TV station is Asheville," she said.

"That's okay. People from here go to Asheville to shop and for concerts. Nothing says people from Asheville won't come to Highridge to hear Trey, who hasn't given a concert in two years. He's got it bad." Marilyn chuckled. "I'm leaving tomorrow, but I'll be back on Friday to help with the engagement party. I'm arranging for the next week off so Mom and I can plan the wedding. Here's my number in New York. If you need anything before I get back, call. We've got to move on this. Get tickets printed today."

"Impossible. I've got to get back to work," Callie said.

"Then I'll take care of it. Give me the details."

"The committee is meeting tonight at my house. We'll have to decide all that then. Want to come? Oh, sorry. It's your last night with Robert."

"I'll be there with Robert in tow. He might have some good ideas, too."

Callie gulped down a last bite of pizza and rushed out the door. She wished she didn't have a full afternoon calendar, but that couldn't be helped. She'd have to have some time off to do all the running around this concert required. She'd probably make a trip to Asheville to deliver tickets once they were printed, unless she could con someone else into doing that.

Don't worry until you have something to worry about, she told herself. *One day at a time. This will get done.*

❧❧

Billy flipped through an old log book until he found the right year. "You just want a guy named Phillips?"

"No, his first name was Phillip. I don't know the last name," Robert said.

Morgan stood behind him in the gatehouse and shifted for a better view. Billy wasn't letting them take the book, but said he'd look up the information for Robert. Morgan moved to Billy's other side and stared at the book on the counter.

They'd come down that morning to discover Billy had gone to town. Because of the card system, Billy wasn't bound to the guard house all day. The residents liked having him visible, since it was double security, but they didn't complain when he occasionally left his post. After lunch, they had checked the gatehouse again and found him.

"Now tell me again why you want this?"

"Just checking a procedure. My character has this same problem to solve. I just wondered how easy it would be to locate someone from the past with only a first name and a brief description."

"I read one of your books," Billy said. "Got it from the library. That Sinclair knows what he's doing. Do you check out all his problems like this?"

"Most of them. That's the log?" Robert pointed to the old ledger that lay open.

"Yep." Billy read down the row, using his finger as a guide. "Phillip Anderson lived here then. His folks had the house. He inherited it."

"You have all the kids' names here, too?" Morgan asked.

"Sure. Had to know which kids to let in. We've only had this card system on the gates for the last ten years."

Billy ran his finger down the row of names. Morgan watched as he turned to another page. "Here's Phillip Bartlett. He doesn't live here anymore. Sold that house to the Sheldons about fifteen years ago."

"And how old was Phillip Bartlett?" Robert asked as he wrote the name down in what Morgan called his clue notebook, since he always carried it with him in case he got an idea for a plot.

"I don't know. Seems like he was a young fellow. Inherited his dad's oil business. See, just the wife and one kid listed with him." He looked up in the air to search his memory. "Yeah, they had a baby when he lived here."

Billy returned his attention to the list and turned another page. "Phillip Baker. Had three boys and one was Phillip Baker, Junior. I remember them. They sold the place at the end of that summer. See, I entered another family right next to their names."

Morgan stared at the name. Phillip Baker, Junior. This had to be the Phillip he was looking for. Since he had moved from Regal Mountain, he couldn't have returned and found that Daisy had borne his child.

"That's it. No more Phillips. You want to try another name? Maybe Sinclair could look for somebody with a real strange name and find it on the first look," Billy suggested.

"No, this is fine," Robert said. "I can't make it too easy for him. I'll have him check out each Phillip. Do you have addresses for these Phillips?"

"Might not be any good any more, that being so long ago and all. People sure move a lot these days. Now, the wife and I have been here at the foot of Regal going on thirty years. Never moved a step."

Robert wrote down the addresses, and then back at Robert's house, Morgan copied the information from the small spiral notebook.

"What makes you think it's Phillip Baker?" Robert asked as he put on another pot of coffee.

"Did I say I did?"

"You looked like it. Is it important that he moved? Why couldn't it be Phillip Bartlett? The age could be right."

Morgan drummed his fingers on the kitchen table and considered what he could tell Robert without breaking his word to Callie. "He had an affair with a local girl," he said at last. "A summer fling. And he never came back."

"Maybe he came back. Maybe he just didn't look the girl up again. Did she check to see that he wasn't here?"

"No," Morgan replied. Robert was obviously getting into Sinclair's character now and was asking too many questions.

"Why not? And why can't she tell you his last name? Did he lie about it or not tell her at all?"

"She's dead. She died before he returned the following summer, if he did return."

"The plot thickens." Robert turned around from the cabinet where he'd returned the coffee canister. "Murdered?"

Morgan took a deep breath. "She died in childbirth."

Robert had a sudden understanding in his eyes, and Morgan knew he had said too much. "And now the child wants to find her father," Robert said. "I'll help any way I can."

Chapter 13

By seven o'clock, the committee members plus Morgan, Marilyn, and Robert were sipping lemonade in Callie's living room. With the organizational skills known to CPAs, Callie checked off the items on the list one by one as the committee made decisions.

"Outside is fine," Morgan said, "but I'll need a raised platform."

"Will a flatbed truck be enough room? We could probably get two. That would make it double wide." At Morgan's okay, Dick Menner wrote that chore on his list.

If all tasks were divided up, this wouldn't be too much trouble, Callie thought.

"We're going to need rest rooms," Marilyn mentioned. "We'll have to rent the portable kind, but we'll need a row of them."

"Do you think we could use the building fund as seed money for this project?" Callie asked the other adult committee members.

They decided they'd have to ask at Sunday school for approval. Meanwhile, they could go ahead and schedule rental for the portable rest rooms.

"What about a sound system?" one of the two teens asked. Both girls stared awestruck at Morgan, barely moving their gazes away from him to enter into the discussion.

"I'll take care of that," Morgan said.

"We should fence off the area," Dick said, "or we'll have people come in without paying."

"We'll need security of some sort," Morgan said. He remembered the second concert on his last tour. He had been pulled off stage by fans who just wanted to touch him. "But I can take care of that, too." He'd have Harry bring security guards from Atlanta. He'd put them up in motels for the night. Harry would squawk about it, since it would be more expense out of Morgan's pocket, but Callie wouldn't know that it wasn't something he provided for every concert. It'd be one less thing for her to be concerned with.

By nine o'clock the meeting broke up. Callie had checked off all her items, and Marilyn had gone through her list, too. She had called printers, checked prices, and arranged for Callie to take ticket information in early the next morning. The printer had guaranteed her he'd have the tickets done by Wednesday noon.

Morgan lingered after the others had gone.

"Would it help if I went with you to the TV and radio stations?" he asked Callie.

"Are you serious? They'd want interviews and all. Are you willing to do that?"

"No problem. Harry will say it'll be good publicity. Walk me to the car, Callie?"

Outside, he slipped his arm around her shoulder and placed her arm around his waist as they walked to the sports car. He explained what he'd found out about Phillip and how he'd done his research.

"Although I didn't tell him, Robert pieced together why I'm trying to find Phillip." He hadn't wanted to tell her, but he didn't want to keep secrets from her. He wanted their relationship based on trust.

Callie was quiet for a long moment. "What did he say?"

"He said he'd help any way he could."

"He's a good friend."

"The best. You can trust him."

Callie smiled and in the dimness of dusk, her expression seemed to Morgan like the sun coming out from behind a cloud.

"What's next? How can you trace these Phillips?"

"I'm not sure, but I'll let you know the minute we find out anything." He drew her into his arms, and she rested her head on his chest.

If only she could stay there forever. After he kissed her good night, she reluctantly let him go.

The next morning Callie arrived at work an hour early and drew up a sample ticket on her computer. She transferred it to a disk and drove to the printer's. Returning to work, she focused on the most pressing problems and arranged to take Wednesday afternoon off.

Callie called radio and TV stations, lining up interviews. She explained the interview agenda to Morgan that night when she went to his house for dinner. She bid farewell to Victoria's family, as they were leaving the next morning for a week in Maine.

"We'll be back for your concert," Vic promised Morgan.

Dorothy was also leaving the next day for Alaska. "Just a little trip with Mary. We're going to take a boat from Seattle. But we'll fly back for your concert, Morgan."

Callie was amazed that they took flying for granted. When money was no object, she guessed one could be almost anywhere at a moment's notice. For someone who had been in only three states, that was a revelation and another reminder that the Duncans and the Rutherfords lived in two very different worlds.

Wednesday morning Callie again went into the office early. She darted to the printers at ten thirty after they called and said the tickets were ready.

"I'll be back in ten minutes," she told Liz, then agreed to pick up some paper coffee cups for the office.

The tickets looked great. She ran into the grocery store on her way back to the office and was standing in the express line when she glanced at the tabloids and froze. Trey smiled at her on the cover— and her own face was looking up at him with love in her eyes.

SUPERSTAR TREY WITH THIS SUMMER'S LOVE AT SECRET MOUNTAIN HIDEAWAY.

She grabbed every copy of the tabloid in the rack and as soon as she'd paid the checker, she ran for the car.

The picture had been taken the night at Murphy's. The man with the camera who had snapped photos of the Prescott family reunion had taken hers with Morgan. She remembered him taking a picture of the Prescott girls with Morgan, but this shot was taken without her knowledge.

She fumbled through pages until she found the story. It was only two columns and contained little information. It didn't mention the town's name, but her name was printed three times. "Is this the love who's keeping him away from his adoring fans?"

"No," she said aloud.

If she'd doubted Morgan before when he'd told her tabloids made up their news, she now knew it for a fact. She stared at the picture again then started the car.

An unexpected client was waiting when she got back to the office. He stood beside Liz, looking at the same tabloid on Liz's desk.

"You won't believe what Sarah found on her coffee break," Liz exclaimed.

"I think I would," Callie said through a forced smile. She realized the futility of buying out the rack. She hadn't even hit the other checkout aisles at the grocery store. Besides, every convenience store and the other grocery stores would have them.

"Can you imagine being linked with Trey? Why, millions of people will know your name, Callie."

"Yes. My fifteen minutes of fame will be on the front page of a tabloid." She turned to her client, dismissing the article as though it had no importance, but inside she was cringing. "Good to see you, John. Shall we go back to my office?"

Callie plunked the coffee cups on Liz's desk and escorted John down the hallway. As soon as she pulled out his file, she focused her thoughts away from the article and onto John's questions on his fiscal year-end report.

But when John left, her mind returned to the picture, and she wondered who had given it to the tabloid. She thought the man with the camera at Murphy's had been one of the Prescott sons. Why would he send the photo to the tabloid?

Dianne. Of course. She would know that Callie wouldn't want this sort of innuendo cast on her. Would she be this devious? Wouldn't she think Morgan would hold it against her, too?

But Morgan didn't take this stuff seriously. He said it was publicity and people didn't believe it. Callie hated to differ with him, but lots of people believed whatever they saw in print. She would have to show Grandma and convince her the headline wasn't true. Callie wasn't a summer fling for Morgan.

Or was she? her dark side argued.

No. He had been going to profess his love the very night that photo was taken.

But he hadn't said anything since, and he'd had the opportunity.

She pushed the argument to the back of her mind and answered Liz's buzz. Then she settled down with her next client.

She scurried home exactly at noon and showed Grandma the tabloid as she gulped down a sandwich. Morgan arrived for her a half hour later. He seemed ill at ease and stood by the front door.

"Oh, Callie," he paused for a moment searching for the right words. "There's a story. . ."

"I read it," Callie said. She had wanted to talk to him about the tabloid and was glad he had brought it up.

"I read it, too," Grandma piped up. Morgan noticed the frown line on her forehead. For every step forward in his relationship with the old woman, he seemed to take two steps back.

"I don't know who sent that in, but I had nothing to do with it. I was surprised when Harry, my manager, called me about it. It's not true, of course."

Grandma lifted her eyebrows.

"It's true that I'm seeing Callie," he quickly added. "I mean the summer love thing isn't true." Grandma's expression had darkened, and Morgan blurted, "Not that I don't love Callie." He glanced at Callie and saw her wide eyes. "Just the summer thing. It's not a summer thing. I mean, I know it's summer, but it's. . ." He stopped mid-sentence. This stammering was not how he intended to tell Callie that he loved her. "What I mean is, I had nothing to do with it. Tabloids make up items all the time."

"They say where there's smoke, there's fire," Grandma said.

"Sometimes the smoke is as simple as a dinner date," Morgan said.

"The fire was invented from the writer's imagination. Occasionally writers might be on target, but likely as not, they add two and two and get thirteen."

"I believe you, Morgan," Grandma said. "All you had to tell me was you didn't know anything about it."

He glanced at Callie.

"Me, too," she said.

He let out a big breath without realizing he'd been holding it. "Okay. Good." He led her out to his car to begin their publicity rounds.

That afternoon, Callie met Trey.

The man she spent the day with was the superstar, the singer who charmed his audiences. The reception at the radio station in Highridge further merged Morgan's and Trey's identities in her mind. By the time they arrived in Asheville at the television station, she was in awe of him.

"You're a split personality," she told him as they waited in the newsroom for an on-camera interview. The news anchor had jumped at the chance to talk to Trey on the air.

"No," he protested. "I'm Morgan Rutherford the Third who happens to be a singer. Singing is part acting. The public expects me to be a little bigger than life, and I try to fit the image they've given me."

"Well, Trey. . ."

"Don't call me Trey," he interrupted. "I'm Morgan to you." He paused. "I guess I am split. But I don't want my friends to think of me as a performer. I want them to think of me as a plain man."

Callie laughed, a high tinkling sound. "I would never describe you as a plain man. Morgan is more approachable than Trey, so you'll always be Morgan to me. But I think you're about to become Trey again." She pointed to the newsman, who was waving to him through the glass.

The door to the on-air room opened, and the anchor popped out. "We're ready for you. We have two minutes of commercials, then we're on. You'll sit in the weatherman's chair."

Morgan took a seat at the news desk while a technician affixed a mini-microphone to his shirt collar and strung the wire behind him.

Callie watched from behind the glass window of the newsroom. Behind Morgan was a large photo of downtown Asheville framed in a window setting to give the illusion of being the view from the on-camera news desk.

The cameraman held up his hand and closed each finger as he counted. "In five, four, three, two, one." He pointed at the anchor.

"A surprise guest wandered off the streets of Asheville today. Vacationing in the mountains, Trey, four-time Grammy winner, has agreed to do a benefit performance in Highridge a week from Saturday. We'll be giving away tickets to his concert. Details on that at the end of the newscast. Now, Trey, our viewers would like to know when your next album will be released."

"I'm writing songs for it now. So it will probably be out in December. I thought I'd try a couple of the numbers on the audience in Highridge."

"How are you inspired? Do you have to be in a certain mood to write a song? Does a woman inspire the love songs?"

Morgan glanced at Callie. "A woman helps," he said and nodded.

"Although our viewers can't see her, I believe you brought with you the same woman who shared the cover of this week's *Inquirer*. Care to comment?"

Morgan laughed easily. "Isn't the standard comment 'just friends'? For now I'll stick with that."

Callie felt heat on her face and ducked away from the glass. She watched the rest of the interview on the small screen TV in the newsroom, marveling at how real the set looked on the TV and how phony it looked in reality.

At the next commercial, Morgan came out the door.

"Do you have the tickets?"

Callie pulled the envelope marked with the station's call letters and address out of her purse. "Ten tickets. Think that's enough?"

"Sure. We want others to buy them. Is the list of purchase places in here?"

Callie nodded. Liz had made calls for her earlier, lining up music stores in each town for ticket sales.

After delivering tickets to another TV station, taping an interview there, since it was after the live newscast, and delivering tickets to music stores, they stopped for dinner.

"We're probably forgetting something major," Callie said over a slab of barbecued ribs.

"I'll talk to Harry tomorrow and have him fax me a list of details he takes care of for each performance. He may have something we haven't thought of. If we forget anything, he'll be there for the concert and can help us out."

"I can't believe you're doing this. Are you feeling apprehensive?"

"Getting scared, you mean? The thought crosses my mind at night. I've dreamed I've forgotten the words."

"You won't. All you have to do is have faith that God will help you with your show. And I know He will help you raise our building fund. You might say He has a stake in this performance."

"You're right. I pray for help before I ever walk out on stage. And I'm preparing. I practiced my new songs this morning, memorizing the words, and I'll rehearse with the band when I go back to Atlanta next week."

Callie looked down at the ribs and knew she couldn't eat another bite now that he had mentioned that his vacation was nearing an end.

"You've been working every day, haven't you?"

"I call my office and check in. I'm not out of touch, but it's different being there to check with the presidents of each company. There's a personal touch that's missing when I'm out of town."

"I suppose." Callie moved her food around on her plate, then looked up at him. "I don't want you to go," she blurted.

Morgan smiled. "Good. But I'll be back—a lot. Atlanta's only a couple of hours away."

❧

The rest of his vacation time sped by.

Saturday night Marilyn and Robert's engagement party was a huge success. The only blot on it for Callie was the appearance of Dianne Prescott and her family. Marilyn had warned her in advance that the Prescotts had been invited.

"My mother wanted the entire mountain invited. To exclude the Prescotts might cause hard feelings among some of their neighbors. The Prescotts have been here a long time."

Marilyn glowed with love, and Robert kept a possessive arm around his fiancee.

"I'll be here until August," he told Morgan. "Then we'll live mainly in New York. But there will always be summers here in the mountains."

Sunday morning in the Sunday school meeting, Callie reported on the open-air concert and the progress that had been made.

"Although we'll sell tickets at the gate, we'll have a pretty good idea of advanced sales before then. We need ticket takers and parking attendants. We're going to use the two fields on the left side of the road adjacent to the field where we'll have the concert." She continued with the committee report and got approval to spend building fund money to pay for ticket printing and bathroom rentals.

After church, which let out late since they had a preacher this Sunday, Morgan took Grandma and Callie into Highridge for Sunday buffet at Holliman's fish camp.

"It's Grandma's favorite," Callie had told him. "She's never been to the ocean, but she loves fried clams."

After dinner, the trio returned to Eagle Mountain, and Morgan suggested he and Callie take a hike up the mountain.

"We need to work off all those clams," he said.

"Maybe I'd better come, too," Grandma said with a grin, and then she burst out laughing. "You should see the look on your face, Morgan. Go on, you two. Git."

They took off on the trail, pushing aside the scrub brush and vines that blocked their way. Mixed in with the dense woods were the ever present wild flowers adding their blues, yellows, oranges, and reds to the green ground cover. The clear blue sky that peeked through the branches above them promised a perfect day.

A perfect day except that Morgan was leaving for Atlanta that afternoon.

They climbed for half an hour, then stopped where the trail turned north.

"If you look through the foliage you can make out one of the houses on Regal," Callie said. "Regal's a lot higher than Eagle. That's how it got its name. It's the tallest around for at least fifteen miles."

"So this is how your mother hiked over to Regal."

"I suppose so."

"This would make a good spot for a house. Look at the view." Callie murmured agreement as Morgan pulled her into his arms. "I need to be heading back to Atlanta," he said reluctantly.

"I know." Her voice was muffled since she had rested her head on his chest, her favorite place in the whole world.

"I'll be back on Thursday. Harry's coming up then, plus the band will be here Friday. I'll call you when we get here, and we'll plan on doing something that night. Okay?"

She nodded, but didn't look up. She found comfort in his arms.

He put his finger under her chin and lifted her face, then leaned down and kissed her. Three times.

"We'd better go back," he said. "Grandma may meet us at the foot of the mountain."

They made their way slowly back down the mountain, walking arm in arm where the path allowed, Morgan taking the lead when the path narrowed and holding Callie's hand behind him.

At the house he declined to go in for a cold drink. "I'd better go on." He kissed her again, and Callie kissed him back.

"God be with you," she said.

"And with you," he echoed. He blew her a kiss as he drove away.

Chapter 14

Back in Atlanta, Morgan called Pete, his arranger, and confirmed that he could get "Callie's Song" finished before Thursday. Morgan drove across the city and delivered the melody and words Sunday night. Pete said he'd have the drum, guitar, and violin parts done within a couple of days. Normally, Morgan wanted his musicians to rehearse a new song many times before they tried it on an audience, but this song was special, and he intended to sing it Saturday night.

Work at the corporate offices fell into a routine for the four days he was there. He found he'd kept well abreast of business while in the mountains, and as a result, he felt confident he could slip off for many three day weekends, if not an entire week here and there, during the summer. For as long as it took to court Callie, he would be going regularly to the mountains. For courting was exactly what he was doing, and he was courting two women, Callie and Grandma.

He also had to find Phillip. He and Robert had agreed that a private detective could be called in now that there were names to be traced. Although Robert had spent several hours at the library, flipping through large city phone books searching for Phillip Baker Junior, he had conceded that he didn't have the time to continue. He needed to finish his manuscript before his August wedding. Besides he could be on a wild goose chase. He might not pick the right city, and Baker could have an unlisted number.

On Monday Morgan hired a detective. By Tuesday afternoon he had a report on Phillip Baker Junior, age thirty-two, now residing in Memphis. He would have been eight that summer twenty-four years ago.

Morgan had been so sure that it was Baker, but he gave the

130

detective Bartlett's name. By Thursday afternoon when Morgan left for the mountains, the detective hadn't located Phillip Bartlett, but would call Morgan in Highridge if he found him.

❧

Callie's week dragged by. She had plenty to do with the final arrangements for the concert, but she missed Morgan. Word of mouth spread the news that Trey was performing, and Joe from Franklin called Callie to make sure it was true.

"He's doing it for you," Joe said. "I'll be there. Anything I can do to help?"

"I'll have a job waiting for you," Callie answered. "Come by the house Saturday afternoon. The concert isn't until eight, but I know we'll have all sorts of last minute emergencies."

On Tuesday Callie received calls from three music stores for more tickets. She had more printed and dispatched the teens to deliver them. At fifteen dollars a ticket, they were hoping to reach more people, but the numbers were staggering. What about the number who would buy tickets at the gate?

Seating was spelled out on the tickets—bring a lawn chair or a blanket. Still the public wanted to see Trey in person.

She called the radio stations and told them to remind people to car pool to the concert as parking was limited. Dick Menner's fallow farm land was the site of the event. Callie called him, and they decided on an additional field for parking.

"Let's hope it doesn't rain," Dick said.

"It's not goin' to rain," Grandma said when Callie confided her fears about the weather. "The good Lord will see to that."

Morgan called Tuesday night and told Callie that one of the Phillips had been eliminated. "It could be that the other one isn't him either. We may have to widen the search to include Highridge." He told her he missed her and that he would see her Thursday evening.

Callie counted the minutes.

❧

Thursday afternoon at two, Morgan ducked out of the office and ran to his car, his heart light. He'd see Callie in a few hours. He grinned at his reflection as he checked his rearview mirror and backed out of his parking space.

The band would be arriving the next morning and all equipment should be there now. He'd given Harry a key to his house and told him to make himself at home and have the sound equipment unloaded in the garage.

The drive north seemed longer than normal, and traffic was fairly heavy. City dwellers heading out of town for the weekend, he decided, getting an early start like himself.

He arrived home in time to say hi to Harry and picked up the phone. He dialed Callie's work number and waited while Liz connected him with her extension.

"I have missed you," he told her as soon as she picked up.

"Me, too," Callie said. "And I've heard your name every time I turn around. Liz is beside herself about the concert and has volunteered hours and hours making calls and running errands."

"Can you come to the house after work? We'll have dinner with Harry."

At five, Callie flew to Regal Mountain. As soon as she parked in his drive, Morgan was out the door and pulled her into his arms. He kissed her soundly.

"It's been a long week," he said.

"I know. And this is only Thursday," she said as they walked arm-in-arm into the house.

Morgan introduced Harry and Callie, and work began. They sat on the deck, and Harry went over a checklist of concert details. Callie was relieved to find they had covered everything.

"Shall we go to Collett's for dinner?" Morgan suggested.

But before they drove into Highridge, Harry insisted on seeing the concert location.

"Where are the concession areas?" he asked.

"We hadn't planned any," Callie said. "It's sort of a picnic atmosphere. People can bring in coolers."

"Just the same, we need to sell drinks. People get hot, faint—we've got to have something to keep that from happening," he said in his gruff way. "We'll get some concessions set up tomorrow. You can make a mint on soda pop. Get it in canisters; sell only two kinds. Make it easy on yourself."

"Okay," Callie said. "We'll work on that tomorrow."

Dinner at Collett's was a noisy affair. On their previous dinner there, people had left Morgan alone, but now the summer was in full swing, and Trey was here for a concert. His name was the buzz word, and the teens swarmed him for autographs.

"Sorry about that," he said when they were safely back in the car. "Normally that doesn't happen here. A few might approach me, like at Murphy's a couple of weeks ago, but not the mob scene."

"Morgan, it's the concert, isn't it?" Callie asked. "It has them seeing you in a different way."

"It'll calm down after it's over. You'll see. In the meantime, we'd better order pizza delivery." He laughed. "Speaking of food, would you mind stopping by the Barbecue Shack? They're catering tomorrow night's dinner."

"That's fine," Harry said. "Callie and I can visit in the car while you run in." As soon as the two of them were alone in the car he started, "So, Callie, what did you think of the tabloid spread?"

"Not much. Do you think the publicity helped Morgan?"

"A picture is always publicity. I just got figures for last week, and album sales jumped twenty percent."

"Can't fight numbers, we like to say in my business."

Harry leaned toward the front seat. "Marriage used to kill a singer, saleswise. These days it's not so bad. Marriage can increase a star's popularity, make him seem more human."

"Oh," Callie said, not knowing where this discussion was leading.

"So, if Trey were to settle down, it wouldn't be the end of his career."

"And it wouldn't hurt his other life, his corporate image, at all, would it?"

"You're pretty sharp, Callie. You know this concert is costing Trey a bundle. Musicians to pay and all."

"I know. But it's for a good cause."

Harry looked her straight in the eye. "Yeah, I guess you're a good cause."

Morgan opened the door and slid inside. "All done. Don't have that to deal with tomorrow."

❧

Callie was glad she'd arranged for Friday off. She spent most of the day with Harry while Morgan and the musicians practiced. "You're a hard taskmaster, Harry," she told him after they'd arranged for soda wagons to be delivered to Dick Menner's farm by ten the next day. They had to be brought over from Asheville.

"Everything has to be in place by four," Harry said. "The place could be full by then. Carnival seating means they'll be early for the best seats—or best plot of ground, in this case."

"But they'll be sitting in the sun."

"Won't matter. You'll see."

Harry excused himself to talk to the electricians who had brought temporary power from the closest electric poles to the make-shift stage. Two flatbed trucks were parked side by side with lumber nailed over the crack between them. "Can't have a musician falling through," Harry had said.

Church members worked Friday afternoon, stringing temporary wire as a fence. Of course, people could duck through if they wanted, but the wire was to keep order.

"We've got a problem, Callie," Marilyn told her that evening when Callie arrived at Morgan's for barbecue with the band. "I went to all of our locations in every small town and Asheville. I've deposited the money in the church account."

"And the extra tickets?"

"There are no extra tickets. All locations are sold out."

"But we printed two thousand tickets!"

"Correction. I had another thousand printed on Wednesday. You were so busy, I didn't check with you. They sold in two days."

"Three thousand. That's forty-five thousand dollars."

"Minus about a hundred tickets that we gave away for equipment rentals and publicity."

"What are we going to do?" Callie asked, her eyes wide.

"We're going to entertain them." Morgan had walked up behind her and put his hand on her shoulder.

"But where do we put three thousand people?"

"Plus those who buy admission at the gate?" Marilyn inserted.

"There will be room," Morgan assured them. "It's a big field."

There was room, but only because the church members took down the wire and let the crowd spread out. Over five thousand people poured onto Dick Menner's farm. The first arrived at eight o'clock Saturday morning. By noon when the church crew was setting up the drink wagons, several hundred people had staked their claims on prime locations.

Cameras had been set up in three places. "You never know when the energy of a concert is exactly what you need in a video," Harry said. "We tape every song he sings, no matter where."

"Good thing we didn't advertise in Atlanta," Marilyn said. "We couldn't handle the crowd. Trey's largest audience was a hundred thousand in L.A."

Callie called and ordered more soda canisters and cups. Joe Lowery picked them up for her. Dick Menner opened the gate for parking in another field and another and still another.

At six o'clock the band members arrived and plugged in their instruments. They tuned up and played a few bars of several popular songs. The crowd noise heightened. Keyed up teens stood on their blankets and swayed with the music.

Callie, who had been on her feet all day, walked slowly to Dick Menner's house, a half mile down the road. Morgan wanted her with him when he arrived at the concert.

Because there was no curtain, Harry had demanded that Morgan be brought to the stage from the back of the field. A four-wheel vehicle would take the long way around the farm so that he could make an entrance.

"Absolutely necessary," Harry had said. "You'd have a riot on your hands if Trey walked through that crowd."

The band members honked as they turned into Menner's drive.

They were to wait at the farmhouse until time to go on stage. They were already settled inside by the time Callie walked into the living room. She glanced around.

"Where's Morgan?" she asked one of the musicians.

"He got a phone call as we were leaving his place. He said something about helping Dinah, but he'd be here on time."

"Dinah? You mean Dianne?"

"Yeah, that's it. He'll be here."

Callie glanced at her watch. Six thirty.

Chapter 15

A t first Morgan hadn't recognize the agitated female voice on the other end of the line.

"Slow down, take a deep breath and start over. I can't understand you," he said.

"Mom, Dad, and P.J. have been in a wreck. I need a ride to the hospital." She was breathless and ran her words together, but he recognized Dianne's voice.

"All right. I'll be right there," he said. "Do you know how badly they're hurt?"

"No. The hospital just called and said they were there and there had been an accident. All the others in my family have their cars at your concert."

"Stay calm. I'll be right there." He turned to one of the musicians. "Go on without me. I need to help Dianne. Tell Callie I'll be there on time."

He picked up Dianne, who jabbered the whole way into High-ridge, her voice so choked with tears that he couldn't understand her words. Obviously, she didn't handle emergencies well. He wasn't sure why he was being so kind to Dianne, since he was still angry with her for her treatment of Callie, but he liked her family and couldn't be unkind to someone in need.

"This is Dianne Prescott," he told the nurse at the desk. "Some members of her family were in a car accident."

"Yes," the nurse answered, consulting a clipboard in front of her. She looked up at Morgan again. "Aren't you Trey?" she asked breathlessly.

Morgan nodded. "The Prescotts?" he reminded her.

"In the first cubicle. This way." She walked toward a hallway with the wall on one side and lined with curtains on the other. Some of the curtains were open, but the first two were pulled closed.

Morgan and Dianne followed her. The nurse drew back the first curtain and let them pass. Cooper Prescott was sitting on a chair, looking pale, but other than that without any visible injuries. Elizabeth Prescott was stretched out on the table, her right arm and right leg in splints. A doctor was examining her ribs, and a nurse was checking the IV that ran into her left arm.

"Cooper, what's the situation?" Morgan asked quietly. Dianne had rushed to her mother's side and was in tears again.

The older man seemed in shock, as if he was looking at Morgan and yet not seeing him. "Elizabeth's hurt," he said in a strained voice. "I swerved to miss a dog and now Elizabeth's hurt."

"Doctor?" Morgan turned his attention to the young man in the white coat.

"She has a broken arm, broken leg, and a few bruised ribs. The leg has been shattered below the knee and will require surgery. He," he nodded at Cooper Prescott, "has a few bruises, but seems okay."

"He had a serious heart attack a few years ago," Morgan said.

"Thanks. He didn't mention that." The doctor turned to the nurse. "Have Carlton bring in the EKG and let's monitor him until the stress situation passes."

"What about their son?" Morgan asked.

"He's in X-ray. He hit the dashboard."

"Trey," the nurse with the clipboard said. "I'll show you where you can wait." She led the way out of the curtained area. Morgan followed and glanced at his watch. Quarter to seven.

"Don't worry," the nurse added. "They'll do everything they can for Phillip."

Morgan nodded at her then did a double take. "What did you call him?"

The nurse glanced quickly at her clipboard. "Phillip. Phillip James Prescott."

P.J. Prescott was Phillip James.

"Could I see that?" Morgan asked and reached for the clipboard.

"Oh, I couldn't, Trey," the nurse protested.

"I just need to know his age," he said. "I thought it would be on there."

She consulted the sheet. "He's forty-three."

Morgan nodded. The age was right. He remembered that Jerry and P.J. were much older than Dianne and her sister. P.J. was tall, and he had dark hair.

"You can sit here and wait." She waved to a wide spot in the hall that held a few vinyl-covered chairs. "I'll come get you as soon as they get him to a room."

Morgan sat down for a few minutes then strode back to the curtained area. Dianne still stood by her mother's side. Cooper was in the next cubicle, fastened to a heart monitor.

"Are you doing all right?" Morgan asked the older man.

"I'm all right. Elizabeth's hurt." Cooper Prescott looked at Morgan through green eyes that rivaled the color of Callie's. Why hadn't Morgan noticed that before?

He wandered back to the waiting area. He couldn't wait much longer to see how P.J. was. Callie would wonder what had happened to him. From the hospital to the Menner farm was at least twelve miles. With the curvy roads, he would need nearly half an hour to get there. He would wait until seven fifteen to find out about P.J.'s injuries, but then he would have to leave.

He paced the hallway, checking periodically on Cooper. Elizabeth was taken to an operating room to cast her leg and arm.

Finally the nurse came back two steps ahead of a doctor. "Trey, this is Dr. Williams."

"Phillip has a broken nose, and his jaw is broken in two places. We're preparing to wire his mouth shut."

"So his injuries aren't life-threatening?"

"No. He'll take awhile to mend, but he'll be fine. He'll breath through a trachea tube while his nose is healing, probably three days or so. And he'll be on a liquid diet for six weeks. But he'll be all right. I'll check with you after the operation."

"Thanks," Morgan called to the doctor's retreating back.

Morgan glanced at his watch again. Seven twenty. He told Dianne what he'd learned and that he'd tell her family after the concert. Then he ran for his car.

He drove as fast as was safe around the hairpin curves out of Highridge. By the time he approached the turnoff for the Menner farm, it was ten minutes before eight.

🌸🌿

Callie paced the living room floor. The musicians had already left for the concert field. Dick Menner had driven them the back way in the Jeep.

"Where is he, Harry?"

"He'll be here. Probably caught in traffic." Harry's voice was gruffer than normal, even though he was offering her some encouragement.

"He hates performing live," Callie said, wringing her hands.

"Tell me something I don't know," Harry barked. "Don't worry," he added in a less harsh voice, "he wouldn't let you down."

God, bring him here safely, Callie silently prayed. She went out on the front porch and looked down the road. Cars were still being directed onto the parking lot fields. She walked down to the drive, then back to the porch. She glanced at her watch. Five minutes until eight.

Car lights approached. Callie watched Dick Menner park the Jeep.

"Any word?" he asked.

"No," Callie said, just as another car passed the parking fields. She watched as Morgan turned in the drive. Relief left her limp.

"Where have you been?" she cried as she rushed to his side.

He explained about the wreck as they climbed in the backseat of the Jeep.

At the stroke of eight, the Jeep's headlights shone as it made its way through the back fields toward the stage.

"Are you nervous?" Callie asked Morgan.

"Petrified."

"Have you gone over the words? Have you asked for God's help?" She held his hand, and he squeezed hers tightly.

"Over and over on both counts."

"He'll help you," she said and prayed silently for Morgan. She had seen the crowd; he had not. There was no way in the world that she would be able to say a word, let alone sing, in front of that many people.

They sat in the Jeep, their heads bowed together; then Morgan opened his door. "Let's do it," he said to Harry, who was already standing behind the truck beds.

At Harry's signal, the band members climbed on stage and picked up their instruments. Morgan and Callie stood hidden behind the Jeep. As soon as the musicians began a low melody, Morgan kissed Callie and walked to the back of the makeshift stage, where steps had been erected.

"Ladies and gentlemen, please welcome Trey," Harry shouted into a mike.

Morgan bounded up the steps. The screams and applause were deafening. Trey took his place at the piano that sat in center stage and immediately launched into one of his number one hits from a few years earlier. He'd sung half of it before the crowd quieted down to listen. At the end of the song, he bowed amid screams and squeals.

Callie stood behind the stage and listened as he sang a slow ballad. The crowd quieted down but erupted again when he finished the song. For the next hour and a half, the high tension between performer and audience never diminished.

Dusk had fallen. The plan had been to end the performance before it got pitch black. Temporary lights had been attached to the few permanent electric poles that marched across Menner's field, but the weak beams didn't light the parking lots, and the new moon would give little light. Since the crowd was used to the lights only on the stage, Callie hoped they would be able to see well enough to clear the fields after Morgan finished.

"This is a new song that's going on my next album," Trey was telling the crowd. "I hope you like it. It's about this area and a very special woman."

Another musician took Morgan's place at the piano, while Morgan walked to the front of the stage with a hand mike. The band struck up a chord, and Morgan crooned:

"Where the Blue Ridge meets the Smokies
Lies the place that I love best.
Where the deep sky meets the mountain peaks
And the tall trees give me rest,
God smiled on this sweet country,
For here I met my Callie.
My Callie. Oh, sweet Callie,
I love you, my sweet Callie. . ."

Callie's hand flew to her open mouth. What was he saying? He had written the song for her!

"He wants you on stage," Harry growled at her. "Go." He pushed her up the steps.

She stumbled at the top for there was no handrail and the lights blinded her, but she regained her balance and walked toward Morgan. He had turned and stretched out his hand to her. She took it and stood beside him as he sang, "Share my North Carolina home? My Callie, oh, my Callie, will you share my mountain home?"

Callie looked into the eyes staring into hers. The two of them were in a world of their own, even though over five thousand people watched them, spellbound.

"Will you marry me?" he whispered, but his soft words carried over the North Carolina field, and five thousand people held their breaths, waiting for her answer.

"Yes," Callie said, and a cheer erupted from the crowd. Morgan kissed her, and catcalls echoed off the mountains.

When the screams and shouts died down, Morgan spoke. "This concert tonight is to raise money for Callie's church, which is in bad need of repair. Lots of folks have worked hard to make sure this performance went off all right. Help them out by picking up all the cups and litter and taking them with you. Could we pick up right now before our last song?"

He laid down the mike and picked up a cup he'd been drinking from and handed it to Callie. She collected paper cups from the other musicians then sat down on the edge of the stage. The audience buzzed as en masse they picked up the litter that had accumulated during the day.

As soon as the noise died down and people had resumed their seats on blankets and lawn chairs, Morgan picked up the mike again.

"I'd like to close with a song that's always been special to me. If you listen to the words, you'll understand the faith I've built my life on. When I finish, if you really liked the concert, would you be silent for a moment and then leave quietly?"

He nodded to the band, and they began the sweet strains of "Amazing Grace." In his strong tenor voice, Morgan sang with an emotion that touched Callie's heart.

With the last note, the stage lights flicked off, except for one dim spotlight on Morgan. He stood still, his head bowed. No one moved. No one spoke. For five minutes the silent ovation continued. Then the few lights on the electric poles came on, and the spotlight on Morgan was turned off.

Chapter 16

"I've never seen anything like it," Harry said back at Morgan's house on Regal Mountain. "Not a peep the whole time they were loading their cars."

The band and Callie, Grandma, Joe, Morgan's family, Marilyn, and Robert had returned to celebrate the fund-raiser. Over seventy-five thousand dollars had been raised to restore the old church.

"Sakes alive, I never thought we'd raise this much money," Grandma said when Marilyn finished with the last of the preliminary figures.

"Of course, we've got a few more bills coming in," Marilyn said. "The electricians and the drink wagons. Wow, did drinks bring in the money."

"We're paying the musicians, too," Callie said. She'd already discussed it with the committee, and they had unanimously agreed that Morgan shouldn't pay the expenses of his band.

"Oh, we've had a meeting, and we decided we'd donate our time," said one of the musicians. "That was quite a concert. We're all glad to have been a part of it."

Grandma shook each musician's hand and thanked them all.

"What I've never seen, and I've been to a lot of concerts," Robert said, "was the way the place was cleaned up. There wasn't an empty cup on that field. That was a stroke of genius, Morgan."

Morgan smiled. "I didn't want Callie up until three in the morning cleaning that place up."

"Speaking of time," Grandma said. "It's past my bedtime now. You want to take me home, Callie?"

Callie glanced at Morgan. She had left her pickup parked at Menner's farm house, and she and Grandma had ridden to the mountain in Morgan's van.

"I'll take you home, Grandma," Joe offered.

"I'll be home soon," Callie called to their retreating backs.

"They're night owls," Morgan said, nodding at the musicians. "Why don't we go get your truck, Callie?"

"I think the newly engaged couple wants to be alone," one of the musicians said. The others teased them, too, as Morgan and Callie slipped out the kitchen door to the garage.

Instead of driving on down the road to Menner's house, Morgan drove into the concert field. He helped Callie out of the van and held her hand as they walked to where the two flatbed trucks were still parked. The headlights from the van illuminated the steps, and they climbed up and sat down on the stage with their feet dangling over the side. Morgan put his arm around her.

"Callie, I didn't mean to propose to you tonight," Morgan said softly.

Callie's heart stopped. He'd been moved by the moment, and the whole thing had been a mistake?

"I intended to propose when it was just the two of us, without an audience. But it just came out of me. I love you, and I couldn't hold it in any longer. I don't even have a ring yet. I hope you don't mind that so many people witnessed our private moment."

"I wasn't aware of anyone else. Just you. It was a perfect night." She traced his cheek with her fingers. "I love you, Morgan."

He kissed her softly and held her close, then let out a long sigh. "I may have found your father," he blurted. She pulled back from him. "Sorry, I didn't mean to say it so abruptly. I just don't want any secrets between us. Tomorrow we'll go to the hospital to see him."

"Hospital? Where? Is he ill?"

"He's in Highridge. He was in a car wreck, but he's going to be okay."

"A wreck?" Callie's mind processed that fact. "P.J. Prescott is my father?" She felt as if someone had punched her in the stomach.

"His name is Phillip James. I don't know that he's your father, but everything points to it. Right now all his family's at the hospital, so it would be better if we wait until tomorrow to see him.

Callie, I don't know if his family will accept you."

"It doesn't matter," she said, but tears formed in her eyes. "I have you. You and Grandma are my family. And Vic and Adam and their kids and Dorothy."

"And we'll have our own children, too," he promised and kissed the tears that flowed down her cheeks.

※

Callie was ready when Morgan picked her up at seven thirty the next morning. He had suggested the early visit to the hospital with hopes that they could discover the truth and Callie could have a little time to recover before Sunday school. If she were terribly upset, the Sunday school meeting would lift her spirits, as a celebration covered-dish picnic was scheduled after the service.

The hospital staff flitted around with the after breakfast routine. Several nurses smiled at Morgan and Callie, and one gave them directions to P.J.'s room.

They walked into P.J.'s room unannounced. It was empty.

"He went to his mother's room," a nurse said from the doorway. "Room one-fourteen. He wasn't content until he could see for himself how she was."

They walked down the hall and found the room. Callie held tightly to Morgan's hand. He squeezed her fingers as they walked through the doorway.

Elizabeth Prescott lay in a hospital bed looking old and haggard, her immaculately applied makeup missing. Her arm and leg were in casts. P.J. sat in a wheelchair, his face badly swollen, a pad of paper and a pencil on his lap, an IV pole beside him.

"Good morning, Elizabeth," Morgan said. "You remember Callie Duncan?"

Something akin to fear lurked in the older woman's eyes. "What do you want?" she asked.

"We wanted to talk to P.J.," Morgan answered.

"He can't talk. He had a tracheostomy. We're both in pain. Could you come another day, Trey?" She didn't include Callie in the invitation.

P.J. scribbled on his pad and held it up.

"Are you related to Daisy Duncan? You look like her," Morgan read. "Yes," he said to P.J. "Callie's her daughter."

Elizabeth Prescott moaned. P.J. paid no attention but wrote another note. "Where are Daisy and Sam?" Morgan read. "I don't know Sam," he told P.J. "Daisy died twenty-three years ago giving birth to Callie."

P.J.'s eyes widened, and he slowly shook his head.

"You didn't know?" Morgan asked.

He shook his head no.

"Please go," Elizabeth said. "We need our rest."

Callie stepped forward. "Before she died she called out, 'Phillip, Phillip.' Are you that Phillip?"

P.J. nodded yes and scribbled on the pad. "I loved her. She married Sam," Callie read. "No," she said to him, "she didn't marry any Sam. She wrote to you that she was pregnant, but you never answered her letter."

P.J. shook his head then grabbed it with his hands, as if he had hurt himself.

"You didn't know?" Callie asked.

He shook his head again.

"But you did, didn't you?" Morgan asked Elizabeth.

"I read that letter and burned it," she spat out. "And I'd do it again. P.J.'s too good to associate with ignorant mountain people, and he sure didn't need a brat around to spoil his life."

"He loved my mother. Did you really believe it was your choice to make? Why did you tell P.J. that my mother had married Sam?" Callie was guessing on that score, but it seemed very possible that Mrs. Prescott had meddled there, too.

"He moped around once we left Regal Mountain. I told him she called and said she was marrying somebody named Sam. Once he knew she'd dumped him, he got over her, even though he started staying at college through the summers and wouldn't come back to Regal with us. He met his wife and got married. Now that you know, get out of my room. Stay out of our lives."

"All right," Callie paused before she added, "Grandmother."

P.J. shook his head and reached for Callie. Tears rolled down his cheeks. Callie took his hand. "She loved you to the end," she said and kissed his swollen face.

"We'll come back later this afternoon, P.J.," Morgan said. "Do you want to be wheeled back to your room?"

He nodded.

"Don't go, P.J.," his mother called, but P.J. wouldn't turn around to look at her.

"Good-bye, Grandmother," Callie said and pushed the IV stand while Morgan pushed P.J.'s chair.

They delivered P.J. to his room, and Morgan helped him back into the hospital bed.

"We'll be back," Callie said. "Do you want us to come?"

P.J. nodded. "Want to know you," he wrote on the pad.

Callie smiled and nodded. "I'll be back."

She held on tight to Morgan's hand as they walked out of the hospital; as soon as they were in his car, she burst into tears. Morgan held her while she sobbed. A few minutes later she dried her eyes with his handkerchief.

"Do you intend to give her another chance?"

"No. I'll see P.J., but not her. She destroyed my mother. That's selfish of me, isn't it?"

"It's very human, but you may change your mind. I imagine your mother would want you to know your father. And God will help you forgive the Prescotts."

Morgan chuckled, and Callie looked at him as if he'd gone mad. "There's a funny side to this, Callie. Dianne is going to be my aunt by marriage."

With the emotional trauma of finding her father and being tossed out by her grandmother, Callie wanted to cry again, but instead, she laughed along with Morgan.

"Let's get to the Sunday school meeting. We have a lot to celebrate," Morgan said. "Time and prayer will straighten out our relationship with that family, but right now I want to concentrate on our own lives. We need to set a date for our wedding."

Epilogue

Callie had wanted Grandma to walk her down the aisle, but Grandma said it wasn't fitting. Although Callie was on good terms now with her father, she didn't think he should be the one to give her away since he hadn't raised her. So she decided to walk down the aisle alone. What really mattered was that Morgan would be at the other end.

Although the wedding had been planned for Sunday afternoon, it had been moved up to midnight Friday to avoid a media circus. Harry had told Morgan that the press coverage would be good for his image, but Morgan had said that though his proposal was public, his wedding would be a private affair. Callie had known it would be at midnight, but the few guests had been called at five that afternoon and told of the change of plans. The air of secrecy had added more excitement to the already keyed-up Callie.

The long summer had gone, and with the last leaves of autumn, renovations on the church had been completed. Callie and Grandma had made several trips to Atlanta to visit Morgan, to see what his life was like. Grandma had insisted that Callie know the winter side of a summer person, and Callie had delighted in her new knowledge of Morgan. She'd seen him as a singer and as a business executive, but knew that his Christian heart controlled both professions.

Work continued on the highest peak of Eagle Mountain on Morgan's and Callie's summer home. Grandma had given them the land as a wedding present but declined to live with them when it was finished.

"My place is in the valley," she said. "At the foot of Eagle, where I've spent my life."

"But you'll visit us in Atlanta, won't you?" Callie had asked. "The winters get pretty cold in the mountains."

"I might consider it my winter home," Grandma had said and chuckled.

A knock on the van door arrested Callie's thoughts. Since there was no place to change inside the church, Grandma and Callie had waited in the van for their entrance.

"It's time." Marilyn stuck her head inside the side door.

"Are they here?" Callie asked.

"The whole Prescott clan," Marilyn said.

"Okay. Give me two minutes."

Marilyn ducked out, leaving Callie alone with Grandma.

"Thank you, Grandma, for all you've done for me."

"Why, child, it's been my pleasure."

"And please be nice to the Prescotts. I know this is awkward, but I wanted to make a gesture of forgiveness."

"Without Phillip, I wouldn't have had you," Grandma said. With a lace handkerchief, she wiped a tear from her eye. "My Daisy made a mistake—but God always seems to take our mistakes and turn them to joy. If He can forgive, then I reckon I can too."

Callie flung her arms around Grandma and whispered, "No matter what my relationship with them evolves to, it has nothing to do with my love for you."

"I know that, Callie Sue. Morgan told me love is the only thing you can divide and it doesn't get smaller. And I believe it. Now don't you start cryin'. He's waitin' for you in there. Let's go."

Callie followed Grandma out of the van into the night. A full moon illuminated the church yard, and lights from the church beckoned them forward. At the door, Grandma arranged Callie's wedding gown that she had sewn then disappeared inside.

Callie waited in the darkness alone until the door swung open. In the flickering candlelight, she could see Morgan. He was waiting for her.

Callie's Challenge

To my in-laws, Merle and Marietta Jones,
for their encouragement and for their fine son.
Thanks to Joan Banks, Dian Doody Blanchard, Bonnie Hinman,
Ellen Gray Massey, and Joan Schenk for their advice on this book.
Special thanks to my sister Elaine Jones
who survived this swimming pool accident.
And of course, thanks to Jimmie, Landon, Morgan,
and Marshall for their patience while I write.

Chapter 1

Callie Rutherford sang as she walked around the swimming pool absently checking the arrangements of plants. A clump of tall potted ferns waved their branches in the warm Atlanta breeze. In one corner a tiered plant stand held a blaze of colored azaleas. Tables, some with umbrellas, and chairs dotted the tiled deck.

"You sure sound happy," Wilda said, "singing in that sweet voice."

"I am happy," Callie told her housekeeper. As much as she wanted to confide her secret, she kept it to herself. Her appointment was in three days, and she'd say nothing until she was sure. She forced her thoughts back to the party and moved an artillery-leafed fern.

"Is that too close to the water?" Wilda asked.

"I think it's all right. Now what's left on our list?"

The party wasn't until tomorrow afternoon, but Callie wanted as much done ahead of time as possible.

"Caterers will set up tomorrow at eleven," Wilda answered. "I could have handled it, you know."

"I know," Callie agreed. "You're the best cook around, but I want you free to supervise changing rooms and such for the guests. I don't know how many will opt to swim, but we should be prepared. I want everything perfect."

This was Callie's first party since she and Morgan had married six months earlier. Although normally they would spend the May weekend in their mountain home in North Carolina, a couple hours' drive away, this weekend would find them entertaining the board of directors of the Rutherford Group.

No stuffy meeting for this group. Morgan had jumped at Callie's suggestion of a family affair. Parents could bring their children, and the older members of the board could bring their grandchildren.

"I'm home," called a deep voice from inside the house.

"Out here," Callie called and watched her husband walk through the French doors that opened from the house.

Every time she saw Morgan P. Rutherford III, or Trey as his country music fans called him, her heart raced. God had smiled on her and given her the love of the kindest, handsomest, most talented man she'd ever know. A six-time Grammy winner, he was also an astute businessman, effectively combining his singing career with managing his family's business empire.

Last week they had been in Nashville for the Academy of Country Music Awards. Callie had stood in awe of some of the music industry's brightest stars until she realized they were all normal people; they just had high public profiles. Their success depended on the public liking their music and their public image.

Trey had won several awards, including Entertainer of the Year. In his acceptance speech, he attributed his success to God and his new wife, Callie.

The best music video winner even featured Callie. Since Trey's manager Harry Caywood had insisted on filming the benefit concert Trey had performed for Callie's small country church, and since Trey had sung a special song for Callie and proposed in front of thousands, the song was a natural for a video—a touching one that fans adored.

But that was last week. This week Trey had taken a backseat to Morgan P. Rutherford III, business executive who ran the Rutherford Group, an enterprise that owned six subsidiaries, from a theater chain to a small airline. Callie was proud that he could balance two such contrasting careers, but in her mind he was neither singer nor businessman. He was the man who loved her—the strong-principled Christian man to whom she'd given her heart.

Now Morgan strode outside by the pool and stretched his arms to Callie, who hugged him and lifted her face for his kiss. Even the little pecks he gave her when Wilda was around turned her inside out.

"Looking good," he said, as he glanced around the pool area. "Anything I can do to help?"

"I think we've got it under control," Wilda answered as she straightened some cushions on a chaise lounge. "We'll keep that filter running a little longer."

Arm in arm, Morgan and Callie strolled back into the house. "Talk at the office is of my clever wife who wants the board to know the executives on a casual basis."

"Good to know, but we'll withhold judgment until tomorrow," Callie said with a laugh, but she was pleased that Morgan's administrative heads were anticipating the pool party. The actual board meeting would be held a week later, an all-day Saturday affair.

After a leisurely dinner, Callie read over her party list and checked off a couple more items. "Want to walk?" she asked Morgan then. Many evenings they walked over their four-acre grounds for exercise.

They crossed through the kitchen to exit the back door. "Are you still here, Wilda?" Callie asked the housekeeper, who was wiping off the counter. "I thought you'd be getting ready for your date. She's going to the movies with Ralph," Callie explained to Morgan.

Wilda was in her early fifties and in the prime of her life, she repeatedly told Callie, who had to agree. Wilda had been widowed at an early age, had no children, had worked for Morgan for four years, and had been seeing Ralph a year longer than that.

"I'll change as soon as I turn off that filter," Wilda said as she hung up the dishcloth.

"Go on," Morgan said. "We'll turn it off on our way back in. By the way, I'm thinking of asking Ralph his intentions. This romance has been going on plenty long. Good thing it didn't take Callie that long to decide to marry me."

"You'll do no such thing," Wilda said with the familiarity of someone long accustomed to Morgan's teasing. She wagged a finger at him, but gave him a grin before leaving the kitchen.

Morgan and Callie, keeping a brisk pace, walked the perimeter of their land. Callie loved the well-groomed lawn with its neatly trimmed shrubbery. At first she'd found the high brick fence smothering, after the views from their mountain home outside of

Highridge, North Carolina. But she'd quickly learned that even in this ritzy part of town, Morgan could easily be swamped by fans if he ventured into the neighborhood for an evening walk.

Being in the public eye had its drawbacks. They couldn't go out in public without causing a stir. Since that spontaneous proposal to her in front of a concert audience, Callie's and Trey's pictures had been splashed all over the tabloids. They had kept the actual wedding date a secret. The press had expected a Sunday afternoon wedding as the announcements had said. However, Morgan and Callie had called the guests at five o'clock on Friday and told them the wedding would be seven hours later at midnight. It had been a beautiful candlelight ceremony in the recently restored country church where Callie and her grandmother were members, and no reporters were around.

That reporters left Morgan alone at the Rutherford Group spoke of how completely he separated his two careers. Still, Callie was always aware that her moves were grist for public consumption, and the high walls around their grounds were a constant reminder.

"Shall we head back for the pool?" Callie asked. "Feels like we could have a shower." They had already walked the perimeter several times, and the evening breeze had turned into strong gusts.

"I'm ready to call it a night. We have a big day tomorrow. Don't worry. Even if it rains tonight, we'll have a good day for the picnic."

"Race you," Callie called over her shoulder as she sprinted toward the pool area.

Morgan caught her in no time, his longer stride on his side.

"Oh, no," Callie moaned, not because of losing the race, but because the wind had blown a fern basket into the pool, clouding the water with dirt and fine leaves. "I guess Wilda was right. I shouldn't have put that fern so close to the pool."

Morgan grabbed a net and fished the plant and basket out of the water, leaving some debris behind. "The filter sounds different," Callie said. "Should we turn it off?" She took the dripping fern from Morgan, who walked over to the pool house and looked at the filter.

"There's a leak around the rim." He squatted down and examined the heavy, two-foot-wide lid, running his finger around the seal. "If I tighten the bolt, that should take care of it."

That was one more thing Callie admired about Morgan—he didn't act like a big singing star or a corporate head. He was handy around the house. If he could fix something, he did.

She watched him locate the toolbox on a low shelf and extract a pair of needle-nosed pliers. And then a horrific bang drowned out Callie's scream as she watched the lid blow off the filter and crash into Morgan's face, knocking him to the ground.

Skin hung from his chin, exposing his jawbone. Blood shot from his flattened nose. "Morgan!" Callie screamed again. She knelt at his side and gasped at the widening circle of blood around his head. No, she couldn't lose Morgan now that they'd found such happiness.

What to do? What to do? She turned off the filter, which stopped the gushing water that soaked him, and then jumped up and ran for the house. Milliseconds later, she returned, shouting into a portable phone and dragging a tablecloth.

"Morgan Rutherford," she told the 911 operator. "Trey. It's Trey." She wasn't above using his fame to get the ambulance here and fast. She gave the address while holding the tablecloth to Morgan's nose, applying pressure to stop the bleeding. A wound in his neck bled, too, but it wasn't gushing like his flattened nose.

"I'm okay," Morgan croaked in a voice that wasn't his own. "I'm okay."

"I've got to unlock the gate." Callie tried to keep her voice calm, now that her initial panic was over. She guided Morgan's hand over the tablecloth. "Push down as much as you can stand. I'll be right back."

She carried the phone with her and dashed back into the house. There were several switches to the gate at the main entrance. She flipped the one in the kitchen while explaining to the operator what she knew of Morgan's injuries.

"Stay on the line until the ambulance gets there."

"I will," she said and ran back to Morgan. The puddle of blood was getting larger. His head, resting on one outstretched arm, was exactly as he had fallen. What she could see of his face was ghostly white against the red-stained tablecloth he still held to his nose.

God, please help him, she prayed silently. *Please, please don't take my Morgan.*

"They're on their way," she comforted him. She took over applying pressure and listened for the wail of sirens.

"I'm okay," Morgan croaked again.

"Yes. You're going to be fine," Callie said. She wanted to hug him to her, but she dared not move him.

After what seemed like hours, but must have been only a few minutes, she heard the scream of the ambulance.

"I hear them," she said into the phone. "Tell them to come around the house on the south side. There's a walkway."

Moments later a team of emergency personnel raced around the house, carrying a stretcher and a medical bag. Callie stepped back while two men hooked Morgan to an IV, applied a pressure pack to his face, and checked for broken bones.

On the count of three they lifted him onto the stretcher, with his head still resting on that outstretched arm. Callie followed them to the ambulance. Once Morgan was loaded, she climbed in beside him.

"Mrs. Trey, you can't ride with us. You'll have to follow in a car."

"No. I'm going with him, but I'll stay out of the way." She plastered herself to the side of the ambulance. The steel look in her eyes must have convinced the attendant that she wasn't budging.

"No time to argue. Let's go," he called to the driver, who turned on the lights and siren as soon as the ambulance left the long driveway. Callie kept her eyes on Morgan's face as they careened around corners and raced through traffic lights. The technician talked to the emergency room via a speaker phone, giving Morgan's vital signs until they arrived at the hospital.

Callie waited until Morgan was unloaded before hopping out of the ambulance. She ran behind the stretcher and into the curtained cubicle with him.

The doctor pulled away the pressure bandage, and Callie gasped. Morgan's face had puffed up, the swelling leaving a fold of skin that completely hid one eye. The other eye was a slit that looked straight at her.

"Okay," he said, or at least that's the guttural sound she thought he made over his raspy breathing.

"I know," Callie replied, holding back tears.

A receptionist came in with a form for Morgan to sign. "Can I sign that?" Callie asked.

"If he can sign, he should," she said.

Morgan's right arm still supported his head, but he moved the fingers of his right hand, motioning for the pen. Although Callie knew he couldn't see the paper above his head, he scrawled his name.

"We've got to stop the bleeding," the doctor said. "We'll stitch it, stabilize him, then operate."

Under protest, Callie was ushered out the door and into the lobby to wait. She used the time to call Morgan's mother from the receptionist's desk and told her what little she knew about Morgan's injuries.

"I'm on my way," Dorothy Rutherford said in a strained voice. The fear in her mother-in-law's voice echoed that in Callie's heart. She stumbled across the waiting room, collapsed in a chair, and cried.

"Oh, God, please help him," she whispered. "He's such a good man, and I love him so."

She took a deep breath and looked up when the receptionist called her Mrs. Trey.

"Could you fill out some forms, please."

"It's actually Mrs. Rutherford. Trey's his singing name," Callie said and sniffed. "What do you need?"

She took the clipboard and filled out all she could, then returned it. "I don't know our insurance number. I didn't grab my purse. Could I use your phone again?" She glanced at her watch. Nine o'clock. Would Wilda still be at the movies?

She looked up the theater number and had Wilda paged. After a couple of minutes, the housekeeper answered. She assured Callie she'd lock up the house and immediately bring the forgotten purse to the hospital.

Callie sat down again, then jumped back up and walked to the drinking fountain. She peeked through the glass in the swinging door that hid the emergency room cubicles from her view. Nothing. What were they doing in there? She paced to the front door and back. How long did it take to sew him up temporarily? And what would an operation mean? She took a deep breath and forced herself to sit down. She prayed again and again, then jumped up when she heard the swinging door open.

"We're taking him up to ICU," the doctor said. "The bleeding's under control, but it's not stopped completely. He's lost a third of his blood. I don't want to give him a transfusion if we don't have to, but we can't operate until his blood pressure is stable."

"What are you operating for?" Callie asked.

"We'll set his nose for one thing. I can't be sure until we get X-rays, but I think his jaws are broken at the hinges. His palate doesn't look good. We'll probably have to put in a trachea tube for a few days, so he won't be able to speak. I don't know the extent of the damage from the blunt wound to his neck, although we're watching the swelling of his larynx. And we need a plastic surgeon to work on his chin. You can see him as soon as they get him settled in ICU. Don't upset him. He doesn't look like Trey. But he's conscious."

Callie nodded then listened while the receptionist directed her to the intensive care unit. She took the elevator up and was whisked inside Morgan's room as soon as she identified herself to the nurse at the desk.

Morgan lay in the bed, holding a plastic suction tube in his mouth. "Oooo-kaaaa," he muttered through huge lips that stretched across his battered and discolored face.

"I know." Callie leaned over, brushed the hair off his forehead, and kissed him on a clean spot. His nose was flat. The multicolored bruises, which covered most of his bloated face, were darker under his slit of an eye. Dried blood covered his neck. Each time he took the suction tube out of his mouth to grab a raspy breath, he dripped blood on himself.

This person bore no resemblance to the dark-haired, blue-eyed, handsome man she'd married, except for the intelligent look in the one eye that stared at her.

"Here's your brother," a nurse said.

Callie glanced over toward the door and unconsciously moved in front of Morgan to block the view. Neither she nor Morgan had a brother.

A camera clicked.

"Get him out of here. He's a reporter," Callie ordered. She wasn't about to move or the man would see Morgan. The camera clicked twice more before the nurse ushered the reporter out.

"Sorry, Morgan," she said. "I'll speak to the nurses. I'll be right back."

Callie stormed out to the desk, where Morgan's mother now stood.

"You won't let her in, but you let in a reporter?" Callie said in a shrill voice. "A reporter with a camera!"

Dorothy Rutherford hugged Callie. "Calm down, honey. He's gone. Let's dwell on Morgan. How is he?"

"He'll be all right." She repeated all the doctor had told her. "You can talk to him, but he only grunts back. And you must be prepared because you won't recognize him. He looks. . ."—she searched for a word—"inhuman."

Chapter 2

Before seven o'clock the next morning, Callie and Dorothy had been joined in the surgery waiting room by Morgan's sister, Victoria, and her husband, Adam; members of Morgan's band; Charlie Lockhard, Morgan's right-hand man; and several executives from the Rutherford Group. Wilda was on her way to North Carolina to get Callie's grandmother. Harry, Morgan's agent, had been at the hospital all night and had gone home for a shower.

Morgan had been in X-ray at six and was now in the operating room.

During the long night, Morgan had demanded a mirror. Dorothy had quickly handed him her compact mirror, so Morgan could examine only a small portion of his face at a time.

"The doctors are going to fix you up as good as new," Callie told him. And she believed it. She had talked with the plastic surgeon, who had assured her that he had seen worse facial injuries, and they had come out fine.

Callie had repeated the story over and over, from the horrific bang of the filter top blowing off to the moment Morgan had been taken downstairs, and she had drunk cup after cup of coffee.

"We've got trouble," Harry announced when he returned around eight. He waved a newspaper in his hand. "It hit the AP wire. That reporter knows the business." He handed the paper to Callie.

On the front page was a color picture of her blocking most of Morgan's face. The side without a visible eye could be seen, but most people wouldn't be able to tell it was his face.

"SINGER INJURED IN FREAK ACCIDENT," the headline screamed.

Callie skimmed the article, which had exaggerated the facts, of course. An unidentified hospital worker had been quoted as saying

Trey had no face.

"This is in every newspaper across the country this morning. No telling what the tabloids will run," Harry said.

"Should you release a statement after we know the extent of his injuries?" Callie asked. The last thing she wanted to think about was publicity, but she knew her husband's fans would want to know.

"I've already talked to a hospital administrator who will do it," Harry said. "We're setting up a press room."

Of course, she should have known Harry was on top of the situation. He was the best manager in the business. She'd heard Morgan say that often enough.

Morgan's minister arrived, followed by several members of the small congregation. Callie had found that his church home in Atlanta reminded her of the one she'd left in the mountains. Again, Morgan's public image led him to find a small church where he could know the few members and be accepted as another Christian there to worship instead of as a celebrity.

By nine o'clock, flowers started arriving, but there was still no word from the operating room.

Callie sat as long as she could then paced around the large waiting room, speaking in polite tones to Morgan's friends, Victoria's friends, and Dorothy's friends, who now numbered at least thirty, standing in clumps or sitting in small groups, all waiting to hear word about Morgan. Callie walked over to the windows and stared out. She had been in Atlanta six months, but during that time she hadn't made any close friends of her own. For the first time since marrying Morgan she felt lonely and longed for the mountains and familiar faces.

Dorothy came over and held her hand. "How are you doing?"

"I'm all right," Callie said, although her nerves were stretched to the breaking point. She looked into Dorothy's eyes and saw the iron strength that Morgan had told her about. When his father had died, his mother had held the family together. Now she remained calm in the face of fear, while a tight fist squeezed Callie's heart.

"Shouldn't be much longer," Dorothy said. "Another hour, maybe.

It's already ten o'clock."

Callie nodded, not trusting her voice. She watched hospital pink ladies carry in more flowers. Every end table was covered, and they were placing plants on the floor.

"I think I'll make a list of flowers," Dorothy said, digging in her purse for a pen and paper. Callie knew Dorothy was as wound up as she felt and needed something to do to pass the last few waiting minutes.

While Dorothy made her list, Callie escaped down the hall and found the hospital chapel. A couple in their forties sat at the back of the tiny room, the woman in tears. Although she had come there for solace herself, Callie stopped by their pew.

"Can I do anything to help?"

The woman shook her head, obviously unable to speak.

"Our son's been in a wreck," the man said. "He's in the operating room now."

"Jeff's only seventeen," his wife choked out.

"I'm sure the doctors are doing what they can," Callie said. "He's in God's hands now."

The woman nodded, and Callie took a seat on the front pew to give the couple some privacy.

"Dear God," she whispered. "Please be with Morgan. He's such a strong man, but he's weak now. And please be with their son Jeff." She wiped a stray tear, refusing to give in to the emotions within her, and sat quietly for a while. She turned when she heard movement at the back of the room.

"Grandma," she said on a breath of relief and flew into the old woman's arms, the tears she'd held back flowing freely. Grandma had raised her from the day she was born, and since Grandpa's death years ago, Grandma had been both mother and father to Callie.

"I knew you'd be here, Callie Sue. Now, now, you dry those tears. God will take care of Morgan." Grandma reached into a deep pocket of her dress and handed Callie a handkerchief.

Callie stayed in the security of Grandma's arms until the storm had passed. "I guess we need to get back to the others," Callie said.

"The doctor should be in soon."

Before they left the chapel, Callie spoke again with Jeff's parents; then she and Grandma walked slowly back to the waiting room. Callie was unprepared for the standing-room-only crowd.

Harry made his way to her side. "We've asked the hospital to keep others downstairs unless they're cleared by Charlie or me. No reporters are allowed up here. They're keeping them in another room. We've got major network cameras now. If this wasn't such a tragic event, I'd be thrilled with the coverage."

Morgan's sister squeezed through the crowd. "News has spread fast. Morgan's on every prayer chain in Atlanta and every other town in America. Don't you worry; he'll be fine." Victoria's eyes shone with unshed tears, but she smiled at Callie.

A moment later the doctor stepped off the elevator. The crowd quieted. Callie and Grandma walked over by Dorothy and waited for the news.

"He's fine," the doctor said first, and Callie could breath again. "As we suspected, both his jaws are broken. He's wired shut and will be for six weeks. He has a new nose. His palate was shattered, and we're surprised he didn't lose more than two teeth with the force that had to have hit him to do this much damage to the roof of his mouth. He's breathing through a trachea tube now, so he won't be able to speak for a few days."

"Will he sing again?" asked someone from the crowd.

"I don't know," the doctor said, and the group gasped. "A blunt trauma to his neck has caused the avulsion of a vocal chord. Time will tell what happens there. With more plastic surgery, we should be able to make the scars on his face less noticeable." He patted Callie on the arm. "He's in recovery now, but he'll be taken to ICU in about half an hour. Someone will come for you when you can see him."

The next half hour dragged by until Callie and Dorothy were ushered behind the closed doors of the intensive care unit. Morgan lay in the first cubicle with his eyes closed, drifting in and out of a deep sleep. His face was bandaged, but the swelling around his eyes was down, and he looked human again.

"Morgan." Dorothy held his hand, and for the first time silent tears flowed down her cheeks as she looked at her bruised son. Callie understood the relief that caused her tears.

"He looks so good," Callie said and meant it.

Dorothy gave a shaky laugh. "Who would have thought that this looks good? But you're right. He looks much better."

Morgan fluttered his eyelids then opened them a second.

"I'm right here, honey. You're going to be fine," Callie said.

He nodded, a brief movement, and a sighlike sound escaped the trachea tube, as if he were reassured by her words.

Morgan's nurse moved in to take vital signs, so Callie and Dorothy stepped back into the ICU waiting room. Jeff's parents stood outside the door.

"How's your son?" Callie asked.

"The next twenty-four hours will tell," said Jeff's father. "He survived surgery."

"Have you seen him?"

"Not yet." He pointed to a sign behind Callie. Visiting hours in ICU were for five minutes every four hours. "They'll let us in at noon."

Callie stared at the sign. She had gone in and out of ICU all night, and so had Dorothy and Victoria. Why, even the reporter who claimed to be her brother had been admitted. Why couldn't this badly injured boy's parents see him? If she had reassured Morgan in some way, and she felt she had merely by her presence, then wouldn't parents have a remarkable effect on a seventeen-year-old boy?

"Your last name is?" Callie asked.

"Richardson, Ken and Marie Richardson."

"Callie Rutherford. I'll be right back." Callie twirled and opened the swinging door. A nurse sat at a desk in front of an aisle with five glass-fronted rooms on each side. Morgan was in the first room, but looking down the hall, Callie saw several empty rooms. In each room that held a patient, a nurse sat on a stool monitoring bleeps on complicated equipment.

"You can go back to him," the nurse at the desk said.

"Thank you, but why? When Jeff Richardson's parents are kept outside?"

"Now, we can't let everyone in here. They'd get in the way of treatment," the nurse explained.

"Then why am I allowed? It's not noon yet."

"Last night Trey told the doctor he wanted you in here."

But Morgan could barely talk last night. Although Callie had realized the rich and famous were treated differently, she naively hadn't expected that special treatment to spill into the medical world.

"So if Jeff said he wanted his parents—"

"He's unconscious right now," the nurse interrupted.

"But we don't know what unconscious people actually hear, do we?"

The nurse fiddled with some papers on her desk. "We're not sure," she admitted.

"What if Trey wants Jeff's parents with him?"

"Don't make this difficult, Mrs. Trey."

"Difficult? That boy could be dying. What if he were your son?"

The nurse actually blanched. "We try not to think in those terms," she said tersely.

Callie stared at her, speechless.

"Okay, I'll let them in," the nurse said as she rose from her chair. "But I'm holding you responsible. The head nurse will be back in a few minutes. If I get in trouble. . . ."

"I'll take the blame," Callie said and followed her into the ICU waiting room. Jeff's parents were led inside, and Callie and Dorothy trailed back to Morgan's room.

Callie watched Jeff's parents. His mother didn't cry now, but stood tall and held her son's hand. Soft crooning noises could be heard. "You're fine, son. Don't worry. Dad and I are here."

The comforting sounds were much like she had murmured to Morgan during the night, and she had seen him visibly relax at the sound of her voice. Callie knew she had done the right thing in interfering with hospital policy.

Morgan still slept, so Callie and Dorothy returned to the surgery waiting room.

"He's much better," Callie told the crowd. "He'll be moved to his own room tomorrow."

"Did he talk to you?" someone asked.

"He can't talk. Remember the tube? But I'll bet he'll be writing notes in a few hours," Callie said.

And he was. By late afternoon, Morgan was talking with his own brand of sign language and scribbling notes on a pad that Callie got at the hospital gift shop.

The crowd had dispersed, although Victoria, Grandma, Harry, and Dorothy remained. Charlie had asked that Rutherford Group executives go home.

"Morgan's orders," he said after making a quick trip into ICU. He held up a scrap of paper to prove his words. "Sorry about the picnic. We'll do it soon," he read.

❧

By that evening, Morgan was moved to his own room with a private duty nurse. Normally a patient with his injuries would have been kept in ICU, but there was too much traffic in and out, the head nurse had said. Callie knew the move was a direct result of her interfering with Jeff's parents, but since she could afford the private duty nurse, she much preferred that Morgan be in a cheerful room than in the trauma atmosphere of ICU.

She told Morgan about Jeff. After their first visit to their son, Ken and Marie Richardson had to wait until the regular visiting time to see him again, so Callie showed up in the waiting room right after each visiting session to get an update on Jeff's condition. Although a fifteen-year age difference separated them, Callie and Marie became fast friends, bonding with the weight of their traumatic experiences.

By bedtime, Callie was exhausted but refused to go home for longer than the time she needed to take a shower and change her clothes.

"You're paying the nurse to stay with him," Dorothy told her.

"I know, but I can't sleep at home. I'll do better with Morgan." Just because Morgan was out of ICU didn't mean he was out of the woods. Even the slightest possibility of hemorrhage meant she wasn't going to leave him.

She spent the night in a reclining chair and got up each time Morgan stirred. He wrote on the pad that he didn't want to take the pain medicine because it clouded his thinking and made him feel out of control. But Callie and the nurse convinced him that he'd get stronger quicker if he could sleep.

With morning came the arrival of more flowers. As soon as new ones were delivered and added to Dorothy's list, Callie set them outside the door for delivery to other wings in the hospital. She had kept about twenty arrangements to brighten Morgan's room, but there was no room for the other three hundred.

"Your fans love you," Callie told him. "And so do the florists in town." He smiled. It was just a millimeter raise of his swollen lips, but Callie knew it was a smile, and it warmed her heart.

"It's a miracle," Marie Richardson cried to Callie after the noon ICU visit. "The doctor says Jeff's improving much faster than expected. He's off the ventilator and breathing on his own."

"It's the power of prayer," Grandma said when Callie announced it to the group that had gathered in Morgan's room.

Morgan was awake again and motioned with his hand for his paper and pen.

"I want to meet Jeff," he wrote.

"We'll arrange it when he's out of ICU," Callie said.

The doctor left orders for Morgan to walk. He would need time to regain his strength, especially since he had lost so much blood, but walking would begin the process of returning his body to normal. Before Morgan was allowed outside his room, Harry sealed off the corridor, closing doors to other rooms and stationing guards at the ends of the halls. He made sure there would be no photos of Trey in the morning papers, although updates of his condition were given on the nightly news.

Callie walked on one side of Morgan with his arm resting on hers for stability. Victoria walked on the other side and pushed the IV pole.

For two days that pattern continued, and Callie slept at home while a nurse stayed with Morgan. The morning the packing was removed from Morgan's nose, the doctor announced he'd take out the trachea tube the following day.

Callie saw the fear in Morgan's eyes even though the doctor assured him he'd be able to breathe when he took the tube out. Several times that day Callie watched Morgan cover the tube with his finger and try to breathe through his nose. Each time, he'd uncover the tube and make an awful gasping sound.

"I'm staying tonight," she told him about dusk that evening.

He didn't protest but nodded in agreement.

"I have only a few more hours before you'll be able to speak, and I want to take advantage of it. For once you have to listen to me—you can't talk back." She winked at him.

The color of his bruises had changed daily, some to a deep red and others a mustard yellow, but although Morgan looked better, Harry was adamant in his stand on crowd control. After the reporter had managed admittance to ICU, Harry had set up a security system the FBI would admire. Besides controlling the group that had waited in the surgery waiting room, Harry kept a plainclothes guard at the door to Morgan's room, restricting visitors. Pink ladies left their flowers at the door. Only Morgan's privately hired nurses were allowed in.

Morgan still hadn't met Jeff. Harry felt a visit outside his wing, which was sealed before Morgan took his exercise walks, could cause problems. They'd arrange a meeting later.

Morgan didn't argue. He'd seen himself in the bathroom mirror, and he didn't want publicity now.

"I look bad," he wrote.

"I've seen you look better," Callie said. "And you will again. This will take some time, but maybe we can spend it in the mountains. Are you ready for another summer in Highridge, like last year?"

She had fond memories of their courtship. Morgan had fought an uphill battle getting her to go out with him in the first place, even though she had badly wanted to. Grandma's prejudice against summer people, who flocked to the North Carolina mountains for extended vacations in their huge mountain homes, had stood in the way of an easy relationship.

Hearing a knock on the door, Callie glanced up from Morgan's writing pad. Dorothy, Victoria, and Grandma had all gone home for the night, and Harry never knocked but blustered his way in.

The nurse opened the door and spoke to the guard. "Dianne Prescott. Says she's your aunt," she told them.

Morgan's eyebrows shot up, and he stared at Callie in silent communication.

"That's the first time she's claimed our relationship," Callie said.

Last summer had also been a traumatic time in Callie's life. Grandma had told her she'd lied about Callie's heritage. Callie's mother, Grandma's only child, had died in childbirth, but the father Callie had thought was also dead was alive, even though Grandma didn't know his whole name. Morgan had helped her find her biological father, P.J. Prescott, a summer person, who had loved her mother.

Dianne Prescott, an uppity socialite, was P.J.'s much younger sister. She'd had no use for Callie, whom she'd thought of as an ignorant mountain girl. P.J.'s mother had been downright hostile. But once Callie had married Morgan, or Trey as Dianne and her mother called him, they had been nicer, if not patronizing. P.J. had tried to make amends to Callie, and they were still working on a rather shaky relationship.

He had called Callie at home last night and reminded her that he, too, had broken his jaw last summer and assured her that Morgan would be fine. "He'll be drinking his meals for a while, then graduate to food from the blender, but that won't last long," P.J. had told her.

Callie had told Grandma about P.J.'s phone call.

"You can't swing a cat around here without hitting someone who's had a broken jaw," Grandma had said.

Even the guard at Morgan's door boasted that his jaw had once been broken.

"Do you want to see Dianne?" Callie now asked, and Morgan

shrugged in answer. She motioned for the guard to let her in.

"Trey, I came as soon as I could. I just got back into Atlanta today." Dianne rushed to his bedside with barely a glance in Callie's direction. "Oh, Trey, what's happened to you?" she moaned.

Callie wished she'd denied Dianne admittance. They had all kept an upbeat attitude around Morgan. Her negativism wasn't needed, especially now when he was worried about the trachea tube.

"He's doing much better," Callie said. "In a few weeks he'll be as good as ever."

"Is it true you won't ever sing again?" Dianne asked Trey.

"Dianne! Morgan can't speak right now, but the tube comes out tomorrow. It's time for you to leave. Visiting hours are over." Callie ushered her to the door and returned to Morgan's side.

"I'm sorry I let her in. Will she ever change?" Callie stared at the frown lines etched on Morgan's brow and leaned down and kissed them. "You're going to be fine," she said and smiled. "Now, are you ready for some sleep? Tomorrow's a big day."

Morgan spent a fitful night. He took one pain shot at Callie's insistence, but it didn't calm the anxiety in his eyes. Twice in the night Callie heard him try to breathe through his nose then quickly uncover his trachea tube and suck in air.

"I'm sorry you had a bad night here," he wrote on his note pad at first light. "I'm ready now." He pointed at his tube.

"I know you've wrestled with it. Did you turn it over to God?" Callie had prayed through the night that Morgan could deal with the procedure.

"I'm okay now," Morgan wrote.

A little after seven the doctor came in. "Ready, Trey? I normally remove trachea tubes in one of the emergency rooms, but your manager is throwing a fit around here about security. Are you sure you're not the president of the United States?"

Morgan smiled, that little lift at the corner of his wired mouth.

"Let's do it," the doctor said, and the nurse helped Morgan sit in a hard chair for the procedure.

Callie stood in the corner and prayed. She looked up when Morgan took a loud breath through his nose.

"Not too bad," he said in a garbled voice through his wired jaws. His next distorted words let her know the agony he'd been suffering silently. "But can I sing?"

Chapter 3

Morgan's eyes slowly opened as Harry entered the room. He didn't think he had the strength to sit up as his manager and the nurse commanded. But it was time to go.

Harry had made the decision to move him home at midnight. That way reporters wouldn't expect it, the halls would be empty, and there would be no pictures of a bruised and battered Trey in the morning papers.

Morgan would have clenched his teeth as he sat up, if his wired jaws had permitted it. As it was, he slowly straightened, took the two steps to the wheelchair, and fell into the seat.

This was no good. He wasn't an invalid; only his face was damaged. His legs were fine, if only he had the energy to move. He had to build up his blood. He'd have to force that liquid iron down, but it tasted horrible and stayed in his mouth for a long time after he swallowed what he could. A straw didn't work well, a syringe didn't shoot it down his throat, so he held a spoon up to the narrow slit between his lips and sipped. But as he was wheeled down the silent corridor, he vowed to take that iron eight times a day if necessary. He wanted to be back on his feet and now.

Morgan had never been a patient in a hospital before, and the experience was not one he wanted to repeat. The helplessness and feeling of being out of control of his life were taking their toll. Maybe returning home would somehow restore his ability to make decisions for himself.

"Where's Callie?" he asked as the elevator doors shut the trio in the confined space. He needed his beautiful blond-haired wife with him. She gave him strength.

"She's at home. I told her I didn't want any wayward reporter who might be watching the house to follow her to the hospital."

"Too paranoid. We not this careful." He knew his speech wasn't clear. The wires made him unable to open his mouth. He mumbled at best in a shorthand language. Talking hurt, and the sound that came out wasn't his voice.

His agent shook his head. "Since your wedding and that video, everyone knows Callie's face. And now, both your picture and hers have been on the major networks every night since it happened."

Morgan nodded. He hadn't watched TV. He wasn't left alone enough to need the distraction. If Callie wasn't with him, his mother or Victoria or Grandma had been there. Plus the nurse. He'd been lucky to get a few naps in during the day. At home it would be different.

Harry wheeled him out to the car, and Morgan climbed in the front seat.

"Thank you," he told the nurse. He wouldn't be needing a nurse from now on. He had Callie and Wilda at home. And he'd soon be able to get around on his own.

❧

The trip home was much slower than the ambulance trip to the hospital had been. When Harry pulled into the long driveway, Morgan could see the lights of the house, from nearly every window, blazing a welcome.

Yellow ribbons were tied on the ornate columns that held up the veranda roof. A banner, WELCOME HOME, MORGAN, was stretched between two columns and flapped in the night breeze.

Callie stood in the open doorway with his mother and family members behind her. Even Victoria's kids were there, despite the late hour.

Callie ran to the car and helped him out. He needed her strength as he walked toward the front door. Love radiated from the people inside, and it gave him the energy to smile, which stretched his lips to the hurting point.

Each took a turn hugging him, and then as if reading his thoughts and his need for rest, his family and Harry left. Grandma excused herself and went to the bedroom suite Callie had decorated for her frequent visits. Wilda went to her apartment, which was off the kitchen wing.

Morgan leaned on Callie and walked with her to their bedroom. His side of the king-sized bed held four pillows arranged in a slanting fashion that resembled the slope of his hospital bed. He crawled in and waited for Callie to join him.

"I need this," he said and reached out for her. Immediately, she took her rightful place in his arms. "I love you, honey."

"Oh, Morgan," Callie said. She choked back a sob then let the silent tears fall.

"Tears, Callie?"

"I'm sorry. You should be the one crying, not me." She sniffed. "I'm being a big baby, but I'm so relieved to have you home."

Morgan squeezed her shoulders and made an attempt to kiss her on top of her head. He sighed, an exasperated sound. He'd increase that iron to twenty times a day. He had to get well and fast. He needed Callie as his wife.

"I can kiss you," Callie said. "At least on the forehead." She brushed his hair out of the way and kissed him.

Morgan made a choking sound. "Not had in mind," he mumbled.

Callie laughed and swiped at her tears. He was glad to see her mood swing the other way.

"You'll be well before you know it, honey. And the best thing for you is a good night's sleep."

But that night Morgan slept fitfully, and each time he shifted on the mound of pillows, Callie woke up.

"Maybe sleep on couch," he told her the next morning.

"Not on your life. I'm so glad to have you home, I don't care if I'm up all night long." She gave him a big hug. "Now you stay here. I'll bring you some breakfast."

But Morgan insisted in sitting in a reclining chair in the den. He sipped his liquid meal and made notes on a yellow legal pad. He didn't know what was happening at the office. Today was Thursday. The board of directors would be meeting in two days. He should be there.

"Walk outside," he told Callie before lunch time. If he condensed his sentences to few words, he didn't hurt so much when he talked.

"You do need exercise, and it's a glorious day out." Callie helped him toward the side door, but Morgan stopped still and motioned toward the French doors that led to the swimming pool.

"Are you sure you want to go out there?" she asked.

He nodded.

With slow, careful steps, and resting a lot of his weight on her, he walked to the pool house. The filter lid had been repaired and the filter now hummed softly. No water leaked from the rim.

He stared at the tiled floor where he'd fallen, but saw no telltale blood stains. He pointed at the spot and raised puzzled eyes to Callie.

"Yes, that's where you hit. The water from the filter diluted the blood; then Wilda cleaned up the rest that night. Morgan, the doctor asked what made the wound in your neck, but I didn't know. Do you?"

He reached for the toolbox and extracted the needle-nosed pliers he'd used to tighten the bolt.

Callie shook her head. "You were very lucky the jab didn't do more damage. It was the blunt trauma that caused a separation of one vocal chord, but it should reconnect to the cartilage in eight or ten weeks. Until it does, you'll be real hoarse. Does it hurt to talk?"

He nodded. "Sing?"

"I'm sure you will. Just a matter of time. Let's go in," Callie suggested. She didn't mention that there was a chance the vocal chord wouldn't reconnect all the way. The odds were in his favor that it would, and she wasn't going to give him more to worry about.

"What caused?" He motioned to the filter.

"Ah. The pool men have an answer for that, but one of them wants to tell you himself. Do you want to talk to him today?"

Morgan nodded. More than anything he wanted to make sure this wouldn't happen again. Callie could have been the one out there when it blew.

❦

Wayne Degraffenreid, the pool man, arrived a half hour after Callie called. When Morgan saw his face, he thought Wayne must still be in his teens.

Callie sat beside Morgan's recliner while the young man shifted from one foot to the other. "Please sit down," Callie said.

"No, thank you. I just need to say this." He took a deep breath, then another. "Okay. I'm the one who caused your accident. I put the wrong size of bolt on the lid. The old one was rusted, and I put a new one on, but I didn't have one big enough. I didn't know it would matter, and I wanted it to look good for you. I'm so sorry."

"How long work with company?" Morgan asked.

"I worked for them a little over a month. But the company isn't to blame. It's me. I should have known better." He ran his fingers through his dark hair and heaved a big sigh. "I want to pay for the damages and your hospital bills. It'll take me awhile. I can pay you some each month."

"Don't need money," Morgan said.

Callie stood and walked toward the young man. "Do you still work for them?"

"No," he said, looking down at his shoes. "They fired me when this happened."

"Where do you work now?"

"I'm looking for something else. I'll find work. I'm a good worker. I just made a mistake. I wouldn't hurt you for anything," he apologized again. "I've always admired your music. I wish it had been me and not you."

Morgan could see in the young man's eyes that he was sorry. "Call you," he said then looked at Callie.

"We'll call you," Callie told the pool man. "Thank you for coming." She walked him to the door then returned to Morgan.

He was on his feet and walking toward his study.

"Can I get you something, Morgan?"

"Come," he said.

Callie followed and watched him find a number in his address book.

" 'Vestigate," he said.

Callie looked at the name and recognized it as the private investigator Morgan had hired to find her father. The PI hadn't found him, but he had eliminated a couple of possibilities.

"You want him to investigate the pool man?"

Morgan nodded.

"Why?"

"Find what kind of person," he said.

"Okay," Callie said and reached for the phone. Morgan sat in his desk chair and listened to the conversation and nodded in satisfaction.

"Now, Morgan," she said after she replaced the receiver, "you need to rest. Harry will be over at one, and Charlie's coming at three. I think I'm becoming your secretary."

"No. Wife," Morgan said and pushed himself out of the chair. He placed his arm around her and pulled her to his side. "Need you. Need iron."

"It's not time for your medicine."

"Take more," Morgan said. "Get strong." He patted her on her behind.

Callie looked into Morgan's teasing eyes and laughed.

"What's going to make you strong is plenty of food and more exercise. You've lost weight, and Grandma and Wilda are determined to get it back on you. You get to graduate to blender food today, and they've been cooking up a storm this morning. I think there's some kind of unspoken contest."

She walked with him, his arm still around her, to the kitchen and pulled out a chair for him. Grandma and Wilda were already at the table, drinking coffee.

"Phillip said his favorite food when his jaw was broken was beef stew, puréed of course." She called her father Phillip, because that's what Grandma had said her mother had called him. "So Wilda's made that. And on the corner burner," she said, sounding a little like a boxing announcer, "we have Grandma's chicken and homemade noodles."

"Are you hungry, Morgan?" Grandma asked. "I'll fix you up just right." The spry old woman got to the blender before Wilda could get out of her chair.

"Two courses," Morgan said.

"You want to try them both?" Callie asked.

He nodded. He'd eat anything they fixed for him. And he'd eat plenty of it, even though it took him awhile to eat.

❧

The afternoon tired Morgan. First Harry visited, purely social, but Morgan could tell something was on his mind. Then Charlie met with him in his study.

While the two men discussed Rutherford Group business, Callie lay down. She could sympathize with Morgan's frustration with his tiredness. She had been up with him in the night, which hadn't helped, but she knew the depth of her tiredness stemmed from another source.

She had kept her Monday morning doctor's appointment, letting Grandma and Dorothy stay with Morgan in the hospital. She knew they thought she'd gone home to rest, but she'd driven straight to the doctor's office and spent an anxious few minutes waiting for the test results.

She had considered a home pregnancy test, but wanted to be absolutely positive and start on vitamins or whatever she needed to make sure her baby was healthy. Having heard stories about inconclusive results from too early testing, she had waited an extra week before going in for the test.

When the nurse had called her into an interior room, Callie didn't want to go. She had lived with the secret hope for a few weeks, and she didn't want to destroy her dream. Slowly, she'd followed the nurse into the room.

"Congratulations. According to the information you gave us with your blood sample, your baby's due December fifth, give or take a week or two. We're more accurate than the weatherman, but not by much."

Callie knew she had grinned from ear to ear, not at the nurse's joke, but at the joy of being pregnant. She was going to have Morgan's baby! "Thank You, God. Thank You," she had whispered. She had picked up vitamins before going back to the hospital to see Morgan, but she hadn't told him her news.

She wanted to tell him now, but she didn't want him to worry about her when he should focus on getting well.

They had talked about having children, and he had confided that he wanted a houseful, but he didn't want her to go through the delivery. Since her mother had died in childbirth, and Grandma had given birth to four stillborn babies, he had transferred those thoughts to her.

Callie had assured him that Grandma probably hadn't had good prenatal care and that her mother had suffered from a hemorrhage that sometimes affected young mothers; neither were inherited conditions. She had no fears herself, but she knew Morgan hadn't been convinced that she wouldn't be putting herself at risk if she became pregnant.

No, she couldn't tell him now. For the moment he had too much to handle. She saw the fear in his eyes whenever his singing career was mentioned. She saw frustration whenever he thought of the Rutherford Group. She loved him too much to add one more worry to his load. She'd wait and tell him as soon as he was well.

Morgan had not performed live on stage since the benefit he had given for the church. He'd never liked performing live, and together they had decided he shouldn't have to give concerts. However, he still intended to continue his studio recording. But had that choice been taken from him now? Of course his hoarse voice sounded different. She knew she shouldn't judge it on the mumbled partial sentences that he muttered, but the nagging thought stayed in her mind. What was it doing to Morgan?

She rolled over on her back and stared at the ceiling and rested her hand on her stomach, wondering about the child inside her. Was it a boy or girl?

In about seven months she would have a son or daughter. What kind of mother would she be?

That thought sent her mind to her new friend—Jeff's mother. She sat up and reached for the phone. Marie Richardson answered after the first ring.

"I walked down to Morgan's room this morning and saw he was gone. Did you get him out without reporters? How's he doing?"

Callie was impressed that Marie could ask about Morgan when her son lay partially paralyzed in bed. He was out of danger, but had a long road to recovery ahead of him. They still did not know if he would ever walk again. Time alone would tell.

"He's tired, but he's glad to be home. When Jeff gets out, we hope you'll bring him over. Morgan wants to meet him, even though it wasn't possible at the hospital."

She shivered at the thought of the hospital. Now that they were home, it seemed like another world. How did doctors and nurses see injured and diseased people day after day and go on without their hearts breaking with each case?

She finished her conversation with Marie, slipped her shoes on, and went to Grandma's room.

"You're leaving?" she asked as she gazed at the opened suitcase on the bed.

Grandma smiled and continued packing. "Now that I've made enough chicken and noodles to last Morgan a week, I reckon my usefulness is done for now. Wilda said she'd drive me back home. Morgan needs privacy now that he's here."

"Grandma, you're part of our family. You know that."

"I know that, Callie Sue. And I know that man needs to hold you every minute he can, and he doesn't need an audience."

"Grandma!"

"While we're talking heart to heart, here's somethin' I want to know. When are you goin' to tell him about the baby?"

Chapter 4

Callie's mouth flew open, and Grandma chuckled.

"How did you know?" Callie asked.

Grandma chuckled again. "I've seen a mighty lot of pregnant women in my life, and they all have that same little secret smile. Even with Morgan laid up like this, you still have it. Now it had to be a baby. Otherwise, nothing would have made you smile."

Callie hugged Grandma and told her the due date. "I'm not going to tell Morgan until he's well. He doesn't need to worry about me while he's worried about singing again and how the company's doing without him."

Grandma nodded. "Probably wise. I'm happier than I can say for you. But now, I need to be getting out of here. You don't need Wilda this afternoon, do you?"

"No. She can take you home. I just wish you'd reconsider. We haven't had time for a proper visit."

"Why don't you bring Morgan to the mountains to rest? Clean air might do him good. Being away from that swimming pool might help, too."

"I've been thinking of suggesting that. After the board meeting on Saturday, I think he'll be content to keep in touch with the company via long distance."

Callie carried Grandma's suitcase to the front entry. Wilda scurried out of the kitchen and explained the supper situation. After a quick good-bye to Morgan, they were on their way to North Carolina.

As Callie turned away from the door, Charlie Lockhard called to her from the doorway of the study. "Callie, would you come in here a minute?" Frown lines around his mouth signaled his mood.

Callie walked inside and saw the exhausted slump to Morgan's shoulders as he sat behind his desk. He looked at her as if she were a lifeline in a storm, and Callie stepped around the desk so she could put her arms on his shoulders.

"Please tell Morgan that he can't attend the meeting Saturday," Charlie began. "He'd be distracting, and we have a lot of ground to cover. I can handle the meeting. The agenda's been set for weeks."

Callie looked down at Morgan and saw the tiredness in his eyes. He'd sat at his desk while Harry was here and for almost an hour with Charlie. There was no way he could handle a day-long board meeting.

"Morgan, Charlie's right. You can't physically do that so soon. In another week, I'm sure you could. However, we can have a conference call on a speaker phone set up so that you can monitor the meeting from here. You can hear all that goes on there and write down any comments. I'll be here to speak your thoughts to board members. Technology will allow you to be there without being there. That won't be hard to set up, will it, Charlie? We'll need a couple of speaker phones in the board room so we can hear all the conversations."

"Consider it done."

Callie massaged the tightness in Morgan's shoulders. "We'll bring the recliner in here, so you can move back and forth when you get tired. We want all the handouts and charts here, too, Charlie."

"I'll personally deliver everything tomorrow."

"All right, Morgan? Will this work for you?"

Morgan nodded. When would this nightmare end? He was so tired. As much as he hated the pain medicine and the out of control feeling it brought, he thought he'd take some and lie down. Then maybe he could sleep for more than an hour.

Charlie arranged to come back the next afternoon then left. Callie helped Morgan to bed.

"Harry upset," Morgan muttered.

"What about?" Callie asked. She had left Morgan alone with his agent, thinking she'd be in the way.

"Don't know," Morgan said. "Find out."

"Okay. You get some sleep. I'll be checking on you."

"Stay?" Morgan patted the bed beside him, and Callie lay down with her head on his chest. About fifteen minutes later, Morgan's breathing became regular, and Callie slowly shifted positions so she could get up without waking him.

In the quiet of Morgan's study, she punched the phone button that was programmed with Harry's number. After she got Harry on the line, Callie went straight to the problem.

"Morgan says you're upset. Why?"

Harry was silent for a long moment. "He's got to perform again. Live."

"Now, Harry, you know he's decided to give up concerts. He'll do more albums, though. I know he'll sing again. It's too important to him." She believed that. She had prayed about it and felt at peace. God had given Morgan a wonderful voice, one He wouldn't take away.

"The albums aren't enough," Harry growled in that way he had. "His fans have to see him. There's been too much publicity. Some of them probably believe he has no face, like that one article said. When he's well again, he's got to sing in public."

"You mean on a TV special? One that could be taped?"

"I mean in a come-back concert. This has to be big, Callie. It has to show everyone that Trey is back and better than ever. That he has conquered a tragedy and lived to sing about it."

"Aren't you a little melodramatic, Harry?"

"No. It's got to happen. And you have to make him want it."

"Me?"

"He'll do anything for you. And you have to want this for him. Believe me, Callie, it means his career. I've been in this business a long time, and I know what I'm talking about. Trey's fans have to see him perform live. Those who can't be there have to see him on videos in front of an audience, so they know there were no special camera angles to make him look good."

Callie twisted the phone cord in her hand. She hated to admit it, but what Harry said made sense. "I'm not going to push him on this now. He needs rest to recoup. He can't be worrying about anything else. He's already scared that he won't be able to sing again, even in a studio."

"He'll sing," Harry said matter-of-factly. "When can we push him on this concert?"

"After the wires come off. Six weeks, the doctor said. It may take longer for the vocal chord to reconnect, maybe eight weeks. Give him time, Harry."

Harry grumbled but agreed. After he hung up, Callie walked outside to the pool and wandered around. If only Morgan had been another two feet away from that filter when it blew. If only she hadn't put that plant so close to the edge, so that it fell in and clogged the filter with dirt and leaves. Guilt rushed at her.

She remembered that afternoon clearly when Wilda had told her that plant was too close to the water. But Callie had insisted it was fine. If she hadn't moved it, the filter wouldn't have clogged.

She could go on and on with what-ifs, but she had to deal with reality. And a big reality was she felt responsible for the accident.

She walked back into the house and tiptoed to their bedroom. Morgan lay propped up on the pillows as she'd left him. She knew it wasn't a comfortable position for him. He liked sleeping on his stomach or his side. If only they could get back to normal. There was that phrase again. If only.

Morgan's face was healing. The deepest bruises around his eyes were still a brilliant red, but the darkest blue areas of two days ago were mustard yellow, and the yellow ones of yesterday were already lighter. Tomorrow the doctor was coming over to take out the stitches that ran from below his nose, through his lips, and all the way under his chin. Dr. Fuhr didn't normally make house calls, but he'd said he understood the pressures of unwanted publicity and would come to the house.

Morgan must have felt her presence, for he opened his eyes, looked at the ceiling, and then found her with his gaze.

"I'm sorry, Morgan," Callie said.

"Not wake me," he mumbled and shook his head.

Callie crossed the room and stood beside their bed. She had to say this. She prayed for courage to make her confession.

"I'm sorry I caused your accident," she choked out.

"You caused? No." He shook his head again.

She took a deep breath and knew what the pool man had gone through that morning. She should have spoken up then, but she had been too ashamed.

"If I hadn't placed that plant where the wind could blow it over, it wouldn't have clogged the filter and caused the water pressure to build up and the top to blow."

Morgan swung his feet to the floor and pushed himself off the bed. "Accident," he said and held out his arms to her.

For the second time in less than twenty-four hours, he held her as she sobbed. He made soothing noises through the wires.

"This hard on you," he said. "Me, too, if it were you."

Callie sniffed and reached for a tissue from the night table. "Yes. It's hard. And I'm sorry for the accident, and I'm sorry for falling apart when you need me."

"Need you to cry for me," Morgan said. "Need you to care." He ran his hands over her back and pulled her closer. "I love you."

"I know. And I love you more than I can ever tell you."

She went up on her tiptoes to kiss him, and he bent down. When she reached for his forehead, he shook his head.

"On lips."

"Oh, Morgan, I don't want to hurt you." But his eyes told her he needed loving, so she gently brushed her lips against his.

"Need take iron," he said. "More iron."

Callie smiled and dried her tears. She knew what he was talking about, and her heart was glad that he loved and desired her.

"Your mom will be over a little later," Callie said. At that moment the phone rang, and she reached for the receiver. Morgan didn't let her move from his side.

"Hi, Phillip," she said as soon as she recognized her father's voice.

Morgan's eyebrows lifted, and Callie nodded.

Phillip had called a couple of times since Morgan had been hurt. In the past, Phillip's few calls from Boston had been strained. For

Callie, trying to develop a relationship with a man she hadn't known existed until last summer wasn't easy.

Morgan had helped track down her father with the sketchy information Grandma had given her. He was a summer person who had gone to the mountains for vacation. Callie's mother, Daisy, had called him Phillip on the day she had died in childbirth, but Grandma didn't know his last name. She had seen him once in town and described him as tall with dark hair and around twenty.

Although Morgan had hired a private investigator, he had discovered Callie's father had been right on Regal·Mountain where Morgan had a home. Until last summer, Phillip had not returned to the mountains since that fateful summer when he'd met Daisy. His mother had destroyed Daisy's letters to him in Boston and told him the love of his life had married someone else.

But now Callie had met her father, and they needed time to get to know each other before they could begin to form the bond of father and daughter. Phillip and his children had attended the wedding, but that was six months ago, and since then Morgan and Callie had been busy making their life together and establishing a new routine.

"He's much better," Callie was saying now to her father. "Getting stronger every day."

"Go to mountains," Morgan muttered. "See Phillip."

"Just a minute, Phillip." Callie looked at Morgan. "You want to go to the mountains after the board meeting? Stay there until your wires come off?"

He nodded, and she relayed the information to Phillip.

"That would be wonderful," she said. She covered the receiver. "He'll come to the mountains soon."

Morgan smiled and nodded.

"Yes. He's had some of your recommended beef stew," Callie said into the phone. "He loved it. He's having it for supper, too. And breakfast tomorrow. Okay. I'll tell him. Thanks for calling, Phillip." She hung up the phone. "He says you'll be back to normal in no time. He's coming to the mountains in another week or so and says he'll stay a couple of weeks until he has to get back for the summer school session at Boston U. We're going to talk about my mother."

Morgan squeezed her shoulders. "Work from mountains. Charlie in charge like last summer."

"Thank you, Morgan. I do want to know my father."

He nodded. "Eat?"

"Hungry again? Good. Because you eat so little at a time, you need to eat more frequently. What will it be? Instant Breakfast, stew, or chicken and noodles?" Again she fixed all three and watched Morgan sip his food.

When Dorothy came, she brought puréed barbecued beef. "It's really watered down to get the chunks out, but I tasted it, and the flavor's still there," she said.

Victoria and the kids came over and brought Morgan's favorite chocolate ice cream, and for a snack he had a malt.

That night Morgan slept fitfully again, but he had at least a few hours rest. The pain wasn't so bad now, but his sleep was disturbed by the uncomfortable position in which he needed to lie. Each time he unconsciously turned his face to the side, the wires would push on his jaw and awaken him.

On Friday, Morgan stayed up longer in the recliner and found he could snooze in it better than in the bed. Harry delivered a large bag of get-well cards from fans. Callie opened them and read him the funny ones. Charlie brought over the material for the board meeting. And the doctor took out the stitches.

That evening, Morgan experienced some flashbacks of the accident. He tried not to communicate his anxiety to Callie. When she sent searching looks his way, he smiled as best he could with the wires restricting movement.

"Seems odd that our lives could be so altered in such a short period of time," she said.

Morgan's keyed up energy allowed him to walk the perimeter of their grounds with Callie. After the exercise, he was worn out and that night he slept better.

The board meeting was scheduled to begin at nine. Charlie called at eight thirty and left the speakers on the phone so Morgan could hear the greetings and noise of the board members and the company executives who would be presenting reports.

Callie sat in Morgan's chair. On the desk was a cup of coffee, which Wilda kept filled, and the same rolls that were being served in the board room. Wilda had made some lemon pudding for Morgan, and he smiled at the pretend world that she and Callie had set up for him.

The meeting went smoothly with Callie reading Morgan's opening remarks and Charlie taking over the meeting after that. Morgan scribbled comments on his legal pad, and Callie voiced them to the board.

During the noon break, Morgan took a nap. During the afternoon session, he sipped food and listened intently.

At the end of the meeting, Callie read a statement about Morgan being in the mountains for the next five weeks and designating Charlie as the one in charge at the corporate offices.

"Morgan will be in touch daily by phone. There will be no break in the regular chain of command, except that it may take a little longer to get decisions made."

"Went well," Morgan said, after the phone connection had been broken.

"Yes. Now, when shall we leave for the mountains?" They kept clothes at the mountain house so they didn't need to pack.

"Now?"

"Oh, you aren't up to that are you?" She glanced at her watch. "It'd be eight before we could get there."

"Go," Morgan said.

Callie found Wilda and told her they were leaving for a few weeks; then she gathered up medicines, placed Morgan's puréed foods in a cooler, and they left for their mountain home.

Chapter 5

The drive to Highridge lifted Callie's spirits. As tired as she was after the long board meeting, she wanted to see the mountains again. She glanced at Morgan, who sat in the passenger seat, his gaze drifting along the scenic road.

She knew spring was his favorite season, and the middle of May had to be about the best time of spring. The trees had leafed out and overhung the two-lane road in places, forming a canopy overhead. The shades of green were fresh and clean, not the dried dusty green of late summer, and Callie was reminded of God's promise of rebirth. She prayed that Morgan, too, would be regenerated by being around nature instead of the concrete of the city.

As they neared Eagle Mountain, the road climbed, turned back on itself, and climbed again. Knowing the road as well as she did, Callie skillfully maneuvered the car.

They had stayed in their new home on Eagle Mountain on several weekends, but they hadn't been there for any extended length of time. Grandma had owned Eagle, and her house rested at the foot of the mountain. She'd given the land to Callie and Morgan for a wedding present. Building had begun on the house before they were married, and the interior had been completed three months ago.

A house of her own was a dream come true for Callie. Not that the Atlanta house wasn't hers, too, but it held Morgan's history. This one would have shared memories.

Callie had wanted Grandma to live in the new house, but Grandma had said her home was at the bottom of Eagle. It was a ramshackle old farmhouse that Callie had fixed up after she had gotten a job as an accountant. Although homey, it was a far cry from the mansion on the mountain.

Something niggled at Callie's mind. What had she forgotten to bring with them to the mountains? She went over the list in her head. Morgan's medicines, her own vitamins—those were of primary importance.

"Oh, no. I forgot to call Marie Richardson and check on Jeff."

"You can call from the house," Morgan said.

Callie nodded. The call would be long distance, but she had quickly become accustomed to the luxuries of having money.

Had it changed her? she wondered. What had happened to the young girl who had received the first college scholarship financed by Trey, the country singing sensation? Was she still inside Callie? She hoped so. That was the girl Morgan had fallen in love with. She shook her head. Strong values, knowing right and wrong, a steadfast belief in God—those things were within her. Knowing she could reach for the phone and call anywhere in the world anytime she wanted didn't change her basic character.

The junction of the highway onto the county road loomed ahead. Callie turned and drove two miles into the country before Grandma's house appeared. Grandma sat in an old rocker on the front porch. She didn't seem surprised when they drove up.

"Welcome back," she called and walked out to the car and stood by Morgan's open window. "How you doing, Morgan?"

"Okay," Morgan mumbled.

Callie ran around the car and hugged Grandma. "We'll be staying a few weeks," Callie announced.

"Good. Do you both good. You need anything up at the house?" She peered in the back seat and obviously saw nothing. "Groceries?"

"I'll run into Highridge tomorrow morning. Maybe you could stay with Morgan while I do?"

"Sure."

"Don't need babysitter," Morgan protested.

Callie leaned in the window and kissed him lightly on the lips. "Yes, you do. Humor me for just another week. Then I'll let you be alone. Promise."

Morgan nodded.

Callie gave Grandma another hug. "I want to get Morgan settled. See you tomorrow."

She climbed back into the car and started up Eagle Mountain. The road was steep with switchbacks every little bit, but the mountain wasn't as tall as Regal where Morgan's summer home was and where her father's parents had a home. Morgan had decided to keep the Regal Mountain home for his family to enjoy. Dorothy and Victoria's family used it regularly.

Near the top of the mountain, Callie glimpsed her home, nestled among trees. She caught her breath as she did each time she saw it. Viewed from below, the cathedral-type structure soared into the sky, with a floor-to-ceiling glass opening onto a large balcony. As she turned on the switchback, Callie lost sight of the house until she came out on top of the mountain. From this side, the high-pitched roof allowed the house to fit into the tall trees around it.

Callie pushed a button and the garage door opened. As soon as she'd parked the car inside, she helped Morgan into the house. They walked through the large kitchen and straight to the long windows. Callie opened one set of doors and seated Morgan on the balcony overlooking a fantastic view.

"Stay here. I'll get you something to eat and bring it out." She went back to the car for the cooler and their medicine bag, then warmed Morgan's puréed stew in the microwave.

She made a mental note to move the recliner out on the balcony for Morgan in the morning. She doubted he'd be up too much longer tonight. He'd been sitting most of the day.

She popped the top of a diet soda and carried it and Morgan's stew out on the deck.

"Glad we came," Morgan said.

"Me, too. There's nothing like these mountains to put life in perspective, is there? We're going to be fine, Morgan. I know it."

He nodded and sipped his supper.

Callie slipped inside, called the hospital, and talked briefly with Marie. Jeff was improving daily. He should be able to go home within a week.

"Morgan, you never got to meet Jeff," Callie said when she returned to the deck. "What do you think of having him and his parents here for a weekend? It would give him something to look forward to. He's quite a fan of yours."

"You like him?"

"Yes. He's a real fighter. He was injured so badly, but he doesn't give up. Did I tell you his accident was a result of a drunk driver? A hit and run, except the drunk also hit a tree at the end of the street, and that stopped him."

"Not say much about him."

"I guess I haven't told you his whole story. Of course, I've been so concerned about you and the board meeting. Doesn't that seem in a different world? That's what I love about the mountains. Cares seem to be as far removed as a rock at the foot of the mountain that's too little to be seen from here."

Morgan put his empty cup on a side table.

"You're tired aren't you? Give me five minutes to put fresh sheets on the bed and we'll lie down."

✄

One entire east wall of the bedroom was windows, just like in the living room. The bed faced them, so the first thing Callie saw when she awoke the next morning was the pink glow of the morning sunrise. She glanced over at Morgan who was still asleep on his hill of pillows.

He hadn't stirred much last night. Callie didn't know if it was due to his exhaustion or to the fresh mountain air.

She'd slept, too, and dreamed about their baby and the day when Morgan would be well. She would tell him about the baby the day the wires came off. Having that goal in mind made it easier for her to stand the wait.

Today she felt ready to face the world. She quietly made her way to the kitchen and made a pot of coffee. When she carried half a cup to Morgan, he was awake.

"Beautiful," he said.

"I know. I can't get enough of the view."

"Not view, you," he said with adoration in his eyes.

Callie laughed. "Flattery will get you a second cup of coffee if you can sip this one. I've let it cool a little bit for you. We need milk before I make you an Instant Breakfast. How about some chicken and noodles?"

Morgan nodded.

While Morgan bathed, Callie fixed his puréed meal.

"Take shower 'morrow," he told her later.

"I'll bet you'll be strong enough then that I won't worry about you standing in the shower."

"Sound like baby. Easy this way. I talk normal again?" She knew he was worried that he'd get so accustomed to his verbal shorthand that he wouldn't form complete sentences ever again.

"Of course you will. There's no need for you to strain yourself any more than necessary. As long as we communicate, that's all that matters."

"You go store. I okay."

"Please, Morgan, humor me. Let Grandma come up for a little while. She hasn't gotten to visit with you, and it'll make her feel needed. In a couple of days, you can go to town with me."

A guarded look came into his eyes, and Morgan shook his head in a negative manner.

"We'll wait awhile, then," Callie said. She called Grandma and set up a Morgan-sitting time.

Morgan walked slowly to the long windows and looked toward town, which was several miles to the north. Although Highridge was a wealthy resort town accustomed to celebrities and therefore didn't make a fuss over them, he knew his bruised face would cause stares and comments. He had tried on sunglasses and liked the way they hid the heavy bruises around his eyes, but they didn't disguise the jagged line on his face. Someone in Highridge would recognize him and tell the press he was here, and then the reporters would descend. No, he'd stay on the mountain until he was himself again.

Morgan turned to watch Callie while she talked. The morning sun shone off her honey gold hair, which she'd been letting grow longer because he'd asked her. His heart was warmed that she wanted to please him. She was a beautiful woman, and she was his wife. He thanked God that he'd met this woman who loved him as much as he loved her.

"It's all arranged. I'll leave you here alone long enough to drive down and bring her back. She said she'd walk up, but it's a steep climb for me. Grandma doesn't need to make it. Anything special you want from town?"

"Ice cream."

"Of course. I'll get tons of it."

Callie moved the recliner out on the deck and laid one of Grandma's crocheted afghans beside it in case Morgan got cold in the early morning mountain air. She walked beside Morgan as he carried a book out on the balcony and sat down.

"I'll be back before you can say Jack Robinson," Callie told him.

"Jack Wobinson," Morgan said, then took a sharp breath. He couldn't say rs. Was it because of the wires or his restructured palate?

"Don't worry," Callie said. "As soon as the wires come off you can open your mouth and yell Jack Robinson so that it echoes off Regal."

She was right. Surely she was right, he thought.

Callie leaned down and kissed him lightly on the lips. He put his arms around her and held her close for a moment before he let her go. As soon as she got back, he'd ask her to sit with him. He wanted to hold her and have her hold him.

With a wave, Callie left, and a short time later Grandma walked out on the porch.

"Well, Morgan, it's you and me," she said. "Want to play dominoes?"

That was Grandma's game, and Morgan knew he didn't stand a chance at winning. But he agreed to play. They sat down at the small round table in the kitchen. A game table was in the den, but Grandma always preferred the kitchen, so Morgan accommodated her. He accommodated everything Grandma wanted, since she meant so much to Callie. He loved the old woman, too, but he knew Grandma had the upper hand in their relationship.

Callie made her way slowly down Eagle Mountain for the second time in the last ten minutes. She slowed at her old home and marveled that she no longer lived there, but at the top of the mountain. What changes the last year had brought.

She touched her stomach and thought of the baby. Not telling Morgan was so hard. Luckily she'd had no morning sickness or any of the other discomforting side effects of early pregnancy. She'd read the pamphlets the nurse had given her, but she wanted to pick up a book on pregnancy. She'd call Morgan's doctor in Atlanta and cancel her own doctor's appointment there. Dr. Doody in Highridge could see them both while they were in the mountains. On Monday she'd take care of those details.

She drove directly to the grocery store. She didn't want to be gone long. Today she'd get only the necessities and make a longer trip during the week. She'd get Grandma to sit with Morgan again, although she knew he'd object. What she needed was an invisible babysitter, someone he was so used to, that he wouldn't think about her being there just to watch him. She needed someone like Wilda, but she couldn't ask her to come to Highridge for several weeks. She had a life in Atlanta, and besides, they needed someone house-sitting while they weren't staying there.

Because they hadn't stayed in the new house longer than a weekend, Callie hadn't thought of hiring a housekeeper for the mountain house. That would be the answer. Maybe Grandma would know someone. She sorted through the members of her church, but couldn't come up with someone who could work a full-time job for only six weeks, or maybe longer since it would be summer soon.

On a sudden impulse, Callie stopped at a pay phone and looked up the number of the receptionist at the CPA firm where she had worked as an accountant before her marriage. Liz answered on the second ring and seemed delighted to hear from Callie. After assuring her that Trey was doing well, Callie asked if she knew of anyone in the community who would want a temporary job as a housekeeper/companion for a few weeks.

"Callie, this is just what my sister needs," Liz said, excitement coloring her voice.

"Jean?" Callie had met Liz's sister on a few occasions. She couldn't imagine why she'd want this type of position.

"Her husband died just after you moved to Atlanta."

"Liz, I'm sorry. I didn't know."

"It's okay. A heart attack. He went suddenly, leaving Jean with two teenaged boys and needing a job. She's been substitute teaching, trying to work into the school system. But that's iffy work. Some days she's called and some days she's not. And school's about out. This would be a perfect answer for her. Let me call her, and I'll feel her out."

"All right. I'm not home right now, but I will be in half an hour. Have Jean call me if she's interested." Callie gave her the number and fairly flew into the store.

She loaded up on milk and ice cream, then pampered herself with a bag of chocolate kisses. Maybe it was a pregnancy craving, or maybe it was just her sweet tooth acting up. She wanted to buy several small bags but settled for one giant-sized bag.

Callie made it home, unloaded, and got Grandma back down the mountain before her grandmother's ride came to take her to church.

"Morgan's been on the prayer list," Grandma said before she got out of the car. "I'll tell them he's home for a spell. Do you mind if people call on you?"

"I think Morgan would like the concern," Callie said.

Jean's call came exactly a half an hour after Callie had talked to Liz. They talked briefly and arranged for Jean to begin the next morning.

For the rest of Sunday, Callie snuggled by Morgan's side. He seemed stronger and wanted her by him. They went on a walk around the top of the mountain, not a long one, but a tiring one. Then again, they snuggled side by side on the porch swing on the balcony.

Morgan seemed in good spirits. When his boyhood friend, Robert Garrigan, called, he mumbled across the phone lines, his first attempt at phone communication.

"This will work," he said to Callie a few minutes later. "I can talk to Charlie every day without you."

"Hey, don't forget you need me, mister," Callie teased, but she was glad he was gaining confidence and was talking in better sentences, too.

"Robert and Marilyn coming to mountains next weekend," he said.

"Great. Can't wait to see them. Will they be here long?"

"Three weeks this time, then they'll be back later in the summer."

Both Marilyn and Robert were summer people whom Callie had met last year. Robert wrote best-selling mysteries, and Marilyn was a stockbroker in New York. They had married a month before Callie and Morgan had walked down the aisle.

Callie's father was coming, their friends would be here, Jeff and his parents might come to the mountains, and Callie had hired Jean to help her out with the house and Morgan. All in all, their recuperating stay in the mountains looked like a good time for all. Just what the doctor ordered.

Chapter 6

Morgan sat on the deck with Callie, enjoying the late morning sunshine. Jean was in the kitchen, preparing some new puréed foods to give him a different taste treat. "Isn't she terrific?" Callie asked.

"She seems nice." He hadn't thought far enough ahead to think they'd need someone up here, but Jean did free them from household chores, so they could do things. If he could do things. Just trying to speak in complete sentences seemed to be all he could do. If he was going to communicate on the phone, he needed full sentences.

Last night some people from Callie's church had come by. He'd met them all last summer and worked with some on the benefit program he'd performed to earn money for much-needed repairs on the old building. They wanted to express their support and concern, and he had spoken in as normal a fashion as he could manage in his hoarse voice.

He was taking his iron supplement and eating every couple of hours, since he ate such small amounts at a time. With every minimeal he felt stronger. He knew he had a long way to go, but he was seeing progress and that was giving him hope.

And he needed all the hope he could muster. His moods swung like a pendulum. When others were around, they bolstered his spirits. When he was alone, even for a short while, he felt tired, no, exhausted and depressed. Once when Callie had the radio on and he'd heard one of his songs, he'd felt like crying. The last time he'd cried was when his father had died. And the time before that was probably in third grade when he'd had a bad bike wreck.

He had to get a grip. He couldn't let Callie know how much he ached for a return to the good life—life before the accident. He would never again take for granted simple things: walking as far as he wanted, eating an apple, or making love to his wife.

"How about strawberries and cream?" Jean asked, pulling him out of his thoughts.

Callie pushed a table closer to Morgan's chair. "That sounds wonderful." Callie was delighted with Jean. The red-headed woman was petite, about her height, with sparkling eyes and a level head on her shoulders. Callie liked her immediately, and Morgan seemed to like her as well.

When Callie mentioned Jean's late husband, the brightness in her eyes hadn't faltered. "We had wonderful years, and I have great memories. He's gotten his heavenly reward. I wouldn't wish it away from him, even though I miss him." With an undefeated attitude, although Callie knew light housekeeping and helping her with Morgan weren't Jean's goals in life, she kept a happy smile on her face and a lightness in her step.

Callie guessed Jean to be in her late thirties or early forties. Her sons were fourteen and sixteen. They might be friends for Jeff if he got to come up for a weekend. She hadn't broached the subject to Marie Richardson, but she would this evening when she called the hospital. Besides getting Jeff into a different environment and giving him the boost of meeting a celebrity, Callie had an ulterior motive. She hoped Jeff's indomitable spirit could help Morgan. He grew despondent with the waiting game of recovery. She could see it in his eyes at unguarded moments, although she knew he was trying to hide it.

Meanwhile, she was hiding her pregnancy. She didn't like being secretive, but she didn't know what else to do. She wanted Morgan to celebrate the baby with her, not mope around worrying needlessly about her. And right now she thought that was what he would do. He had too much time on his hands, not much energy, and too much to think about.

"What would you like to do this morning, Morgan?" she asked when they had finished their snack.

"I'm going to set up office hours," he said. "That way Charlie can depend on me talking to him around ten, after the mail comes and manager reports are completed. Then in the afternoon I can call again around four to catch up on the events of the day."

"Excellent idea," Callie said. "While you do that, I thought I'd go into town to the library. I'll pick you up a mystery or two."

※ ✔

They parted, Callie feeling easy with Jean in the house in case Morgan needed anything. She didn't plan on being in Highridge long and parked on Main Street by the bookstore. She didn't want a library book on pregnancy, since Morgan might be with her when she'd need to return it, and she had no intention of letting him see this book until she could tell him about the baby. After poring over the baby section, she chose a book and then browsed a moment in the children's section.

Someday soon she'd have a little one who'd want storybooks read to him at nighttime. Him? Was she thinking of their child as a boy? She really didn't care which gender it was. She'd heard other pregnant women say the important thing was a healthy baby, and that was exactly how she felt. She walked outside into the spring sunshine and looked down the street toward the candy store. Dare she indulge herself? She still had a few chocolate kisses left, but her supply was dwindling. This store was famous for its hand-dipped chocolates.

As she stood by the car debating, Joe Lowery walked out of the bank a few doors down. "Joe," she called. She'd met him at the University of North Carolina at Chapel Hill when she'd answered his note on the bulletin board asking for a rider to share gas to Franklin, a town only a few miles away. They'd become close friends, and whenever he'd been on business in Highridge, he'd come out to Grandma's for a visit and a meal.

When she called his name again, he turned and walked down the street toward her. "Callie Sue," he said when they met and hugged. "I expected you'd turn up here soon. How's Morgan?"

"Doing better. Thanks for your calls to the hospital. We've been busy, or I'd have gotten back with you. What are you doing in Highridge?"

"Our bank has bought out the one here, so I'm liaison man right now, making sure the new procedures are in line with our policies. I may be moving here; it's all up in the air right now."

"Can you come out for supper tonight? I know Morgan would like to see you."

"Sure," he said without hesitation.

"Good. See you at seven."

Callie picked up some books from the library for Morgan, and within an hour she was back on the mountain.

※

Morgan had just walked outside for some exercise when he heard the motor pulling the car up the steep inclines of the mountain road. He chuckled. Callie had driven a manual shift pickup when he'd met her, but she'd never been smooth at shifting gears. He listened to the grind as she shifted to low in the sports car they'd driven from Atlanta. He should give her lessons on listening to the engine and knowing the exact moment to shift. He waited until she came around the last switchback and waved as she pulled into the garage.

She glanced guiltily at the seat beside her and leaned over before he could open the door for her. Was she hiding something from him? She climbed out and kissed him, then reached back in and picked up some books. She grabbed a sack, and he read the logo on the side. Now he understood what she'd been doing. "Callie, you don't have to hide candy. It doesn't bother me for you to eat in front of me."

Callie looked startled for a moment before she sighed. "Are you sure, Morgan? I couldn't pass the candy store without stopping in. Oh," she hurried on, "I ran into Joe, and he's coming to supper. I'd better tell Jean. How was your call to Charlie?" She knew she was rambling, but he'd almost caught her with the baby book. She'd stuffed it under the passenger seat and would have to retrieve it later when he took a nap.

※

Dinner that night was a huge success, Callie thought. She had missed contact with Joe, who reminded her of her single days at the university. He also had news of people in the Highridge community and filled her in on what was happening with the local people. Morgan seemed comfortable with Joe, although she remembered the first time they'd met, she'd thought Morgan was jealous. Morgan and Joe had gotten to know each other better during last summer's concert, and Joe had been one of the few invited to their secret marriage ceremony.

After dinner they sat on the balcony and talked some more. Morgan listened politely, but he was tired and he was feeling sorry for himself. He knew he had told Callie that she could eat anything in front of him, but the steaks she and Joe had cooked on the grill for dinner had him salivating. He was hungry for real food—for a salad and hot rolls. He'd eaten some warmed up chicken casserole, puréed of course, that Jean had prepared before she'd gone for the evening. But even the chocolate malt Callie had fixed hadn't done away with the empty feeling he had inside.

After Joe had left and Callie was sleeping peacefully, Morgan quietly got up and fixed himself an Instant Breakfast. The silence in the house penetrated to his soul, and he sat in the dark living room and stared at the blackness outside the windows.

Why had this happened to him? Was there some divine plan he had no notion of? Was it a random act of cosmic violence? Why? Why? Was there a reason that could make sense of this?

In the wee hours of the morning, Callie reached out for Morgan and touched nothing. Alarmed, she crawled out of bed and called his name. She heard a soft mumble from the living room and found Morgan sitting in the recliner.

"Are you hurting?" she asked and kneeled beside him.

"No. Got hungry and ate. I'm hungry again. Hungry for you." He reached for her, and she climbed onto his lap.

Callie saw the adoring look in his eyes and knew her eyes reflected back the overwhelming love she felt for this man. She took the initiative and kissed him on the forehead, on his cheek, on his lips, on his neck. She hugged him close then slid off his lap, and, taking his hands, led him to the plush rug in front of the fireplace. Man to woman, woman to man, they expressed their love.

"I have missed you so much," Morgan said.

"I know. Why is it that physical love makes us feel so close? Has God made us fit together so perfectly because it makes us see ourselves as one? Makes us united in body as well as spirit?"

"Don't know," Morgan said. "Just know I love you so much."

"Come on, let's go back to bed," Callie said. "You need to get some rest."

"Feel rested now," Morgan said. "Feel whole again."

Callie laughed, and arm in arm they walked back to the bedroom.

❧

The rest of the week fell into a routine. Morgan called his office as he'd planned. When he was closeted in his study, Callie read her baby book and felt guilty that she hadn't shared her joy with him. But she had made her decision to tell him when the wires came off, and she knew that was the best thing for Morgan.

She had taken Morgan to the doctor in Highridge. Dr. Doody had agreed to examine him once a week to ensure against infection and pain. A trip back to Atlanta wouldn't be necessary until it was time for the wires to come off. On another day, Callie saw the doctor by herself and was reassured that she was doing all the right things for her baby's health.

Jean was working out like a dream, and every day Callie liked her more. Her bubbly personality lightened the place, and she made it her mission in life to prepare tasty treats for Morgan.

Callie called Marie Richardson each day and got updated reports on Jeff's condition. Marie couldn't believe Callie and Morgan really wanted them to visit in the mountains, but after she'd talked the invitation over with her husband, they had decided to take them up on it. Jeff would be released from the hospital on Friday. He'd spend a week recovering at home, then Marie and Ken would bring him to the mountains for the weekend.

On Friday, Robert and Marilyn arrived from New York. They came directly to the house from the airport without stopping at their own house on Regal Mountain. Morgan laughed, more of an inward sound than an out loud sound, when he saw his best friend.

He and Robert had gone through a lot in their growing up years and, as men, had grown even closer. Robert wrote mystery novels, and when Morgan had needed help discovering who Callie's father was, he'd turned to Robert, thinking that if he could make his fictional detective, Sinclair, solve so many mysteries, maybe he could help with the mystery of Callie's father. Robert had been glad to help. His wife Marilyn was a wonderful person, too. She and Callie had formed a solid friendship bond.

Although Robert's eyes showed concern when Morgan first saw him, he didn't show pity but compassion. "Didn't I give you a black eye once back when we were around eight?" Robert asked as they all sat on the balcony with a big pitcher of lemonade. "It looked about like that."

"Wasn't it the other way around?" Morgan asked in his hoarse voice. "Didn't I give you one?"

"Maybe we both looked a little beaten up after the big fight," Robert said.

"What were you fighting about?" Callie asked. The two men looked at each other.

"Haven't a clue," Robert said.

"I can't remember, either."

"Probably some little blond," Marilyn teased. "They've always claimed to be big ladies' men. Even at eight, they must have been charmers."

Callie looked at the two friends and thanked God that they had come. Just that morning she had seen that look of despair in Morgan's eyes. He was so good at hiding it, or maybe it just came and went. She didn't know. And they didn't discuss it. When she'd asked him if anything was wrong, he'd said he was fine. Now he looked happy, his eyes shining with pleasure.

"What caused the accident?" Robert asked. "Can it happen to any pool filter?"

Callie explained what she knew of the problem, and Morgan elaborated. "Investigator looking into background of pool man," he said.

"You think someone did this on purpose?" Marilyn said with a gasp.

"No. Just wanted to know about him. He was willing to pay for hospital bill," Morgan said. "He seemed very sorry."

"You know," Robert said thoughtfully, "this could be a plot for Sinclair. This could be made to look like an accident, but be carefully orchestrated. Could the blow have killed a person?"

"Morgan could have bled to death," Callie said and shivered involuntarily. "He lost a third of his blood. That's why he's still so weak. In another few days we should see major changes in his energy level."

"This has real possibilities. Do you mind if I enlarge it a bit and use it for a book? I could set the murder in an isolated place, say a mountain top in North Carolina," he said and looked around. "No close neighbors, no ambulance service. Hey, this could work."

"Well, good to know that I've provided a plot for you," Morgan said. "I knew there had to be some good come out of this."

Callie looked sharply at Morgan. Although he was teasing his friend, she heard a bitter ring in what he said, and for a brief moment that haunted look had returned to his eyes.

Chapter 7

This will be good for you," Callie said and straightened Morgan's tie. "It's been two weeks now, and you need to get out and see people. I wouldn't count one quick trip to Highridge to the doctor as getting out. Especially since you went in the back door and saw only Dr. Doody."

"They don't need to see me," Morgan mumbled. He'd let Callie talk him into going to church, and now he was regretting that decision. "God understands why I'm not in church."

"I'm sure He does. But He'll be proud of you for making the effort, especially since He knows what it costs you."

Morgan took a deep breath. Several of the church members had been by in the last few days and had seen the way he looked. But a whole group was different than one or two at a time. They wouldn't gawk at him, would they?

Callie drove them to the bottom of Eagle in the van they kept at their mountain home. Grandma was going with them, and the little sports car wouldn't hold all three of them.

Grandma was waiting on her porch. She climbed aboard, and the trio set off for the little country church where Callie and Morgan had been married.

The old church, dedicated in 1804, was as solid as the year it was built. The money that Morgan's concert had raised for the church had assured that. A shored-up foundation, a new roof, new windows, and a new coat of white stucco over repaired cracks made the church look brand new again.

No extra space had been added. It was still a small one-room church with a center aisle and antique pews on each side. But the fifty members didn't need special classrooms. They merely divided into Sunday school classes by sitting in different areas of the small sanctuary. A circuit preacher ministered to the church every other Sunday. This week there would be no sermon.

Morgan walked into the church wearing dark glasses to hide the worst of his bruises. He felt silly with them on inside the sanctuary, and although he didn't want to expose his face to curious looks, he took them off.

Around forty people stared at him for all of three seconds, just as they would anyone who entered and walked to the second pew.

"Glad to see you out, Morgan," one member said.

A couple of the teenagers came over to him and told him how sorry they were that he'd been hurt.

From behind the podium, an elderly man called the Sunday school meeting to order. The combination secretary/treasurer read the minutes and gave the treasury balance. Then the congregation stood for a prayer followed by a hymn.

Morgan tried to sing. When he talked, he formed his words slowly so that he could be understood, but he couldn't keep up with the pace of the song, even though "In the Sweet Bye and Bye" wasn't sung at a fast clip. He knew the wires hampered him, but was that all? He tried humming along and heard his voice crack, and the hoarseness in his voice wouldn't go away.

As if reading his thoughts, Callie turned to him and smiled. "It will be all right," she said.

The Sunday school lesson was on the prodigal son, a lesson that Morgan had never really understood.

"There will be more rejoicing in heaven over one sinner who repents than over ninety-nine righteous persons who do not need to repent," Tommy Ray read from the quarterly.

"That doesn't seem fair," Morgan spoke up. He had never questioned that before. He had merely accepted it. "Why should we live good lives if we'd be more celebrated if we led bad ones then changed?"

A lively discussion of the parable ensued with Tommy Ray summing up the consensus. "The son who had worked the land with his father was reassured that his inheritance was his, and the son who had taken his inheritance and spent it wasn't going to get more. The prodigal son would have to live with what he'd done, but he was forgiven for it. Isn't that right?"

"Jesus said He had come to save sinners, not punish them, but that doesn't mean they won't be accountable for their actions in this life," another member spoke up.

"The whole thing is about forgiveness," Callie said. "And that's what we as Christians should dwell on."

The piano player started up a lively tune that signaled the end of Sunday school, and the members moved back to their regular seats for the closing hymn.

Over the Sunday dinner table at Grandma's, the discussion turned again to the prodigal son.

Grandma took her turn at explaining the parable. "I think living a good life gives its own rewards—like how others treat us and the good feeling we enjoy while we're on this earth. At the same time, we oughta forgive those who do what we think is wrong. We can't know what's in other people's hearts. We can only know what's in our own."

As Grandma said this, Callie looked at Morgan and wished she knew more of what he was feeling.

❧

On Wednesday morning, Callie knew she was going to be sick. She felt it before she even raised her head from the pillow. With quick, purposeful movements she threw off the covers and dashed for the bathroom.

As soon as he heard her, Morgan was beside her, holding her head. He had been afraid that she'd have some sort of reaction to her father coming to the mountains. A nervous stomach hadn't crossed his mind, but here it was.

When Phillip had called earlier in the week to announce he'd be there on Wednesday, Morgan had watched Callie alternate between excitement and apprehension. They hadn't seen Phillip since the wedding, and now that they were going to have a couple of weeks in close proximity, Morgan realized she couldn't handle the uncertainty of what their relationship would be.

Grandma hadn't helped. She'd been as moody as Callie. Morgan had finally talked to Grandma about how important this was to his wife, and that they needed to play it up as a positive thing, not dwell on the negative. Grandma had sniffed and said she knew Morgan was right, but it was hard.

Now looking at a pale Callie, Morgan knew he'd underestimated what this first heart-to-heart encounter would be like for her.

"I'm all right," Callie said. She looked up at him with guilt in her eyes.

Why would she feel guilty about her sickness? It wasn't every day that a woman got to talk to a father she didn't really know about a mother she'd never met. Although the two had spoken on the phone several times, they had never broken down the barriers of the past. Today was the day. Phillip had even mentioned it when he had called.

Morgan washed Callie's face with a cold washcloth. He felt odd taking care of her when she had been taking care of him. He'd been taking advantage of her, he realized, relying on her strength to carry him through this hard time. Well, she could depend on him to get her through her hard time.

He led her back to bed. "Can I get you some crackers and a soda?" That had been his mom's remedy for an upset stomach. Surely it would work for Callie. He'd never seen her sick before, and he didn't like seeing her lie there so helpless and pale.

"Crackers sound good. I'll be all right. I'm not really sick," she said.

"I know. But I'll stay right by you when he comes, Callie. We'll learn about your past together." He was stronger now. Two weeks and five days had gone by since the accident, and for the last few days he'd felt physically better and better. Emotionally he wasn't exactly solid, but maybe he'd been feeling sorry for himself. That wasn't his normal way, and he'd watch that in the future. "I'll get those crackers."

Callie couldn't believe that Morgan had misinterpreted her

sickness, but she wasn't going to correct his mistake. She hoped this wasn't the beginning of a streak of morning sickness episodes. Grandma had said some pregnancies had isolated incidents, and she prayed this was one.

"Here you go." Morgan put a plate of saltines and a can of soda on the night stand. He gathered some throw pillows off the floor and piled them behind Callie's back so she could eat. He smiled that wired-mouth smile that Callie was getting used to. "You're going to be fine."

"I know. Thanks, Morgan. I love you so much," she said and then dissolved into tears.

"Honey, it's going to be fine." Morgan climbed into bed beside her and pulled her into his arms. He stroked her hair as she nestled her head on his chest.

"I know. This is silly."

"No, it's not. Just nerves. You'll be fine."

In half an hour she was over the nausea—and found herself ravenous instead. Chocolates ranked high in her mind, but she settled instead for the toast and tea Morgan fixed her. He drank his ever-present Instant Breakfast.

Sunshine filtered through the leaves of the trees overhead and speckled the table on the balcony where they ate. A gentle morning breeze reminded her that it was still May, and Callie pulled a sweater closer around her.

"Shall we have lunch out here? It'll be warmer then, and I imagine Phillip would like the view."

"Good idea. I'll do my office stuff early, then we'll get everything ready," Morgan said.

Jean arrived, and she and Callie worked on a fruit salad in the kitchen. "He's probably as nervous as you," Jean said.

Callie had explained about not knowing her father and the importance of this meeting that Phillip had said would answer all her questions. The problem was, she didn't know what questions she had. He'd answered the most important one last summer—he had loved her mother.

By ten o'clock everything was in readiness. Callie paced the wide balcony, listening for the sound of a car. Once she heard a motor, but it stopped at Grandma's. Unexpected company, she imagined, since Grandma hadn't mentioned anyone coming over this morning.

A few minutes later she heard the unmistakable sound of a car making the laborious assent up Eagle Mountain. She ran into Morgan's study.

"He's on his way," she said breathlessly.

Morgan rose from his chair and walked with her to the living room. He put his hands on her shoulders and faced her. "This is going to be fine. You already know a lot of their history. This will just finalize it." He kissed her forehead.

When the doorbell rang, Callie answered it and stood open-mouthed as Grandma swept into the room in front of Phillip.

"Hello, Callie," Phillip said. "Since I promised you we'd talk about your mother, I thought Mrs. Duncan should be here, too. I hope you don't mind."

Actually, Callie was relieved. She'd known she would have to repeat to Grandma everything Phillip told her anyway; this would be easier. Callie glanced at Morgan who was shaking hands with her father.

"Welcome, P.J. Please come in and sit." Morgan had known P.J. as Dianne Prescott's much-older brother. They had never called him Phillip, or Morgan might have made the connection between the unknown Phillip who was Callie's father and P.J. Prescott.

"Grandma, why don't you sit right here?" He motioned for her to sit in his recliner. He opted to sit beside Callie on the couch to give her his physical as well as moral support. But when he glanced at Grandma, he wondered if she might need him more.

She held her head in a straight upright position as if she were a mannequin in a chair. Her gaze stayed on Phillip. Morgan knew if this meeting was hard for Callie, it was doubly so for Grandma. Callie had never known her mother, but Daisy had been Grandma's only child.

Callie had met Phillip when he was in the hospital recovering from a car accident. When he was discharged, he had gone back to Boston, where he lived. They had talked on the phone, and he and his children had attended the wedding, but this was the first opportunity Callie had had for a face-to-face meeting.

The tension in the room was a palpable thing. Callie put her hand over her stomach, thinking this time she might really be sick from nerves. Grandma's posture was belligerent. Did Phillip have a chance of explaining his love for her mother?

"How have you been, P.J.?" Morgan said.

Phillip looked from Morgan to the women. "I think we'd better skip the small talk and get right down to why I'm here," he said. "I want to know my daughter better, and I know that won't happen until I've told all of you about Daisy and me."

He had sat in an overstuffed chair opposite the couch, but now he stood and walked over to the glass wall and looked out toward Regal Mountain. "Twenty-five years ago my dad bought a house on Regal Mountain, and I came to the mountains with my family for the summer. I was nineteen and had finished one year of college. I came to the mountains to figure out what I wanted to do with my life. My dad had been such a success as an inventor, and I felt I needed to succeed as well as he had. But I had no inclination toward engineering. I was much better at memorizing history dates than at plugging in numbers in a formula. I needed to declare a major in college, and I didn't know what to do. I needed time to think."

He motioned toward the view. "I hiked a lot that summer, on my own. That is, until one day in June when I was climbing this very mountain and saw the most beautiful girl in the world, sitting right here at the top."

Grandma gasped.

"That's right, Mrs. Duncan. It was Daisy. She was so bright-eyed, trusting, and innocent. We talked that day." He waved his hand as if correcting himself. "Actually, I talked and she listened. As we got to know each other, I listened to her dreams, too.

"We knew we couldn't see each other. My mother would have

been displeased, to say the least, to find I was in love with a mountain girl. Mother has always been a social climber. When Dad bought the house on Regal, it was the beginning of her life as a socialite. And Daisy knew you wouldn't like her seeing a summer person, as you called us. She said you labeled us 'putting on airs people' and had no use for us."

For the first time Grandma took her gaze off Phillip and looked at the floor. Callie could only guess what was going through her mind.

"Daisy and I met here every day, and then we started meeting at night between here and Regal. There's a path—"

"I've been on it," Callie said and knew that several times she and Morgan had followed the same path that Daisy and Phillip had taken.

"Daisy encouraged me to do what I wanted in life. Which I have. I majored in history, and I teach it at Boston University, but you know that. Our plan was for us to complete more schooling. Then I'd come back for her, and we'd be married.

"I left with that understanding. However, Daisy never answered my letters, and I heard from her only once, indirectly. Mother said she had called and said she'd married a man named Sam. As you know, Mother intercepted Daisy's letters to me, and I believed her when she said Daisy had married someone else. There was no other explanation for why she didn't answer my letters. Of course, I now know she didn't get them. Mother took them out of the mailbox when I'd put them out to be picked up by the postman. So Daisy must have believed I didn't love her, just as I believed she didn't love me."

He walked back from the windows and plopped down in the chair, as if his tale had exhausted him.

"I never returned to the mountains until last summer. I stayed at school in the summers, and four years later married Louise. I thought I loved her at the time, but she never took the place of Daisy in my heart. We were married for eleven years when she died. And we did have some good years together. You've met your half brother and half sisters." He looked at Callie as he spoke. "They'd like to know you better, too."

Callie swallowed hard and squeezed Morgan's hand.

Phillip reached into the pocket of his sports coat and withdrew an envelope. "These are the only pictures I have of Daisy. One evening we went into Highridge and played in the photo booth by the hotel. I had copies made for both of you." He handed pictures to Grandma and Callie.

There were four pictures with typical snaps of the two of them crammed in the booth. In two pictures they were clowning around, laughing. In one they were kissing. And in the last one they were looking at each other, love shining in their eyes.

"And now I'd like to know what happened to Daisy." This time Phillip turned his gaze to Grandma.

She sat statue still, with tears flowing down her cheeks. She opened her mouth, then shook her head and looked at Callie.

Callie took a deep breath. "My mother wouldn't tell my grandfather your name because she was afraid he'd hurt you. On the day I was born, the day she died, she called *Phillip* over and over. That was all they knew of you."

Phillip bowed his head and cried.

Chapter 8

Callie closed her dry eyes and leaned against Morgan. What could she do for her grandmother and her father, these two who were hurting so? The picture of the mother she'd never met had touched her soul. She looked young, bright, happy, and so in love. But Daisy Duncan was only a picture to Callie. She wasn't a real person.

Grandma and Phillip had known this happy girl. They had both loved her. And Callie saw clearly that they both blamed themselves for her death.

"I should have been with her," Phillip moaned. He rocked back and forth holding his head in his hands.

Grandma still sat upright, mopping her tears with a hanky. After a long moment, she rose and walked over to Phillip and patted him on the shoulders. "There was nothing you could have done except love her. I should have let her see you. I didn't know. I suspected she had a thing for a summer boy, but I didn't want to know for certain. I was too scared of losin' her. And I lost her anyway."

Phillip stood and hugged Grandma. "I'm sorry," he choked. "But please understand that I loved her, too."

Grandma sniffed. "I can see that in the picture."

Callie turned to Morgan, still at a loss for what to do. He stood and pulled her up with him. "Part of Daisy still lives," he said and urged Callie to go to them.

"She has your green eyes," Grandma said to Phillip as she reached for Callie.

"But otherwise she looks like Daisy," Phillip said. "I'm glad we have you, Callie." He pulled her into the circle but turned his attention to Grandma. "Mrs. Duncan, forgive me."

217

"I do. Forgive me, too."

"Yes."

Now Callie couldn't hold back the tears. She broke away from her father and grandmother and reached for Morgan.

"Is now a good time for dinner?" Jean asked from the doorway.

"Perfect timing," Morgan said.

The mood of the group on the balcony was calm like a rainbow after the storm, Callie thought. God's promise to the world. There would always be an ache in Grandma and Phillip for Daisy, but the first offerings of peace had been extended and accepted. Callie hoped they could build on their shared love for Daisy, her mother.

Callie insisted that Jean join them for soup, shrimp salad, and fruit salad, feeling that another person might help with what might be a strained conversation. Then she offered a simple prayer. "Thank You, God, for bringing this family together and healing its wounds." The clanging of silverware brought a lighter conversational tone.

"Are you still eating beef stew?" Phillip asked. "I tried everything that could be beat to a liquid, and it was my favorite. But wouldn't you give anything for a thick steak?"

"I miss potato chips," Morgan answered. "Sometimes I get out the bag and smell them."

Phillip laughed. "Yeah, I remember. But it won't last forever. My wires came off in five weeks. Maybe you'll get yours off early, too."

Hope sprang in Morgan. "Just over two weeks and I could be okay?" he asked.

"Could be."

"Morgan's going to our doctor in town tomorrow, just for his weekly checkup," Callie said. "We've kept in touch by phone with his Atlanta doctor, but I don't think a trip back is necessary yet." She didn't want Morgan's hopes to be raised and then be plunged downward again if he had to wait the full six weeks.

Callie asked Phillip about his life in Boston and included Jean by talking about her search for a teaching job.

"Are you thinking of relocating or staying in the area?" Phillip asked Jean.

"Whatever's necessary. I like it here, but we could always come back summers."

What an odd turn of events, Callie thought. Here was Jean, who had lived here all her life, thinking of becoming a summer person. And Callie herself was now a summer person. Grandma's old adage about summer people and year-rounders not mixing was no longer applicable to their lives, if it ever had been. People were people, no matter where they lived at certain times of the year. Though unfortunately, there were those who were uppity, like Phillip's mother, Elizabeth.

She wondered what Phillip's relationship was with Elizabeth Prescott, but didn't get to ask until later that afternoon after Jean had delivered Grandma back down the mountain. Phillip and Callie went for a walk while Morgan lay down to rest.

"Things are very distant between my mother and me," Phillip said. "Once when I called to talk to Dad and she answered, I hung up. I wasn't proud of doing it, but something in me just slammed down that phone. I've spoken to her, but the last time I saw her was at your wedding. I need to talk to her like I've talked to Mrs. Duncan today. I need peace, Callie. I need to move on in my life. I regret a lot about my marriage to Louise, but I had three great kids with her, so there was good, too."

Callie walked arm in arm with her father and thought about the half brother and half sisters that she'd met but didn't know. They lived in Boston, so getting to know them would not be easy, but perhaps she could join them for a holiday sometime.

Again, she was becoming accustomed to money and what it could buy. All she had to do was call for a plane reservation and she could be anywhere in a matter of hours. When money wasn't an issue, overcoming obstacles was easier—if the obstacles weren't emotional problems of the heart.

Phillip left with the promise to return for another visit. Although they'd made great strides today, Callie wanted to know still more about her father.

Now that he was feeling stronger, Morgan prowled the house

like a caged tiger. "I want to be normal again, get back to work. Do you think I could get these wires off in two weeks?" he asked. "Could we go to Atlanta to talk to the doctor? He'd be the one to take them off, wouldn't he?"

Callie glanced at her watch and saw she had just enough time to reach the office. Her call netted an appointment for the next day. Again, the power of celebrity and money spoke volumes.

"Do you want to spend the night? See Charlie and Harry?" If he met with them, perhaps she could sneak off for an appointment with her doctor.

"That'd be good," Morgan said. He went out on the deck and left Callie making phone calls to set up his meetings. First she called her doctor and confirmed that he would work her into his schedule Friday morning. At the same time, she set up meetings for Morgan and called Wilda to tell her they'd be returning the next day.

Jeff and the Richardsons were planning to come on Saturday, but Callie would be back Friday afternoon in plenty of time to make last-minute arrangements for their visit. She smiled as she remembered her last phone conversation with Jeff.

"Wait until I tell my friends I spent the weekend with Trey," he'd said, excitement coloring his voice. "They won't believe it."

Callie felt good that she could help this boy who had been through so much.

✄

At the crack of dawn on Thursday, Morgan was up and ready to go. Although Callie had told him there was no use in hurrying, since his appointment wasn't until one o'clock, he wanted to get back to Atlanta. He knew he'd get a good report from his doctor. Hadn't Dr. Doody in Highridge told him how quickly he was healing?

Oh, there were still yellow bruises, especially around his eyes, but that was minor. His chin had an angry looking scar, but that was going to be worked on. Maybe he could schedule that today. And what about getting those two front teeth? As soon as the wires came off, he wanted to be fitted for a bridge. Not that he minded the time in the mountains, but his time there this time wasn't a self-imposed exile, but a forced retreat.

When he couldn't make decisions for himself, he felt out of control, not a feeling he liked. He had always enjoyed doing for others, but he didn't like others doing for him. Again, the issue was control.

Because of Morgan's insistence on an early start, they reached Atlanta in time for morning rush-hour traffic. By the time Callie turned the van into the long driveway of their home, her patience was worn thin, and she was glad for Wilda's welcome.

Yet, for the first time, Callie felt discontent in the Atlanta house. In the mountains she felt at peace. Here her thoughts immediately went to the accident. Surely in time, that feeling would go away.

Morgan also felt haunted by the accident. Odd, it hadn't bothered him to see the swimming pool before they had left for the mountains, but seeing it now brought back that night in pounding intensity. It would be three weeks tomorrow, but he felt half a lifetime had gone by since that filter had slammed into his face.

Wilda showed Morgan the mail that had accumulated. "I was going to send another packet to the mountains today," she said. "This letter looked important."

Morgan studied the return address—the private investigator. He took the letter and a cup of coffee into his study. The pool man, Wayne Degraffenreid, was twenty-two and a high school dropout. He had found a day job just last week at a shoe factory. At night he played piano in an espresso bar. He'd worked a variety of jobs, mostly unskilled labor and always for minimum wage, and the location of his gigs had changed through the last five years, but he had always played music. He'd played with several bands. Sometimes he played keyboard instead of piano, but the hope was the same. Someday he'd get his big break and make records.

"Good news or bad?" Callie asked from the doorway.

Morgan explained the investigator's report. "It would take him forever to save enough money to pay the hospital bill. No high school diploma, but a love for music. I wonder if he's any good. I could put in a word for him as a studio musician."

"Could you use him?"

"No." Morgan chuckled in his closed-mouth way. "He plays piano—like me."

"Could we go hear him?"

Morgan lifted his eyebrows and that guarded look came back in his eyes to be replaced a moment later by a thoughtful expression.

"I could wear that fake beard and glasses. No one would recognize me. Why not? I've got plenty of strength now."

"You mean that beard you wore in the Christmas pageant in the mountains? It wasn't bad," she said. "Let's see what the doctor says. I should think an outing of an hour or so would do you good."

The doctor agreed that Morgan could do anything he felt he could handle. "But don't overdo," he cautioned Morgan. "We don't want any setbacks when you're doing so well."

"What about the wires?"

"The X-rays look good. I'll see you in two weeks, and we'll make our decision then."

"What about the scar work?" Morgan asked. He wanted everything done now.

"We'll sand it, and it'll look much better. When the wires come off, we'll discuss it."

"Can't you do it now? Then when the wires come off it'll be healed, too?" Any delay only meant drawing out the time he couldn't be back to normal. "And my teeth?"

"Your dental work can start as soon as the wires are off. I suppose I could work on that scar. It's healed nicely, but I don't want to overload you."

"I can take it. Now?"

"Tomorrow morning, early. I can do it first thing. . .around seven or it'll be next week when I can get to it."

"I'll be here," Morgan said.

❧

The espresso bar looked like an old warehouse with a high ceiling and exposed heating ducts. The old wooden bar area, complete with bar stools, was in the center of the large room. Round tables dotted the space around it; at one end of the bar was a piano on a raised platform.

Morgan, disguised in his beard and dark glasses, and Callie sat as close to the piano as they could. At odd intervals noise from the espresso machine drowned out the sound of the piano.

Callie giggled and took a sip of her latte. "If this was the sixties, you'd fit right in," she told Morgan, "although you'd need a more colorful shirt, maybe with a rainbow on it. At this yuppie hangout, you stand out."

Morgan chuckled. He lifted his cup of cappuccino to her and carefully took a sip. He hoped no one could tell he couldn't open his mouth.

Wayne Degraffenreid sat at the piano and played old favorites. He swayed with the music as though feeling every note.

Someone requested "Autumn Leaves," one of Morgan's favorites for the piano. The trilling of the notes sounded like the leaves drifting from the trees to the ground.

Morgan leaned toward Callie so she could hear him. "He's good. Maybe I could get Harry to come listen to him."

"I like his sound. He enjoys his music," Callie said.

"He has a good ear."

They stayed for a few more songs; then Morgan escorted Callie to the car. "Why don't you let me drive?" he asked. "I know you don't like driving the van in city traffic."

"Not yet, Morgan. Didn't the doctor say you shouldn't drive for six weeks?"

"But I'm strong again. I'm almost back to normal."

"I think it has more to do with the anesthetic and delayed reflexes," she said. "Come on, think of it as being chauffeured."

He smiled and tried to think of it in her way, but this was one more area in which he felt out of control.

"How do you feel about helping Wayne Degraffenreid when his carelessness caused the accident?" she asked after they'd arrived back home. "I don't think I could be so kind about it."

Morgan was silent for a long moment. "I'm not sure how I feel.

I wish it hadn't happened, but I know he didn't do it on purpose and that he is truly sorry for it. That doesn't excuse his actions, but I need to forgive him and forget it. If I can point him in the right direction in a career, it will help me make sense of all this."

"You're a good man, Morgan Perry Rutherford the Third," Callie said. "And I thank God every day that I'm married to you."

"Words are cheap," he said with a teasing glint in his eyes. He put his arms around her and ushered her toward the bedroom. "Show me."

Chapter 9

If Morgan had had any idea how much the sanding of his scar would hurt, he wouldn't have done it.

First the doctor gave him four shots in the chin and another above his lip. The physical pain was there, but the emotional pain was worse. The needles took him back in time to the night in the emergency room when he'd held the skin over his jawbone.

Then the doctor took an electric handheld machine and sanded his skin. It was a disk of tiny metal razor blades. When it touched his skin, flesh and blood flew everywhere. What was left of his chin looked like a piece of bleeding raw meat.

Morgan didn't refuse the pain medicine the doctor gave him. Nor did he object when a ghostly white Callie took her place behind the wheel of the van.

"Why don't you lie down until Charlie gets here?" she suggested, and he went straight to the bedroom.

"I have some errands to run," she told him. "I'll wait until Charlie comes before I go."

How could she leave him when he felt so bad? His chin was on fire, he couldn't eat anything but watered down junk, and he needed her. And she was going to run errands? What was so important that Wilda couldn't do it?

When Charlie arrived, Morgan walked to his study and sat down heavily behind his desk. He heard the door shut behind Callie as she left.

"What happened?" Charlie asked, his eyes wide.

"This is plastic surgery. To remove the scar. Remind me never to have a face lift," Morgan said without a hint of humor.

Charlie had brought lots of papers for Morgan to sign, some just letters, but he asked Morgan to sign them to show the company was running on an even keel.

"I'll keep faxing you the day-to-day reports," Charlie said. "Everything's going smoothly. No strikes this summer." He referred to the threatened walkout by airline stewardesses last summer. Morgan was glad he didn't have to sit in on any labor negotiations. No union contracts expired this year.

Callie wasn't back by the time Charlie left, so Morgan sipped a teaspoon of pain medicine. Now that the deadening shots had worn off, the pain was becoming intolerable.

Another half an hour passed before Callie returned without carrying any packages.

"How are you feeling?" she asked the moment she was back in the house.

He grunted a reply just as the phone rang.

Callie answered and immediately said, "What's wrong, Marie? . . . I'm so sorry. Where is she? . . . Just a minute."

Callie turned to Morgan. "Marie's mother had a stroke. Would you mind if I offer to take Jeff back with us? Then she could devote her time to her mother, and Jeff won't be disappointed."

Morgan shrugged.

Callie took that as a yes and made arrangements with Marie. "It's no trouble. We'll get a therapist in Highridge. Don't you worry about it. We'll bring him back whenever you need him."

Callie hung up and again turned to Morgan. "I arranged to pick him up before three. That way we can get out of town before traffic picks up. Would you like me to get him then come back for you?"

"Yes." He didn't want to meet the Richardsons looking like he did.

"Harry's coming for lunch. Are you going to mention Wayne Degraffenreid to him?"

"No." He didn't feel one bit of charity toward the man who had caused this accident. Morgan closed his eyes to shut out Callie's questioning look. He didn't want her accusing him of going back on his word about helping that man. Had he actually said that helping Wayne would help him forgive him? He must have been affected by the man's music. Or was the effect of the pain on making him so angry right now?

He lay down again until Harry arrived shortly before noon.

"Lunch is ready, honey," Callie called, and he forced himself to get up.

Lunch. Ha! His first course would be Instant Breakfast, chocolate flavored, followed by the ever-present beef stew. If he didn't take too long to sip those courses, he'd have time for ice cream before the others had finished dessert—but if he did take too long, then the others would sit watching him spoon each tiny morsel into his wired mouth. He was lucky he was missing his two front teeth so he had a hole through which to poke his food.

Feeling the drowsiness of the pain medicine, Morgan stumbled into the dining room.

"What happened to you, Trey?" Harry demanded.

"The doctor's working on his scar," Callie explained. "It should be healed in three or four weeks."

"Three or four weeks? What are we talking about all together? Another month or two before he's ready for the concert? Tomorrow's the first of June. That means the end of July or first of August before we can do it."

Morgan shook his head. The pain medicine was doing more than making him woozy. Now he was hearing things and seeing things. He saw Callie shoot Harry a warning look.

"What concert?" he mumbled.

Harry exchanged a secretive look with Callie.

"What concert?" he asked again. Something was going on and he wanted to know what. Had they been plotting behind his back?

Harry cleared his throat. "Have a seat, Trey." In an uncharacteristically mild manner, Harry said, "I know you prefer not to perform live anymore. However, that decision's been taken from us. Your fans need to see you in person on stage, singing like normal. Your career depends on it. They won't buy a studio shot or a video. We need the biggest concert of your life to show them that Trey's back."

Morgan was glad he was seated or he would have fallen over. "No way," he mumbled through his wires in his hoarse voice.

"Morgan, I believe Harry's right about this," Callie said then turned to Harry. "Although now was not the time to discuss it."

Even she was against him.

"We don't even know if I can sing," he said.

"Of course you can sing," Harry said. "It'll take you a little while to get your voice back in shape, but we'll get you a voice coach. No problem. We have some details to work out. Where do you want the concert? New York? Los Angeles?"

"No concert," Morgan said.

"Trey, I appreciate how you must be feeling," Harry started.

"No, you don't," Morgan muttered.

"I said this means your career, and I believe it. Fans aren't going to buy records if they think they're getting old songs that we just hadn't released before. You need to be working on new material, and you need to be seen. This could be the biggest come back show ever. Barbra Streisand, move over. Trey is back!"

Morgan closed his eyes and wished his manager was back in his little office downtown.

"You can do this, Morgan. I know you can," Callie said.

"If you think it's so easy, you do it," Morgan said.

"I never said it was easy," she amended. "But I could do it, if I put my mind to it. Just like you can and will."

His chin had burst into flames; he knew it had. His mind was cloudy with pain medicine that wasn't working except to dull his thought processes. And Callie was talking to him as if he were a little kid.

"I'll do it if you'll do it," he said.

Callie, her mouth hanging open, looked at him. Harry's eyes were bugging out of his face.

"I'm not a singer," she finally said.

"You said you could do it if you wanted. Well, how bad do you want it?"

"Morgan, you're tired, and I know you're in pain."

"Yes, I'm in pain. I've been tired for weeks. And I'm sick of this.

Take it or leave it. Will you sing or not?"

Callie glanced at Harry, not knowing how to handle Morgan. She'd never seen him in a mood like this.

"Humor him," Harry said in a low voice.

"What?" Morgan demanded.

"Do you mean a duet?" Callie asked. "We'd sing together?"

"Sure. A duet. Can you do it?"

Callie took a deep breath before she committed herself. Of course, once Morgan was out of pain and was himself again, he'd renege on this agreement. This was pain talking, that and the weeks of uncertainty that had dragged by.

"Sure, I'll do it. I'll have to have a few lessons. The voice coach can help me, too."

"Shake on it," Morgan said.

Callie stuck out her hand, and he took it in his much larger one. There was no gentleness in their touch, merely a formalizing of a business agreement. Callie blinked back tears and left the room.

❧

As soon as Harry left, still growling as he walked out the door, Morgan went in search of Callie, but she was nowhere to be found. He wandered from their bedroom to the spare bedrooms to Grandma's room before he asked Wilda where she'd gone.

"She's getting Jeff Richardson. She said it would take awhile to get him loaded. She'll be back for you by three."

He didn't feel like being polite to a stranger. Morgan didn't want to admit that he was jealous of an injured boy, but he needed Callie, and she seemed more concerned with Jeff.

In a moment of lucidity, he knew he was being ridiculous and unfair, but that moment was fleeting. He took more pain medicine, even though it wasn't time for another dose, and lay back down. He was asleep when Callie came for him.

She hated to wake him up. If he felt half as bad as he looked with that bloody face, then she could excuse his behavior today. She hoped he'd fall asleep once she got him in the van.

She'd left Jeff in the van since she could hardly get him out on her own. Ken Richardson had lifted his son and belted him in a seat. Marie and Callie had wrestled the wheelchair into the van. Jeff had taken steps between parallel bars, but he couldn't walk on his own. The prognosis was good, but he had weeks of intensive physical therapy before he could graduate to crutches.

She was counting on Morgan helping her get Jeff out of the van. If Morgan wasn't feeling strong enough, and she'd been well aware of his staggering walk at lunch, then she'd call Phillip. She'd forgotten to call her father and tell him that she and Morgan were leaving the mountains for two days. He'd planned to spend time with her every day while he was in North Carolina.

Callie felt defeated. She'd been on a teeter-totter of emotions today. From the pain of seeing Morgan's face this morning to leaving him when he wanted her to stay. Seeing the obstetrician had given her new hope. With state-of-the-art Doptone equipment, she'd heard the baby's heartbeat for the first time through ultrasonic waves. But Morgan's reaction to Harry's concert ultimatum had reaffirmed her decision not to tell him about the baby until he had healed. He had too much to handle right now. Unneeded worry about her and the changes their lives would undergo with the addition to their family were concerns he could deal with after he was well. She had to protect him from those thoughts.

This wasn't a good day to bring Jeff back to the mountains. Morgan felt crummy and was acting worse, but knowing Jeff was in the mountains under the care of a therapist would take a load off her friend Marie. But how heavy a load could Callie handle?

She sat on the edge of the bed and touched Morgan's hand. Somehow she'd get through this day, and tomorrow would be better.

"Dear God, please help us all work together and get through these trying times," she whispered.

Morgan opened his eyes. "I'm sorry," he said.

"I'm sorry, too," she said. "How are you feeling? Any better?"

"Still hurt. Time to go?"

"Yes. Jeff's waiting in the van." She helped Morgan get ready and said a quick good-bye to Wilda.

Jeff seemed thrilled to meet Morgan, and Callie could tell Morgan was trying his best to be kind to the teenager. Morgan explained that he was on pain medicine, and Jeff seemed to accept that explanation when Morgan fell asleep minutes after they left Atlanta. Callie used the drive time to chat with Jeff, enjoying the scenery and the peace that the mountains brought her.

With a much lighter heart, she pulled off the main highway onto the county road that led to Eagle Mountain. She stopped at Grandma's and introduced Jeff.

"Oh, Morgan," Grandma said when she saw him. Her expression showed her revulsion and pity. "Is it paining you?"

"Don't ask. My face is supposed to look better when it heals."

"It will. I reckon them doctors know what they're doing."

"I'll see you later," Callie said. "I need to get these guys home and fed. I've heard their stomachs rumbling over the motor." She put the van in low and started the hard pull up the mountain.

Phillip's car was in the driveway. What luck. Between him and Morgan, they could easily carry Jeff into the house. Callie ran inside to get her father and found him and Jean in the kitchen. They hurried outside and a few minutes later had Jeff installed in his wheelchair on the balcony.

"What a view," he said. "This is fantastic!"

"Yes," Callie agreed. "I never grow tired of it. None of us do." She glanced around and was surprised to see Phillip and Jean standing close together and smiling at each other. Something was going on. It was in the air between them.

"I'm sorry I forgot to tell you we were going to Atlanta," Callie told her father.

"It worked out fine," Phillip said. "Uh, when I came over yesterday, Jean and I got to know each other better. Tonight we're taking in a movie."

Jean raised her eyebrows at Callie. "I hope you don't mind."

"Mind? Of course not," Callie said. "Enjoy."

After a lasagna dinner that Jean had left for them, Morgan took more pain medicine and leaned back in the recliner. He'd helped Jeff into the bathroom and now that the boy shouldn't need anything for a while, Morgan could rest.

This might have been a mistake bringing Jeff to the mountains. He needed help getting in and out of his wheelchair, and he needed to exercise every day. Getting real exercise equipment and a therapist would have to wait until Monday. Meanwhile, Callie had asked Morgan to rig up an exercise bar outside tomorrow, and Phillip had said he'd help.

Morgan looked over at Callie and Grandma and Jeff playing dominoes at the game table. Jeff didn't have a chance of beating those two sharks, but he'd find that out for himself.

Jeff seemed like a nice enough boy. He had blond hair and was tall, if his sitting height was any indication. His dark eyes held a sparkle that being in a wheelchair hadn't destroyed. Or had it been even brighter before?

He didn't seem to be in pain, or if he was he hid it well. Not like the pain Morgan was feeling. He hurt. He hurt on the outside, and he hurt on the inside.

How could Harry insist on a concert? And why did Callie agree with him? *Because fans are fickle*, a little voice inside told him, and he knew it was true.

After an accident like this, he had to make a public statement. He couldn't possibly answer all the cards that had come. He had to publicly thank his fans. And the only statement was a song. Center stage and personal—in front of thousands.

But why did the thought terrify him? God had always given him the strength to sing in spite of his stage fright. Wouldn't He help him now?

Morgan didn't know. He didn't even know if he could carry a tune. Would the hoarseness ever leave his voice? Why had God done this to him? Until he had an answer to that question, how could he sing?

Chapter 10

Morgan laid Jeff on the floor for his exercises.

"Marie gave me a list," Callie said.

"I know them," Jeff said. "Twenty-five lifts on each leg; then I do the elastic pull twenty-five times."

"Does it hurt?" Callie asked.

"No. Oh, a little," he revised his negative answer.

"Callie, I need more ointment put on," Morgan said. Horrible smelling stuff had to be put on his chin to keep the top skin from scabbing over and to let the bottom layer heal first. His face still looked like raw meat.

Callie glanced over at him. "Just a minute, honey." She handed the wide elastic band to Jeff; then she got the salve and gently touched Morgan's face.

"I'll put it on again around noon," she said. "How does it feel?"

"Better," he said. "Is it time for more medicine?"

"Not yet." She turned her attention back to Jeff. "How much weight do you put on the parallel bars when you're walking?"

"All of it," he answered with a grimace as he lifted his left leg a few inches off the ground.

"What could we use, Morgan?"

"I don't know," he said. That guarded look was back in his eyes, but she didn't know what to do about it. She could handle only one problem at a time.

"Could we use Grandma's sawhorses and nail a couple of long boards to them?" she asked.

"The runners should be round so he can grip them," Morgan said. "Long shovel handles from the hardware store might work. What time is Phillip coming? Maybe he could pick them up."

"That's a great idea. Why don't you call him while I help Jeff with the elastic pull?"

"You should take the van into town to get the handles," Morgan told Callie after he had spoken to her father. "Phillip doesn't think it would be safe sticking wood out his windows. He wants you to pick him up on Regal, and he'll go with you."

"Okay. Will you help Jeff while I go?" She smiled up at him.

"Sure," he said.

The minute Callie had left, Jeff said, "You're not like I expected."

"What did you expect?" Morgan asked.

"Someone bigger. Stronger."

Morgan drew himself up to his full height. "I'm six foot two," he said.

"Yeah, I know. I guess I meant bigger than life. I've seen you on videos."

That was common. Many fans thought of Trey as more than a simple mortal. Because his name was a household word, Trey was expected to live up to the image the press made for him. Well, he couldn't do that. He was just a man.

"You're just a guy who whines a lot."

Morgan took a step back.

"Callie, will you put some ointment on my face?" Jeff mimicked. "You should try being me and see how it feels to not be able to walk."

Morgan turned and walked out. This was not going to work. When Callie got back with the wood, he'd tell her to take Jeff back to Atlanta.

"Morgan," Jean called a few minutes later. "Could you help Jeff into his chair?"

Morgan marched back into the den and glared at Jeff on the floor.

"Thanks," Jeff said.

"No problem," Morgan said shortly. He lifted the boy back into the wheelchair and pushed him out onto the deck. "Would you like a blanket?" he asked. "Early June mornings in the mountains aren't like the steam heat of Atlanta."

"I'm okay," Jeff said. "I like the cool."

"Fine. I have office hours. If you need something, call Jean." He was trying to be the adult here and be civil to the boy.

The twinkle in Jeff's eyes, which Morgan had mistaken last night for the sparkle of life, was pure mischief. Morgan pivoted and made for the sanctuary of his office. Catching Charlie in the office on a Saturday morning was a balm to his wounded ego. He had decisions to make. He was a person in charge. And he wasn't a whiner, no matter what Jeff thought. Was he?

When Callie returned with two extra long shovel handles and the sawhorses from Grandma's, Morgan had finished his call and helped Phillip unload the van.

"This should be fairly easy," Phillip said. "We can't drive a nail through these handles, but we can use nails as guides."

Morgan had no idea what he was talking about, so he just held the handles in place while Phillip drove several nails on each side of them.

"How's he going to get inside this thing?" Morgan asked. Sawhorses at each end blocked access to the parallel bars.

"We'll have to lift him over then help him turn around."

"It'll work," Callie said. "It's just a temporary measure. He won't be walking on his own for another six weeks, at the earliest. His physical therapist gets him upright every day. That's why I wanted this contraption."

"Let's get him to try it out," Phillip suggested. He disappeared into the house and returned pushing Jeff's wheelchair with Jean following behind.

"Morgan, give me a hand here," Phillip said. Together they got Jeff standing and lifted him over the bars so that by putting his weight on his arms and hands he could support himself.

"Can you put any weight on your feet?" Callie asked.

"I'll try," Jeff said.

In Morgan's opinion Jeff was playing the hero for Callie and Jean.

Why couldn't they see through him? The kid felt as sorry for himself as Morgan did. *Wait a minute*, Morgan thought. He didn't feel sorry for himself. Did he? Did the others think he did?

He looked at Jean, but she wasn't watching him or Jeff. She had eyes only for Phillip. Just what he needed, a moon-sick housekeeper. And Phillip stood beside her with his hand resting on her shoulder.

Morgan glanced at Callie to see how she was taking this. She'd finally accepted her father and her mother as a couple, as ill-fated lovers, and now Phillip was making a play for another woman. Okay, maybe he wasn't being fair to Phillip. Callie's mother had been dead for twenty-five years. A quarter of a century. Phillip had been a widower for ten. It was time for him to make a new life for himself. But Morgan didn't want Phillip's new life to hurt Callie.

"Thanks for making this exercise bar," Jeff said in a polite voice. He placed weight on his left foot and grimaced. In slow motion he moved his right foot in front of it, then the left, then the right.

"You're doing great!" Callie exclaimed. "Who knows what fresh mountain air and outside exercise will do for you."

Jeff sent her a doubtful glance. The kid wasn't as much a Pollyanna as he acted sometimes.

"Let's help him turn around," Phillip said.

Morgan took his place on one side of the makeshift parallel bars and lifted Jeff so that he could turn. At least, he thought, he was strong again. Oh, he got tired easily, but he could walk and lift things, and he was thankful for that.

After ten more minutes, Jeff declared he couldn't stand anymore, and the two men lifted him back into his chair.

Lunch was served in the dining room so that Jeff had plenty of room for his chair at the head of the table. Morgan sat on one side with Callie and sipped his soup. Jean and Phillip sat across from them.

"I called the office," Morgan said to make conversation. "Charlie was in catching up on what he missed yesterday. He's one dependable man. I don't know what I'd do without him."

Callie agreed. "What about Harry? Did you call him and work out the concert details?"

"No." Morgan didn't want to talk about the concert. He knew he had to do it, but he wasn't ready to work on it.

"You're doing a concert?" Jeff asked. "Can I go?"

"Probably not," Morgan said. "It'll be in New York or L.A."

Callie shot him a sharp look. "Actually the details haven't been worked out," she explained. "Harry would like a large audience. If you're walking by then, perhaps you could go with us." She smiled, then turned to Jean and said, "I was hoping your boys could come over tonight for a while. Maybe play board games with Jeff."

"I'll ask them," she said. "Phillip was coming over for dinner to get to know them, but it might work better if we all came here."

"That would be perfect," Callie said. "Let's have a cookout. Barbecued ribs, corn on the cob, potatoes in the coals." She cast an apologetic glance toward Morgan. "Would that be all right, honey? We could purée some meat for you."

Was this a social center? Morgan wanted a quiet night, just him and Callie, cuddled on the couch watching a DVD.

"That'll be fine," he said. He got up from the table and walked to the balcony. He couldn't refuse Callie the chance to spend time with her father. And he couldn't refuse her request to have the boys over for Jeff, but he felt as if he were being manipulated. Again his life was out of his own hands. He wanted control.

By six thirty everyone was gathered around the picnic table, gnawing on corn cobs and ribs. Everyone but Morgan. He stood by the brick barbecue grill and watched the others. Grandma had joined the festivities along with Ray and Brandon, Jean's sons. Before dinner the boys had played Frisbee with Jeff, making sure the disk was thrown straight at Jeff each time, so he could catch it. They were all getting along like a house afire, laughing and talking. Meanwhile, sitting at a dinner table and watching others eat was getting harder and harder for Morgan.

Grandma and Phillip were talking, both a little reservedly, but still they were communicating. Morgan thought their relationship had helped Callie more than her getting to know Phillip herself. But he didn't know. He and she hadn't talked about it.

How he loved Callie, and how he wished he had her alone. He wanted to return to the days of April before any of this had happened. Maybe the two of them could go for a walk later tonight. A path led around the top of the mountain, dipping lower here and there, then climbing back up to the house. They'd enjoyed it in April, feeling so close to the moon and the stars and God.

God seemed to have deserted him now. He felt Callie drifting away from him, too. At times she was so preoccupied. Of course, there was her father. And he knew his accident had taken a toll on her. Now she had Jeff to think about, too.

Did whatever was going on between Phillip and Jean bother her? He hadn't had a chance to talk with her about it. Tonight they would. Surely the others wouldn't stay late.

His mind was clearer now that he hadn't taken any pain medicine since this morning. His face hurt less, and he'd put the salve on it himself, twice now. He toted the pan of leftover baked beans and joined the procession as the picnickers carried empty plates into the house.

"We'll have Grandma's homemade ice cream pretty soon," Callie announced. "I couldn't eat another bite right now."

The phone rang, and she grabbed it. After a moment, Morgan heard her invite Robert and Marilyn over for dessert.

"Robert finished the rough draft of his book," she said. "He's been a hermit since he came to the mountains," she explained to the others. "He's been too busy writing to socialize up until now."

When the newcomers arrived, the group settled down to a game of charades with one team against the other. Jean's sons and Jeff had never played the game, but they joined in with the exuberance of youth.

When ice cream was dished up, Morgan and Robert sat in a corner of the balcony.

"Well, what did your private detective come up with?" Robert asked. "Anything good?"

Morgan explained about hearing Wayne Degraffenreid at the espresso bar. "He's a good musician. I thought about putting in a good word for him with Harry. He might be able to hook him up with some studio work."

"But you haven't yet?"

"No, not yet. I didn't talk to Wayne. Callie and I went incognito. I wore a beard and glasses." Morgan stroked an imaginary beard.

"That was before you went for the rugged look, huh? That has to smart." He pointed at Morgan's chewed up chin.

"It hurts all right, but it's better now than yesterday. That was an all-time low. Now I just look like a piece of raw meat."

"Too bad I can't use that look in my book. Of course, a corpse wouldn't have a need for plastic surgery."

"So you really did kill a man off with my accident?"

"Worked like a charm—a carefully engineered feat of death. However, the bad guys were out to get Sinclair. Instead, they killed his friend. Morgan, this is the best book I've written. Now that I have the plot down, I have to fine-tune the murder and the consequences. But Sinclair isn't working for a client this time; he's working for himself and has a personal stake in the outcome. I've put more emotion in this one than any other book. Probably because I imagined you as the friend who took the hit."

"Glad I could be of use. Now I just wish this nightmare was over."

"Few more weeks, then you can talk and eat again?"

"Yes. And start dental work. Harry insists that I do a concert to prove to the world that I'm all right. He says my career depends on it. Callie agrees." He was asking a question without saying the words.

Robert rubbed his chin. "I suppose they're right. The sooner you do it, the more dramatic it will be. You don't want to do it?"

Morgan made a strangling sound through his wires. He didn't even know if he could sing.

"Well, old friend, I guess this is one of those times that separates the men from the boys. You'll do fine."

"Private conversation?" Callie asked from behind them.

"No," Robert said. "Just doing a little more work on my book."

"I thought you'd finished it."

"The rough draft. That's the quick part. The revisions take much longer."

"My accident worked as the murder," Morgan said. He handed Callie his empty bowl. "Good ice cream."

"Grandma makes the best," Callie said and smiled.

Morgan didn't get to talk to Callie that night. After their guests left and Morgan had helped Jeff to bed, he found Callie had already fallen asleep.

Morgan doctored the raw wounds on his face and slipped quietly in beside her. She murmured his name and turned over. He watched her sleeping peacefully. Her golden hair shone in the moonlight, and her steady breathing was a whisper of life to him.

He cherished this woman who had pledged her love to him, but he knew he hadn't shown it lately. Tomorrow would be different. They'd talk again like old times.

Chapter 11

I'm not going, Callie," Morgan said. "I'll help you load Jeff, but there will be plenty of help at church to get him out."

"Why won't you go?" Callie asked. Her face had clouded over, and he hated seeing that look in her eyes.

"Look at me. I'd scare half the people there."

"You went last week. They didn't care what you looked like. Didn't you notice that?"

"They were very nice. But this week I look worse. Please, Callie, I'd rather stay alone."

"Oh," she said in a small voice, and he knew he'd hurt her. She'd misinterpreted what he meant. Or maybe she hadn't.

A few minutes later he lifted Jeff into the van and folded the wheelchair and stowed it behind the seats. As soon as Callie started the slow descent of the mountain, Morgan set out for a walk.

He'd wanted Callie with him, but he needed to commune with nature. To find God again. He'd done a lot of thinking last night as he lay in the dark with Callie asleep beside him. In the quiet, pain had returned, and the deepest pain of all, the sense that he'd been deserted by God, came back to him now, clear and sharp.

Many times he'd asked why this had happened to him. He'd given surface answers, like helping Callie know Phillip, but that would have happened without the accident. That Phillip came to the mountains now was a direct result of Morgan's retreat to heal, but father and daughter would have rendezvoused in the mountains sometime this summer anyway.

Certainly Robert would have come up with another idea for a book without Morgan's getting hurt. Robert never had a shortage of ideas in his mind. Morgan had always accused him of being the one who hatched the plots that had gotten them in trouble as youngsters.

There was the matter of the pool man, but Morgan hadn't made up his mind about helping Wayne Degraffenreid get work in the music field. Perhaps his talent would be discovered without any interference from Morgan.

So, what was the reason Morgan had been injured? Did God have some divine plan for him that he couldn't see? Or had God turned his back on Morgan P. Rutherford the Third?

He walked from the house to the opposite side of Eagle Mountain and sat on a huge rock that jutted out, forming a precipice. From his vantage point, he could see miles and miles. Regal Mountain wasn't far from here as the crow flew. Although fully leafed trees hid most of the houses, he could make out a rooftop here and there.

A robin sang a song from a tree behind him. Other birds answered his call. Here, high above the rest of the world, Morgan found a little peace.

The rhythm of the wind as it tossed the tree limbs back and forth made a natural sound that God had ordained. If there was order to the world, and God had created that order, then why had He allowed Morgan to be hurt? And when would this ordeal be over and life return to normal? Was there a lesson to be learned from this? If so, what was it?

Morgan stared at the sky above the peaks of the Blue Ridge Mountains and the far distant peaks of the Great Smokies. Was there a prettier place in the world? He doubted it. He was one of those summer people that Grandma had distrusted, but he felt as if his heart belonged in these mountains where Callie's roots were and where their future would be.

The Atlanta house was in another dimension, another time and space where corporate decisions were made. This place was Morgan and Callie's home. This land inspired him.

With a purpose to his step, he followed the path back to the house. For the first time in over three weeks, he sat down at the grand piano in the living room and played "Amazing Grace." It was the first song that came to mind, probably because he sang it at every concert.

It was his closing song.

Now it was his beginning. If he was going to sing in public again, and in a big way if Harry had anything to do with it, he needed some new material.

He pulled out blank sheet music from the piano bench and penciled in notes and words as they came to him. This was going to be his finest concert. If he could sing again. But he pushed that negative thought from his mind.

Callie heard the music as soon as she entered the house, and her heart was gladdened. She'd wondered how long Morgan would take to get back to what he loved best.

She walked up behind him and put her arms around him. "Solitude must have done you some good," she said and kissed him on the neck.

He pulled her around until she was sitting on his lap. His kiss was still tentative. In two weeks he would be able to kiss her in the old way with no wires to hamper him.

"Jeff's in the van," she said.

"Okay," he said in his hoarse voice. He kissed her once more then walked hand in hand with her to the door.

Grandma sat in the van with Jeff. She gave Morgan the straightforward searching look that she was famous for, then nodded. "Feeling better?" she asked.

Morgan nodded and turned his attention to setting up the wheelchair and getting Jeff into it.

Callie and Grandma got busy in the kitchen while Morgan wheeled Jeff out to the balcony, where the boy normally sat. Morgan sat in the porch swing and pushed himself off with his foot.

"We got off to a bad start yesterday," he said. "I'm sorry I was so short with you. But I'm not a whiner. You met me at my worst time."

Jeff eyed him suspiciously, but when Morgan walked over to him with his hand outstretched, he shook it.

"New start?"

"New start," Jeff said.

"So, how was church?"

"Small, but there were two or three cute girls there."

Morgan smiled. Jeff was a normal seventeen-year-old boy. Why hadn't he looked at him as a boy/man who needed help instead of lashing out at him as he had yesterday?

"That Darlene's something, isn't she?"

"Yeah. She's a good-looking girl and nice, too. She have a boyfriend?"

"I don't know. You ought to ask Callie. The girls confide in her. Did they talk to you?"

"Yeah. They asked me how it happened and all."

"You know, I don't know how it happened. Callie mentioned a drunk driver."

"Head on. The guy hit me not two blocks from my house. I was lucky he wasn't going any faster or he could have creamed me. I'd been to a baseball game and had dropped a friend off at his house, so I was alone.

"I couldn't believe it when his headlights came at me. I honked my horn, but they just kept coming straight at me." Jeff's voice rose as he recounted the events of that night.

"I thought he'd veer to the right, but he never did. I got as far over as I could. I guess that's why he hit my side so hard. It's like it happened in slow motion."

"I know what you mean." Morgan told the story of his accident and the way he'd seen the filter lid fly at him. "Was the other driver hurt?" he asked.

"Broke his arm. That's all. I hope it was the arm he used to lift his beer to his mouth. Maybe it will keep him off the streets for a while. It was his third time to be picked up for driving under the influence."

"I'm surprised he had a license."

"He didn't. It was suspended, but that didn't stop him. He goes to trial the last part of June. This time I hope they throw the book at him." Jeff's tone had gotten louder and louder. "The guy's got money and power. If it's possible, he'll beat the charge." He looked down at his legs. "I don't know why this happened to me instead of him," he said vehemently. "Why am I the only one to suffer? I have to work and work to get back to normal. And he has a cast on his arm. It's not fair."

Morgan was silent for a moment. This boy was going through the same thing he was. "Seems like there should be a reason, doesn't there? There should be a lesson learned by that man or by you or by someone. Some good should come out of this."

"But what?" Jeff raised his hands up, acknowledging he had no answer.

"Dinner's on," Callie called from inside the house.

Morgan pushed Jeff inside and stopped the wheelchair at the head of the table. Today he didn't feel the animosity he had yesterday at Jeff's taking his traditional seat. He gave the boy a smile then bowed his head to ask the blessing.

"Dear God. Thank You for this day and this food You have given us." He paused and glanced at Jeff, then closed his eyes again. "We need Your help today. We need to know why our accidents happened. Is there a reason? Are You teaching us something? Please show us why. Amen."

"Amen," Grandma said. "So you two want to know why? I've asked that question a lot in my life, and there's not always an answer we see. We have to accept what happens and go on."

Callie glanced from Morgan to Jeff. Were they getting along now? Yesterday's animosities hadn't escaped her, even though both males had tried to cover their feelings. She'd prayed they could help each other through their trials, and God seemed to have answered her prayer already.

"What possible good could come out of your accident?" Callie asked Jeff.

"Nothing."

"Oh, think about it. Could this serve as an example to other teens? Could they understand the importance of not drinking and driving? Could they see what happens? Could they learn how to drive defensively? Not that there was a thing you could have done differently. By pulling over and slowing down, you may have saved your life."

"And how am I going to be an example? Who do I tell?" asked Jeff.

"Seems to me there was a big wreck with a singer some time back. One of the Mandrells," Grandma said.

"Barbara," Morgan said. "She posed for a poster promoting the use of safety belts after she and her kids were hit head on. She said the belts saved their lives."

"Well then, you do the same," Grandma said.

Jeff waved his fork at her. "Who would listen to me? I'm no big star." He pointed his fork at Morgan.

They were all looking at him. "Hey, I'm not going public with a face like this."

"Maybe you wouldn't have to show your face," Callie said. "What if you and Jeff did an interview with a magazine. The reporter could take pictures of the back of your head and Jeff in his wheelchair. I'll bet Harry would jump on the idea."

"We want to reach teenagers, not music fans."

"If one person, no matter what age, listens and learns, then you've got a reason to go through this." Callie motioned to the wheelchair.

"What about Robert?" Grandma asked. "He might know a writer for a teenagers' magazine."

"Robert wrote for magazines before he sold a novel. He might be interested," Morgan said.

"Would you call him? Please?" Jeff asked.

"Can't hurt to ask," Morgan said, getting caught up in the enthusiasm. Maybe some good could come out of Jeff's being hurt.

❧

Later that afternoon Robert came over.

"I haven't written for magazines for over ten years, but I don't think I've lost my touch. I'll have my agent market an article, offering only one-time rights, so we can hit as many magazines as possible. Let's make a list."

He had brought along an old market book that listed magazines and their addresses.

"Most of the teen magazines are aimed at Sunday school audiences,"

Callie said as she flipped through the pages.

"You want to hit those, too," Grandma said. "Even Christian kids with good values go astray now and then. You've got to warn everybody."

"Grandma has a point," Robert said. "We'll let my agent worry about the markets. Let's get to work on the article. We'll need pictures of you and Morgan out on the exercise bar. I could get a photographer from the Highridge paper to come out and snap a few thirty-fives. Tell me everything you remember about the wreck, and I'll work something up tonight. Then tomorrow we'll get the pictures."

As she listened to Jeff's story, Callie wiped away tears. She already knew the story, but she was so emotional these days, the result, she knew, of all the extra hormones coursing through her blood.

"Jeff is only telling you half the story," she said. "The other half is from his parents' point of view. Marie and Ken have been through so much with this. While Jeff was unconscious, they didn't know if he would live or die. The parents' story is one that should be told, too."

"I have to work Trey into it, too," Robert said. "Using your influence is how we'll get this into print."

"Having a famous mystery author write the story isn't bad, either," Morgan said. "Editors would have to be nuts not to go for this story."

The next afternoon Robert brought a photographer with him and set up the photo shoots.

"Careful to get Morgan in the shots, but keep his face in shadow," Robert directed. "We want to see these pictures tomorrow." He had interviewed Marie and Ken via phone and had his agent making calls. "There's nothing new about this story. It's repeated over and over every day. But my agent says with Trey involved, it's a story magazines will buy. I'm going to mention that you two were in the hospital at the same time. That's the connection—recuperating together. I'll touch briefly on your injury, Morgan, but not take the focus off drunken driving."

The following day, Morgan, Jeff, Robert, and the photographer were poring over photographs.

"This one on the exercise bar is excellent," Morgan said.

"Yes, but we'll use this one of you lifting Jeff over the side rail to get him standing up. Shows teamwork," Robert said.

Morgan looked at Jeff, whose eyes were sparkling again. He had insisted on doing double time on the exercise bar that day. Jeff wanted to walk, and he wanted it now.

Morgan wanted to be well, too, but there was nothing he could do to help himself. No amount of exercise would help him get the wires off any quicker. But the excitement of the article made him make a decision about Wayne Degraffenreid.

He called Harry.

"All I want is your opinion. Listen to him play and see if you think he could be a studio musician. If you don't want to take him on as a client, that's your business." Morgan also told him about Jeff's article, and Harry was all ears.

"We need a headline in the tabloids, too. That'll hit the stands a lot quicker than magazines with a big lead time. Everybody reads the front pages in the checkout lines. The in-depth stuff can come later."

"Whatever you think," Morgan said.

"I'm going to leak some information on a comeback concert," Harry told him. "Know where you want to do it?"

Morgan noticed that his agent took it for granted that he would be singing. "New York."

"Central Park? Yankee Stadium?"

"You work out the details. That's your job. I'm writing new songs."

"Best news I've heard all day," Harry said. "Look for your name in the papers."

Chapter 12

Callie was sick again. She'd hoped that last week's episode would be the one and only, but a few days later she woke up early and knew if she moved, she'd throw up.

With iron determination, she slipped out from under the sheet, covered her mouth with her hand, and ran noiselessly down the hall to a guest bathroom. She sank to the floor beside the toilet and emptied her stomach.

"Callie?"

She should have known. He slept so lightly these days. Morgan got her a wet washcloth and helped her to her feet.

"I think I ate too many sautéed mushrooms last night. Or maybe it was the butter. Sometimes I react to too much butter." The excuse was the best she could think of. "I think in this case you're lucky you aren't eating solid food yet," she tried to joke.

"Are you all right? Ready to get back to bed?" He led her back down the hall. "Why didn't you go to our bathroom?"

"I didn't want to wake you."

"Callie, I'm here for you. Don't ever worry about waking me up if you're ill. Now how about some ginger ale and crackers?" Again, he relied on the only remedy he knew.

"Okay, thanks." She rested with a cloth on her forehead until Morgan returned.

"Just a sip, then you have to eat a cracker," he instructed, just as he had a week earlier. "I don't like seeing you like this, Callie. We've got to make you well."

"I'm all right."

He sat on the bed next to her. "I've been wondering how you feel about Jean and Phillip."

"I think they deserve each other. They both can make their own happiness, but they'd be better off together. Did you think it would bother me?"

"I didn't know. Since you're just getting to know him as a father, to throw in Jean, too, seemed a bit much."

Callie shifted on the pillow, and Morgan lay down beside her and slipped his arm around her. "He will never be a father to me. Not like. . .well, since I've never had one, I'm not sure what I'm saying, but not like your father was to you. Didn't he teach you right and wrong and play baseball with you? Didn't he hug you and love you?"

"My father was the best. He did all the things a father should do. He was a good provider, but he made time for his kids. Vic and I had our private line to his office. No matter what meeting he was in, if we called, we were to be put through immediately. I remember once I called when he was having a board meeting, much like the one I missed a couple of weeks ago. Mom had said I couldn't go skating with some friends, and I wanted a second opinion. He said I should never question my mother's decisions. And I didn't get to go skating for two weeks."

"You'd make a good father," Callie said.

Morgan raised his eyebrows. They had discussed this before, but he wasn't willing to risk Callie's health to have a child. She had told him that Daisy's death from childbirth wasn't due to a genetic defect, but he also knew that Grandma had had four stillborn babies. He wasn't going to put himself or Callie through anything so traumatic. Maybe they would adopt.

"Thanks," he said and switched the topic. "How about another sip?" He held the glass of ginger ale for her and handed her another cracker.

Callie was sick once more before she was able to crawl out of bed and into the shower. Then she felt normal again.

Jean eyed her suspiciously when she appeared in the living room. Callie averted her gaze. Grandma knew; she felt sure that Jean knew, and she didn't want to talk about it until she could tell Morgan.

"Could we talk a minute, Callie?" Jean asked.

Here it comes, Callie thought. "Of course. Is this a private conversation?" she asked and waved toward the den where Morgan and Jeff were playing chess.

"For now," Jean said. "Join me in the kitchen?"

Callie watched Jean make hamburger patties for tonight's cookout when her sons were coming over again to see Jeff. The sight of raw meat made Callie clutch her stomach. She sat on a bar stool and turned toward the window.

"It's about your father," Jean said. Callie felt relieved but didn't answer. She couldn't face that meat again. "Uh," continued Jean, "I know we've known each other only a week, but we've been seeing each other a great deal. Not just the time he spends over here, but in the evenings, too."

"Yes, I know," Callie said.

"I think I love him," Jean said softly. "I know it's soon after my husband died, but my feelings for Phillip don't diminish my feelings for David. It's like two different parts of my life."

Jean walked behind Callie, forcing her to turn around. With the intention of reassuring Jean that she was glad she had found love, Callie gasped instead as her eyes fell on the hamburger patty Jean was holding in her hand. Callie ran for the bathroom.

A few minutes later, Callie returned to the kitchen. "Jean, I'm sorry. I was sick this morning. I think too much butter last night. Sometimes it affects me that way. I'm delighted you and Phillip have found each other."

From Jean's look, Callie didn't think she believed her excuse about the butter, but she didn't know what else to say unless she told her the truth about her illness. *What a tangled web,* she thought, remembering the old adage about lies. Even little ones told to help others grew and grew until they ended up hurting others anyway.

"I'm sorry," she blurted. "It wasn't the butter. I'm pregnant."

"Ah," Jean said as if that made sense of everything. "The raw hamburger?"

"Yes. I haven't told Morgan because he needs to concentrate on himself, not me. Please don't tell anyone, not even Phillip. I want Morgan to be the next to know."

"I thought it upset you that Phillip and I were getting close."

"I know or I wouldn't have told you my secret. Promise me."

"Oh, I promise I won't tell, but it's not something you can keep a secret for long. Have you seen a doctor?"

"Both here and in Atlanta. I'm healthy and taking vitamins," she said as Jean ushered her to a chair. "And I'm not an invalid."

Jean laughed. "My natural instinct is to protect a pregnant woman."

"That's one reason I'm not telling Morgan yet. When the wires come off and his face is healed, he'll be able to concentrate on my pregnancy better."

"You're probably wise. His moods swing even more than yours . . . and I remember what pregnancy does to your emotions. Did you realize he and Jeff were at war for a while?"

"I knew they resented each other."

"I heard them Saturday when they didn't know I was around. I'm glad they've made peace. Wonder what did it?"

"Prayer changes things," Callie said. "And I prayed mighty hard about it. So did Grandma. God knows I needed them to help each other."

Morgan poked his head into the kitchen. "Are you feeling all right?" he asked.

"I'm fine."

"Do you feel like running an errand into town? We need to get a walker for Jeff."

"Do you think he can use a walker already?"

"No, but the physical therapist thinks it would be an incentive. He could stand up in it in the house and get in more exercise than with the bars in the yard."

The therapist hadn't been able to come on Monday when Callie had called, but she'd come out Tuesday morning and had already been here today. Callie had talked to Jeff's mom and assured her Jeff was doing his exercises. Since Marie's mother was still in the hospital, she agreed that Jeff could stay in the mountains until she could care for him again.

"I'm on my way," Callie said to Morgan. "Do you want to ride along?" Morgan's only trips to town had been to the back door of the doctor's office.

"No," he said quickly. "I'm headed for my office."

Grandma went to town with Callie, and they hit the grocery store as well as the library. They stopped at the bank and had coffee with Joe. He accepted an invitation to the cookout. Why not turn it into a real celebration? Callie wondered. She wasn't sure what she was celebrating, but she had a new life in her, Jeff and Morgan were friends now, and Morgan was playing the piano again. The old Morgan wasn't back yet, though. This Morgan was still subject to high and low swings instead of the even balance of the old Morgan. But he was on a high now, and she wanted to capitalize on it.

❧

Back on Eagle Mountain, Callie called Marilyn and Robert and invited them, too. As soon as she hung up the phone, it rang.

"Callie, my folks are here," Phillip announced without preamble. "I thought they were coming up next week after I left, but they decided to come early."

"I see," Callie said, but she didn't see what Phillip wanted from her.

"Would you like them to come to the cookout tonight? I've talked to Mother, and she's apologized for lying about Daisy and keeping her letters from me." A long moment passed. "I'd like them to meet Jean." Another long moment. "Callie? Are you ready to make peace with them?"

No, she wanted to scream. "Please bring them," she said instead.

Callie ran for Morgan's study. "Cooper and Elizabeth Prescott are coming tonight," she said. Morgan stood and reached for her, and she flung herself at him and hugged him close. When she looked up at him, though, all she could see was his raw chin. It hadn't bothered her before, but now it reminded her of raw hamburger and that thought sent her running to the bathroom.

Morgan followed her and got the cold washcloth as he had earlier. "You've got to settle this thing with Phillip's family," he said. "I hate to see you tearing yourself apart like this."

Once Callie was lying on the bed, with her gaze averted from Morgan's face, he paced back and forth.

"If you don't want them here, I'll call and tell Phillip not to bring them," he said. "But you have to face it sometime. You said you felt better about Phillip and your mother after you talked with him and Grandma. Do you think it would be the same if you talked to the Prescotts in the same way? Not tonight with the others around, but now. Or this afternoon."

"She hates me," Callie said, and Morgan didn't have to ask who "she" was. Elizabeth Prescott had made no secret of her dislike of Callie when she'd learned about her granddaughter. Only after hearing that Callie was engaged to Trey had she changed her attitude, and that fit with what Phillip had told them of her social climbing ways.

"You can't let someone else have control over your emotions," Morgan said. "If you hate her back, you're giving her power over you . . . and you're using energy in a negative way." He sat down beside her, but Callie still wouldn't look at him.

"I admit I didn't feel charitable toward the pool man who put the wrong size of bolt on that filter. Now that I've worked through it a bit, I feel better, though. Harry should have gone to hear him play last night."

"I didn't know you'd told Harry," Callie said. Why were they keeping things from each other? In the past they had shared everything.

"I called him yesterday, but I guess I forgot to mention it to you," Morgan said. That eased her mind somewhat. At least he hadn't intentionally not told her information. "Now, back to Elizabeth Prescott. What do you want to do?"

To know Phillip better meant understanding his family. But she didn't want to see Elizabeth. She'd rather be stung by a hundred wasps, but she recognized that this was not something she could avoid. Better to get it over with and move on. Elizabeth's rejection had lurked in the back of her mind for too long. "I want to see her this afternoon."

"Good. Do you want me to go with you?"

"Yes. Do you mind?"

He leaned down and kissed her. Callie closed her eyes so she wouldn't see his face.

"Callie Duncan Rutherford. I am your husband, and I will always be here for you. Just like you've been here for me through the accident." He kissed her again then reached for the phone.

❦

Later that day, Callie said to Elizabeth, "I wanted to see you this afternoon to get rid of bad feelings between us."

The older woman, carefully made up and with every dyed chestnut hair in place, sat in a wing chair in the great room of the Prescott home on Regal Mountain. Cooper, her husband and Callie's newfound grandfather, shared the couch with Phillip. Morgan and Callie sat together on the matching love seat.

"Phillip and I have been through this," Mrs. Prescott said with a lift of her chin. "I believe that was sufficient. It's a family affair."

"But I'm family," Callie said.

"Yes, Mother. Callie is my daughter." Phillip turned to Callie. "I understand that what Mother did, she did thinking it was the best thing for me. However misguided her motives, she was thinking about me. I accept that. Now she must see how her decision affected others."

For the first time Mrs. Prescott looked directly at Callie. "I suppose you want me to say I'm sorry."

"I want you to say what you feel," Callie answered. "I'm sure it's hard knowing you have an illegitimate granddaughter. It was hard for me to accept that myself. I thought I was an orphan, and believe me, that was easier to take. Until last summer, I didn't know my father was alive. But now I'm delighted to know him." She smiled at Phillip. "And I know he loved my mother."

"They were too young to know what love is," Mrs. Prescott said. "They would have ruined their lives."

"Did you know my mother?"

"No. But I could tell from her letters that she wasn't who I had in mind for Phillip. I wanted him to be happy."

"And you were the judge of his happiness?"

"You don't know what it's like to be a mother. When you have children and are concerned about their marrying the right type of person, then you'll understand."

Callie sat rigid. Didn't she already feel protective of her unborn child? Would she be as interfering a mother as Elizabeth Prescott? No, she would not. She would remember how lives could be destroyed or changed forever as a result of one person's choices. She would teach her child right and wrong and pray that her child made correct decisions. And she would respect her child's choices. Phillip was nineteen when he had met her mother. That was young, but it wasn't the same as a fifteen-year-old boy having a crush. Still, she could see that a mother might have a hard time realizing when her child was mature enough to make wise decisions.

She didn't want to understand Mrs. Prescott's actions, but now, in spite of herself, she found she did. But could she forgive her? She would try.

"Thank you for sharing that," Callie said. "I understand your actions, although I don't agree with them." She stood and said good-bye. She shook hands with Cooper Prescott and then held out her hand to Mrs. Prescott, who finally reached for it with a limp handshake.

❧✦

"That wasn't exactly a meeting of the minds, but it may be all you ever get out of her," Morgan said as Callie drove them back to Eagle Mountain. "She's a cold woman."

"Yes, but I feel better for going over there. Do you think they will come tonight?"

Callie had her answer when Mrs. Prescott sent her regrets with her husband.

"Elizabeth has developed one of her headaches," Cooper said. "But I wouldn't miss this cookout for the world."

Chapter 13

During the following week, Callie's nerves were on edge. She experienced no more morning sickness, but she dreaded waking up in the mornings, not knowing if she'd feel sick or how to cover it up if she was.

Morgan worked on songs, but as the date neared for the return to Atlanta and the wires to come off, he was short-tempered. When he voiced his doubts that he'd ever sing again, Callie would reassure him, and that seemed to help for a little while. Then she could tell from his attitude that his doubts had returned.

Meanwhile, Callie watched Jeff struggle with pain, exercising his legs until he neared exhaustion. His parents had agreed he could stay until Morgan returned to Atlanta to have his wires removed. Jeff vowed he'd walk off that van when he returned home.

Phillip came over every afternoon to visit and left with Jean when her workday was over. Mrs. Prescott did not call or send any messages via her son. Callie truly didn't care. She had found a measure of peace in herself by understanding the woman's motives. She had forgiven her, although she didn't care if she ever saw the woman again.

Grandma watched Callie like a hawk and fussed at her about nutrition. "You're eating for two now, Callie Sue. You make sure you give my great-grandchild a good start in life."

On Wednesday Jean fidgeted as she worked around the house at the top of Eagle Mountain. "I got a contract to teach in Highridge next year," she told Callie. "Fifth grade. What do I do? Sign it and obligate myself for an entire year or wait until Phillip says something?"

"What do you expect him to say?"

Jean laughed, a self-conscious sound. "The big four words: Will you marry me? Why would he when we've known each other only two weeks and he leaves on Friday?" She plopped down on the couch in the living room and burst into tears. "What should I do?"

Callie put her arms around Jean and cried tears of empathy. Her father was leaving, and they were now friends. They'd talked about Callie's going to Boston to visit with Phillip and his kids, her half brother and half sisters, but they hadn't finalized anything. Not that she should cry about that, but she cried at anything these days.

"What's wrong?" Morgan asked from the doorway. He crossed the room in quick strides and pulled Callie into his arms. "Are you hurt?"

"We're okay," Callie said and took the handkerchief Morgan offered her and mopped at the tears that wouldn't stop. "Jean got a teaching job."

"Congratulations, Jean. So these are tears of happiness?"

"No. She wants to marry Phillip," Callie said and sobbed.

Morgan's eyebrows shot up. "Does he know that?"

"Of course not," Callie said. "She can't tell him."

"Why not?"

"Morgan, you don't understand," Jean said. "This job in Highridge is an answer to prayer, but now I want to go to Boston."

"What's wrong?" Jeff wheeled himself into the living room.

"Nothing," Morgan said. "It's too complicated for mere males to comprehend."

"Not funny, Morgan," Callie said. "This is serious."

"Then Jean had better talk to Phillip, but we don't need to interfere."

"Morgan, I can't just call Phillip and tell him I want to marry him. I have responsibilities, two sons to raise. That's a lot to ask a man to take on," Jean said.

"True," Morgan said, "but how else will he know? Give him a chance. The worst he can say is 'no.'"

"Someone's coming," Jeff said and wheeled himself over to look out the east wall of windows. The sound of a motor, chugging up the mountain got louder and louder.

A few moments later a florist truck pulled up to the house. All four of them watched as the delivery man carried a giant bouquet of roses to the door. "Flowers for Jean Garvey," he said.

With shaky hands Jean took the roses and carried them to the dining room table.

"Let me guess," Morgan said as Jean picked the card out of the bouquet and read it. She placed her hand over her heart.

"Phillip wants to take me to dinner tonight. Just the two of us."

"All right!" Callie exclaimed. "This is your golden opportunity. Go call him and accept. What will you wear?"

"This is out of our league," Morgan said to Jeff. "Ready for exercises on the bar?"

The two males left for outside, and Jean made the call. She came back into the kitchen with her face glowing.

"We're going to Collett's. Fancy. This must mean something."

"Of course it does," Callie assured her. "You must leave here early so you have plenty of time to get ready." The phone rang, and she said, "I'll get that."

The superintendent of the Sunday school had talked to several members of the small congregation who wanted to have a surprise party for Morgan. "He was so good to raise all that money for our church last summer. Now that he's hurting, we want to do something for him. Do you think he'd come to the church tomorrow night or should we come to him?"

Morgan had refused to go to Sunday school for the second Sunday in a row. His face looked much better now. It no longer had the raw meat look, but had scabbed over and looked like a giant strawberry that baseball players sometimes get when they slide into home.

"I can get him to Grandma's if you could hold it there." That way Morgan could claim tiredness and retreat to the top of the mountain if he wanted. She had no idea if a party would cheer him up or not.

They arranged the covered dish dinner and music party. Callie immediately called Grandma, who had already talked to several people about the party. "This here's a perfect place," she said. "We're having us a music party. Think that'll make him happy?"

"I don't know, Grandma. He's up one minute and down the next. He wants so desperately to sing, and he's afraid. We'll know more Friday when the wires come off. This can't be a late party, because we'll head to Atlanta by six the next morning."

Callie almost asked if Jean and Phillip and Marilyn and Robert could come but decided against it. Although Grandma had come a long way toward accepting summer people as regular folks, others in their church were uncomfortable around the wealthy summer crowd. This was a church picnic, and she guessed it should stay that way.

Callie wound up her talk as Morgan came in pushing Jeff in front of him.

"Grandma wants us to come to dinner tomorrow night. Around six. Is that all right?"

"Sounds fine. Jeff's going to walk now. Want to see?"

Callie followed them to the hallway that led to the bedrooms. Morgan set the walker exactly in the center between the walls and wheeled Jeff to it. "Careful to balance before you move it," Morgan said as he helped Jeff stand. Callie pulled the wheelchair a few feet back.

Jeff clutched the walker as he had been doing all week. He'd stood for as much as fifteen minutes in the past, although his arms had borne most of his weight. This time he started as he'd practiced. He took a deep breath and lifted the walker. Before he could set it back down and move his feet, he tumbled face forward and landed in a crumbled heap on top of the tipped-over walker.

"Are you all right?" Callie exclaimed.

"I'm okay," he said. "I thought I could do it." Frustration made his voice rise in pitch.

Morgan helped him up. "You pushed your hands to the center before you lifted the walker. You have to lift it from the side to keep your balance. Now, let's try again."

Callie scooted by them and repositioned the walker. She stood in front of it and held it in place as Jeff took his place.

"Okay, move out, Callie. I'm ready."

"Can I hold it in place, so you won't go down again?"

"No. I'm going to do it by myself."

Callie stepped back and watched the determined teenager. He gritted his teeth and painstakingly moved the walker forward a few inches. His left foot took a step followed by his right.

"I did it!" he exclaimed, his face brightening with joy.

"Again," Morgan said calmly.

Jeff repeated the slow process four more times. "That's enough for now," Morgan said. "We'll try it again in an hour." He moved the wheelchair behind Jeff and helped him sit.

"Didn't your therapist in Atlanta say there was no way you could walk for at least six weeks?" Callie asked. "If she thought you could make this much headway so quickly, I doubt she'd have okayed your coming to the mountains without her supervision."

Jeff's grin stretched from ear to ear. "Won't she be surprised? Wait until Mom and Dad see me."

"They'll be thrilled," Callie said. She leaned over and hugged the boy. "I knew the mountain air would do you good. This is a healing place. We're high in the air, closer to God." She glanced at Morgan and hoped he'd agree, but he merely nodded.

When his Highridge therapist arrived, Jeff showed off his new skill. The rest of the day Jeff practiced with the walker for ten minutes at the stroke of the hour. He fell three more times, but only, he stated, because he got overconfident and didn't take his time. By nightfall Callie was exhausted by his efforts and didn't know how he could even stand up to try again. He went to bed early with the promise of starting the regime again the next day. "We can take Grandma's sawhorses back to her tomorrow when we go to dinner," he said as Morgan helped him get into bed.

By eight o'clock the next morning, Jeff had already had his first walking session. He and Morgan sat on the balcony. With the sound of Jean's car climbing the mountain, Callie rushed out the kitchen door, waiting impatiently for the news.

"Well?" she said as soon as Jean stepped out of the car.

"It didn't come up," she said.

"You didn't ask him how he felt?" Although Callie understood why Jean couldn't say anything, she knew the clock was ticking away the minutes until her father would be leaving for Boston.

"I thought he'd say something. We had a wonderful time, and I told him about the teaching contract." She shut the car door.

"What did he say about it? That should have made him make a move," Callie said as they walked into the house.

"I thought so, too, but he said he was glad I'd gotten what I'd wanted."

"Well, don't sign that contract until he's gone."

"That's tomorrow, Callie."

"But you never know the difference a day can make. Just think, if you two married, you'd be my stepmother, wouldn't you?"

"I guess in a way, I would," Jean said wistfully. "I'm going to make something special for Morgan, since we hope this is his last day to eat puréed food. Has he already eaten?"

"He's had an Instant Breakfast, but he's always hungry." Callie took her cue from Jean and turned to a different subject.

Later that morning she talked to Phillip and arranged for the two of them to go into Highridge for tea. It would be their last time together since he was leaving the next day for Boston at about the same time that Callie was leaving for Atlanta. "I'll pick you up," she told him. She wanted to check with Grandma and see if she could get any supplies for the picnic while she was in town.

"Everybody's bringing their own table service," Grandma said when Callie suggested she pick up paper plates. "I'll take care of you and Morgan and Jeff, so Morgan won't suspect anything."

"What about balloons? Can I supply those? That would lend a festive air. We could tie them to the poles on the front porch."

"Good idea," Grandma said. "Balloons are good."

Callie left Grandma's house and drove straight to Regal Mountain. Phillip was sitting in the yard waiting for her, so she didn't have to go up to the Prescott house. She wondered if he had done that so she wouldn't run into Elizabeth Prescott. Callie really didn't care anymore, but she imagined he would take awhile to realize that. He seemed subdued on the curvy ride into town.

When they were seated on the open-air balcony of the Highridge House overlooking Main Street, Callie brought up the subject of Jean. Morgan had said she shouldn't get involved, but she hated seeing two people she loved so unhappy. And unless she missed her guess, Phillip's mood was directly related to Jean.

"She's going to teach next year. That's what she wanted. She told me she was praying for a contract when we first went out," Phillip said.

"Maybe that's what she wanted before she got to know you," Callie said as nonchalantly as she could then took a big bite out of a cookie.

"Do you know something I don't know?"

She chewed slowly and swallowed the cookie while she studied his face. "I doubt it. Of course you know she loves you."

With a bang, Phillip set his glass of lemonade down on the table. "She loves me? She didn't tell me."

"Of course not. Did you tell her that you loved her?"

"No. I didn't want to cloud the issue. She got the contract she wanted that lets her stay in the mountains. I knew she wouldn't want to leave."

"Men! Why can't you read minds?" Callie said and looked up at the ceiling.

"What should I do?"

Heeding Morgan's warning not to interfere, although she already had, Callie said, "That's between you and Jean, but I think you should be honest with each other." She saw him glance at his watch. "Are you ready to go? I need to pick up some balloons."

Phillip helped her stuff the car with helium-filled balloons, allowing only enough extra room for the two of them. "Would you mind helping me unload these and tying them on Grandma's porch? I can take you home after I check on Morgan," Callie said, hoping that Jean would be driving Phillip home.

He consented and, from the look in his eyes, Callie figured he knew the way her mind worked. Maybe there was something special to this father/daughter thing.

At the top of the mountain Callie climbed out of the van and invited Phillip inside. They'd left Grandma's porch looking like a carnival booth.

"I'll just be a minute," she said. "I want to make sure Morgan doesn't need anything."

Phillip followed her into the house and into the kitchen where Jean was whipping up a pudding treat for Morgan.

"Could we go for a walk?" Phillip asked.

Jean glanced at Callie, who looked as innocent as she could manage. "Go on," Callie said. "I'll finish this." As they walked outside, Callie poured the instant pudding into a bowl and carried it to Morgan.

He was in his study, just hanging up the phone.

"Harry," he told her. "He's heard Wayne Degraffenreid play several times now and took George Warner to the coffee shop, too. Wayne has a short-term contract to go on the road for two months while George's keyboard man is home on leave. The keyboard man's wife is having a baby in a week or two, and he's taking off to be with her now and after the baby's born."

When he mentioned the word "baby," Callie unconsciously put her hand to her stomach. Realizing what she had done, she quickly removed it and clapped her hands. "That's great news, Morgan." George Warner wasn't a giant name in the business yet, but he would be. For now he was the opening act for other singers. This job was bound to lead to others for Wayne Degraffenreid.

"Yes. It's another good thing to come out of this accident. Pudding for me?" He nodded toward the bowl Callie still held.

She handed it to him. "Uh, Jean fixed it special for you. She and Phillip are on a walk."

Morgan raised his eyebrows. "Do I smell a meddler?"

"Not really. I just told him they should be honest with each other."

"Honest? As in, you love her and she loves you, so why don't you do something about it?"

"Now, honey," Callie said. She walked around the desk and sat down on his lap. "Love is something to celebrate. It's not something to miss just because you misinterpreted the other person's actions. Take this action." She kissed him tenderly on his lips. "How would you interpret that?"

"I need another sampling before I can make a clear decision," Morgan said.

She kissed him again. "And now?"

"Callie!" Jean shouted from the hallway. "Where are you?"

In her haste to get off Morgan's lap, Callie nearly fell. "We're in the study," Callie called. Oh, no. Jean sounded as if she were boiling mad. Had Callie done the wrong thing telling Phillip how Jean felt? In her mind, Callie regressed to fifth grade when she'd told a boy that her best girlfriend liked him. Morgan had been right. She should never have meddled.

"Callie," Jean called again. She appeared in the doorway with Phillip on her heels, her face glowing, her eyes dancing. "I quit," she said. "I'm getting married."

Chapter 14

"Wow! I mean congratulations." Callie hugged Jean and then Phillip. Morgan shook hands with her father.

"When's the happy event?" he asked.

"The boys and I are going to visit Phillip in Boston in a couple of weeks. As soon as I can get things worked out," Jean said. "Then we'll set a date. Phillip thinks it's only fair the boys see what life will be like in the Northeast. We can come back to the mountains for summers. Phillip won't be teaching every summer session like he is this one."

So another year-rounder would become a summer person.

"And you're walking out on the job, are you?" Callie asked. "Good thing we're headed back to Atlanta tomorrow."

"I could come back for another week, if you need me." Jean offered.

"No need. Now that Morgan's strong again, I can handle things," Callie said.

"You mean Jean was a babysitter?" Morgan asked.

Callie opened her mouth then closed it. The others laughed, and even Morgan smiled as much as his wires would allow.

"Now why couldn't I see through this situation before?" Morgan asked.

"You've had a lot on your mind," Jean said. "Callie didn't want to add to it by making you aware you needed someone with you."

The two couples walked back to the kitchen. Jean told Jeff her news and said good-bye. "I know you'll be walking in no time."

"We're going to Regal to tell my parents," Phillip said, "then we're going to talk to Jean's sons."

"I'm so happy for you," Callie said and kissed her father good-bye.

266

"Have a safe trip tomorrow."

"You, too. I'll be calling you, Callie, to arrange for a visit." He hugged her and whispered, "Thanks for telling me to be honest today." Then he let her go and climbed in the passenger seat of Jean's car.

"Call when you get back to the mountains. If you need me, I'll come help," Jean said.

"I'll call, whether I need help or not," Callie said.

She and Morgan waved good-bye as Jean backed the car around and headed down the mountain.

"Well, since you brought those two together, I guess you're all right with it?" Morgan asked. "It doesn't bother you that your father is getting married again?"

"No. I hope he is happier this time. He deserves a new start in life."

"An example of the prodigal son?" Morgan asked.

"Yes, in a way. Yes."

✤✦

Callie and Morgan walked back inside in time for Jeff's hourly ordeal with the walker.

"Can I take the walker to Grandma's tonight?" he asked.

"I don't see why not," Morgan said. "You can show her your stuff."

When it came time to go to the foot of the mountain for the surprise party, Callie loaded Jeff's wheelchair into the van. She wanted him to be mobile with all the others around. He could show them his walking progress, but she didn't want him in danger.

Morgan was looking backward as he talked with Jeff, so he didn't see the cars at the foot of the mountain when they came into view.

"Morgan, close your eyes," Callie said. "Grandma wanted your last night on puréed food to be special, and I helped her decorate for her dinner. I don't want to spoil her surprise."

"Close them now?" he asked, although she could see that he'd already followed her request.

"Yes. We put balloo . . . Wait, I'm not telling what we did. Just keep those eyes closed tight. I'm not much good at keeping secrets from you," she said, although she'd done an outstanding job at keeping the biggest secret of her life.

"Jeff, watch him. Don't let him peek." Callie winked at Jeff, who knew all about the surprise.

Jeff laughed. His mood, which had climbed higher with every step he took, was contagious.

Callie maneuvered the van close to the porch. Other vehicles were parked up and down the lane from the highway. The crowd of about thirty people stood around the porch and waited in silence for Callie to come around to Morgan's side. First she opened the sliding door, so Jeff could be part of the surprise; then she opened Morgan's door.

"Keep them closed until I say you can open them," Callie instructed. "Watch your step. Okay, now open."

"Surprise! Surprise!" the group yelled in unison.

If it could have, his mouth would have dropped open. As it was, Morgan's eyes widened, and he raised his hands up as if to say, "How did you manage this?"

Grandma stepped off the porch and hugged Morgan. "We want to send you off to Atlanta in a big way," she said. "When you come back, we know we'll have a hard time keeping you quiet."

"This is wonderful," Morgan said, although he knew that not many of them could hear him. He said it again, as loud as he could, and church members shushed each other.

"I'm deeply touched by this party. I didn't have any idea. Callie said I had to close my eyes because of some decorations." He motioned to the balloons that adorned the spindly porch columns of the old farmhouse. "How could you all be so quiet? Did you hold your breath?"

The crowd laughed.

A fiddler struck up a tune, and the group launched into "For He's a Jolly Good Fellow." A couple of other musicians with guitars jumped in. When the song ended, the crowd cheered.

The superintendent of the Sunday school stepped forward. "You were here for us when we needed our church repaired. Now we're here for you since you need to be repaired. So let's pray before we dig into this delicious food."

Members bowed their heads, and the old man continued. "Lord, we want to thank You for this and every day You give us. Bless this food for the nourishment of our bodies and bless those who prepared it. And help this fine man find inner peace and let him sing for our enjoyment again. Amen."

"Amen" resounded through the group before several conversations started at once.

"Morgan, you get to lead us through the line," Grandma said. "Point to anything you think can go in the blender, and I'll mush it up. Callie, you fix a plate for Jeff." Someone had helped Jeff into his wheelchair and had pushed him to a spot not far from where the musicians had drawn up chairs.

Callie followed Morgan through the line. He settled for the chicken and noodles that had become a staple in his diet and took a piece of lemon meringue pie for dessert. He couldn't eat the crust, but he could slowly manage the filling.

The Sunday school superintendent sat down beside Morgan on the porch. "We've missed you the last couple of Sundays." It wasn't an accusation, just a statement of fact.

"I looked so bad, I didn't want to scare the congregation," Morgan said.

"They wouldn't have been scared. You might have found some answers."

"To what questions?" Morgan asked. He wasn't sure where this conversation was going.

"What questions do you have?" The old man asked a question of his own.

Morgan sighed. "Several. The biggest question is why did God do this to me?"

The screen door slammed behind Grandma as she came out of the house. "Here you go, Morgan." She handed him the same bland-looking puréed gunk he'd been eating for five weeks.

"Thanks," he said and stirred the thick liquid. Would he really get to eat solid food tomorrow?

Grandma moved back to the food line, and the old man picked up the conversation where it had left off.

"God didn't do this to you. As I understand it some young man made the wrong decision about a bolt on a filter. The filter clogged because of dirt and the pressure blew the top off. You can't blame God for this. We all make choices, be they right or wrong. God knows which one we're going to make, but He lets us choose."

Morgan looked into the old man's clear gray eyes. He had seen so much in his eighty-some years. Surely experience had given him this wisdom to see what Morgan couldn't see.

"So accidents happen," he said.

"Yes, as a result of our choices. What has happened to the young man who chose the wrong bolt? Have you forgiven him for making the wrong choice?"

"The man's a nighttime musician. I asked my agent to listen to him play and maybe hook him up with a job that he'd know how to do."

The old man smiled. "Did he get a job?"

"Yes. Just today."

"You're a good man, Morgan."

"No. I didn't want to help him. I could have called my agent a couple of weeks before I did."

"But you did call. That's what matters. God didn't make the decision for you. He gave you time, and you did the right thing. I'm sure He approves." The man stood up. "I've got to get in line or all of Grandma's fried chicken will be gone."

Morgan stared after the old man. He thought his name was Mr. Burch. He'd have to ask Callie, because the old man had made more sense out of this accident than anyone else had. It was an accident, plain and simple. Accidents happened because of people's carelessness or ignorance or both. God didn't have it in for Morgan. He had let others make choices.

"Our choices affect many people," Morgan told Callie, when she sat down beside him on the porch.

"Yes, they do," she said. "And we try to make good ones."

"We try. But we don't always. Is that Mr. Burch?" He pointed to the old man.

"Yes. He's been superintendent of the Sunday school for almost thirty years. He's never abused the power, so he's reelected time and again."

"He told me that God didn't cause this accident. People's choices caused it."

Callie put down her plate and looked at Morgan. "I know. Do you remember our conversation in Atlanta? I told you I caused the accident or I contributed to it by placing that plant too close to the edge of the pool, so when it blew over, it went into the water."

"But you couldn't have known the wind would come up."

"No. I didn't know. But I made the choice to set that plant stand where I did. If I had set it back another three feet, the filter wouldn't have clogged." Callie sniffed. They had been through this before, but obviously the issue wasn't settled.

"It would have clogged another time and blown, and you might have been injured. That would have been worse."

"I would have rather it had been me," Callie said.

In spite of the others around them, Morgan kissed Callie. "I'm glad it was me. Now enough of this. We're at a party to celebrate my wires coming off. Let's eat." He lifted up his bowl of gruel as a toast.

As soon as all had eaten and covers had been put on the leftovers, the musicians tuned up, and the folks sang in an old-fashioned hootenanny. Morgan hummed along. He had worked at saying clear, full sentences in conversations, but he didn't struggle with the words of the songs.

Tomorrow. It couldn't come soon enough.

The party broke up around ten, and Morgan loaded Jeff into the van. Amid cheers, he'd shown the church members his walking ability.

"I can't wait until tomorrow," Jeff said as the van climbed Eagle Mountain. "Mom and Dad aren't going to believe this." Morgan knew exactly how he was feeling.

They left even earlier than they'd planned. Morgan was awake by five, and Callie didn't think that Jeff had slept at all. Both males shifted nervously in their van seats, a feat that Jeff hadn't been able to do just two weeks earlier.

"I told Grandma that Phillip and Jean were getting married," Callie said. "She took it okay. She likes Jean, too."

"Good," Morgan said.

"Good," Jeff said.

"I told the man in the moon that we'd fly up there for dinner," she said.

"Good," Morgan said.

"Good," Jeff said.

"All right, guys, I'm through talking, since you're not listening. Let's listen to music."

"Good," Morgan said.

"Good," Jeff said.

Callie found a station and drove the rest of the way humming along by herself as the two nervous males fidgeted.

First stop in Atlanta was Jeff's house. His parents were out the door before Callie shut off the motor.

Ken opened the side door, and Marie climbed in the van and hugged her son. "I've missed you so much," she said. "Did you have a good time? Did you do your exercises?"

"Every day," Jeff said. "How's Grandma Hinkley?"

"She's much better," Marie answered.

"Hey, would you and Dad get my wheelchair out of the back?" Jeff asked nonchalantly.

His parents went to the back of the van and pulled the wheelchair out. While they were out of sight, Callie set up the walker on the driveway, and Morgan lifted Jeff out of the van.

"I won't be needing that," Jeff said as his parents wheeled the chair to the side of the van. He took a few tentative steps.

Callie grinned at the expression on the Richardsons' faces. "He's not real mobile yet, but he's been walking for a couple of days now."

"I can't believe it," Ken said. "This is impossible. You weren't to be walking for a few more weeks, if then."

"Good mountain air and a positive attitude got this boy on his feet," Morgan said.

"We can't thank you enough," Marie said.

"We didn't do it," Callie said. "He did."

After walking a bit more, Jeff allowed himself to be carried into the house since there wasn't a ramp for the wheelchair. He submitted to the chair again, but not for long, he assured them. He was going to continue his every-hour walking routine until he didn't need the walker anymore.

Callie and Morgan stayed for coffee, and Morgan took a pill the doctor had prescribed he take before the wire removal procedure. They left the Richardsons with promises to return in a few days.

"Next stop, wire removal. Are you ready?" she asked as she drove them to the doctor's office.

Morgan took a deep breath. He felt more out of control than he ever had. The pill had taken effect, and he could barely keep his eyes open.

He was taken right into the office, and the doctor came at him with shot after shot. Just as the last time he was in the office, he experienced déjà vu. He relived the night of the accident, and the emotional scars within him bled, revealing themselves in tears that stained his cheeks.

Callie held his hand as the doctor used pliers to untwist the wires and pull and tug and jerk them out. He gripped her hand as if it were a lifeline, squeezing hard. It was her lifeline, too, as the room spun and she fainted and sank to the floor.

Chapter 15

Through the pain, Morgan knew Callie had gone down, and he called to her in a muffled voice. The doctor's hands were still in his mouth, but Morgan shoved them away with his free hand. His left hand still held Callie's. In his drug-induced stupor, Morgan crawled off the high examination table and crouched down beside her.

"Get a wet cloth," the doctor ordered, but the nurse already had one on Callie's forehead and another at the back of her neck.

"Callie, can you hear me?" Morgan asked. He could barely talk. One loosened wire dug into his tongue.

She moaned.

"Honey, wake up. Wake up."

She was out for only a moment, but it was a lifetime to Morgan. If anything ever happened to Callie, he didn't know what he'd do. She meant everything to him.

She fluttered her lashes, as if it was too great an effort to open her eyes.

"Callie."

This time she opened them and took a shallow breath and then another.

"What happened?" she asked in a small voice.

"You fainted. Did I squeeze your hand too hard?"

She lifted her hand to wave his question away, but it was too heavy to keep in the air, and she let it fall down to her side. Her head ached.

"Let's get her up on the table," the doctor said. Although Morgan had been drugged, his mind was now crystal sharp, and he lifted her and placed her on the examining bed. He took a chair beside her.

"Are you all right?"

"I feel weak, but I'm okay. Sorry. This whole thing got to me."

"Nurse, stay with her," the doctor said. "I've got to get these wires out while he's still somewhat numb."

"No. I'm okay." Callie sat up on the table and motioned for Morgan to take her place.

"Honey, you'd better lie back down."

She shook her head. "I'm okay. Let's get this finished and get home."

She sat in the chair Morgan vacated and again held his hand as the doctor wrestled the wires out of his mouth. Morgan didn't squeeze her hand this time, although she knew the pain had intensified as the pain killer wore off.

When it was over, Morgan and Callie took a cab home. "Neither one of us should be driving now," he had told Callie. "We'll send someone back for the van."

❧

After returning a call to his mother, Morgan lay down and insisted Callie join him. "I know you were frightened for me, but you're still looking pale. And I need you with me."

Callie needed the rest. She'd had an early morning filled with anticipation and pain. But she slept as fitfully as Morgan, who felt as if he'd been in a fight and come out the loser. His face ached, and his mouth was full of the metallic taste of blood.

Dorothy and Victoria delivered the van and were waiting to see them when they got up a couple of hours later.

"Oh, Morgan, how do you feel?" his mother asked. "Your chin is healing. Can you talk?"

"I can open my mouth all right, and I'm hungry for something that I can chew. Problem is," he said with a lisp, "I need my two front teeth." His voice was as hoarse as ever.

"Morgan sees a dentist on Monday," Callie said. "In a couple of weeks he should look much better." She felt rested now and ready to cope with Morgan's pain again.

Although he didn't mention how he felt, the frown lines on his forehead had deepened, and she saw pain in his eyes.

"What about the concert you mentioned last week when we talked?" Victoria asked. "Have you scheduled it, and are you giving us tickets?"

"Always after a free ride, Vic," Morgan teased, but the frown line remained etched on his forehead. "I don't know when it is, but we've decided on New York.

"Where the Blue Ridge meets the Smokies," he sang, "Lies the place that I love best." He was actually singing, but the hoarseness wouldn't go away. "Where the deep sky meets the mountain peaks and the tall trees give—"

He stopped when his voice cracked, and he looked with fearful eyes at Callie.

"It'll take awhile to get back in the swing," she said. "Maybe we should look into that voice coach."

He nodded. "I'll take some lessons with you. Get my voice back in shape."

"Callie, you're taking lessons?" Dorothy asked.

"No, well . . . ."

"Callie's singing a duet with me at the concert," Morgan announced.

She had thought he'd forgotten about that promise that was made when he'd been in such pain from the plastic surgery. Surely he wasn't going to hold her to it.

"It was one of the conditions of my doing this concert. I'm writing a special song for us." He crossed over to the piano and sat down. He'd thought of letting Callie out of the deal, aware that she'd agreed to it only to get him out of the doldrums and back into his old life again. But at times lately she'd seemed so distant. He'd catch her with a faraway look on her face, and when he'd asked about her thoughts, she'd said she just had a blank mind. He didn't buy that. Something was bothering her, and he couldn't break through the barrier that she'd thrown up between them. Practicing together, a situation that brought down a person's defenses, might help her open up to him. He didn't want secrets between them. He loved her with all his heart and wanted them to always be close.

He played the melody with one finger, all he could manage in his current state of mind and body.

"Sounds lovely. This should be a real treat to your fans. After 'Callie's Song' won video of the year, they want to see more of her, don't they?" Victoria asked.

"Yes. She's definitely the better half of this whole," Morgan said. "A lot of the cards and letters we've gotten are giving her support because I'm hurt." He understood that. He would've needed support, too, if their roles had been reversed.

Dorothy and Victoria stayed for lunch and seemed to enjoy watching Morgan eat solid food as much as Callie did.

"Any more chips?" Morgan asked. He could chew fine with his back teeth. His front bottom teeth felt odd, but then, they had no top teeth to match up with.

He took a bite of a ham and Swiss cheese sandwich, not his choice in what his first meal should be, but Wilda had explained she didn't know exactly what he'd be able to handle. He wasn't tasting much anyway, since his mouth and tongue were still stinging.

"Fried chicken for supper?" Morgan asked and the housekeeper promised to fix the special meal.

"Mashed potatoes and gravy?" she asked.

"No. More potato chips," he said and took a handful from the bowl she had refilled.

⁂

Dorothy and Victoria left shortly after lunch, and Morgan lay down again. As soon as she was sure he was asleep, Callie called her doctor and told him about fainting.

"I'm sure you're fine, but if you want to come in, we'll listen to the baby's heart to make sure."

Callie lost no time in driving to the office, where the nurse ushered her in and hooked her to the listening device. The heartbeat was loud, and Callie breathed a sigh of relief.

"Are you taking your vitamins?" the nurse asked, and Callie assured her that she was. Fainting that morning had been a fluke.

Seeing Morgan's anguish was more than she could handle. She felt certain it wouldn't happen again.

She left with a lighter heart, but with another decision confirmed in her mind. She'd planned on telling Morgan about the baby today, but she'd wait until he was better. His concern for her in the doctor's office reaffirmed her thought that he needed to concentrate on himself and not on her health. She'd see how the visit to the dentist's office went on Monday. Then she could tell him.

※ ✄

On Monday, Morgan was more than ready for his trip to the dentist, a place that from childhood had given him a stomach-tightening feeling. Each time he looked in the mirror and stared at the unsightly hole in the front of his mouth, he more desperately wanted teeth. His bottom ones didn't feel right, either, and he had given them a pretty good working out, eating everything he'd been craving for five weeks.

Callie seemed more secretive. He hoped his imagination was working overtime, but he felt she was keeping something from him. He set up a voice lesson for Tuesday, and had the voice coach come to the house. Singing in front of a critical audience might make her open up. He knew his attempt at psychology probably wouldn't measure up to any scientific approach, but it was the best he could do.

The dentist took molds for his front teeth, promising a new permanent bridge within ten days. He put temporary teeth in place, but they were yellow and too big.

"Your bottom teeth are dead," the dentist told him. "That's why they haven't felt right to you. We'll start root canals on Wednesday."

"He could have said we're putting you in front of a firing squad, and I'd have been more relieved," Morgan told Callie on the way home. "I wish I could get over my fear of the dentist's chair." On the positive side, he was behind the wheel for the first time since the accident, and he felt good to be in control again instead of being a passenger.

That's what he had been for the last five weeks—a passenger in life. Finally he was taking control again, bit by bit.

He headed for the office as soon as he took Callie home. Now that he could open his mouth without a black hole, he felt he could face his employees. He wasn't ready for his fans yet, though. They expected a bigger-than-life persona. He wasn't there, yet.

As soon as Callie got into the house, she called Grandma. "I've waited too long. Every time I set a time to tell him, something else comes up and I delay. Now it's gone too far. I don't know how to tell him about the baby."

Grandma chuckled. "If you don't tell him soon, he'll notice on his own. You can put it off another month, but is that fair to Morgan? Callie Sue, you've got to tell him tonight."

But she didn't. He was full of office talk. Even though he had been on top of the business via the phone, that wasn't the same as being there in person to read expressions on faces. He was going back tomorrow after their morning voice lesson.

That thought paralyzed Callie. How could she go through with a duet? At least he didn't expect her to sing alone.

❧

At ten the next morning, Callie sang scales for her new voice coach.

"She has good pitch," Annette Hamilton told Morgan, as if Callie weren't in the room. "She could be very good."

For the next hour, Callie practiced singing from her diaphragm. Morgan's lesson was less intense, since his hoarseness continued.

"What did the doctor say about your vocal chord?" Annette asked.

"In another week or so it should be reconnected to the cartilage," Callie explained. "Then the hoarseness should disappear." She knew Morgan had hoped he'd speak normally when the wires came off, but they were still playing the waiting game.

Morgan went to work, leaving Callie to practice on her own. She sang as she went about the house. She was having fun learning to sing the right way. Her voice was more forceful, but the thought of singing in front of thousands made her stomach churn.

With Morgan dreading the dentist's chair, she didn't tell him about the baby that night. After his root canals the next morning wasn't a good time to tell him, either. And she was no closer to an idea of how to break the news to him.

That night, Robert's phone call caught Morgan in the study. Callie was in the den reading.

"Hey, you're talking better," Robert said. "The wires came off all right?"

"They're off," Morgan said. "It wasn't easy going for me or for Callie. She fainted."

"Fainted? Odd. She was so strong during your hospital stay. And from her description, you looked inhuman."

"Well, this was a lot of pain. Not something I want to repeat." Morgan held the phone a moment while Robert repeated the conversation to Marilyn.

"Good news here. My agent sold Jeff's story to the Sunday supplement of the Johnson chain of newspapers. They're all over the country, so you'll get better coverage there than in any one single magazine."

"Great news. When will it be out?"

"The end of July. The lead time is usually longer, but the editor decided an article that he'd already scheduled didn't work. So I imagine that picture of you and Jeff will be the cover. Just a second, Morgan."

He heard a muted conversation between Marilyn and Robert.

"Marilyn's concerned about Callie. She wants to know if Callie's been sick?"

"No. Well, she had a nervous stomach a couple of times when we were in the mountains, but that was because her father was coming over."

Again Robert repeated the conversation to Marilyn.

"Was this sickness the first thing in the morning?" Robert asked.

"Yes. She woke up sick a couple of times. Once she emptied her stomach, she was okay. I've been worried about her. I think Phillip's presence in her life after all these years has really affected her. I know something's bothering her, and if it's not that, I don't know what it is." Morgan held on again and listened to a female squeal at Robert's end.

"Morgan, are you putting us on? Is this a secret?" Robert asked with a chuckle.

"Let me in on the joke," Morgan said.

"You really don't know?"

"Know what?"

"Put these words together and see what conclusion you draw. Callie's upset, morning sickness, fainting spell."

Morgan didn't reply. His mind reeled. Was Callie pregnant? Surely not. As much as they wanted a family, he'd told her how afraid he was for her to have a baby. What if it was stillborn like four of Grandma's babies? What if Callie died in childbirth like her mother?

"Morgan? Are you still there? Morgan?"

"I've got to go," Morgan said in a stunned voice and hung up the phone without saying good-bye.

His mind flashed back to Callie, sick in the mornings, eating crackers in bed. She'd cried when Jean was offered the teaching job. At the time he thought she was being a little emotional, but again he'd chalked it up to her new relationship with her dad. The secret, faraway look on her face that she wouldn't explain. Everything came back to him in a flood. Why hadn't he seen the obvious?

And why hadn't she told him? Did she think he'd be upset? Actually, he didn't know what he felt. He wanted to be a father, but his first concern was for Callie. Had she been to the doctor? If not, she was going right now, even if he had to cart her to the emergency room. If she had to lie in bed for nine months or seven months, or however long it took, he'd be at her side the entire time. He wondered when the baby was due. He needed some answers, now.

Chapter 16

Morgan bowed his head.

"God, I don't know how to ask her. She's the most important person in my world, and I'm afraid to ask her. What if I'm wrong? How will that make her feel? What do I say? Please guide me."

With a resolute squaring of his shoulders, he walked into the den. Callie sat with her head resting on the back of the rocking chair and her eyes closed. An open book lay in her lap.

Morgan sank to his knees in front of her. He closed the book and laid it on the floor, then took her hands in his.

She opened her eyes and sat up straight. For a long moment they stared at each other, both with unanswered questions, then Morgan placed a hand on Callie's stomach. Quick tears formed in Callie's eyes and rolled down her cheeks.

"We're going to have a baby, Morgan. I want you to be happy about it."

With a purposeful move, Morgan lifted her out of the chair and sat down, holding her.

"Now, Callie," he crooned. "Are you all right? Why didn't you tell me earlier? And when?"

"How did you know?" she said and sniffed, then added, "December."

"December. A Christmas baby. Have you been to the doctor?"

"Yes. I'm healthy and I'm taking my vitamins. I even went Friday after I fainted, but I'm fine. And the baby's heart is as strong as ever."

"You've heard it?"

"Yes," she said and smiled. The same faraway look he'd seen before came in her eyes.

"Callie, I'm scared for you."

She turned in his arms and kissed him. "You have no reason to be scared. I'm healthy, I'm the perfect age for having a baby, and I want this baby so much."

"But Grandma. . ."

"Grandma's babies were stillborn almost fifty years ago. Great medical strides have taken place since then. Don't you worry. This baby is going to be healthy and happy and loved."

Morgan rocked back and forth, holding her close to his heart. "Why didn't you tell me?"

"At first, I didn't want to tell you until I knew for sure. My doctor's appointment was on the Monday after your accident. I found out then, but I couldn't tell you. You couldn't talk; you were in pain. I thought you should concentrate on getting well and not worry about me." Callie took a deep breath. "I knew you had reservations about me being pregnant, and I didn't know how you'd feel about it. I didn't get pregnant on purpose. I wouldn't have consciously made that decision without you feeling the same way."

Morgan kissed the top of her head and continued rocking. "You know I'd like a houseful of children. But I want you more. I didn't want you taking risks with your health."

"But I'm not, Morgan. Come with me to the doctor next time, and you can talk to him. Oh, you can hear his heartbeat, too."

"His heartbeat?"

"I call the baby a him, but I don't know. What would you like?"

"A girl just as beautiful and kind as her mother."

Callie leaned away from his chest so she could look in his eyes. "I've kept this secret, but I thought I was doing the right thing. I didn't think you could handle it along with your injuries. You seemed so distant from me sometimes—like you were suffering alone. And I was here for you."

"Oh, Callie. I didn't want to burden you with how scared I was. It didn't seem manly, and it seemed pretty vain. It wasn't the pain so much as the emotional aspect. What would I look like? Would the fans accept me? Would I sing again? There were so many questions.

And right there on top was why did God do this to me?"

"But He didn't."

"I know. We make choices. . .free will. But He's with me, and He's healing me, from the inside out. I've been out of control. I need to feel I'm controlling myself. I know I can't control others."

"I think we ultimately must turn over control of our lives to God. Master control. If we let Him influence our decisions and choices, then we can't go wrong, can we? Not really, anyway." She wiggled in his lap. "You want some chocolate?"

"Chocolate?"

"It's the one thing I'm crazy for. The best ones are those chocolate kisses with the nuts."

"And I thought you were crazy for me," Morgan said.

Callie laughed. "I am. If you were chocolate, I'd eat you up."

She started to get up, but Morgan held her firmly. "One more thing, Callie. We can't keep secrets from each other ever again. I couldn't explain your preoccupation, and I thought you were drifting away from me. You had good reasons for not telling me, but they were unfounded. Of course I worry about you, but I could have taken it and been as excited about the prospect of becoming a father as I am now. No more secrets?"

"No more secrets," she agreed.

He kissed her, and she kissed him back with all the love they shared between them.

"Now I'm getting some chocolate."

The phone rang, and Morgan answered while Callie put chocolate kisses in a bowl and brought them to the den.

"Were we right?" Robert asked without saying hello.

"Yes. Callie and I are having a baby in December."

"Congratulations, old man. You'll make a great dad, but you have to remember some of the scraps we got into and not be too hard on the little fellow."

Morgan laughed. "Just a minute," he said into the receiver. He explained the earlier phone conversation to Callie. "Should we ask them to be the godparents?"

"I can't think of anyone I'd rather have." Marilyn had helped her through a rough time last summer and had helped plan Morgan's concert for her church. Robert had been Morgan's best friend forever, well, until Callie had come on the scene. Callie smiled and repeated, "I can't think of anyone I'd rather have."

Morgan asked and waited until Robert conveyed the request to Marilyn. "They'd be honored," Morgan told Callie. "Marilyn wants to talk to you."

Callie took the phone and explained why she'd kept the news a secret. When she hung up, she turned to Morgan. "We need to tell your mother."

"What about Grandma?"

"She knows. She guessed almost before I knew. If we'd been around your mother more, I'm sure she'd have known, too. Mothers seem to have this intuitive instinct about other pregnant women."

Morgan phoned his mom and Victoria; then Callie called Grandma and explained that Morgan knew.

❧

The next morning Callie told Wilda and experienced the pleasure of being able to talk about the changes that were taking place physically within her.

"A baby," Jeff said, when Callie called him. "You should name him Jeff."

"I'll give it some thought," Callie said, "but remember that Morgan is the third. He might want a fourth, and let the tradition live on. Of course, it could be a girl."

"How about Jeffaleen? Jeffilou? Jeffereena?"

Callie laughed. "I'll mention your suggestions to Morgan." She called her father, and she called Jean. She told Harry when he phoned.

"Congratulations, Callie," he said then switched the conversation to the concert. "We've set the date for August fifteenth in Yankee Stadium. How's Morgan doing with the voice lessons?"

"He's not there yet. Another week and the chord should be completely connected. He's still hoarse." Callie twisted the phone cord around her finger. "I'm taking lessons with him for the duet. I didn't think he'd make me do that." She had thought of asking Harry to talk him out of it, but then she remembered their new understanding not to keep their feelings from each other.

When Morgan came home from the office, and they were on their exercise walk around the grounds, she brought up the subject.

"Why do you want me to sing a duet with you? I'm no singer."

Morgan stopped walking and faced her. "On the day I mentioned it, my face had been cut to shreds, and I was striking out at anything. I didn't think you'd agree, and that would give me the perfect way out of doing a concert. Then after awhile I thought that voice lessons, having to sing in front of me and a voice coach, might wear down your resistance to talking to me about what was bothering you."

"Then your reasons are no longer valid," Callie said.

"No. But I like singing with you. You have a good voice, and we harmonize well, even with my croaky voice. But you don't have to go through with it. It's your decision."

"But you've written a song for us."

"True. But I can get backup singers to take your part. It's up to you, Callie. I should never have put you on the spot. I'm sorry."

She didn't know if she could do it. She prayed about it, and she continued with the lessons, practicing her part when she was alone. During the next few weeks, Morgan didn't press her about it, even when his hoarseness disappeared.

Finally the vocal chord had attached completely, and his voice was his own again. He thanked God that his ordeal was over at last. Callie was jubilant with Morgan's complete physical recovery, but as the time neared for the concert, she still hadn't made a decision about singing with him. Did he really need her on stage now that he knew he could sing again?

≫≪

Callie and Morgan left for New York two days ahead of the scheduled concert. Morgan's new front teeth couldn't be distinguished from his own. His chin held only a small scar that Callie told him gave him character.

Grandma had agreed to come with Dorothy and Victoria's family.

Jeff had conned tickets out of Morgan, and he was flying in with the others. "I won't be a burden," he'd said. "I can walk alone okay."

He was still a little unstable on his feet, although he'd graduated from the walker to crutches by the middle of July and had been walking alone now for over a week. By getting in the stadium early with Morgan and the others, he wouldn't be subjected to the jarring crowds of a couple of hours later.

Robert's article on Jeff and Morgan and their struggle to overcome their accidents came out three weeks before the concert date. Letters against drunk drivers had poured into the newspaper offices, and loyalty to Morgan had precipitated a sold-out concert.

The day before the performance, Callie went with Morgan to Yankee Stadium to look at the stage that had been erected. Sound equipment was being connected, and Morgan sang a few songs, without one crack in his voice and absolutely no hoarseness. When he started on the duet, even without the backup singers, Callie joined in.

She didn't know if she could sing it with him the next night, and he had told her she could decide at the last minute. Stage fright could paralyze her; he knew because he suffered from it. Less now than in the past, and knowing how close he'd come to never performing again, he'd come to grips with it. He didn't want to give up singing. If his career required a concert a year, filmed for TV viewing later, he'd do it.

On the day of the concert, Morgan and Callie stayed in the hotel until after the others had arrived late that morning. This was Grandma's first trip to New York, and she was all eyes and open mouth at the sights as a limo carried them around Manhattan. Robert and Marilyn invited everyone to their apartment for lunch and after another hour of sightseeing for Grandma, the group relaxed in the hotel.

At three thirty they left for the stadium for the eight o'clock show. Touring the stadium, eating in the restaurant, and watching final preparations for the performance filled the hours until show time.

"This is different than the concert we arranged for Morgan last summer," Marilyn said. The fallow land of a church member had been used for parking, and the audience had sat on lawn chairs and blankets. Two flatbed trucks had served as the stage.

"But the same excitement is here," Callie said. The group sat in the dressing room, waiting for the big moment as fans noisily filled the stadium.

Morgan had decided against a warm-up group. This was his come-back concert, and it would be his alone. He'd give the fans two hours of songs. "If you want to sing," he told Callie, moments before walking onto the field, "be ready by nine-thirty. It's the next to last song."

Callie nodded. Morgan always closed with "Amazing Grace." He'd use the spot before it to plug his new song. It hadn't been recorded as a single yet, but that was scheduled for back in the studio next week. Unless, as Harry had said, it went so well tonight that it would be released as a live recording, complete with the response of the crowd.

At five minutes before eight, Morgan's band walked to the stage and tuned up their instruments. Morgan and Callie stood together in the tunnel that led to the field and asked God to bless the concert and to give Morgan courage to sing in public.

"Ladies and gentlemen," the announcer's voice came loud and clear over the sound system. "In his first appearance since his accident last spring, please welcome Trey."

Morgan walked onto the field, cameras capturing his image on the brand new scoreboard. The fans roared and stood in an ovation for him before he'd sung a note. Morgan was so choked up at their support that a full five minutes passed before he started his first song, but the fans' cheers hadn't died down by then anyway.

He started with "Callie's Song" and interspersed some of his old hits with new songs he'd written. The only break he took was when the band played an instrumental.

When the time neared for the duet, it was Callie's turn to ask God for courage. She knew Morgan wanted her to sing with him, and she wanted to. She knew the words by heart. Now if she could only get them out in front of sixty thousand people.

When he started the song before the duet, she walked to the stage and sat on the steps, waiting for her cue. At least she could stand by him even if she couldn't get one word past the huge lump in her throat. She waited for the audience's applause that signaled the end of the song, then she climbed the stairs and walked to Morgan's side.

He didn't have to explain who Callie was when she joined him. The crowd knew. He put his arm around her and drew her toward the mike. In a wifely gesture, Callie reached up and brushed back the hair that had fallen on his forehead. She looked into his eyes, saw his love, and knew she could sing for him.

"Callie and I are proud to share our joy with you," he announced, and his arm tightened around her. "We're having a baby in December." It hadn't been in a press release, no rumors had leaked out, and the mood of the crowd was that these dear friends had just shared a secret with them, all sixty thousand of them.

When the crowd noise died down, the band began on the duet. Callie took a deep breath, then sang in a clear sweet voice:

"Our lives are joined with love's promise,
 Old as time, but still brand new."

Then Morgan sang,

"With the joy of song and laughter,
 We come to share our lives with you."

Their voices combined in a rich harmony:

"We walk, we run, we climb, we stumble
 Through life's triumph and its woe.
 But through it all God gives a strength
 We wish that every heart could know."

When they finished the song, Morgan and Callie held hands

and faced each other, as they had done when they had taken their wedding vows.

"You are wonderful," Morgan whispered.

"I love you," Callie whispered back.

The crowd erupted. Callie stayed on the stage while Morgan sang his traditional final song; then together they walked off the field.

"What are you going to do next year for an encore?" Harry said as they entered the dressing room. "Last year you asked her to marry you. This year you tell the fans you're having a baby. How can you top that?"

Morgan laughed. "We'll give it some thought," he said.

Epilogue

"Push, Callie, push," Morgan urged. "I can see the head."

She'd been in the hospital only five hours, and he had expected a longer labor than this. He'd read everything he could find on natural delivery and had gone through classes with Callie. Now that the moment had come, he couldn't believe that he was actually witnessing the miracle of birth.

She squeezed his hand, stopping the circulation in his fingers, but he didn't care. She could have cut off his hand if that would have made this easier for her. Morgan wiped the perspiration from her forehead.

"All right, push again," the doctor said in a calm voice. "This is it."

Callie grunted as she gave a final push.

"It's a girl," the doctor announced.

Callie exhaled as relief flooded through her. She glanced at Morgan, whose eyes were shining with joy.

"It's a girl," she echoed the doctor's words. "Is that okay?"

"It's perfect." Morgan took the baby from the nurse, who had quickly wiped her off and wrapped her in a pink blanket. He laid the baby next to Callie and kissed first his wife and then his child, all the while giving thanks to God that they were both all right.

"Do you have a name picked out?" the nurse asked.

"No," Callie said.

"Yes," Morgan answered at the same time.

"We do?"

"I'd like to name her Daisy," he said.

"You want to name her after my mother?"

"Without Daisy, I wouldn't have you. I owe her more than a namesake."

Tears streamed down Callie's face. "Hi, Daisy," she whispered to the child. "I love you."

An Ozark Christmas Angel

To Vicki and Mike,
with love.

Chapter 1

Lyndsay, I have a great favor to ask." Anita Jane Wells's normally powerful voice came across the telephone line as a whisper.

"Just name it," Lyndsay replied without hesitation. "Are you all right? What's wrong?" There was nothing she wouldn't do for Anita Jane, her mentor, who'd paved Lyndsay's way into the country music scene.

"The doctor says pneumonia can be very dangerous."

"Pneumonia? Are you in the hospital?"

"Yes," Anita Jane croaked. "I'm in Branson, and I need you to fulfill my contract. I can't leave the theater in the lurch. I know it's a lot to ask, since this is your composing time, but I'll be on my feet in a week or two. Certainly before Christmas."

"Do you have a show tonight? I don't know if I can get a flight that fast."

"There's a one fifteen out of Dallas this afternoon. I've taken it before."

Lyndsay glanced at her watch. Almost ten. "I'll be on it. What about backup singers? Are yours there?"

"Oh, yes. It's my usual Christmas show, and the manager has agreed that you can step in. All you have to do is bring your guitar. My secretary will have a ticket waiting for you at the airport, and someone will pick you up in Springfield. The doctor is here, so I'd better go."

"Could I speak with him? Please?" She knew Anita Jane would gloss over the severity of her illness. Lyndsay had seen her walk on stage when she'd had a burning fever, spouting the line, "The show must go on." She must be gravely ill to have Lyndsay replace her for two weeks.

"Dr. Hamilton," a baritone voice announced.

"This is Lyndsay Rose. How is she, really?"

"She's doing fine and should be out of here soon. Don't be overly alarmed."

"She said pneumonia—"

"Yes," he interrupted. "Pneumonia can be a killer, but I'm certain Anita Jane will be fine. Some rest will work wonders for her."

Lyndsay let out a deep breath, unaware that she had been holding it.

"Okay. Take care of her, Dr. Hamilton. I'll go to the hospital as soon as I get to Branson."

There was a pause on the other end. Then, "She'll be fine, Miss Rose. I'll see you later today."

Lyndsay hung up the phone and pulled suitcases from a large storage closet. She mentally made a list of costumes to take and street clothes as well. What was the weather like in Missouri? Hadn't Anita Jane mentioned wading through deep snow last Christmas?

❈❈

"She sounds like a nice person and is very concerned about you. Why are you doing this to her?" Dr. Hamilton asked in a gruff voice as he helped his older friend with her coat. He stood in front of the door to the hospital corridor and waited for a reply.

"I told you she needs to be with people at Christmas," Anita Jane said in her normal voice. "For the last three years, since her husband died, she's isolated herself with the pretense of writing songs. I'm doing this for her." Anita Jane chuckled. "Hey, I could be a Christmas angel, going about doing good."

Will Hamilton laughed and studied the country singer. She was sixty-four, but her energy level, her skin tone, and her heavy dark hair belied her years. Oh, there were character wrinkles and some gray hairs among the brown, but this woman stayed young without the help of cosmetic surgery and hair dye. Still, she wasn't his idea of a Christmas angel. An exceptional individual, yes. A headstrong woman, yes. An unconventional woman, yes. But never a Christmas angel.

"What about this afternoon when she gets to Branson?"

"Will, I was hoping you'd help me out there."

"I've already lied for you," he said.

"No, not lied. Lyndsay's a stickler for lying. You never said I was a patient here. Or that I actually had pneumonia, and neither did I."

"I was careful about what I said, but that isn't what she heard, and you know it. She thinks you're on your deathbed."

"I'll straighten her out in a few days. After you pick her up at the airport and take her to the theater to sign the contract. And after she's done a couple of shows and realizes how much she needs this."

"I'm going to pick her up?" Will stared at his friend. How had he let her talk him into helping her? Probably because she reminded him of his aunt, who also got her way when something was important to her. This morning, Anita Jane had called and asked if she could meet him at the doctor's lounge. When he'd told her it was his day off, but he would be checking on a few patients, she'd conned him into seeing her. Now she wanted him to pick up Lyndsay Rose?

"Please, Will. It would mean so much to Lyndsay if you reassured her that I would be mending quick." When he didn't immediately answer, she continued.

"Remember that benefit I did for the children's ward? You said anytime I needed anything, anything at all. . ."

"Okay. Okay. Then we're even." He didn't appreciate spending his day off driving an hour to the Springfield airport even if it was to pick up the beautiful Lyndsay Rose. He'd planned on fishing.

Anita Jane smiled at him, one of those cat-who-ate-the-canary smiles, and he opened the door to the hallway. Together they walked to the parking lot.

"You're in your bachelor car. Where's your four-wheel drive?" she asked when he stopped at his little sports car.

"At home."

"Better take it. Lyndsay's never learned to travel light."

❧

Lyndsay peered out the window as the plane descended and headed for the runway. What a small place compared to the massive Dallas/Ft. Worth airport she had left a little over an hour ago.

No snow. Maybe she'd been wrong about the weather in Missouri. She'd never played in Branson, although she'd performed in Kansas City on her last tour. But that had been in the summer, and she'd been in that city for less than twenty-four hours before she'd taken off for Denver. Tours wore her out. She much preferred studio work, but it was hard to sell records if she didn't hit the road.

The plane set down with a couple of thumps, not the smoothest landing Lyndsay had ever experienced. She wondered who would be picking her up. Probably Anita Jane's secretary, Rowena. That woman could organize anything on a moment's notice.

The last time she'd seen Rowena was at Trevor's funeral. The cancer had been quick. Four months after it was discovered, her husband had died. Although Anita Jane had been the strong one for Lyndsay, Rowena had been there in the background, quietly organizing everything, making phone calls, and making sure the family were where they needed to be when they needed to be there.

Anita Jane and Lyndsay's mother had been high school friends who had roomed together in Nashville while Anita Jane had been trying to hit the big time and Melinda worked as a secretary for a recording company. Melinda was actually instrumental in getting Anita Jane's big break. But as she'd told Anita Jane countless times, if she hadn't had the talent, getting Melinda's boss to listen to her wouldn't have done any good. Anita Jane had repeated the story to Lyndsay and echoed the same sentiment when she'd gotten a record producer to listen to Lyndsay's demo.

That had been eight years ago, when she was twenty. A lot had happened since then. Her career had skyrocketed, and then her mother had died, later Trevor, and now Anita Jane was ill. Wasn't pneumonia what people got right before they died? Even cancer victims like Trevor ended up with pneumonia. Once the lungs filled, death was inevitable.

With a heavy heart, Lyndsay automatically donned sunglasses, joined the group of passengers exiting the plane, and walked through the tunnel into Springfield's terminal. She should have no trouble finding Rowena in this place.

She looked for the tall redhead in the crowd of some forty people in the waiting area, but she wasn't there. Her first thought was that Anita Jane might be so ill that Rowena wouldn't leave her. Lyndsay whipped off her sunglasses, thinking whoever was to pick her up might not recognize her with them on.

She stepped over to the side to wait when a huge bear of a man approached. He was a basketball coach's dream and a football coach's dream at the same time. He wasn't heavy, there appeared to be nothing but muscle on his tall frame, but he was huge, and she'd guess he was somewhere in his early thirties. She looked up at deep brown eyes.

"Lyndsay Rose, I'm Will Hamilton."

She didn't recognize the name and shook her head.

"Dr. Hamilton. We spoke this morning about Anita Jane."

"Oh, no," she gasped. Had the doctor come to tell her the bad news? *Dear God, please don't let her be gone,* Lyndsay prayed. She groped for the nearest seat and sat down hard.

Will watched Lyndsay's face turn a ghastly white.

"Are you going to faint?" he said and hunched down beside her chair. "Put your head down." He gently pulled her toward him.

"Anita Jane?" she mumbled.

Realization hit him. "She's fine. Anita Jane is fine!" But she wouldn't be for long. He might put her six feet under for what she'd put this woman through.

"She's still alive?"

"Very much alive. I had the afternoon off, so I came to get you as a favor to Anita Jane. We'll talk as soon as you're feeling better."

"I'm okay now."

"You're getting some color back, but sit here a few more minutes while I get your suitcase."

She handed him five baggage claims.

"I'll get these loaded and be back in a few minutes."

Will strode toward the baggage area. Anita Jane had gone too far this time. She'd always been a bit eccentric, but her antics had never harmed anyone before. Maybe he should leave Lyndsay's suitcases and get her on the next plane back to Dallas. No, she should have the opportunity to look a healthy Anita Jane in the eye and ask her what she could possibly mean by getting her to Missouri under false pretenses.

He carried two cumbersome bags to his Suburban and moved his car to the ten-minute loading zone. Two more suitcases and a wardrobe trunk later, he returned to the waiting room to find Lyndsay signing autographs.

For a moment he'd forgotten she was a big star. He'd seen her as the victim of unforgivable meddling.

She looked up and smiled at him.

"Just a moment, Dr. Hamilton, and we can go."

Where had all these people come from? Of course they would recognize her. Dark glasses no longer covered her face, but even with them, her trademark waist-length blond hair was a dead giveaway. She signed another twenty autographs, giving her complete attention to each fan, before they made their getaway to his car.

He snatched the parking ticket from under the windshield wiper and vowed to bill Anita Jane.

As soon as they were on the road Lyndsay turned to him.

"So Anita Jane is all right? She's responding to treatment?"

Will took a deep breath. "Anita Jane doesn't have pneumonia. She wanted you to think that so you would come down here and not be alone for Christmas."

"What!"

He glanced at his passenger, whose expressive eyes that had earlier held panic and grief now were saucer-sized in disbelief.

"She says that since your husband died you pretend to write songs in December and become a hermit. She thinks you need to be around people."

"You're not making this up?"

He shook his head.

"It's true that I don't go on the road in December. Trevor died December fifth, we were married on the fifteenth, and his birthday was the twenty-first. That's an awful lot of memories for one month, and sometimes they get me a little down. But I have always spent

300

Christmas Day with family. If I'm not at my brother's, I go to my in-laws." She shook her head. "I'm not lonely, even though I miss my husband. I can't imagine what Anita Jane was thinking."

"I don't know that she's thought it through, but she sees herself as some sort of Christmas angel, spreading joy and good cheer. I just can't picture her sprouting a couple of wings. And a halo is out of the question."

Lyndsay laughed, a bit out of relief and a bit at the improbable word-portrait that Will Hamilton had painted of her friend.

"What's your part in this little farce? You told me she had pneumonia."

"Not exactly." He gave a blow-by-blow of his morning conversation with Anita Jane.

"So she was in the doctor's lounge when she called. She's good," Lyndsay said and nodded her head in thought. "But she has met her match. I'm not sure what I'm going to do, but are you willing to help me?"

"Whatever it is, count me in."

Chapter 2

Will drove Lyndsay directly to the theater where she would be performing that evening.

"Her plan is for you to sign the contract right off. Once you've signed, she thinks she'll have you down here for at least a couple of weeks. Do you want to do that?"

"It's okay. Since I'm here, I'll play along until we figure out what else to do. I've already cleared this with my agent. I taped a Christmas TV special last month, so I have a show all worked up."

Will ushered her through a side door into the theater and introduced her to the manager, who had the contract sitting on his desk.

"It's wonderful of you to fill in for Anita Jane like this," the manager gushed. "I'm sure she'll be well soon and can take over before the winter season starts."

Lyndsay exchanged a glance with Will. Was the manager in on this game, too? Will raised his eyebrows as if to say he didn't know. Oddly, she'd known the doctor for only an hour, and yet they could communicate without words.

Lyndsay studied the contract. It ran through the middle of December with no days off. On Sunday she'd lead a gospel music service.

"When does the winter season start?" she asked.

"After the New Year. We take a couple of weeks off before we begin again. Not too many tourists are here for the actual holidays, but they do like the Christmas shows, so this week and next will be busy."

Lyndsay glanced at her watch. Already four o'clock.

"I'd like to check with Anita Jane and then rehearse before the show."

"Anita Jane set a rehearsal for four thirty. Some of the musicians

302

are already backstage. Here's the program she's been doing and the music," he said and handed her a stack of papers, "but I'm sure you'll want to add a few songs of your own."

The manager showed them to Anita Jane's dressing room, then a stagehand left with Will to unload her wardrobe trunk and suitcases.

Lyndsay collapsed on the small sofa. What had she gotten herself into? Taking over someone else's show was a monumental task. Well, she wouldn't get it done by moaning about it. With a prayer for help and new resolve, she sat up straight and flipped through the sheets of musical numbers, mentally matching the music with the costumes she'd brought. They would work. The songs were mostly traditional Christmas carols, so she knew the words. A few arrangements had an Anita Jane twist, but she could mimic that. She'd grown up with Anita Jane's music, and she knew her musical mannerisms and show style.

"Do you want all of these?" Will asked from the doorway.

"These two have street clothes." Lyndsay pointed to the smaller suitcases.

"I'll take them to your suite," Will said. "Anita Jane has a cabin out at Big Cedar, but she's arranged for you to stay in the main lodge."

"Why don't I stay with Anita Jane? Doesn't she have an extra bedroom?"

"I'm sure she does, since those cabins have several rooms, but she asked that. . . Oh, good idea, Lyndsay. She's supposed to be in the hospital anyway. Let's see her wiggle out of this one."

"Exactly. She'll have to fake her illness and stay in bed while I'm there or confess. As a matter of fact," she said as she picked up the phone from a small end table, "I think I'll ring her right now and let her tell me she's been dismissed from the hospital."

But it wasn't Anita Jane who answered. Rowena told Lyndsay that Anita was in the hospital.

"I have a rehearsal in a few minutes, but I'd like to check on her. Do you have the hospital number?" Lyndsay wrote it down. "Rowena, Will says I'm booked at the lodge, but I'd much rather stay at Anita Jane's. While she's in the hospital that shouldn't be a problem, and while she's recuperating, I can help take care of her. Will can drop my suitcases by there. . . No, I insist. I want to be near her." Lyndsay grinned at Will. "I've got to run. See you soon."

Lyndsay read the phone number to Will. "Is this familiar?"

"That's the hospital. I wonder what she's up to now."

The information desk answered the call. "The receptionist says she's in room 255," Lyndsay told Will as she waited for the connection.

"There isn't a room 255. She's probably. . ."

Lyndsay waved her hand to shush him. "Anita Jane? How are you? . . . I'm at the theater now. Will's going to take my things to your cabin, but I'll come to the hospital immediately after the show."

Lyndsay handed the phone to Will. "She wants to talk to you."

She couldn't tell much from Will's half of the conversation. It was partly in code, since most of his answers were of the "yes" and "no" variety. He motioned for her to go out of the room, so Lyndsay stood in the hall outside the open door.

"I can talk freely now. She's stepped out for a minute." Will winked at Lyndsay. "No, she's determined to stay with you and take care of you. Are you sure you know what you're doing, Anita Jane? She's stressed out about this. . . All right, but I don't approve. Where are you now?"

He motioned Lyndsay back into the room. "Lyndsay's back. Did you want to tell her anything else? Fine. I'll be over to see about your release." He hung up the phone.

"Well? Where is she?"

"She's been standing at the information desk waiting for your call. Now she's decided I can dismiss her with a private duty nurse, because she hates hospitals. That means the extra bedroom is out for you. She sure covers all the angles."

"All right. I'll stay in the lodge, but I'll be dropping in on her at all hours."

"She'll expect you tonight after the show, and she'll try to arrange any other visits. What we have to do is decide where she wants to be, and be there first. That way she'll have to stay home. Last year, she made all the Christmas parties. I'll make a list and see what we can do. This is going to be fun."

"Excuse me." A woman stood in the doorway. "Miss Rose, I'm from wardrobe."

Lyndsay held up one finger, "Just one minute and we'll get to work." She turned her attention back to Will. "Why did you have me step into the hall?"

He shrugged. "Anita Jane said you were a stickler about lying. So I'm playing the game by your rules." He glanced at his watch. "I'm headed to the hospital to check on patients and see Anita Jane. I'll be back here when your show is over and take you to the lodge. Around nine?"

"Okay."

He carried her two suitcases with him as he left.

A whirl of activity engulfed Lyndsay. A makeup artist, the wardrobe mistress, and the band leader swarmed in. She carried on three conversations at once and tried to take direction herself.

By five forty-five the rehearsal ended so the entertainers could get dressed for the seven o'clock performance. They'd run through most numbers once, but hadn't practiced any of the songs Lyndsay would be adding to the show. She felt comfortable enough to sing them without backup, but tomorrow she'd make sure they rehearsed. Harmony added to the depth of her music, and she wanted the audience to get their money's worth. As it was, she worried they would feel cheated that they didn't get to see the legendary Anita Jane Wells.

❦

So this was how a double agent felt, Will mused as he prepared to take on Anita Jane. Because he knew she would expect him to protest, he did just that and with a vehemence, since his heart was in it.

"You should have seen her at the airport. She thought you were dead, and I was there to break it to her," he explained as they sat at a table in the doctor's lounge. "You should be ashamed of yourself."

"Will, you don't understand. In the long run Lyndsay is going to thank me for this. She's a beautiful woman, isn't she?"

That was an understatement. Her beauty wasn't just physical; it was in the depth of human understanding in her eyes. Not that she had merely survived some hard emotional times, but that she had accepted them and gone on with her life. He didn't know exactly how he knew that, but he did. She had inner peace. That's what he'd seen in her deep blue eyes.

"Yes, she's beautiful, but I think you underestimate her. She's grieved for her husband, but she's come to grips with it."

Anita Jane gave him a long look. "I know her very well, and I believe I know what's best for her. I was there when she was born, I was with her when her mother died, and I was there right after her husband died. In a couple of weeks, she'll be a different person, and she'll have me to thank for it. Now, are you available to take her to the lodge tonight? Or do I need to get someone else? Dave Robbins would probably do it."

Was she crazy? He wouldn't trust Dave Robbins within twenty miles of Lyndsay. The man might be a professor at the College of the Ozarks and be one of his good friends, but he wouldn't welcome any competition from Dave. Competition? Now why would that enter the picture? He pushed the thought out of his mind. "I've already arranged to pick Lyndsay up after the show."

"Fine. Here," she said and dug a ticket out of her purse, "in case you get there early. Well, I've got to run. Rowena's interviewing nurses for me since Lyndsay's thrown a kink in some of my plans. I thought of just getting someone from a temp agency, but Lyndsay's sure to question her about her credentials. This is getting to be an expensive ordeal. I just hope Lyndsay appreciates what I'm doing. After all, I am her Christmas angel." She straightened an imaginary halo and laughed, then turned and left.

"Christmas angel—bah, humbug!" Will exclaimed to the empty room. No self-respecting Christmas angel, even a pretend one, would introduce Dave Robbins to Lyndsay Rose. His friend might be a charmer, but Will wouldn't trust him with his sister, and he certainly wouldn't trust him with Lyndsay. Oh, he was going to enjoy teaching Anita Jane Wells a lesson about meddling in other peoples lives.

He ordered opening night roses for Lyndsay, made his rounds, then drove to his home on Lake Taneycomo and studied his calendar. There were the usual number of Christmas parties and special events held around Branson, and they were all important to Anita Jane.

She prided herself in being not only a country singer, but being part of the community. That was how he'd met her in the first place. She'd volunteered for a committee to study the traffic situation in Branson. With all the music theaters on the strip, there was a continual traffic jam from April to November. While the highway department put in new roads, the committee came up with alternate routes for the locals and smart tourists. They'd also requested that the music shows stagger their hours so all the shows wouldn't let out at the same time. He'd met Anita Jane at the first meeting, and they had hit it off. She wasn't at all what he thought of as a celebrity but was a down-to-earth person. This was her third year to return to Branson for part of the tourist season and to stay through Christmas. Twice she'd come to him as a patient—once for asthma and once for a sprained wrist. But their relationship wasn't really professional; it had been sparked by mutual respect and genuine friendship.

But that was in the past. Now he was ready to do battle with Miss Christmas Angel. She had hurt an innocent young woman, no matter what misguided good intentions she'd had. She should learn to think matters through before acting on them.

He made a list of events Anita Jane wouldn't want to miss and canceled other plans he'd had so that he could attend them, escorting Lyndsay Rose. Anita Jane would have to stay away from the festivities or give away her deception in getting Lyndsay to Branson.

He fixed a quick sandwich, showered, dressed, and drove to the family theater where he saw the marquee announcing Lyndsay Rose in a Christmas Spectacular.

Before the opening curtain, the manager made a quick appearance and announced that Lyndsay Rose was replacing Anita Jane Wells; however, he didn't give any reason. The audience didn't seem to care. They sat spellbound as Lyndsay's clear, sweet voice gave new meaning to old carols. The sets sparkled with artificial snow and Christmas greenery, giant red bows and ornaments. Backup singers wore elaborate costumes that glittered and shone.

But the star was Lyndsay Rose. Whether flanked by others or sitting on a stool alone on the stage, she commanded attention. At one point she asked a couple of children from the front section to join her on stage. They sat in a sleigh while she sang "Jingle Bells" and two mechanical horses pulled them across the stage. After the song, she handed each child a present she selected from those under the giant Christmas tree at stage left.

She ended the show with "Silent Night," and a more eloquent version he'd never heard. The audience burst into applause. Lyndsay bowed again and again. The stage manager presented her with a bouquet of roses, and the audience clapped even louder. Lyndsay read the card attached to the ribbon, looked directly at Will in the second row, mouthed "Thank you" and smiled, then walked gracefully offstage.

Chapter 3

Wonderful show," the theater manager said. "They loved it." Echoes of the same sentiment came from all sides as the cast congratulated each other.

"And that was with one rehearsal," a backup singer told Lyndsay. "Imagine what we'll be doing by next week."

"It's Anita Jane's program," Lyndsay said. "She's great at developing a show." She looked down at the roses she held. Will was a real sweetheart. She'd seen him the moment the curtain had opened. It was hard to miss a man that big.

"How about dinner?" another backup singer asked.

"Thanks, but my ride is here, and I've not even checked into my room yet. It's been a long day."

The singer squeezed her arm. "Yeah. And I'll bet the delicious Dr. Hamilton is your ride."

"You know Will?" Lyndsay asked.

"I saw him bring you this afternoon. He's a friend of Anita Jane's, so he's been backstage before. He's a hunk and eligible." She raised her eyebrows in speculation.

"He's very nice," Lyndsay said. "And I need to get out of this outfit, so I can go. I'll see you all tomorrow—around six?" With the success of the show, she decided they didn't need to rehearse again before the evening performance. The cast members' cheers of agreement followed her to her dressing room.

Will was leaning against the wall beside her door.

"Wonderful show," he said. "You were marvelous."

"Thanks. And thank you for the roses. You're very sweet."

Sweet? Will couldn't remember that he'd ever been called sweet. It didn't sound like a masculine characteristic, but coming from Lyndsay, it sounded like a great compliment.

"I'll only take a minute to change," she announced and disappeared inside the dressing room.

Will exchanged hellos with cast members as they drifted to other dressing rooms. Within five minutes Lyndsay reappeared, this time devoid of stage makeup and dressed in the jeans and sweater she'd worn when he'd picked up her at the airport.

"Well," she said when they were settled in his car. "Did you release Anita Jane from the hospital?"

"She's home all right. And I think she'll be there for some time. I have a plan."

He explained his schedule of events and how he'd arranged for them to attend festivities that Anita Jane would normally attend.

"I realize you won't be able to go places during your performances, but when you're finished for the evening, we can make an appearance, just like Anita Jane would have done."

"Are there events during the day that I could attend on my own?"

"Well, there are some, and I'm on a light schedule, so I can take you around." He didn't mention that he'd rearranged his on-call time and traded time off with his partner in his family practice so he would be available to squire her around.

"This sounds crazy, but medicine is a cyclical business. People would rather spend money on Christmas presents than on doctor bills, so in December they don't always go to a doctor when they should. Of course, many end up in the emergency room."

"And do some get well without medicine?" Lyndsay asked.

He glanced over at her and saw her teasing grin.

"Yes. Some do. But you've got to admit there's a lot to peace of mind, and that's what some people get from visiting a doctor."

"Can't argue with that," Lyndsay said. "How much farther? Haven't we gone several miles?"

"We're almost there. The lodge is on Table Rock Lake, and the drive is worth the great view you're going to have. Another night, when you're not so tired, I'll show you the million Christmas lights."

"Sounds great. Don't you think I should spend some time checking on Anita Jane? Otherwise she might get suspicious."

"True. We want to flush her out of her scheme but not before she has to suffer for it." He didn't mention that he wanted their time together to go on for a while. He didn't understand why that thought even occurred to him. He hardly knew Lyndsay, but he knew he wanted to know her better.

"You are bad, Will Hamilton."

He grinned. He accepted that as a compliment.

"Is this a town?" Lyndsay asked as Will pulled up in front of a magnificent lodge. They'd passed several cabins and another huge rustic building.

"No, but it appears that way. There are three lodges and a hundred private cabins. Anita's cabin is down that road. Do you want to see her first or check in?"

"Let's go straight to her. That would be my normal reaction."

Will turned the car down the narrow road and soon parked at Anita Jane's. A light blazed from the front window.

Their knock was answered by a woman in a white uniform. Will exchanged a glance with Lyndsay and whispered, "She doesn't skimp on anything."

Lyndsay nodded and followed the nurse into the cabin. A fire burned cheerily in the fireplace, and a robed Anita Jane sat in a recliner, covered with a quilt.

Lyndsay rushed to her side and hugged her.

"How are you feeling?"

"Better, now that I'm home," Anita Jane said in a husky voice. "Thank you so much for coming. I knew I could count on you." She coughed.

Will reached for her wrist and felt her pulse as he looked at his watch, "Could I see her latest readings, nurse?"

The nurse handed a clipboard to Will.

Lyndsay glanced at the fireplace. "Do you think it's wise to have a fire? I know not much smoke escapes, but there's bound to be some. Will?"

"Lyndsay's right. Don't build a fire tomorrow," he instructed the nurse, then turned back to his patient. "Delicate lungs don't need any further complications." Lyndsay was brilliant. Anita Jane enjoyed a fire, more for the esthetic value than the heat. Having no fire would keep her aware of Lyndsay, even when she wasn't there physically. "And the real Christmas tree ought to go," he added. "With your allergic tendencies, you're running the risk of a flare-up with the spores from a live tree. An artificial tree would be okay."

Lyndsay turned to take off her coat, and Anita Jane glared at Will and shook her head.

"You'd better go on to the lodge, honey. I'm going to bed. I stayed up just to see you for a minute."

"Anita Jane, I'll be happy to stay here with you."

"Any other time I'd love that, honey. But the nurse will take care of me, and I'm up and down in the night, taking medicine and all. I want you to rest undisturbed." She coughed again then continued, "I heard the show went off without a hitch."

"It went fine. You have a good program lined up."

"I'll take Lyndsay to the lodge," Will said, "and I'll check on you tomorrow, Anita Jane." He bent over and kissed his friend on the cheek, then hustled Lyndsay outside.

"She's quite an actress," Lyndsay said once they were inside the car. She coughed in Anita Jane's style.

"No fire. A stroke of genius," Will said.

"Thanks. I thought it was a nice touch. And that bit about the live tree was excellent. She loves the smell of an evergreen at Christmas."

Will parked the car in the lot and escorted Lindsay to the lobby. While she checked in, he returned to the car for her luggage.

He stepped into the lobby in time to hear Lindsay cry out and run into the arms of another man.

"It's so good to see you, Morgan," she said then hugged the woman beside him—a woman Will hadn't seen at first. "Callie, what are you doing here?"

"Grandma's always wanted to see Branson, so we brought her down for the Christmas shows," Callie said. "We'll be here until Saturday."

"Oh, Will, you won't believe who's here," Lyndsay said and waved him over to the group. She made the introductions, and Will breathed an inward sigh when he learned the couple were married.

"Morgan is known as Trey to his fans," Lyndsay explained, and Will understood why the man looked familiar. "We only see each other at country music award shows," Lyndsay explained, "but we get in all the visiting we can then. Did you bring Daisy?" she asked, then turned to Will again. "She's their darling little baby."

"She'll be one on Thursday, so she's hardly a baby," Callie said. "She took her first step three weeks ago, and now she thinks she's conquered the world. Sorry, I sound like a new mother, don't I? Daisy's upstairs with Grandma. We took in one of the shows tonight; then Morgan and I went for a walk by the lake. Isn't this the most romantic place?"

"I just got here. I'm filling in for Anita Jane."

"What happened?" Morgan asked.

Will shot Lyndsay a warning glance.

"They can be trusted," Lyndsay said, "and they could be good accomplices."

"Okay, but we can't let it be general knowledge, or Anita Jane will never forgive us."

"Promise you'll never repeat what we tell you?" Lyndsay asked. "It wouldn't do Anita Jane's career any good."

Callie nervously glanced around. "Is there something illegal going on?"

"You know me better than that," Lyndsay said then explained the situation. "Don't you agree she needs to be taught a lesson?"

"Wouldn't hurt," Morgan said. "What can we do?"

The foursome walked to a sitting area in front of a massive fireplace. Callie and Morgan sat on one couch, and Will and Lyndsay sat on another facing them.

"We saw Anita Jane's show on Saturday night," Callie said. "She's one of Grandma's favorites. We went backstage after her show, and I know Grandma would love to be in on this scheme. We could visit Anita Jane tomorrow morning and take one of

Grandma's home remedies for a cold."

"You have one with you?" Will asked.

"No, but there are all sorts of wild herbs for sale at a store we shopped at yesterday. We can get the ingredients and have Grandma cook it over at Anita Jane's. She'll have to pretend to be sick while we're there."

"Great," Lyndsay said. "I hope it tastes horrible. But can you make sure she takes it?"

Callie laughed. "Few people can cross Grandma. She'll make Anita Jane swallow it."

"I'll watch Daisy while you all take your turn with Anita Jane," Lyndsay offered. She'd fallen in love with the little girl when she'd seen her in Nashville in October at the awards show and welcomed the chance to spend time with her. Trevor had wanted lots of children, and just days before he'd gotten sick, they'd talked about starting a family.

"Wonderful," Callie said. "It might be easier if you came to our suite instead of us carting all of Daisy's belongings to you. Amazing what one little person requires in an hour's time."

They exchanged room numbers, and Will stood up, effectively ending the conversation. Now that tomorrow morning was planned, he wanted to get Lyndsay up to her room. She had to be tired, both emotionally and physically.

"Lyndsay hasn't seen her suite yet," he said as he picked up the two suitcases once again.

They said good night to Morgan and Callie and climbed the wide staircase to the second floor. Will opened the door to Lyndsay's suite and carried the suitcases through the living room and deposited them on the bedroom floor. When he returned to the living room, he found Lyndsay reclining in an overstaffed chair, her feet on the ottoman, her eyes closed.

"Tired?" he asked.

"Exhausted." She was also hungry. She'd not eaten since that sandwich on the plane. "Is there a restaurant here?"

"Of course. Would you like to go there or have something sent up?"

Lyndsay glanced around the pine walls of the rustic room. The stuffed head of a deer stared at her from above the fireplace. "Does the lodge have room service?"

"Don't let the decor deceive you. Although it looks like a turn-of-the-century hunting lodge, it has all the modern conveniences. Even indoor plumbing," he said with a chuckle.

"Then I'd love to have something delivered."

Will located a menu in a desk drawer, read it aloud, then called in their order. "Fifteen minutes, guaranteed," he said.

Lyndsay leaned back in her chair and closed her eyes again, thankful that Will had ordered some food and would stay to eat with her. Odd how relaxed she felt with him.

"When I got up today I planned on Christmas shopping for my brother's family and working on a new song. Instead I'm here in Missouri, and I've performed on Branson's famous strip. Who'd have guessed it?" She opened her eyes and looked at Will. "What about you?"

"Since it's my day off, I'd planned on making early rounds and then fishing."

"Instead you ended up hauling me around."

He nodded. "And it's been much more exciting than throwing a line in the water."

This time she nodded in agreement. "And more exciting than deciding which scarf to get for my sister-in-law."

Chapter 4

C ome get this, Daisy," Lyndsay said. She shook a stuffed raccoon to get the little girl's attention.

Daisy toddled over and grabbed the animal. "Da, da, do," she chanted.

Those were her favorite sounds, Lyndsay had decided, since she said them no matter what they were playing with.

Morgan, Callie, and her grandmother were at Anita Jane's, doing their part to make her life miserable. Lyndsay chuckled at the thought of Grandma. She was a wiry little woman whose iron will was apparent at first meeting. Anita Jane had met her match in that woman.

"Da, da, do," Daisy said and pulled Lyndsay's arm.

"Whatever," Lyndsay said. "Want to go for a walk?" She picked Daisy up and hugged her. When Daisy hugged back, Lyndsay sighed. "Oh, precious." What she would give to have a little darling of her own.

She put Daisy's coat on her and carried her down the stairs. A walk by the lake would be a fine morning outing. How could she have associated Missouri with snow? Today was a gorgeous day, bright sun and not a cloud in the blue sky. The temperature must have been fifty, and it was the third of December. This was almost Dallas weather.

Lyndsay carried Daisy along the water's edge and pointed out birds and an occasional fish that surfaced for food then left widening circles behind. She let the little girl walk for a few minutes and tightly held her hand. Then she carried her back to the lodge.

Will Hamilton stood on the wide porch.

"Will, what are you doing out here?" Lyndsay called. A wide smile expressed her delight at seeing him again.

"Making a house call." He held out his hands to Daisy and she reached for him.

"I guess she doesn't know a stranger," Lyndsay said, a bit miffed that Daisy would so readily leave her.

"Kids like me," he said. "Actually they like high perches," he admitted. "And deep voices."

He certainly could provide both, Lyndsay thought, looking up at him. Each time she saw him, he seemed bigger, more impressive.

"Da, da, do," Daisy said and pointed.

Lyndsay turned and saw Morgan, Callie, and Grandma crossing the parking lot.

"She's fit to be tied," Grandma said after she'd been introduced to Will. "I told her you thought my remedy would do her good. She about choked on it, but she got a tablespoon down. I'm going back this afternoon to give her another dose."

"What's in this potion you've concocted?" Will asked.

"Can't give away my secret recipe or you'll be using it on all your patients, but she'll have garlic on her breath for a while."

Will laughed and handed Daisy over to Morgan. "I believe I'll pay her a visit. Come with me, Lyndsay?"

"Sure. Callie, you have a little angel here."

"Was she good?"

"Couldn't have been better. I'll stay with her again if you all want to go out during the day."

"Thanks. I'll keep that in mind," Callie said and followed her family inside.

Will retrieved his bag from his car, and he and Lyndsay walked to Anita Jane's cabin. Will pointed to the chimney. "No smoke." Her Christmas tree, now unadorned by lights and ornaments, stood in its stand on the front porch.

They found Anita Jane as they had left her the night before, sitting in the recliner.

She smiled at them. "Good to see you again, honey. Did you sleep all right?" she asked in her hoarse voice.

"I'm supposed to be asking you that," Lyndsay said and hugged her friend. "My suite is wonderful. Now how are you?"

"I had a good night. I'll be on my feet in no time. Can't keep me down." This time her voice sounded more normal.

No, but they were going to try to keep her down, Lyndsay thought.

"You don't want to rush anything," Will said. He listened to her heart and her lungs. "Your lungs are doing better. Are you taking your medicine?"

A stubborn look crossed Anita Jane's face. "Of course, Will. And I took some horrible poison from Callie Rutherford's grandmother. That woman's trying to kill me."

"She means well, and there's nothing in her natural cure that will harm you."

"Where's your nurse?" Lyndsay asked.

"She'll be back tonight. I just sent Rowena on a couple of errands, but she'll be right back, and she'll stay with me during the day. About tonight, Lyndsay. My driver will take you to the theater at five thirty. I can arrange for a friend to bring you back."

"I'll pick her up after the show," Will spoke up. "I promised her I'd show her the Christmas lights."

"Okay. That's arranged for tonight. Tomorrow—"

"Tomorrow we're going on the lake, and Thursday night we're invited to the party at the college. Next week we'll take in the Chamber's bash and the Grand Palace party for the entertainers."

Anita Jane's eyes grew wider with every plan Will announced.

"Sorry you won't be able to go, but right now you need to get some rest. You're talking too much. You don't want to overexert yourself. Can I help you into bed?"

"No. I breathe better sitting up. I'll be fine," she snapped.

"I'll check back with you before I go to the theater," Lyndsay said before she and Will stepped outside.

They didn't talk until they were out of earshot of the cabin.

"She's getting testy," Lyndsay said.

"Sure is," Will said with a grin.

"Will, you said you weren't lying about things, just walking around them. What about Anita Jane's lungs? You said they were better."

Will looked thoughtfully at the calm lake then looked back at Lyndsay. "What do you know about asthma?"

"Is that an evasive response, so I don't get into the patient-doctor confidential area?"

Will nodded.

"Okay. I know she has asthmatic tendencies that flare up from time to time. I won't ask any more questions."

"There's no need for other questions. She's not having an episode." Will reached for her hand and held it quite naturally as they walked toward the lodge. Lyndsay hoped his medical training didn't allow him to feel her pulse through her fingertips, for she was sure her heart was beating a hundred times a minute.

He was only holding her hand, but a man had not held her hand in this companionable way since Trevor had died. It was both alarming and quite satisfying at the same time.

When they reached the lodge, Will said good-bye and promised to pick her up immediately after the show.

Lyndsay climbed the stairs in a daze. How could a hand offered in friendship affect her this way? Was she actually interested in a man? Wasn't that being disloyal to Trevor?

She paced her living room, restless to go out, yet not knowing where to go. A hike along the lake might be the answer. She pulled back her trademark long hair in a ponytail and stuffed it under a hat. Sunglasses completed a disguise that had worked very well for her for years. The lodge wasn't packed with tourists who had recognized her, but she had noticed a few stares when she and Daisy had taken their walk. She wasn't in the mood for signing autographs.

For an hour Lyndsay strolled along the water's edge, skirting soft areas. She rested on a fallen log and looked up at the tall hardwood trees with their winter silhouettes devoid of leaves. In spring this area would take on a whole new look—green renewal, the promise of new growth.

Maybe it was time for her to have a new growth, too. Her life with Trevor was finished, but her life wasn't over.

As always, when faced with difficult thoughts, Lyndsay turned to God.

Is it time to move forward? Lord, I don't know what to do. And I may be premature in even speaking of this. I've known Will only a short time, but I know I'm attracted to him. What I don't know is how he feels. Even if he isn't interested, I need to know how to handle this new feeling. How do I act? What do I do? I need direction.

Lyndsay bowed her head and cried healing tears. Her tears were for Trevor, for uncertainty, and for loneliness. After a few moments she rose from her perch on the log and retraced her steps toward the lodge. Her heart felt lighter, refreshed.

And she needed to talk to a friend. She followed the narrow road to Anita Jane's. In bringing her here, her older friend had started her on a different road of recovery. Maybe Anita Jane had had her best interests at heart.

Lyndsay rapped on the door and hugged Rowena after she opened the door. Out of the corner of her eye, Lyndsay saw Anita Jane dive for the recliner.

As much as Lyndsay wanted to let her friend off the hook, she couldn't since she'd agreed with Will to teach her a lesson. Maybe their farce wouldn't be carried on much longer. On the other hand, once the pretense was over, she'd be on a plane returning to Dallas and her life there. She frowned at that thought.

"Something wrong?" Anita Jane asked. Her hoarse voice was back.

Lyndsay shook her head. "No. Just checking to see how you are and to ask a question."

A concerned look crossed Anita Jane's face. "Ask."

Lyndsay sat down on the couch. "This is a little awkward, but I'd like to know more about Will Hamilton."

Anita Jane's face lit up like a light bulb.

"He's a true friend. You like him?"

"I don't really know him yet, but he's an interesting man. Tell me about him."

"He's a gentleman. Played football in college, but you may have guessed that from his size. Football and medical school seem a remarkable combination, but he's a remarkable kind of man. Is that the kind of thing you want to know?"

Lyndsay nodded. "Go on."

"He likes fishing, a real nut about it, but I don't know why. What's important is he's a Christian, and he puts others' needs ahead of his own. As far as medicine is concerned, he's an outstanding family doctor. His talent is in diagnosing. One of my backup singers went to him after being treated for diabetes. Will examined him and just by touching him, located a lump. That night they operated on him and found a tumor which had caused the diabetes."

"Pretty impressive. Is the singer all right?"

"He's had chemo and is in remission. And all thanks to Will Hamilton."

"Anything you don't like about him?" Lyndsay asked with a smile.

Anita Jane studied the ceiling. "He works too hard. Even on his days off, he's checking on patients. And there's one thing worse than that. His fishing. He'd rather fish than about anything."

Lyndsay laughed. "That's the worst thing?"

"That's it."

"Well, thanks," Lyndsay said and stood up to leave. "Sorry to have you talk so much. I know Will wants you to get some rest. I'll check back with you later."

Lyndsay enjoyed the walk back to the lodge. She ate a leisurely lunch at the restaurant, took a nap, read part of a mystery, and dropped in on Anita Jane again before time to get ready for the show.

Again the performance went well. As soon as the final curtain dropped, Lyndsay hustled to her dressing room. Will was already there, leaning against the wall and conversing with one of the staff.

As quickly as she could, Lyndsay took off her stage makeup and changed into street clothes. Again she stuffed her hair under a hat, then joined Will, who whisked her into his car.

"We just have time to make it to Silver Dollar City. It closes at ten, and I want you to see the big tree."

"The lights all along the strip are magnificent," Lyndsay said.

Every theater and hotel sported string after string of lights. Some trees glistened with white lights only, others were multicolored.

"Just wait," Will said.

When they arrived at the 1890s theme park, they left the car in a huge lot and rode the shuttle to the main gate. Lights sparkled from every possible location, but the wire tree in the village green area surpassed them all.

Animated lighted ornaments, perfectly choreographed to music, brought the tree to life. It positively radiated warmth and good cheer. Lyndsay glanced at others around her. Not a solemn face looked up at the tree, but eyes were filled with wonder, and not just in the faces of youngsters. Senior citizens also gazed in awe at the spectacular tree.

Will held Lyndsay's hand and led her to a tiny wooden church where a pianist played carols. From inside she could see across a valley where lighted figures on the hillside appeared to be suspended in air.

They exited the church and walked the perimeter of the park, with Lyndsay's "oohs" and "aahs" joining the voices of other light-seers.

"I want to come back here again," she told Will when they arrived back at the car.

"We will," he promised. He drove downtown, and they strolled hand-in-hand along the lake where more animated lights held her spellbound.

"The whole place is a wonderland," she said as they stood and gazed on a lighted nativity scene.

"Life takes on a special glow at Christmas," Will said and pulled her into his arms. He looked down at her with tenderness in his eyes, and then he kissed her.

Lyndsay thought she'd never breathe again.

Chapter 5

I've wanted to do that since we met," Will said and this time kissed her on the forehead. He kept his arm around her shoulder as they walked back to the car.

"I've wanted you to do that since we met," Lyndsay said then wondered why she'd been so forthright with him.

Will grinned, an ear-to-ear type of grin. "Then maybe we should try this once more." He turned her in his arms and kissed her again. And again Lyndsay's heart stood still.

When they pulled apart, Will asked, "Would you like to go fishing tomorrow afternoon?"

"Fishing?" she whispered. It was all the voice she could manage.

"I have the afternoon off and thought you'd like to see some of the natural wonders of the area." He didn't add that he'd had his schedule juggled so he could take her out on the lake. "And Thursday night is a party at the college that Anita Jane wouldn't miss for the world. It's one of her charities. I thought we'd make an appearance."

"Sounds like fun."

Will helped Lyndsay into the car and drove her home, detouring by sections of town that had more elaborate light displays.

He walked her to her suite and finally thought to ask, "Did you have dinner? Are you hungry?" He'd been in such a hurry to get her to Silver Dollar City that he'd forgotten that she might not have had time to eat before the show.

"I ate a sandwich around five, so I'm fine."

"Well, then, I guess this is good night." He wasn't about to let her go without a good-night kiss. She felt so right in his arms, even though she only came to his shoulder. He felt protective toward her, and more than that, he felt. . .love.

That thought jolted through him, and he ended the kiss and

turned to leave. "I'll pick you up around one thirty," he said and bolted down the stairs.

Love? What was he thinking? He'd only known her a couple of days. He'd felt sorry for her because of what Anita Jane had planned for her, and he felt anger at Anita Jane for manipulating Lyndsay, but love?

"Will Hamilton, get a grip!" he mumbled under his breath.

Instead of heading home, he went by Anita Jane's. The light was still on.

She opened the door and croaked a welcome.

Looking behind him, she asked, "You alone?" in a normal voice.

"Yes. I just dropped Lyndsay off. When are you going to tell her? Hasn't this gone on long enough?" He didn't want it to end, but he wanted it over. He wished he could straighten out his feelings, but his mind was mush.

"Oh, I think she needs a little bit longer. Not much. She seems to be healing faster than I thought."

"Maybe that's because she didn't need healing. Maybe she's gone through all the mourning steps and is just living her own life in her own way without you controlling it."

Anita sat down in a chair and looked hard at Will, who paced back and forth. She didn't say a word, but raised her eyebrows at him.

"Maybe she should go on back to Dallas. Now. Tomorrow."

"I thought you were taking her out on the lake tomorrow."

"I am, but I can cancel that and take her to the airport instead."

"Why does her being here bother you?"

Will stopped his pacing. "She doesn't bother me. I just feel you shouldn't be so deceitful."

"Oh. So you're worried about my mental well-being."

"Something like that."

Anita smiled and nodded. "That's very kind of you, Will. But I'll suffer through in my present state of mind for a few more days. Then I'll tell Lyndsay. If she bothers you, stay away from her. I'll arrange for others to occupy her time."

"I told you she doesn't bother me," he said in a forceful voice and walked toward the door. "She doesn't bother me," he said again. "Good night."

He was starting to lie as much as Anita. "She doesn't bother me," he said with a harsh laugh as he climbed behind the wheel. "Right."

Lyndsay was ready by the time Will picked her up the next afternoon. She'd never been fishing in her entire life, so she was looking forward to a new experience. Anita Jane had told her to wear jeans and a heavy coat since it was colder on the water than on the shore. The temperature that morning when she'd walked to Anita Jane's had been just below freezing, but the sun had melted the frost and now the thermometer read in the upper forties.

"Which lake are we going to?" Lyndsay asked.

"I live on Taneycomo. It's actually the White River dammed up on both ends. Great rainbow trout. You'll see."

Will seemed unusually quiet, although Lyndsay reminded herself that she didn't know him well enough to make that determination. It just seemed that her every waking minute in Branson was spent with him.

"This is your home?" she asked, when he parked the car next to a rustic log house. It would have fit in perfectly with the building code at the lodge complex.

He nodded. "What do you think?"

Was it her imagination or did he sound defensive?

"It's so peaceful, and it fits right in with the woods."

He opened the door for her and showed her around the living room and kitchen, then asked if she'd make coffee while he changed clothes. He'd picked her up wearing a sport coat and tie, and she guessed he'd come straight from his office.

When he reappeared in a sweater, jeans, and hiking boots, he poured the coffee into a thermos.

"It gets a little chilly on the water," he said and picked up the cashmere coat she'd laid on a chair. "This black coat's a little fancy for the lake. You'd better wear one of mine." He hunted through the hall closet then handed Lyndsay an old brown quilted jacket. "That's the smallest I have."

Of course it swallowed her, but she rolled up the sleeves as best she could and once they were in his fishing boat and on the lake, she was glad the length came down to her knees. A wind blew steadily and dropped the temperature by ten degrees.

Will gazed openmouthed at her when she asked him what to do with the pole.

"You don't know how to fish?"

"Well, I've seen fishing in movies, but is there something more than holding this pole in the water? I want to do it right."

"You've never fished?" He still had that disbelieving look on his face.

What was wrong with him? Why couldn't he grasp what she said?

"I'm a city girl. Born in Nashville, but raised in Dallas. I'm sure people there fish, but I don't think my dad did. He died when I was three. And I can guarantee my mom didn't fish."

He let out a long breath. "Okay. Rainbow trout should be biting this afternoon, and they don't care if you have a live worm wiggling at the end or an artificial lure."

Now it was Lyndsay's turn to let out a long breath. Her lucky day. She wouldn't have to fish with live worms.

Once he helped her put her line in the water, she watched Will change the piece of plastic on his hook and throw in his line.

"When the fish takes the bait, you reel him in. You can feel the tug."

"Like this?" she asked. Her pole was bowed from the weight of a fish on the other end.

"You've got one. Reel him in."

"It doesn't work." She tried to wind the string, but she couldn't turn it.

"Unfasten the clamp," he said and reached for her pole. While he wrestled with it, he stuck his pole under his arm and fidgeted with hers. "Wow, it's a big one. Pull up on your pole and wind."

As he handed her pole back to her, a fish bit his bait and jerked the pole out of his precarious hold. All he could do was watch his favorite pole sink into the water.

"I've caught one," Lyndsay shouted. "Look at the size of this fish. Isn't it big?"

Will turned back to her and saw one of the biggest fish he'd ever seen come out of Taneycomo. He helped her land it and stared at it, then at her, then at the spot where his pole lay on the bottom of the lake.

"Should we throw it back in and catch it again?" Lyndsay asked. She didn't want to think about killing the poor fish. And from the way Will was acting, she didn't think he was too excited about it, either. She'd heard that fishing wasn't about catching fish but about appreciating time and nature. The latter fit more into Will's character as she knew him than a hunter who would purposefully kill helpless fish.

"Throw it back?" Will asked. This woman was exasperating. The fish was mounting size, and she wanted to throw it back. She should be wanting to get it weighed. "It'll probably tip the scales at fifteen pounds."

"Well, I sure don't want to kill it, but I don't want to touch it either. Will you throw it back in?"

Will took her pole and unhooked the fish which had been flopping on the floor of the boat. It arched and skimmed the water when he dropped it overboard.

Another boat approached them, and he waved to Kevin, a lake patrol officer, who had another man with him.

"Having any luck?" Kevin asked as he drew his boat beside Will's.

"We caught a big one, fifteen pounds, but we threw it back," Lyndsay said.

Kevin shot a questioning glance at Will. "Usually you throw back the little ones," he said. "This is our new officer, Tom Whiting. I'm teaching him the ropes. Could you show him your fishing license, Dr. Hamilton? Ma'am?"

Will dug his wallet out of his back pocket and showed his license. Lyndsay sat still in the front of the boat.

When the officer turned to her, she held her hands out, palms up.

"I don't live here. I'm just visiting, and I don't have a license."

"Dr. Hamilton?" Kevin said.

"It didn't cross my mind that she'd need a license."

"Well, she does. But it looks to me like only one of you is fishing anyway. One pole, no fish, except the fifteen-pound one that you threw back in," he said and chuckled. "I guess she doesn't need a license this time. But before you drop a line in the water, you need to get a license." He stared at Lyndsay as if trying to place where he'd seen her.

"Okay," Lyndsay said. "I'll get one. Thanks."

The officers shoved off and soon disappeared around a bend in the long lake.

"Where's your pole?" Lyndsay asked.

"I dropped it in the lake," Will muttered.

"Oh," she said, wondering when he'd dropped his pole. "So, what do we do now?"

"Well, since you can't fish and don't want to hurt them anyway, I suggest we go back home."

Lyndsay glanced at her watch. "Could we go for a little ride first? I don't have to be back at the lodge for a couple of hours."

Will took a deep breath and studied the beautiful woman in his old brown coat. He wasn't being a very good sport about this. It wasn't her fault that she'd caught a bigger fish than he'd ever pulled out of the lake. And it wasn't her fault that he'd dropped his pole.

"Why don't you pour us some coffee, and I'll get this motor going. This isn't a speed boat, we'll just take it nice and easy."

He'd forgotten to bring an extra cup, so they shared the cup that served as a lid to the thermos. As they puttered down the lake, Lyndsay watched some ducks drop out of formation and land on the water.

Bare-limbed trees in a thick forest on one shore gave way to high bluffs. Every curve and bend brought a new sight.

"It's beautiful here," she told Will. "I can see why you love it so much."

"You should see it in spring. There must be fifty shades of green everywhere you look. The summer's good, too. Hot sun, cool water. Fall's gorgeous with all the burnt oranges and red of the leaves."

"You ever think of running an ad agency?"

Will laughed. "I do sound like an advertisement, but there's no place like the Ozarks to live. It's a place of change." He handed her the cup of coffee so she could take a sip and took her free hand in his own.

A place of change, Lyndsay thought. She held his hand and looked at the man who had made her feel like a woman again. Yes, it was a place of change.

Chapter 6

"Did you ask Anita Jane to come?" Lyndsay asked Callie.

Daisy's first birthday was being celebrated in style. A private dining room at the lodge had been transformed into a wonderland of colorful balloons.

"Yes, but she declined. I told her we'd take her a piece of cake later."

Daisy sat in a high chair with a pie-sized cake of her own. Most of the icing was on her face, and part of the cake was on the floor.

Her guests were a who's who of performers in Branson. Of course, Morgan knew them, and although they didn't know Daisy, the party was a chance for the entertainers to get together on a personal basis, and that was an opportunity rarely afforded them. The award shows they attended had pre-gala events, but then the singers were too nervous to enjoy each others' company.

Lyndsay had found a log cabin doll house for Daisy. She'd have to be a little older to appreciate the line craftsmanship that went into it and to have the memory that she'd celebrated her first birthday in Missouri, but Lyndsay knew Callie would put it on a shelf for a few years.

Will showed up at the party for about half an hour, and Lyndsay introduced him to the celebrities he didn't know. Odd to be in his town, yet be the one to know the party guests. Will fit right in, not standing in awe of celebrities like some people did who weren't part of the entertainment industry. Of course, he knew the singers who made Branson their year-round home, but many were booked at theaters for a month or two run then went back on tour.

Since touring wasn't high on Lyndsay's list of favorite things to do, Branson was growing on her. She performed at night, but she wasn't packing up and flying to a different city during the days. Those hours were free, and she liked having the best of both worlds. The audience gave her affirmation of her talent, and they came to her; she didn't travel to them. She could see why Anita Jane spent several months here.

Will left the party with the promise to take Lyndsay to the local college's Christmas party that evening. With that in mind, Lyndsay wore her red silk dress when she delivered Anita Jane's promised piece of birthday cake and left from the cabin for the theater. As soon as the evening performance was over, she changed into the red silk again and met Will.

"Tonight's party will be a hundred eighty-degree change from that birthday party. A few celebrities might drop in after their shows, the ones who live here year round, but mostly it will be community people and those who teach at the college."

He drove them south of Branson to Point Lookout where the College of the Ozarks was built on a plateau overlooking lower hills and valleys.

This time it was Will who did the introducing. He let her meet several couples, all the time keeping a possessive arm on her shoulder or holding her hand. Several times he steered them away from Dave Robbins, but finally got cornered by his friend, who demanded an introduction.

"So you're filling in for Anita Jane. She and I are good friends. I've been meaning to drop over and visit with her while she's recuperating. Perhaps you'll be there when I come."

"That would be nice," Lyndsay said politely. Dave looked every inch the college professor from his tweed jacket with leather patches at the elbows to his polished loafers. "How do you know Anita Jane?" she asked.

"She's one of the big contributors to the college. We're a very different college. All our students work their way through school by jobs on campus. Kids who wouldn't be able to afford college, but are dedicated to the pursuit of knowledge, will find a home here."

"An unusual approach," Lyndsay said. She was interested in the college, even if Dave sounded like an ad for the school. Although she'd accused Will of doing the same thing for the Ozarks, somehow it had sounded different coming from him.

"Would you like to see the facilities?" Dave asked. "We have a first-rate restaurant at the gate. We could go there for a cup of coffee, and we have an Ozarks' museum and even a fruitcake department that is a very busy place this time of year." He flashed a charming smile.

"A fruitcake department at a college?" Lyndsay asked.

"It's where all the nutty professors teach," Will said.

"That's Will's favorite joke. He usually adds that I'm the chair of the department, but I'm not," Dave said. "We're famous for our fruitcakes. And our orchids."

"Orchids in the Ozarks?" This place was intriguing. Maybe a little tour would be fun.

Will's pager beeped, and he looked down at the number.

"Sorry, I've got to call the hospital. I'll be right back." Although he'd managed so far to reschedule his on-call time, tonight he'd found no one to take over for him. He didn't want to leave Lyndsay with Dave, but he had no choice.

He stepped in the hall to use his cell phone and quickly determined that he'd have to leave.

Lyndsay was still talking to Dave, exactly where he'd left her. She seemed fascinated by what he was saying.

"I'm sorry to interrupt, but I've got to check on a patient." He took Lyndsay's arm.

"I'll be happy to take Lyndsay home," Dave offered, "so she doesn't have to leave the party. You can run along, Will."

Will looked at Lyndsay. He didn't want to leave her, but he had no choice. He didn't have time to take her back to the lodge, but he didn't want her with Dave.

"Thank you, Dave, but I'll go with Will," Lyndsay said, interpreting Will's thunderous look to mean she had come with him and had better leave with him. "I need to be getting back to check on Anita Jane."

"What about a tour tomorrow?" Dave asked. "I'm out of class at one. We could have lunch at the Friendship House, and I could show you around Anita Jane's favorite charity. She'd love for you to see the place."

Lyndsay smiled. Probably Anita Jane would like that since Will had also mentioned she was a big donor.

"That'll be fine. I'll meet you at the restaurant tomorrow," she said. "One o'clock." She turned and left with Will and had to hurry to keep up with his brisk pace.

At the stoplight, Will turned north instead of taking the road south to the lodge.

"I'll find someone to give you a ride home," he said. The hospital was little over a mile away; he could be there in two minutes versus the twenty-five minutes it would take to deliver Lyndsay to her door and get back. "I might not be too long."

"I don't mind waiting," Lyndsay said. "What's the emergency?"

"One of my older patients fell and broke his hip. The surgeon has been called, but Mr. Coble has asked for me. He's scared. And I'm scared for him."

"It's that serious?" A broken hip didn't sound like such a terrible injury.

"Mr. Coble's in his nineties. The kind of immobility we're talking about will limit his recovery. In a lot of cases with the elderly, a broken hip is the beginning of the end."

Will parked the car in the doctors' parking area, and they entered through the emergency room door.

"As soon as I check on him, I'll either come get you or find you a ride," Will said. "Sorry about this."

"It's all right," Lyndsay said, although she wondered why he'd looked so upset when Dave had offered her a ride if he were just going to find her another one. She'd had the impression they were friends.

Will disappeared through a swinging door, leaving Lyndsay in the waiting room. A gray-haired couple sat on one side, and a mother with a crying baby sat facing them, while on the far side an entire family of five alternated walking to the emergency room door and peaking in. Lyndsay walked around, studying the pictures on the walls, and could feel the gazes of the others on her.

She'd left her hair down. There had been no time to arrange it artfully on top of her head, and she couldn't stick it under a hat to go to the Christmas party. But now everyone recognized her.

"Are you Lyndsay Rose?" A little girl from the family group had wandered over to her.

"Yes, I am. What's your name?"

"Jan Coble. I'm seven just yesterday."

"Happy birthday, Jan. Has your grandpa been hurt?"

The little girl's mouth dropped open. "Do you know my grandpa? He broke his hip. Did you come to sing to him?"

"Well, if his doctor wants me to," Lyndsay said.

"His doctor wants you to." Will stood holding the swinging door open. "Actually Mr. Coble is a fan of yours. He didn't believe me when I said you were here."

Lyndsay let him usher her back to a curtained-off area where a frail-looking man lay on a hard table. His face was almost as white as the sheet under him, but his eyes became more animated when he saw her.

"Hello, Mr. Coble," Lyndsay said. "I just met your granddaughter Jan in the waiting room."

"That girl don't know a stranger," he said through clenched teeth. "You really been out with Doc? I told him he didn't need to leave some good-looking gal to come see me, and he told me you was with him."

"I'm with him all right."

"Well, I'll be." Although the pallor of his skin didn't change, his eyes seemed to twinkle, "Doc here's been holding out on me. It's time he settled down." He coughed, and his small frame shook, and with it his broken hip. He moaned.

"You're fine, Mr. Coble." Will took his hand. "That pain killer should be taking effect by now." Will studied the drip of the IV. "When the surgeon is ready, we'll take you down and get those bones pinned together. Then you'll be all set."

Lyndsay patted Mr. Coble's other hand. "I'll get out of the way, but I'll check on you tomorrow," she promised.

"I'll be out in a few minutes," Will said, and Lyndsay walked back into the waiting room.

"Did you see Grandpa?" Jan asked immediately. It wasn't Lyndsay's place to talk to the family, but if she were in their position, and she had been when Trevor had been so ill, she'd want to know everything that was going on.

"He's getting ready to go to surgery," Lyndsay addressed the family. "The doctor will pin his bones together, so they'll mend. He seems in good spirits, and that's so important."

Had he actually said Doc needed to settle down? She wished she'd taken in Will's reaction to those words.

Twenty minutes later Will exited the swinging doors. If he didn't know better, he'd say Lyndsay was giving a press conference, but instead of cameras and reporters with notebooks and tape recorders, hospital personnel and people in the waiting room were asking questions.

"I guess my favorite song would be the one I'm working on now," Lyndsay was saying. "Every time I start a new one, my favorite changes." She caught sight of him. "One last question. Jan?"

"Do you like my grandpa?"

"Yes, I do. And I'm going to come see him tomorrow."

Will made his way to her side and helped her with her coat, which she'd tossed in a chair.

"You've been a good audience," Lyndsay said. "My show starts at seven. Hope to see some of you there tomorrow night."

Calls of "Thanks," and "See you then," followed them outside, and Will noticed several people held up complimentary tickets.

"You gave out passes?"

"Anita Jane gave me a stack of them, and I hadn't given out any yet," she answered with a shrug. "How's Mr. Coble?"

"He's in surgery now, I'll check on him after I get you home. Seeing you did him a lot of good. Are you really going to visit him tomorrow?"

"I wouldn't have said I would if I didn't intend to."

She sounded a bit put out. "I know," he said. Anita Jane had told him she was a stickler about lying, and she'd apply that to herself above all others. But he knew that about her without remembering Anita Jane's words. He regretted his question, but a big star like Lyndsay Rose didn't drop in on an old man she'd just met and talked to for five minutes. But Lyndsay Rose was more than a big star. She was a woman who had known tragedy and overcome it, and she would remember how it felt and help others.

❧

"Thanks for a most interesting evening," Lyndsay said a few minutes later at her door.

"The pleasure was mine," Will said. He tenderly kissed her. Then again and again. "Well, good night. I'll see you after your show tomorrow. Oh, have me paged when you come to the hospital."

She nodded. "Good night, Will."

She waltzed into her room and saw the light blinking on her phone. The message was to call Anita Jane.

She dialed the number, knowing what a night owl Anita Jane was, even though she was playing the invalid.

"Honey, I just wanted to make sure you were doing okay today, being the fifth and all," Anita Jane said.

Lyndsay nearly dropped the phone. Since she'd been in Branson, she hadn't been aware of the calendar, just of leaving for the show at five thirty. Four years ago today Trevor had died.

Chapter 7

How could I have forgotten my husband's. . ." Lyndsay trailed off. She couldn't call it his deathday, but that was exactly what it was. The opposite of birthday. She paced Anita Jane's living room. Although it was closing in on midnight, she had walked down to Anita Jane's cabin.

"Honey, is that a day you should remember?" Anita Jane asked. "Would Trevor want you to remember it with pain?"

"No, of course not. I just somehow feel disloyal."

"Nonsense. I think that's a sign of healing." She hummed a few bars of a song.

"Is your voice getting better?" Lyndsay asked as she tried to place the melody. "You don't sound so croaky."

"I'm not ready to sing for an audience, but I'm getting stronger. It's time I got out of here. Cabin fever's going to get me long before pneumonia ever could. How was the party tonight?"

Lyndsay knew Anita Jane was changing the subject for her benefit, and she went along with it, explaining about leaving early with Will for the hospital and about Will returning there now to check on Mr. Coble. "I'm going to meet Dave Robbins at the Friendship House for lunch tomorrow. He's going to give me a tour of the college."

"That college does a lot of good. If I get Will's okay, would you mind if I go with you? I haven't been out there in some time, and you wouldn't be gone too long, would you?"

"No, but are you feeling up to it?" Lyndsay wouldn't mind Anita Jane coming but knew Will would veto it. They were trying to keep her housebound to teach her a lesson.

"I'm feeling much stronger. You said Will was going back to the hospital?" At Lyndsay's nod, Anita Jane dialed the hospital number and had him paged. "I told you he worked too hard. See what I mean?" She turned her attention to the phone and explained to Will about the next day's outing.

At the other end of the line, Will Hamilton breathed a sigh of relief. He didn't want Lyndsay spending one minute with Dave Robbins. Anita Jane just might be a Christmas angel after all. She was sure helping him out right now.

"Are you ready to tell her the truth?" he asked.

"No. I'm not strong enough to sing yet, but I'd like to get out of this place for an hour or so. We wouldn't be gone long."

This was getting better and better. It would ensure that Lyndsay didn't spend much time with Dave.

"Okay, I'll tell her you can go."

Anita Jane handed the phone to Lyndsay.

"I think we'd better let her get out before she does something rash," Will said. "Besides, she might catch on to us if I told her she couldn't go, since it is with you, and since she is pretending to feel better."

"If you think that's wise," Lyndsay said.

"It'll work out fine. Oh, Mr. Coble is in recovery and doing fine."

"Already?"

"The procedure only takes thirty minutes. It was a lag screw and plate job. He was lucky he didn't need a prosthesis. This could have been much worse, but now I'm optimistic for him."

Lyndsay didn't understand what he meant by lag screw or prosthesis, but the important thing was the optimistic part.

"I'm glad," she said. "Are you headed home?"

"Pretty soon. I'll wait until he's awake enough to reassure him. I'll see you tomorrow. Will you drop by after your tour of the school?"

"Yes. Good night." Lyndsay hung up the receiver and looked thoughtfully at Anita Jane, who was humming that tune again. "Well, it's all set. I was going to ask if I could use your driver. Is he someone on call, or can I rent a car?"

"Oh, I'll take care of that. Be ready at twelve thirty, and we'll pick you up. Now I'd better get my beauty sleep. And, honey, I'm glad you're doing all right."

Lyndsay nodded, knowing she was referring to Trevor. She hugged her friend and then walked the narrow road back to the lodge.

It took some time for her to fall asleep. She thought of Trevor. And she thought of Will saying it was all right for Anita Jane to get out. Was he wanting to end this farce? Was he wanting to end their time together?

"Dear God," she prayed aloud. "I feel like I'm at a turning point in my life, and I don't know which way to go. Please direct me. Please."

❦

Anita Jane was right on time. Lyndsay had been watching out the window of the lobby and walked outside before the driver climbed the steps of the lodge. Her friend looked the picture of health in a navy blue wool coat buttoned up against the weather that had turned frigid during the night.

"What happened to warm afternoons?" Lyndsay asked once she was settled in the backseat with Anita Jane.

"They tell me there's an Ozark saying: If you don't like the weather, stick around ten minutes and it'll change. But I don't think it's likely to change back to warm anytime soon."

"It can't be over twenty. With the wind chill it's easily in the single digits. Are you sure you should be out in this?"

Lyndsay wasn't about to let Anita Jane off the hook.

"I'm bundled up."

"All right. But if you get tired, say the word and we'll leave. This tour isn't that important. Dave said you would like for me to see the college, and he'd asked to take me home last night, but I wanted to go with Will, and I didn't want to hurt Dave's feelings, but I didn't want to encourage him. Sorry, this isn't making much sense, is it?"

"Perfect sense. This is much safer."

Lyndsay raised her eyebrows. "Exactly."

At the Friendship House, the two women sat at a table and waited for Dave. When he arrived, he glanced at Anita Jane then at Lyndsay.

"You brought a chaperone," he said. "Was this Will's idea?"

Anita Jane grinned. "No, I asked myself along."

"Why would you think Will had anything to do with this?" Lyndsay asked.

"I can read his signs. I've known the boy all my life."

The boy? Never in her wildest imagination would Lyndsay call big Will Hamilton a boy.

"You're wearing a hat," Dave commented.

"Yes. It's cold outside," Lyndsay said with a smile. It was a perfectly good small-brimmed hat that matched her black coat, but she wasn't about to take it off even inside. She had pulled her hair back in a ponytail and stuffed it under the hat. She wanted an easy afternoon, not one where she had to sign autographs.

She steered the conversation back to Will and over lunch Dave entertained them with tales of Will and himself as lifelong friends, fishing Ozark waters and dating the same girls in high school.

After lunch, Dave drove them around to the different buildings. Lyndsay had to admit it was interesting. Seeing seven thousand orchids in the greenhouse stunned her. The fragile flowers seemed out of place. The weaving studio and grain mill were much more in keeping with what she thought of the Ozarks.

Before they ventured into the museum, Anita Jane said she was feeling tired, and they'd better cut their tour a little short. Dave drove them back to the Friendship House where their driver was waiting.

"I'm glad we left early," Lyndsay said as they pulled out of the gate. "It's a fascinating place, but I want to go to the hospital this afternoon. I promised Mr. Coble that I'd visit him today. Remember, the man with the broken hip? Would you mind if I borrowed the car after we drop you off?"

"I'd like to meet him myself. Billy, take us to Skaggs Hospital."

"But if you're tired. . ."

"I'm not that tired. Is Will at the hospital? Maybe he'll take time to listen to my lungs and tell me I'm all right now."

"I'm supposed to page him when I get there."

Anita Jane smiled and hummed that tune again until they arrived at the hospital. What was that song?

At the information desk, Lyndsay asked for Mr. Coble's room.

"Two-fourteen," the receptionist said. "I had instructions to call Dr. Hamilton when you arrived."

"Good. Please tell him we'll be in two-fourteen," Lyndsay said.

Mr. Coble's daughter, whom Lyndsay had met the night before, sat in the only chair in the hospital room. Mr. Coble's eyes were closed.

Lyndsay motioned for the woman not to disturb her father.

"Pappy would never forgive me if I didn't wake him up to see you," she said in a raised voice. "He talked about nothing else all morning. Is that Anita Jane Wells with you? She's his favorite singer. Oh, no offense, Miss Rose."

Lyndsay grinned and looked at Anita Jane. "They're more the same age," she said and winked. "Hello, Mr. Coble." Obviously their conversation had awakened him. She walked to his side and took his hand that wasn't attached to the IV. "I've brought you another visitor."

"Anita Jane Wells! Is that really you?"

Anita Jane laughed. "How are you, Mr. Coble? I heard you had a fall. Are they treating you all right in here?"

"They're not feeding me. I want fried chicken, not this here colored water they call soup."

"You'll be on solid food soon, Mr. Coble," Will said from the doorway. He moved over by Lyndsay. "How'd it go at the college?" he asked in a low voice.

"Very interesting. But we didn't stay long. Anita Jane was tired."

Will nodded. She was earlier than he expected, although he'd been waiting impatiently for the receptionist's call. It had been a good day at the office with patients early and appointments running ahead of schedule. He had two more routine physicals scheduled and had only fifteen minutes before he should walk back to his office in the building next door.

"Would you pop in and see another patient of mine?" he asked Lyndsay. Anita Jane had settled in the chair the daughter had vacated and was visiting with Mr. Coble about the way the music business had changed and what had become of the old sound, when a fiddle and guitar were the main instruments instead of an orchestra playing behind the singers.

Will led Lyndsay from room to room introducing her to his patients.

"Do you usually make hospital rounds during the afternoon?"

"No. I do it in the morning and again in the evening, around six or so."

"But today is different?"

"Yes. When I saw what you did for Mr. Coble, I figured you could raise the spirits of my other patients, too. I can see why Princess Di made hospital visits. And now I have to get back to the office. Thanks for doing this."

"You're welcome," she said as he walked her back to Mr. Coble's room. "Oh, Anita Jane said something about getting you to listen to her lungs. Is that for real, or is it part of her plan?"

Will asked Anita Jane to step into an empty room while Lyndsay talked to Mr. Coble. Her lungs were clear, not even a whisper of a wheeze from asthma, but he didn't expect to hear one. She was as healthy as a horse.

"You could be singing."

"Soon."

"Could I have a time table on this? When are you telling her the truth?"

"That depends on her. Her contract ends a week from Saturday. I'll tell her before then, so she can make travel arrangements."

Will frowned. He didn't want to think about Lyndsay leaving. But what could he do? What did he really feel towards her? Last night he'd been afraid to look at Lyndsay for her reaction to Mr. Coble's comment about settling down. He'd known Lyndsay only a few days. He couldn't base a relationship on a few hours spent together. Oh, there was chemistry between them, he couldn't deny that.

"Will?" Anita Jane's voice sounded as if she'd said his name more than once.

"Yes?"

"I asked where you were taking her tonight?"

"I'm not sure. Going out yourself?" he asked with a wicked grin. "You wouldn't want her to see you. This little outing has worn you out. I'll be sure and tell her so."

"You want me to tell her the truth now?" Anita Jane asked.

"Yes," he said, but his heart cried "no." Lyndsay couldn't leave now. They needed more time together. More time to know each other. More time to share their deepest secrets and their highest goals.

Anita Jane frowned with her mouth and with her eyes and with the line on her forehead.

"Well, I can't yet. I just can't." She stormed off muttering something about hardheaded men.

What was with his old friend? One minute she was as sweet as lemonade on a hot day and the next she was all frowns and anger.

He followed her to Mr. Coble's room and arranged with Lyndsay to take her to dinner after tonight's show and to his office party on Saturday night. Sunday he'd attend her gospel singing show in the morning and take her out afterward for Sunday dinner. Then maybe they could go for a long drive, and he'd show her more of the wonderful area he loved. He wanted her booked up. He wouldn't let Dave weasel his way in again.

Chapter 8

The Friday show went off without a hitch and, like her other performances, was a sellout. When she walked on stage, Lyndsay waved to the folks from the hospital waiting room who sat in the front row of the side section. She was glad they'd come and felt as if they were family. Odd. She'd only met them the night before, but maybe when people were thrown together in an emergency room, they tended to bond. She called Jan Coble and her cousins up for the "Jingle Bell" sleigh ride number and gave them gifts from under the giant Christmas tree at the end of the song.

After the show, Will took her out to dinner at a small steak house where their booth was at the back. They talked about Will's patients she'd met, and he told her about growing up in Branson and his friendship with Dave.

"Morgan and Callie are leaving tomorrow," Lyndsay told him over dessert. "Did you know Grandma's been forcing that remedy of hers on Anita Jane every day?"

"So I've heard. That's probably been harder on her than staying home."

"Do you think we've taught her a lesson yet?" Lyndsay didn't want to know, yet she had to find out if he wanted out of squiring her around. "Is this one of Anita Jane's favorite places?" It was a romantic little place, but were they there to keep Anita Jane from showing up?

"She loves this place, but I don't think she'll show up tonight. She wants to keep you in the dark awhile longer, and I'm not sure why. She got angry this afternoon when I told her she should tell you."

So he did want it over. He'd asked Anita Jane to tell her the truth. What a topsy-turvy world she was in. One minute she thought he cared for her, and the next minute he was telling her he wanted to get rid of her. Oh, he hadn't said it in those words, and certainly his kisses didn't communicate that sentiment. What did he want from her?

"Could we go now?" she asked. She smiled, but it was forced. She needed the privacy of her room to evaluate this bit of information. And she needed to be away from him.

"Sure." He signaled for the bill. "Tired? The hours I've been off work, you've been working."

She smiled instead of answering. Her throat was filled with the tears she wouldn't let show. What was wrong with her? On the way home, she answered his questions with monosyllabic replies. Her mind whirled with thoughts and emotions. She'd been crazy to think that Will cared about her. She'd been crazy to think of loving again.

She hummed that song that Anita Jane had been humming the last couple of days. It had been in her mind, but now she remembered the name. "Only Love Can Break a Heart; Only Love Can Mend It Again." Gene Pitney. A song from long ago. How ironic that she remembered it now. Well, Gene was wrong. In her case, love broke a heart, and broke a heart again.

When they arrived back at the lodge, Will took the road to Anita Jane's. "Just to make sure she's in," he said.

In the streetlight Lyndsay could see a wisp of smoke from the cabin's chimney.

"She's burning a fire," she commented. "Pull in, Will."

He glanced at her but parked the car in the narrow drive.

"I want it over with." Lyndsay opened her door and stepped out before Will could turn the engine off. A few steps before she reached the cabin, Will caught up to her and placed a restraining hand on her arm.

"Why, Lyndsay? Why now? We still have a week together."

Lyndsay looked up at the big man. "I don't like games, and I don't like deceit," she said in a louder voice than she'd intended.

"Who's out there?"

Lyndsay turned back toward the cabin, even though Will didn't release her arm. "It's Lyndsay."

The door opened, and light spilled out onto the sidewalk, silhouetting Anita Jane's form. She looked at Lyndsay then at Will.

"Are you fighting?"

"No," Lyndsay said.

"Yes," Will said at the same time.

"Come on inside, and we'll straighten this out."

Lyndsay removed Will's hand from her arm and strolled ahead of him into the cabin. She took a seat in a chair opposite Anita Jane's recliner. Will stood by the fireplace.

"Well?" Anita Jane asked.

Now that the game was up, Lyndsay wasn't sure how to start. Attack Anita Jane for being insensitive, not only to her emotions but also for using Will's time, or merely ask for an explanation? They hadn't planned this part. But then this wasn't a mutual decision. For some reason Will wasn't ready, although earlier he'd said. . . It was too confusing.

"I know you're not sick," Lyndsay blurted out.

"Yes, I know you know," Anita Jane said.

"Why did you do this? Why did you bring me down here under false pretenses?" Now that she had started, the going was easier. "Didn't you know how I would feel? Didn't you care that I'd be devastated knowing one more person I loved. . ." She stopped when Anita Jane's answer registered. "You know that I know?"

"Of course. Once Will Hamilton saw you, I knew he'd never let you think I was next to death's door. He has more compassion than that."

"You set me up?" Will asked. He'd been leaning on the mantel, but now he stood straight and tall. "Why?"

"I told you. I'm your Christmas angel."

"Nonsense," Will said. "You have purposely manipulated two lives." His voice was rising with each word.

"Yes, I have," Anita Jane said calmly and with a smile on her face.

"Anita Jane." Lyndsay strove for calmness in her voice. "Please explain your actions. And don't pull that Christmas angel thing. Will told me you wanted me to be with people, but you know I'm not a recluse in December. I'm with people I choose to be with. And I really do write songs in December."

"I know. I did this for Will."

"For me?" he asked.

Lyndsay glanced at Will, who looked as bewildered as she felt.

"Yes, you. All you do is live at that hospital. And fish. That's it. You need more. You deserve more. So I decided to get it for you."

"I'm the more?" Lyndsay asked. She had never blushed before in her life, but she felt hot and knew she was beet red.

"What about Dave? If you brought her here for me, why did you keep pushing her toward him?" Will asked.

"Oh, that." Anita Jane dismissed his question with a wave of her hand. "A decoy. He didn't know anything about my plan, but I knew you wouldn't want him becoming friendly with Lyndsay. And that would make you spend more time with her yourself."

Lyndsay's humiliation was complete. "You've really manipulated Will and me. Why didn't you try honesty?"

"If I'd asked you to come down for a few weeks because I wanted to fix you up with a nice man, would you have come?"

"No."

"That's what I thought," Anita Jane said with a nod.

"But your plan didn't work. Just tonight Will told me he wanted you to tell me the truth. He wants me to go."

"No, I don't." In two quick strides, Will reached Lyndsay and pulled her out of her chair. "I never said I wanted you to go. I wanted everything to be honest, but I don't want you to leave—ever." He held her shoulders in a tight grip.

Lyndsay looked up at the big man. "Then what do you want?"

"I want time. Lots of time with you. I want to learn all there is to know about you. I want you to learn about me and learn to love me. . . like I love you," he said in a soft voice.

Lyndsay gasped. She'd prayed for God to give her directions for this crossroads in her life. The direction couldn't be any clearer.

Will still held her by the shoulders, and she reached up and placed her hands on his arms. "I do love you. But we've only known each other a few days."

Will smiled and bent down and kissed her.

"Then what we both want is time. Will you stay here in Branson through Christmas? Please?"

"Yes."

"We'll get to know each other—what we like and what we don't like. We'll give our relationship time to grow. A courtship period, that's what we need."

Lyndsay threw her arms around him. "Right now I feel this could be the shortest courtship in history."

Anita Jane cleared her throat. Will and Lyndsay turned toward her.

"Am I to take it this Christmas angel is forgiven for her meddling?"

Headlights coming down the road shined in through a gap in the drapes at the front window, and for an instant the light settled around Anita Jane's head.

Will and Lyndsay glanced at each other.

"Did you see a halo?" Lyndsay whispered in awe.

Will laughed and shook his head to dislodge the image. "If I did, it was a tarnished one."

A Letter to Our Readers

Dear Readers:

In order that we might better contribute to your reading enjoyment, we would appreciate your taking a few minutes to respond to the following questions. When completed, please return to the following: Fiction Editor, Barbour Publishing, Inc., P.O. Box 719, Uhrichsville, OH 44683.

1. Did you enjoy reading *Callie's Mountain*?
   ❑ Very much—I would like to see more books like this.
   ❑ Moderately—I would have enjoyed it more if _____

   _____

   _____

2. What influenced your decision to purchase this book?
   (Check those that apply.)
   ❑ Cover   ❑ Back cover copy   ❑ Title   ❑ Price
   ❑ Friends   ❑ Publicity   ❑ Other

3. Which story was your favorite?
   ❑ Callie's Mountain   ❑ An Ozark Christmas Angel
   ❑ Callie's Challenge

4. Please check your age range:
   ❑ Under 18   ❑ 18–24   ❑ 25–34
   ❑ 35–45   ❑ 46–55   ❑ Over 55

5. How many hours per week do you read? _____

Name _____

Occupation _____

Address _____

City_____ State_____ Zip _____

E-mail_____

If you enjoyed

Callie's Mountain

then read:

APPALACHIA

Love Nestles into Four Mountain Towns

Afterglow by Irene B. Brand

Still Waters by Gina Fields

Come Home to My Heart by JoAnn A. Grote

Eagles for Anna by Catherine Runyon

♡

HEARTSONG
PRESENTS

If you love Christian
romance...

$10.99

You'll love Heartsong Presents' inspiring and faith-filled romances by today's very best Christian authors...DiAnn Mills, Wanda E. Brunstetter, and Yvonne Lehman, to mention a few!

When you join Heartsong Presents, you'll enjoy 4 brand-new mass market, 176-page books—two contemporary and two historical—that will build you up in your faith when you discover God's role in every relationship you read about!

Imagine...four new romances every four weeks—with men and women like you who long to meet the one God has chosen as the love of their lives...all for the low price of $10.99 postpaid.

To join, simply visit www.heartsongpresents.com or complete the coupon below and mail it to the address provided.

✂----------------------------

YES! Sign me up for Hearts♥ng!

NEW MEMBERSHIPS WILL BE SHIPPED IMMEDIATELY!
Send no money now. We'll bill you only $10.99 postpaid with your first shipment of four books. Or for faster action, call 1-740-922-7280.

NAME_____

ADDRESS _____

CITY _____ STATE _____ ZIP_____

**MAIL TO: HEARTSONG PRESENTS, P.O. Box 721, Uhrichsville, Ohio 44683
or sign up at WWW.HEARTSONGPRESENTS.COM**

ADPG05